MW01710525

DAWNBRINGER

FORGOTTEN REALMS®

SAMANTHA HENDERSON

DAWNBRINGER

D&D®

DAWNBRINGER
©2011 Wizards of the Coast LLC

All characters in this book are fictitious. Any resemblance to actual persons, living or dead, is purely coincidental.

This book is protected under the copyright laws of the United States of America. Any reproduction or unauthorized use of the material or artwork contained herein is prohibited without the express written permission of Wizards of the Coast LLC.

Published by Wizards of the Coast LLC. FORGOTTEN REALMS, WIZARDS OF THE COAST, DUNGEONS & DRAGONS, D&D, and their respective logos are trademarks of Wizards of the Coast LLC in the U.S.A. and other countries.

All Wizards of the Coast characters, and the distinctive likenesses thereof are property of Wizards of the Coast LLC.

Printed in the U.S.A.

The sale of this book without its cover has not been authorized by the publisher. If you purchased this book without a cover, you should be aware that neither the author nor the publisher has received payment for this "stripped book."

Cover art by: Matt Stawicki
First Printing: May 2011

9 8 7 6 5 4 3 2 1

ISBN: 978-0-7869-5794-1
ISBN: 978-0-7869-5917-4 (e-book)
620-31448000-001-EN

U.S., CANADA, ASIA,
PACIFIC, & LATIN AMERICA
Wizards of the Coast LLC
P.O. Box 707
Renton, WA 98057-0707
+1-800-324-6496

EUROPEAN HEADQUARTERS
Hasbro UK Ltd
Caswell Way
Newport, Gwent NP9 0YH
GREAT BRITAIN
Save this address for your records.

Visit our web site at www.wizards.com

DEDICATION

For all my friends who keep me sane….

Welcome to Faerûn, a land of magic and intrigue, brutal violence and divine compassion, where gods have ascended and died, and mighty heroes have risen to fight terrifying monsters. Here, millennia of warfare and conquest have shaped dozens of unique cultures, raised and leveled shining kingdoms and tyrannical empires alike, and left long forgotten, horror-infested ruins in their wake.

A LAND OF MAGIC

When the goddess of magic was murdered, a magical plague of blue fire—the Spellplague—swept across the face of Faerûn, killing some, mutilating many, and imbuing a rare few with amazing supernatural abilities. The Spellplague forever changed the nature of magic itself, and seeded the land with hidden wonders and bloodcurdling monstrosities.

A LAND OF DARKNESS

The threats Faerûn faces are legion. Armies of undead mass in Thay under the brilliant but mad lich king Szass Tam. Treacherous dark elves plot in the Underdark in the service of their cruel and fickle goddess, Lolth. The Abolethic Sovereignty, a terrifying hive of inhuman slave masters, floats above the Sea of Fallen Stars, spreading chaos and destruction. And the Empire of Netheril, armed with magic of unimaginable power, prowls Faerûn in flying fortresses, sowing discord to their own incalculable ends.

A LAND OF HEROES

But Faerûn is not without hope. Heroes have emerged to fight the growing tide of darkness. Battle-scarred rangers bring their notched blades to bear against marauding hordes of orcs. Lowly street rats match wits with demons for the fate of cities. Inscrutable tiefling warlocks unite with fierce elf warriors to rain fire and steel upon monstrous enemies. And valiant servants of merciful gods forever struggle against the darkness.

FORGOTTEN REALMS®

A LAND OF UNTOLD ADVENTURE

CHAPTER ONE

OUTER BANKS, THE MOONSEA

1460 DR—THE YEAR OF THE MALACHITE SHADOWS

The midday sun blazed white in a cloudless sky as they threw the last bodies over the side. Gareth Jadaren wiped the sweat from his forehead with his sleeve and lashed a heavy, flat-stone ballast from the merchantman between a woman's ankles with a strip of leather. The woman lay on her back, her face oddly placid considering the bone-deep slash across her throat. Her unblinking eyes seemed to be contemplating the blue sky, ignoring Gareth's fumbling between her feet.

Acutely aware of Helgre behind him, Gareth concentrated on his work. With a grunt, he tightened the last knot. The leather, like his hands, was sticky with blood.

"Check her pockets," said Helgre.

Gareth obeyed, wiping his hands on the woman's leggings before gingerly dipping his fingers into the pockets roughly stitched into the fabric at the hips. There was nothing there, but, beneath the thin linen of the blood-soaked shirt, Gareth found a small leather pouch, the strap that had secured it around its owner's neck severed by the same blow that had ended the woman's life. Helgre extended her hand over his shoulder, and Gareth placed the sticky pouch on her palm. He didn't look at her but heard the clink of a few coins as she opened it.

"Over the side with her," she said, and he heard her walk away, likely enough to rejoin Ping at the helm. He shivered. Helgre's voice was beautiful, a singer's voice, deep and clear as the sound of temple bells. It was hard to reconcile such a voice with the brutality of the woman who possessed it.

And never, not even on warm summer evenings when the stars were scattered thick in the sky, the lanterns glowed golden on the deck, and the crew, forgetting their harsh profession, sang the songs of many lands, not even then had Gareth ever heard Helgre sing.

Gareth quickly tugged the wet red fabric of the woman's shirt over her exposed breast. He didn't want to drag her over the deck, but he was worried that the deeply bisected neck would give way and the head fall off if he picked her up in his arms. As carefully as he could, he lifted the body by the feet and pulled it over the deck, trying not to let the dead sailor bump against the boards. There was a great pool of semi-congealed blood where her body had lain, and a scarlet smear followed as he dragged her, as if pointing him out to any gods overhead. Gareth swallowed nervously, although he had not been the one to cut the sailor's throat.

He'd done enough under Ping's command to earn condemnation.

A space was notched into the railing around the deck, with a hinged door that could be opened and shut for ease of loading and unloading. Another of the *Orcsblood* crew helped Gareth roll the body to the edge. Below them in the pink-tinged water, sea creatures thrashed, fighting for a mouthful of the unexpected feast the pirates' raid on the merchantman had created.

Gareth swallowed hard as he shoved the corpse clear of the ship. Limp-jointed as a doll, the woman fell, hit the churning water, and was tugged under the surface in a flash of silver scales and teeth. Almost unconsciously, he muttered a prayer half-remembered from his childhood. As he raised his head, his eyes met those of the other crewman, who had only recently joined Ping's crew. Ivor was his name, he recalled—a well-built, dusky man from Turmish, with the muscles of a dockworker.

Sweat prickled cold on Gareth's body. Ping didn't tolerate sentimentality in his crew.

Ivor held his gaze a few seconds and nodded once. Gareth relaxed.

They both looked at the merchant ship lashed to the *Orcsblood's* side, her decks smeared with the blood of her defenders and dotted here and there with the fallen. Movement down the side attracted Gareth's attention, and he saw Helgre grab a rope and swing from the *Orcsblood's* deck to the other, landing lightly with a skill born of years of experience. She drew a long knife from her belt and prowled the silent deck, examining the bodies for any sign of life. As he watched, she bent over one twisted form. Her knife flashed in the sun, and Gareth fancied he heard an agonized groan from the man at her feet.

She glanced their way, and both Gareth and Ivor instinctively backed away from the side, looking away from her and up into the half-furled sails of the merchantman.

"Nice lines," said Ivor. "It's a pity she's to burn."

"Agreed," returned Gareth, with more feeling than he intended.

He was beginning to regret signing on to the *Orcsblood.* It seemed a good idea at the time—bad luck and worse timing had wiped out his profits on the goods he'd brought from Turmish to sell in Mulmaster. Everybody had been willing to pay fair coin, but unfortunately not for the goods he offered. So, when he was bereft of everything but a change of clothes, a fair sword, and a better dagger, Ping's bargain, put forward over the greasy and pocked wooden table in an ill-lit and sour-smelling tavern in the insalubrious district of Mulmaster, sounded appealing.

He would have a fair share in all the booty and a head start if he decided to leave.

"You'll understand that in my business an encounter with a . . . former colleague, shall we say . . . could be embarrassing, on either side," the pirate said, his grin showing an impressive expanse of ivory teeth that looked as if they'd been filed to points. "Especially if a former member of my jolly crew had decided to ally himself—or herself—with more or less law-abiding associates. Should we part ways, it's better we don't meet again."

It sounded reasonable, and the offer of a life sweeter than a slave's, if not as honest, was too good to refuse. Gareth was a realist and had lived a bandit's life before this. He resigned himself to piracy aboard the *Orcsblood*, even when he met Helgre. Ping's second-in-command greeted him pleasantly enough, but no warmth reached her penetrating gray eyes. It was the cold expression in those eyes that chilled Gareth, not the vicious, long-healed slash that marred the left side of her face from eyebrow to chin, twisting the corner of her mouth into a one-sided smile.

Nevertheless, he had left childish ideals in childhood, and serving under a killer was better than starving virtuously, or rotting in prison for debt.

But Ping's practice of destroying ships and slaughtering any potential witnesses sickened even Gareth's sensibilities, and he soon suspected anyone who chose to leave Ping's crew was not in fact given a fair "head start" but disappeared, likely with a slit throat, in the wake of the *Orcsblood* in the middle of the night. He'd made discreet inquiries, but the other members of the crew were reticent on the subject.

Someone struck him lightly on the shoulder, and he turned to see Din, a tall, thin-faced easterner who had signed on shortly before Gareth. He grinned and held out a bucket. His naturally pale skin had burned, then browned, in the months they'd spent on the *Orcsblood*, and he didn't seem at all disconcerted by the slaughter of the merchantman's crew or passengers.

"Ping says to sluice down the decks before we unload," he said as Gareth took the bucket. "Clean decks for clean cargo."

Gareth nodded and lowered the bucket over the side on its rope, avoiding the pink stain where the bodies had been dumped. The waters were quieter now, the victims of Ping's ferocity sunk to the bottom and the scavengers' hunger sated for now. Ivor found another bucket and did likewise, and together they had the deck clean of blood in a short time.

It was late afternoon before they had the cargo—silks from Imaskar and a load of exotic woods—piled on deck. The shipwright had already scavenged anything he could use from the merchantman, and now thick black coils of smoke rose from the hapless ship as she was cut free of the *Orcsblood*. A breeze was freshening, and crew clambered like spiders in the sheets above, for Ping wanted to be long gone before the smoke from the burning ship attracted undue attention.

Others unpacked the crates while Ping and Helgre examined the goods. The crew was cheerful. The slaughter was over, and there would be a generous bonus for all when Ping sold the booty to his contacts on the north shores of the Moonsea. In the meantime, there was food and drink for all, and their captain was pleased with their work.

Gareth stood, stretching his sore shoulders, and watched the merchantman burn. He'd had more than his share of fighting and lifting loads this day. Ivor joined him as a spurt of flame burst from the merchantman's side, and the drifting vessel listed heavily to one side.

"Why waste a good vessel when we could strip her of identifying marks and sell her?" Ivor kept his eyes on the doomed ship, as if he were speaking to himself.

"Each ship has her idiosyncrasies," said Gareth, keeping his voice indifferent. "Ping knows she would be identified eventually."

"But we would be long gone with a decent purse before that happened. And why kill crew and passengers who could be ransomed, or sold far south in the Beastlands, or anywhere the slave trade flourishes?"

Was it his imagination, or was there anger beneath Ivor's carefully modulated voice?

"It does seem wasteful," Gareth said, blinking against the ash in the air as the prow of the merchantman began her long, inexorable slide beneath the surface of the Moonsea.

Two tendays later, Gareth Jadaren didn't have time for moralizing as he blinked the blood out of his eyes. The cut across his forehead smarted, but he'd been lucky. The sellsword had slipped in the gore on the surface of the deck, and the blow meant to split his skull glanced sideways. Gareth had skewered the hapless sellsword as he lay sprawled and stunned, and his sword still quivered in the wooden deck, piercing the mercenary through the torso.

Gareth wiped away another handful of blood, looking around for something to staunch the bleeding. His late opponent wore a jaunty twist of a scarf around his neck that wasn't too grimy, so Gareth bent and flicked it away with two fingers, wadding the scarf against the wound. It stung and would leave a scar, but that was of little consequence.

He glanced about the deck of the *Starbound*. The smell of char was heavy, and small flakes of burned canvas floated in the air. The remaining masts were blackened, and the mainmast lay across the deck, embers glowing along its split-asunder length. Here and there the remaining defenders of the *Starbound* fought in fierce pockets of resistance, but they were outnumbered and couldn't last long.

Ivor loped across the deck toward Gareth. The long knife he preferred for close work was clotted with gore to the hilt; he must have been on mop-up duty. Gareth swallowed the acid that rose in his throat at the sight. He shouldn't let it affect him—he knew he wouldn't long survive his stint on the *Orcsblood* if he was maiden-squeamish about slaughter. And he did mean to survive and accumulate coin enough to start an honest—well, mostly honest—business far from here, enough to protect him and his from the brutality of such as Ping, and those whom Ping succeeded in making like himself.

Ivor pointed at the bow, where Ping stood surveying the carnage.

"Ping wants us to check belowdecks," said Ivor, catching his breath. He surveyed the man Gareth had affixed to the deck.

"Lucky blow," he said in approval, and kneeled to wipe his blade on the mercenary's trousers. From the bow, Ping caught Gareth's eye and pointed at a spot on the deck to Gareth's right. Gareth glanced that way and saw a trapdoor that had been flung open, with the rope that secured it snaked carelessly across the decking. Ping crooked his fingers and thrust his palm down. His meaning was clear.

Gareth nodded. Ivor sheathed his knife and drew a short sword, and Gareth pulled his weapon from his late opponent. Together they approached the trapdoor cautiously.

Ivor pointed at the deck. Dark splotches led directly to the gloomy entrance. When they glanced down into the dark maw, they saw fresh drops of blood soaked into the worn wooden steps leading below.

Gareth ventured down, making sure his booted foot was secure on one step before he attempted another. Four steps down he gestured to Ivor to follow. He heard the steps creak under the Turmish man's weight. Halfway down he paused, blinking to accustom himself to the dim light of the ship's interior. Squinting, he surveyed the hold and the various-size boxes piled along the walls. The only sound he could hear was Ivor's regular breathing behind him. He sidestepped the rest of the way down, making it to the slippery floor without incident.

"Nobody here," he whispered over his shoulder to Ivor.

He saw the flash out of the corner of his eye. On pure instinct, he ducked, hitting the slimy floor, froglike, as a long, snaky stretch of blue-green lightning seared the space where his head had been. Ivor yelled something inarticulate as the step he was standing on shattered and he fell the rest of the way into the hold, landing with an oath heavily beside Gareth.

Something moved in the shadows before them. Sword extended and poised, Gareth rose quickly, knees bent and ready to move. Ivor was still cursing and trying to untangle himself from his weapon. An odd smell, not quite like a campfire and not quite like an alchemist's shop, but evocative of them both, lingered in the musty air. No doubt it was due to the strange electrical attack.

Between two tall boxes a pale shadow shifted, then

advanced into the dim light that the hatch overhead admitted. Half-light illuminated a fierce, feral face. At first Gareth thought it was an elf, or perhaps a massively overgrown gnome. But this creature was far more gaunt than any elf or creature of the Feywild. Its sunken cheeks and high, sharp cheekbones gave it a predatory look, and its nose was reduced to an abbreviated bony ridge with two elongated slits for nostrils. Its huge black eyes glittered with desperation and hatred. One hand was clutched tight to its chest, as if it had been injured, and the other was stretched toward Gareth, the thin fingers impossibly long, the fingernails curved and sharp as claws. It stared at him, hissing in pain or, with his luck, preparing another deadly, electric blast.

Its face was tattooed all over with what looked like scrolling runes, scattered throughout with dots and spirals—or perhaps those were its natural markings. Similar markings decorated its tattered robe, gray-blue in the dim light.

With a quick, supple movement, it thrust its hand toward him. Gareth threw himself to his left, as much to draw fire away from Ivor as to avoid the blast himself. He staggered against the interior wall, scraping his cheek on the rough wood, as another bolt of snakelike lightning surged from the extended palm and crackled past his ear. The singed-air smell intensified, and an electric prickle tingled unpleasantly through his bones.

The tattooed creature moaned with the effort of spellcasting and bowed its head from pain or weariness. Gareth caught a glimpse of long pointed ears, exaggerated as a lynx's with what looked like a frill along the outer edge. He took advantage of its distraction to sidestep away from the wall, jumping surefootedly over bags scattered across the floor as he did. His cornered adversary must have taken refuge belowdecks to hide or protect some object of value. Gareth had seen none of those distinctive blue-green bolts in the fighting on the deck.

The glossy, insect black eyes in the elaborately scrolled face turned back to him, and there was no mistaking its expression of malevolence. It raised a sinewy arm in its shredded blue silk sleeve toward him again, and Gareth could feel the air around him contract and flex, as if it were made of tiny components that had become charged with static electricity.

But the creature had forgotten Ivor, or considered him out of combat, and was taken by surprise when the stocky Turmish man charged, slashing sideways with the short sword.

The startled spellcaster turned, and the snake of blue-green force coalescing from its hand knocked the sword from Ivor's hand. But the sword was only for distraction. Ivor drew his long knife from his belt with his left hand and slashed at the creature's forearm with a vicious back-hand stroke. The blade bit deep and the creature cried out, falling back against the wall. Ivor's right hand dangled uselessly at his side, but he retained his grip on his better weapon. Still holding the knife in a back-hand stance, he lunged at the wounded thing, aiming for the throat.

It flung up a long-fingered hand. Gareth saw nothing but sensed that the air in the hold had shifted. A ripple like the surface of a windblown pond emanated from the bone-white palm, and Ivor fell back heavily, as if struck by a long staff.

Gareth knew they had no time to reason or negotiate. Darting forward in the gloom, he knocked the creature's arm up with an underhand blow of the solid hilt of his sword. Off balance and clutching both hands to its breast, it staggered against the wooden board at its back. This was no time to hesitate; with only a breath and a slight back step, Gareth thrust his blade through the creature's sleeve, down and under the top of its rib cage and into the space where he hoped its heart would be.

He must have guessed right or hit some vital organ regardless, because the creature opened its mouth in a final inarticulate cry and its body spasmed, almost pulling Gareth's sword from his hand. He pulled his blade from the body, hopping back a pace and ready in case it managed to come at him. Finally it stilled and lay collapsed across a couple of packing boxes, staring at the irregular angle where wall met splintery ceiling, as if it saw infinity there.

Something trickled down Gareth's face, and his head throbbed acutely—the fighting had reopened the cut on his forehead. Cursing, he dabbed it with his sleeve. He was going to have a perishing great scar if he was ever given a chance to heal up.

There was a heartfelt groan behind him. Gareth jumped and whirled around, sword up. He prayed it wasn't yet another of those things.

Ivor grinned at him, the tip of Gareth's sword just touching his chest.

"Jumpy, aren't you?" he said, shaking his right hand as if it pained him.

"And how." Gareth turned back to the body and shifted his weapon to his left hand. Bending gingerly over the strange humanoid, he pulled at the elongated hand that curled against its chest. Between its fingers it held a round of metal.

"Lucky thing you're left-handed," he remarked over his shoulder as he plucked the object away and examined it, frowning. It was a rather plain bracelet, made like a small torque to slip over the wrist. It didn't look like anything worth dying over. Surely there were richer pickings in the hold. But the creature had been clutching *this.*

"It's proved useful," said Ivor, and Gareth heard him slide his knife back into place at his belt. Gareth silently agreed. Few opponents in battle, facing a weapon wielded in the right hand, expected the dominant attack to come from a smaller, left-handed weapon.

Ivor leaned close to his shoulder to look at his prize. Gareth examined it as best he could in the dim light. The bracelet was a pale metal, too dull to be silver. Yet it didn't have the heft or feel of pewter. It was simple, with no embellishment save three red stones—possibly garnets—set evenly along its length. The surface of the metal was polished, smooth to the touch, but looked crosshatched by tiny, even marks. Gareth turned it over in his fingers, frowning. It felt warm. And, oddly, the warmth fluctuated ever so slightly against his skin. It was if the piece had its own tiny heartbeat.

The fluctuation was becoming a flutter, as if he held a small, frightened bird in his hand. Instinct told him to drop it, but curiosity compelled him to hold it. On his upturned palm he could see it quiver, the movement slight but visible.

"Strange thing," remarked Ivor. "Do you think . . . Bane's blood!"

They both jumped. The bracelet *flexed,* one end butting against Gareth's hand like a blind worm.

"Sweet Mother's milk, throw the damned thing away!" said Ivor.

But Gareth couldn't. He was frozen with an otherworldly fascination with the thing, watching as the strange metal writhed and elongated. Beneath his feet, the wide wooden floorboards shifted up and down as the ship lurched in the water, and he adjusted his balance automatically.

"It's not doing anything," said Gareth. "Nothing dangerous, at least."

Ivor whistled soundlessly. "You know best. It's you down with the fishes if you're wrong," he said. He nudged at a small bag of rough muslin, one of several scattered about the floor, with the tip of his boot. There was a satisfying clink of metal.

"I wonder if that's what our late friend was so eager to keep from us," he said. "Let's have a look."

Gareth watched as Ivor kneeled and loosed the thin cord tied about the mouth of the bag. He chuckled in satisfaction and held up a couple of elongated coins for Gareth's perusal.

"Silver?"

"No, my rustic friend," replied Ivor. "Platinum, or I'm a mermaid." The coins were stamped with a pattern unfamiliar to Gareth, not unlike the markings on the elflike creature's robe. He glanced again at the staring blind eyes, wishing he could have asked it about the scrolling runes, about how a member of such an alien race came to be on a merchant freighter on the Moonsea, about the object stirring in his hand. He wished it weren't necessary to kill it.

But kill he would, if he must to stay alive. To make a safe place in this world, he would see Ping's ship and all on her destroyed, if that's what it took.

Between one heartbeat and the next he made a decision.

"Friend Ivor," he said, casting a quick glance at the hatch overhead. "Would I be wrong to guess that life aboard the *Orcsblood* has little delight for you?"

Ivor glanced up from sifting through the contents of the bag—all foreign platinum coins, as far as Gareth could see—and narrowed his eyes, considering.

"Not very wrong," he said. "I find Ping's policies . . . unnecessarily harsh and wasteful. And I fear a reckoning is coming. I'd just as soon not be here to taste my share."

"We think alike," said Gareth. "And yet it's my suspicion that for all Ping's talk of fair share of the spoils and a blessing for the road, none leaves the *Orcsblood* save in a shark's belly."

"Worse. I think he gives them to Helgre," said Ivor. They both looked nervously at the hatch. The sounds of battle had faded, and they heard the calls of their crewmates, one to another, on the deck of the doomed merchantman. The smell of smoke was heavy in the air.

"Two may have a better chance than one, working together," said Gareth. "If they can trust each other."

"If," agreed Ivor. Carefully he pulled ten of the coins from the bag and transferred them to his own pouch. Six other bags were scattered about—probably fallen from one of the shattered packing boxes. Ivor gathered the bags together, taking ten coins—no more—from each. Before he tied the pouch shut, he went to the corpse and pulled a few—not all—of the gem-set rings adorning the creature's fingers. Golden rings pierced the frilled ears, and Ivor considered them, then shook his head.

"Being greedy won't help us," he said. "See. . . ."

He held up the bulging pouch before Gareth's eyes.

"If two could trust each other, they could see that those on night duty drank more than their fill tonight," he said quickly. "If they were quick, they could climb over the side and cut the dock boat free. Two could row as far as Mulmaster. And seventy platinum is a good start for two. Two who trust each other."

"Do we?" said Gareth. "You could have taken me from behind after the thing was dead."

"And you could have skewered me neatly, as you have at least two others this day, as I counted the coin," replied Ivor, tucking the pouch into the front of his breeches. "There. Let that scarred siren look for it there."

Gareth nodded. "Equal shares?"

Ivor glanced at the bracelet still squirming on Gareth's palm. "All save that thing, which you're welcome to. It gives me the shivers as bad as Helgre."

The bracelet stretched and coiled. Gareth heard the heavy scrape of a boot at the hatch above, and the living metal paused, as if it heard, too. Then, so fast he barely registered it was happening, the bracelet elongated, becoming little thicker than a wire, and darted under his cuff and up his sleeve like a grass snake. It was a startling and strange sensation, the cool smoothness of the metal and the three small bumps that were the gemstones winding up his arms, across the crook of his elbow, around his shoulder.

Around his neck.

Startled, Ivor cursed. Gareth grabbed at the metal snaking around his neck, praying he could rip it away before it choked him. The weird, bolt-casting creature would have the last laugh here, he thought.

But instead of wrapping tight around his windpipe and cutting off his air, as he expected, it lay loose like a necklace.

Cautiously he felt it between his fingers. It *was* a necklace. The smoothly forged metal had become small flat links, inset at even lengths with the garnets, just long enough to lie out of sight beneath his jerkin.

Ivor's eyes were wide, his mouth open. Gareth shushed him as they were hailed from above and the silhouette of a head appeared in the square of light of the hatch above.

"Hoy! Are you gentlemen planning on joining the rest of us soon, or will you malinger all day?" It was the unmistakable voice of Ping, friendly and joking on the surface, with a deadly edge beneath.

"We've been dealing with a holdout," called back Ivor. "And the ladder was damaged in the process. We'll need a rope to get out."

Ping called back over his shoulder for someone to bring a rope.

"Anything worth saving down there?" he said, turning back. Gareth stifled a cynical grin at the again-innocuous words, the trap set underneath.

"You'd better come see," he called in turn. "Bags of coin, and boxes worth searching."

A rope snaked down, and Ping descended it quickly. Blinking in the darkness, he called to the heads clustered above for a witchlight. It was swiftly tossed down, and he held the blue glowball up high, surveying the bags Ivor had thoughtfully piled together, the singed and shattered steps, and the strange, tattooed body. Under his breath he muttered something in his native tongue.

"Go up and help with the cargo, and then rest. You've earned it." He laid his hand on Gareth's shoulder in a friendly gesture. Gareth steeled himself not to flinch. He nodded, aware of the tickle of the small metal links against his chest. Ping carried no weapon, but tiny scarlet specks were scattered thickly over his cuff.

He swallowed away a sudden surge of nausea that had nothing to do with the wound on his forehead. He wished he'd thought to shut the creature's eyes before Ping arrived. Now there'd be a bustle of unloading loot and other unsavory, urgent business, and he'd have no other time to do it.

"I'll have some of the others help you haul this stuff over to the *Orcsblood*," said Ping. "We can dump the rest of the bodies down here before we scuttle her."

Ping's eyes gleamed as he looked over the bags and wooden boxes with their port seals, indifferent to the dead body sprawled in front of him or to the carnage above.

Gareth followed Ivor up the rope, swearing to himself that as far as it lay in his power, no Jadaren would ever turn to piracy again.

Something seared over Fandour's flesh, just for an instant, like a thread of white-hot fire. He flinched and concentrated, trying to follow the fading sensation as a dog would follow the scent of a rabbit gone to ground.

Somewhere on that distant plane his sundered avatar stirred. The Rhythanko artifact, in which an essential piece of himself was forged, link by link and jewel by jewel, was no longer shielded by the gith.

The scent was lost on the winds and current between the planes, and Fandour subsided into himself, inside the walls of his ancient prison. His avatar had forgotten him and no longer sought reunion.

But Fandour knew he had a chance of finding it now. Now it was loose in Faerûn, that strange plane.

CHAPTER TWO

The Mulmaster Docks

1460 DR—The Year of the Malachite Shadows

Gareth's cramped fingers slipped on the slick wood, found a crack between two boards, and grasped it. The rotted wood crumbled, and his fingers lost their grip for the last time. He scrabbled desperately as he slid down the rough lip of the dock, hearing the water churn over the black rocks far below. Somewhere far below them their boat bobbed, dangerously near the sharp edges of those jagged boulders, tied to a barnacle-encrusted pier. The thin chain around his neck flexed slightly, as if realizing how close they were to falling. Gareth prayed it wouldn't decide to cling on tight and strangle him in the process.

He cursed their turn of luck. It had gone well enough so far. Din and Barneb, assigned to second watch, had been happy to share in the strong wine he and Ivor had brought to break the tedium of the night hours, and in the musky vintage the guards hadn't tasted the mild drug Ivor had slipped into the second bottle. Once Din and Barneb fell into a deep sleep, Gareth and Ivor had secured them against the side of the ship to prevent them from rolling around on deck, called the half hour themselves, and turned the glass. Gareth and Ivor were set to take third watch, so there was a good chance no one would come by to find the post abandoned.

They scuttled down the side of the *Orcsblood* undetected, cut the small boat free, and made for the distant, tarnished lights of Mulmaster as fast and silently as they could. They were both strong rowers. There was only one pair of oars secured in the boat, and one of them took over the chore of rowing the instant the other faltered, so although they were weary and sore when they reached the ring of anchored craft that bordered the town harbor, they made good time.

They glided between the ships, hung with green and yellow witchlight that reflected in the quiet water. Some of the craft were dead quiet, and sometimes a low conversation or the calling of the watch came to them on the gentle breeze from the decks high above. Ivor paddled, avoiding splashing, and Gareth took the tiller, straining to avoid coming too near to any craft. No one hailed them or warned them off, but they both knew that sharp eyes were following them at every moment.

Allies of Ping would betray them to the pirate. Enemies of Ping would hunt them down as suspected pirates. There was no help for them here.

Past the inner circle of craft they saw the docks of Mulmaster, with their red glass lanterns hanging from their piers. Here and there a figure stood on the planking, silhouetted by the soft yellow glow of the town's lights behind them.

Ivor lifted the oars, drops of water reflecting the light of the dock lanterns and falling like rubies into the dark water. Gareth pointed at the shadowy pillars of the piers of one of the docks that loomed, dark and abandoned, over a barrier of sharp rocks that the low tide exposed. The only illumination came from the light of the fat crescent moon shining on the choppy water and a dim green swirl as some sea creature occasionally came close to the surface.

Ivor nodded silently in agreement. It would be better to creep into Mulmaster unperceived than to risk a challenge at the more populated dock.

They made the boat fast and started up the slippery piers, finding protuberances of reinforcing metal and bulges of overgrown barnacles to aid their climb. Both men were sea trained and used to clambering all over a ship, both in calm and in storm. But they had the effort of rowing all the way from the deep water behind them that night, and before that the task of bringing the *Starbound* to heel. Fatigue made Gareth's arms tremble, and more than once he almost lost his footing. The thought of the fatal fall onto the rocks below gave him new strength and determination, but he was mere flesh after all and prayed to whatever god might be listening to give him just enough strength to make the dock.

Perhaps one was listening, for he did. Perhaps it was a capricious god, because he quickly realized that an abandoned dock was an ill-kept dock, and this one's boards were rotting in the damp sea air and spray. He sprawled on the slick edge and wondered if he could fall free of the rocks, and if whatever lurked down there making green swirls in the water would prove to be hungry.

Something wrapped around the biceps of his left arm, something that felt like a band of steel. Gareth felt helpless as a fish on a hook as he was lifted clear of the edge, hauled a few feet over sodden wood to the comparably solid surface of the dock, and deposited in a boneless heap on the slats.

He looked up at his rescuer, who stood over him, fists on hips and side-lit by the moon. Anyone would seem tall from Gareth's position, but this man was well above average height, and broad shouldered to match. Instinctively Gareth noted the wide-bladed dagger thrust through a double-thick belt, the outline of a longbow slung across the man's back, and also the fact that he made no move toward his weapons.

The man wore a simple garment that recalled robes Gareth had seen merchants from Imaskar wear, with wide strips of fabric that crossed the shoulders and chest. There were no sleeves, however, even in the chilly night breeze that soughed from the water, and the man's muscular arms were left bare. The robe parted at the waist, allowing access to the weapon at his belt and no impediment to the legs.

All this Gareth noted in an instant, his gaze traveling up the man's form. When he stared into the figure's face, he gasped.

He looked like a man, albeit orc-tall and similarly broad. But his face, otherwise human of feature, was striped like the hide of the beast Ping had on the floor of his chambers, a great cat from the jungles of Durpar. In the moonlight, he couldn't tell what color the stripes were, but they were dark and looked painted over the pale surface of the figure's face. His hair, long and thick, was tied back, but Gareth could see that the stripes that marked the face continued where they met the hair, which likewise alternated pale and dark.

A muffled grunt made him turn his head, and he saw Ivor a few feet away, similarly sprawled on the wide planks of the dock. A second figure grasped him firmly by the collar. This one was slightly smaller than the first, but still imposingly tall, with a similarly draped garment with loose sleeves. The figure let go of Ivor and straightened, and Gareth saw it was female. She wasn't tiger-striped as her companion, but she wore a wide mask of some pale, thin fabric stretched across her eyes. From two oblique holes in the mask her wide, liquid-dark eyes surveyed the scene. Her dark hair was partially braided in rows back from her face, and the ends fell free over her shoulders. Gareth could see the hilt of the sword she wore strapped across her back, and his quick eyes noted that she, too, carried a dagger thrust beneath her belt.

Gareth heard Ivor coughing and, drawing his cramped legs beneath him, focused on standing up without falling over. Their rescuers, imposing as they might be, didn't seem to intend them any harm—at least not yet. And if they did intend to attack, he'd rather meet them on his feet.

Getting his balance on the gently rocking dock was easy after the months aboard the *Orcsblood*. He untangled his traveling cloak from his sword belt and scabbard, but he was careful to make no sudden movement toward the hilt. The tall, striped man didn't move as Gareth inclined his head slightly.

"My thanks to you, goodsir," he said, then, with a nod to the female figure, added, "And to you as well, fairlady."

Ivor was also standing, but his coughing kept him from replying. He hit his own chest with a balled fist and nodded his agreement.

The man tilted his head.

"What think you, Lakini?" he called to his companion, in a deep voice that had something of a tiger's growl to it. He never took his eyes off Gareth. "Pirates, or fleeing from pirates?"

"Both, as I see it," she replied, in a soft, clear alto. Her masked eyes stared unblinking at Gareth, then flicked back to Ivor, as if looking for clues.

"We're not pirates," Gareth said, trying to sound indignant. Both of their strange rescuers turned to regard him, their gaze unblinking and their bodies absolutely still, even on the swaying dock. The seconds stretched out, and he sensed they were ready to stare him down forever. He opened his mouth again and closed it, unsure of what to say.

Ivor cleared his throat. "We're not pirates *now,*" he said in a hoarse voice, shaking his head at Gareth's frown. "But I will admit to you fair folk that yesterday night we *were.* But we are no longer."

"Reformed pirates, then," said the woman. Both she and her companion fixed Ivor with that steely gaze, and Gareth saw him shrink beneath it.

"As it happens, we're looking for pirates," said the tiger-striped man.

"Would that we still were, for your good people's sake," said Gareth. "But, alas, we have thrown off the life."

"Lusk and I are looking for particular pirates," said the woman. "Or, rather, a particular pirate ship and her crew."

"A ship that kills other ships, leaving no survivors," said the man. "A ship well-known for her cruelty, even in these wicked days. With a master with no respect for the sanctity of life or mercy for those who would surrender."

"Or desire for the ransom that might be earned from surrender," said Ivor ruefully.

"Even so," said the man.

"Leaving such a ship might have been a wise choice for one who chooses to be an ex-pirate," said the woman. "And an even better decision for two."

"We hope as much," said Gareth. "And begging your pardons, but the sooner we can slip up a back road and find a place to roost in Mulmaster, the happier these ex-pirates will be."

The woman stepped toward him, and, hypnotized as a sparrow by a snake, he couldn't help looking into her eyes. With an inner start, he realized that she wore no mask at all—the band across her eyes, paler than the color of her face, was either painted on or part of her facial coloration. The hair braided back from her temples continued the pale stripe.

It didn't look like paint.

"We have business with these pirates, although they don't know it yet," she said, looking down at him, for she topped him by two fingerbreadths. "We would like to know where to find them."

Gareth considered lying, but there was something very compelling about her request. If Ping heard they'd put mercenaries on his track, however . . .

"*Very* much like to know," she said.

Gareth made a quick decision. "The *Orcsblood* lies at anchor there, two degrees from the light of that barge tethered there." He pointed at the tenuous point of yellow light that looked like a tarnished star fallen to the ground. "And if you visit that fair vessel tonight, you'll find that two of the watch were careless of their wine this night." He swallowed and continued. "There's a boat, late of the *Orcsblood*, made fast to a pier beneath this dock, if you're of a mind to clamber down and get it. I don't think we've a need for it anymore."

Gareth's eyes met Ivor's questioning glance. He understood without words—it was one thing to slip away, to desert the ship in the middle of the night. It was another to put this pair of—what were they, anyway? Paladins, sworn to rid the world of Ping and his ilk? Thieves, in search of the treasure a pirate ship might hold? Pirates, looking to seize a vessel for themselves?

Whatever they were, it was another thing entirely to put them on Ping's wake.

The woman smiled. "Many thanks, for the information and the means."

She backed away a few paces. "I hope you prosper well, and honestly, in Mulmaster." Her companion ignored them, staring intently into the purple-tinged darkness of the Moonsea as if he could see the *Orcsblood* if he concentrated enough.

It was clearly a dismissal, or at least Gareth chose to take it as such. The strangers watched them in their strange, stone-still way as Gareth took Ivor by the arm and pulled him toward the dim, irregular line of lights that marked one of the streets of Mulmaster.

The breeze was stronger now, and cold. His arms ached where his perilous climb had skinned them. His shoulders and legs were sore, too—in fact his entire body protested its treatment this night.

But it was good to be off that ship.

"They mean to destroy Ping," said Ivor, breaking in on his thoughts as they hurried along. "And I don't say he doesn't deserve it. But the rest of the crew . . ."

"They had the same choice before them as we did," said Gareth curtly. "And with luck it'll distract Ping from hunting us down. And do you think that pair could take down the entire crew of the *Orcsblood*?"

Ivor looked behind him. "It wouldn't surprise me."

Gareth couldn't help a backward glance at the abandoned dock and the crescent moon hanging low in the sky. There was no one there now. It was as if the strangely marked couple had never existed.

Something moved around his neck and he jumped, startling a curse from Ivor. It was the chain, unhooking itself from around his neck and slithering down his arm, snakelike, under his filthy sleeve. When it reached his wrist, it coiled around it and solidified, thickening until it again took the shape of a torque.

"I still think you should get rid of that thing," muttered Ivor.

"Not yet," said Gareth. "Not till I've found its uses."

The mage's chamber was dimly lit and smelled strongly of chemicals, with an underlying prickle of burned hair. Gareth stifled a sneeze. Mulmaster's air was not the most refreshing, but the honest smells of the street overhead would be less oppressive than this. Mage Magaster stood, arms folded, on the other side of a battered worktable. Beneath his blue-black robe, stained here and there with streaks that might be the result of experiments gone awry or perhaps simply sloppy table manners, his lank frame seemed to be trying to stretch as tall as possible. In the shadows beside the door stood the hooded figure of the mage's apprentice, head bowed and ready to answer Magaster's summons. It was impossible to determine the sex or race of the slight figure beneath its robes, but the soft voice that had greeted Gareth at the door suggested it was female.

Gareth cleared his throat. "I want to know what this is." He took the bracelet from an inner pocket and placed it on the acid-charred wood of the tabletop. The mage looked at it, unimpressed.

"I should think that was obvious," he said in a voice that implied he'd seen many worthless goods and fools in his life. "It's a bracelet."

Gareth grinned humorlessly. "Sure it is. Except, Master Mage, when it's a necklace. Or an armband. Or none of those things, particularly."

From the corner of his eye he saw the hooded figure shift slightly. The mage raised an overgrown eyebrow. "This object changes shape? On its own?"

"And hence my understandable curiosity. Also, its previous owner died rather than give it up, and I'd like to know why."

To be entirely honest, Ping would have ordered the weird creature in the ship's hold killed, whatever he did. But Gareth didn't feel it necessary to go into all that. The less said about Ping, the better.

The day after he and Ivor had taken refuge in the dubious safety of Mulmaster, word had come of a pirate ship, the scourge of the Moonsea, found adrift with all on board slaughtered. Stranger still, rumor said that the slain had not been left to rot where they fell, but that they had been laid out neatly, their weapons at their feet, as if somebody had taken the time to commend them to their respective gods. Ivor and Gareth had looked at each other over the greasy tavern table when they heard the word, silent by unspoken mutual agreement. The news was a relief, but the idea that they had set the mysterious, otherworldly strangers upon the ship they'd served was uncomfortable.

The mage grunted skeptically, unfolded his arms, and poked at the bracelet with a long sharpened fingernail, stained ocher and yellow with the chemicals of his trade. The metal around Gareth's wrist remained a bracelet. The mage rubbed his calloused finger on the front of his robe as if Gareth's questionable treasure were no more than particularly unpromising fewmets.

"The gems are unknown to me, and doubtless of no particular Power or value," he declared in his sonorous voice. "I am unfamiliar with these chicken scratchings on the metal, and I doubt if they even come from the alphabet of any advanced race. It's a trinket some charlatan cobbled together, either to gull a mark or to give a sweetheart, and has no intrinsic magical Power whatsoever.

You could give it to some trollop if she fancies it. Otherwise it's worthless."

Indignant, Gareth snatched up the bracelet before the mage could say more.

"Very well," he said. "You've made your point. I should have saved my coin for the whore. I would have had more enjoyment from it."

He was irritated at more than the man's dismissal of an object he'd hoped to prove valuable, and, as he blinked in the sunshine outside the mage's dim lair, he realized why that was. By saying the bracelet was valueless, fit only to buy a doxy's favors, the mage implied the strange creature on the ship died for nothing. And Gareth realized he was obscurely offended at the insult.

He tucked the bracelet away in a pouch beneath his shirt and made his way down the greasy cobbles, automatically avoiding the refuse that ran down the ditch in the middle of the street. He'd return to the Throatcut Sparrow Tavern that afternoon, and see if he and Ivor could hire on as mercenaries or even mule-hands with a caravan headed south. He didn't see much chance of their establishing a foothold here, unless . . .

He passed a queer sigil burned into a splintered door and shivered despite the noontide heat. No, there wasn't much chance, unless they were willing to join the lower echelons of Bane's dark brotherhood. And Gareth wasn't that desperate—not quite yet. He hadn't left Ping's murderous ways behind to join the Dark Lord's ranks.

He sensed something move behind him and swung around, his hand on his sword hilt. All he saw was a double row of shadowed doorways and the cobbled street, empty save for some dull-colored fowl that pecked at a pile of refuse.

Gareth shifted his pack and continued his course. As the sun reddened in the east, the near-empty streets began to fill with all manner of folk going about their business after the midday warmth. Instinctively, Gareth let his right hand hover near the coin pouch on his belt, under the fold of his shirt, for the pickpockets had left their noontide rest and returned to their trade as well.

Before a dark archway overhung with a tavern sign that depicted a bird in flight with a scarlet splash across its neck, Gareth paused. He'd been walking uphill, and here, through a gap between two tumbledown buildings, he had a good view of the pink-streaked waters of the Moonsea. A sluggish warm wind working between the buildings was tainted with the stench of tar.

He and Ivor had made inquiries about the drifting pirate ship and her load of corpses. Only two of that dread crew concerned them. The first was Ping, who was found laid out on his own quarterdeck, an arrow wound in his throat. The second was Helgre.

Rumor said nothing of the body of a woman with a scarred face.

If Helgre lived, they were not safe in Mulmaster, or anywhere on the Moonsea's shores.

He put a hand on the great slab of oak that served as a door for the Throatcut Sparrow, then paused. Out of the corner of his eye he caught the flicker of a dark-clad figure ducking into a doorway down the street behind him.

It wasn't his imagination, then. Someone had been tracking him ever since he left Mage Magaster's rooms. Could it be a local thief, suspecting he had something valuable and following him in case he proved inattentive and therefore vulnerable to sly fingers in his purse or to a slim blade between his ribs? Or might it be a spy of Bane's fellowship?

Or could it be Helgre, with vengeance on her mind?

Despite the warmth of the day, Gareth shivered.

Two sturdy fellows, dockworkers, judging by the bulk of them, clattered up behind him and interrupted their banter to call out to him that if he insisted on being a door, he'd better open. He grinned at them good-naturedly and opened the door with a flourish, bowing and gesturing for them to precede him into the tavern's dark interior. With a guffaw and a slap on the back they did. Before he entered himself, Gareth glanced quickly down the street. There was no sign of his follower.

Very well. He hadn't survived this long by not being alert at all times. It was a reminder to always stay alert, to always check behind him, and never assume he hadn't attracted the interest of something malevolent.

Once his eyes adjusted to the gloom inside the tavern, he spotted Ivor talking to the innkeeper, a dwarf of gloomy mien and a magnificent braided beard. Ivor dropped a couple of coins in the dwarf's palm and nodded to Gareth. He had sold two of the tattooed creature's rings to one of the least dishonest jewelers in the Mulmaster gold district—evidently his education in a merchant town in Turmish had given him a fair instinct for when he was being cheated. The platinum coins would bring unwanted attention, he had told Gareth, especially with the possibility of Helgre on the loose, so they had divided the elongated coins between them and used the proceeds from the rings for day-to-day expenses.

But that store of coin was going fast. They needed to find a way to replenish it or get out of Mulmaster—preferably both. He was tired of looking for Helgre behind every corner.

It was the faint scrape of iron on iron that woke him. Every muscle in his body tensed, but he remained still. He reached for the knife he kept beside his bed, his hands tight on the sheath.

His cot was on one side of the room, Ivor's on the other, equidistant from the door. Gareth had barred and bolted it before retiring. Now in the darkness he saw a faint green glow around the bolt. He watched, fascinated, as the forged metal cylinder worked itself free as if by disembodied hands and slid back from the loop affixed to the doorway. The light faded, and there was a pause, as if the spellcaster on the other side were taking a deep breath.

Gareth made himself breathe deeply as he counted: one, two, three. He'd reached fifty when a tiny worm of green light insinuated itself from the crack where the door met the doorsill and snaked around the thick, heavy slab of wood that served as a bar. He wondered if Ivor was awake.

Gareth pushed aside his coverings and rose, still grasping his knife. Silently he approached Ivor's cot, but his friend gestured him back with a two-fingered wave. The Turmish man's short sword hung beside his head. Silently he reached for it with his left hand and drew it from its scabbard with scarcely the ring of metal. They both watched as the green worm divided and spread over the wood, individual threads of it nosing all over the surface as if they were exploring the grain. Soon the whole bar was tainted with its light.

Making a sign to Ivor to wait, Gareth took his thin pillow and humped it under the sheets, shaping the bedcover into the approximate bulk of a sleeping man. He left his boots standing beside the bed and tiptoed to one side of the door. Drawing his knife, he put his back against the wall, making sure he would be out of the light that would illuminate the room when the door opened. Ivor did the same with his own bed and likewise ranged himself on the other side of the door.

The green-glowing bar shifted in its wooden cradle, then slowly started to lift. Impressed, Gareth watched as it floated free of its restraints, then was slowly lowered to the floor, where it landed with the softest of *thunks.*

In the green glow, Ivor lifted an eyebrow. Whoever was on the other side of the door knew what he was doing.

Again the unnatural light faded, and there was another long pause. Seconds stretched to minutes, and Gareth was about to seize the door and fling it open for the satisfaction of taking the thief by surprise, when a crack of yellow light showed the invader was finally entering.

A slim hand pushed the door open just enough to allow entry, and a dim triangle of light from the flickering torch in the hall outside fell into the room. A shadowed, robed figure inched into the doorway. A hood hid its face, but it didn't seem to spot him as he leaned against the wall beside it.

Despite the danger, a wave of relief passed across Gareth's body. The thief was much too small to be Helgre.

The hooded head turned from one bed to the other, where their improvised decoys lay.

The figure ventured forward another step. It lifted its left hand, and a small ball of blue light flared and formed there. Cautiously the figure moved all the way into the room. Its right hand was raised in a warding gesture, the fingers slightly spread. It didn't hold a weapon, but then, a spellcaster didn't have to in order to be a deadly threat.

It paused as if making up its mind, then moved silently toward Ivor's bed. The wrinkles in the coverings were cast into sharp relief by the blue glowball as the figure approached. It paused and drew breath.

Surely it was about to utter an incantation. Gareth was about to shout a warning, when Ivor launched himself at the invader.

It didn't see him. Just before Ivor made contact, Gareth heard a feminine voice say, "Excuse me."

There was a muffled shriek as Ivor bore the intruder down on the bed, grasping it by the approximate location of its neck and drawing the short sword back with the sharp point under the intruder's chin. The blue glowball went out with a fizzle, and the hood fell back from the face.

It was a young woman, staring up at Ivor with wide, startled eyes. Gareth kept his knife ready. He knew enough women, old as well as young, who were as deadly as the most brutal pirate.

One of them *was* the most brutal pirate.

Ivor's face was inches from the girl's, his muscular right arm heavy across her chest and neck, her legs pinned to the bed by his own. They stared into each other's eyes with mutual astonishment. Then, with an oath, Ivor pulled away his sword and scrambled off her slight body. He muttered something that sounded like an apology.

The girl didn't move, but she opened her lips to speak. Gareth swore to himself as Ivor stood staring at her like a poleaxed ox. He shoved Ivor aside and clasped his free hand over her mouth.

"I'll have no spellcasting, you understand me?" Gareth said in a hoarse whisper. "Try anything like that and I'll cut your throat before you can get it half out."

He turned to Ivor, who stood opening and closing his mouth like a fish. "And you—get your wits about you and check the hallway. We'll get knifed from behind while this one charms us."

Ivor nodded and moved to the half-open door.

Gareth turned back to the girl. "Silence, mind. And keep your hands where I can see them. Am I heard?"

Beneath his hand, she nodded. He paused, assessing her. But she remained still, and she didn't glance behind him as she might if she expected help. Ivor vanished into the hallway and swiftly returned, shaking his head.

"No one out there," he said. "Let the girl up, Gareth. She can't do much with the two of us here."

"You're naïve," said Gareth, but he backed his weight off the intruder, allowing her to sit up. As she did, the hood fell completely free, exposing thick brown hair braided back from her face.

He studied her in the dim light from the hallway. She was human, mostly, dark skinned, with wide-set green eyes in a catlike face. High on her left cheek was a small rune drawn or tattooed on her face. He frowned, reminded of the markings of the strange creature on the *Starbound*. But this mark, whether a sigil or a letter of an unfamiliar alphabet, was nothing like those markings.

He gestured at her with the knife, and she flinched back. "Explain," he said.

"Easy, Gareth," murmured Ivor at his shoulder.

"I came to warn you," she said, with only a slight tremor in her voice.

"You might do that anywhere other than our chamber in the dark of the night," Gareth said. "Or you might have knocked rather than unlocking the door from the wrong side. You should be careful about doing that if you're likely to get caught. People tend to take it the wrong way."

"I wasn't going to hurt you, or rob you," she said, glancing from his face to Ivor's. "I'm supposed to, but I won't."

"That's kind of you." He lowered the knife but didn't sheathe it. "Would you care to illuminate us?"

Carefully she lowered her hands and shifted her weight to make herself more comfortable. He watched her narrowly but allowed it. Something about her shape or the fall of her robe reminded him of something. Or was it her voice? It was the same as the soft voice at the entrance to the mage's chambers. He snapped his fingers, making her jump.

"Mage Magaster!" he said. "You were there when I consulted him today. Did he send you?"

She inhaled sharply. "In a manner of speaking." She nodded at the door. "Privacy would be prudent. Do you mind?"

Ivor pushed the door shut and replaced the bar. The girl pushed back her sleeves, and Gareth tensed. She smiled.

"Just making a little light," she said, palm extended. After an instant he nodded and sheathed his blade. Perhaps he was as naïve as Ivor, but she had an air of truth about her. And few spellcasters bothered saying, "Excuse me," before they tried to kill someone. Some did, he was sure, but not many.

The blue ball of light reappeared in her palm. With a few muttered words she released it, and it floated to the ceiling, illuminating the room reasonably well, if casting sharp shadows against the floor and walls. He folded his arms and watched with Ivor as she rose and went to the door, then spread her fingers over the lock while muttering under her breath. The now-familiar green light flowed from her hand to the bolt, and as she fisted her hand, it flared briefly, a deep emerald, before the light faded away completely.

"That should hold, and ward against listening as well," she remarked, as much to herself as to them.

"You mentioned a warning," said Ivor, sounding impressed.

She turned away from the door toward them, watching both of them closely with her wide cat eyes. He saw her robe was belted securely around the middle, and that beneath it she wore leggings that looked like leather, tucked securely into soft boots. A knife with an intricately engraved hilt hung at her belt. It was almost ridiculously small, and it didn't seem likely to make an adequate weapon. She'd made no move toward it when Ivor jumped her, Gareth remembered. It must have something to do with her Art, which seemed to have more to do with undoing locks than with offense.

"My master told you there was nothing special about that bracelet you brought him," she said to Gareth. "He lied."

"I knew it," said Ivor. He reached for the girl's arm, then seemed to think better of it, and stood, looking awkward, his hand splayed near her elbow. "I knew that thing was cursed."

She cocked her head up at him. "Cursed? I don't think so. But that's a powerful—and potentially very dangerous—nexus of magic. I was across the room, and I could feel it."

She glanced at the door nervously. "Magaster sent me to spy on you, and to steal the bracelet if I could."

A thrill of anger went through Gareth—and more: a not-unpleasant prickle of anticipation. "That old cheat. I should go and shake the coin I paid him out of his pockets."

She shook her head. "That would be unwise. Magaster's negotiating an alliance with the Dark Lord's sect, and he seeks to become a power in Mulmaster. It's easy to sink a trackless wanderer or two past the mouth of the bay with a boulder at their heels, and what possessions they have divided between Bane's minions."

Gareth paced the floor. Ivor was still staring at the girl, goggle-eyed as an astonished frog. "If he wanted the thing, why not strike me down there, within his bailiwick, and take it?"

"He didn't know what to do. The kind of magic that thing manipulates is unlike anything he's ever encountered. He wouldn't be able to tell you anything about it even if he was honest, even if he wanted to. The mystery of it confounded him, and he's not used to that. He told me to follow you, to find out what I could about it, where you might come from, where that thing you showed him came from. And if the opportunity arose, I was to steal it from you."

Her gaze flickered over to his bed, and then down, to where his boots stood side by side at the foot. She pointed.

"It's there, isn't it?"

Gareth was impressed. He had secreted the bag with the bracelet in one boot, and the coin pouch in the other, and he didn't think the mage's apprentice meant his coin.

"You can tell where it is?"

"Yes—mind you, I know less than my master about such magic. But it has a powerful aura about it. And also . . ."

"What?"

She looked again, almost longingly, at the bracelet's hiding place. "May I look at it?" Gareth saw her fingers twitch.

"Very well." His knife was close at hand in case he needed it. He moved to stand beside Ivor at the door.

The mage's apprentice stepped quickly across the room and picked up the left boot, upending it over his bed. The pouch landed on the mounded coverlet. She made a gesture with her forefinger and the blue glowball lowered, spreading its azure glow on the bed. Hesitantly she shook the bracelet out of its pouch and it lay there, looking, as the mage had said, like nothing impressive. She reached out her hand to the thing, hesitated, and drew back.

"And also?" queried Ivor.

She sighed and looked up. "You might have noticed I've a knack for locks."

"It had not escaped our attention," said Gareth.

"Locks and wards, making and breaking them. It's my only talent, really. I may not know much, but I know about locks. And this"—she indicated the dull metal semicircle—"this is a lock, and also a key."

Gareth and Ivor looked at each other quizzically. Ivor lifted an eyebrow, and Gareth turned back to the girl. "Why warn us? Why defy your master? I can't imagine he'll look on you kindly after this."

She made a face. "I want to get away from the stink of Mulmaster, with its fish and rust and smoke," she said. "And I know my master plans to join the devout of Bane, and if I'm to prosper here, I must bend my neck to them as well. And the thought turns my stomach."

She sat on the bed, suddenly looking very young. "Magaster sees little use for locks and keys save to secure a room, and little use for me. He tolerates me against those times he needs me to steal something. He can't understand the beauty of a well-constructed trip latch or a spell that works, bit by bit, on opening a door starting from the very grain of the wood. He certainly can't appreciate this." She picked up the bracelet gingerly between two fingers and placed it in her palm. "I can't begin to imagine the skill of the people who constructed this."

There was a pause.

"What's your name?" Ivor asked her.

"And what do you want from us?" said Gareth.

She grinned up at them, looking even more catlike. "Jandi, Jandi M'baren. I thought if you had something like this, you might want to use it. And if you wanted to use it, that I might be able to help you."

"Why would we need your help, Jandi?" asked Gareth. He felt Ivor stir by his side. Fool, he thought indulgently, to be charmed by a pair of pretty cat eyes.

She pursed her lips. "Do you know anything about locks? Do you know how a key can be made that will unfasten a man from the liver outward, and unlock his flesh with a word? Do you know how to ward a house so that each lock will whisper the name of the last being that opened it?"

"No," he admitted.

"Well, I do," she said. "And while I admit that the secrets of your pretty trinket here are beyond my knowledge, they won't be for long. Just give me a little time."

Gareth was intrigued. "What can you do with a key—or a lock—like that?"

She turned it over in her fingers. "There's a great Power that runs through it. It keeps something shut and enclosed, and it is able to tap into it and magnify its own strength, and its ability to keep it imprisoned." Jandi tilted her head and considered. "That's very clever, you know. If it imprisons a living being, the entity's struggles will only strengthen the lock. It would trap itself further, like a bird caught in a wire."

Gareth felt a flare of excitement. He stepped closer to her. "Could you use it to secure something against all comers? A ship, maybe?" He thought of a ship of his own, a merchantman proofed against all of Ping's ilk.

Why stop there? "Or a house. A big house. A . . ." *Dream big.* "A fortress."

"Using the Power of whatever it imprisons?" She lifted it and looked through it like a keyhole. "I bet I could do it," she said reflectively. "I bet I could."

"I bet you could, too," said Ivor, staring at her.

"Then Jandi M'baren and Ivor Beguine," said Gareth. "By the Nine Hells, I think it's time all of us got out of Mulmaster."

Again he experienced awareness, like a flaming whip. This time Fandour seized it, ignoring the pain, and the burn faded away along with his connection to the Rhythanko. But before it did, he had a clear image graven on his mind—a creature of the strange plane held the Rhythanko and knew its nature—he knew it as few ever could. He clutched at the image, but it slipped away, leaving him bereft. For a long time Fandour floated static in the iron egg of his prison.

Then he turned his consciousness back to the Nexus, the place in the strange plane where over the centuries he'd been able to make contact, to touch those alien minds, and to begin to understand them. With understanding came control. From one mind, if he was sufficiently rooted, he could reach out and touch another, both gathering information and influencing behavior.

In Faerûn, his mind grew. He had infinite patience. It had taken an eon to realize he was imprisoned and to remember how that came to be, another to learn to send his consciousness to the plane where his avatar had wandered, another to begin to manipulate, one by one, the inhabitants there.

Eventually the net would be cast wide enough. Eventually he would find the Rhythanko and make it remember. Eventually he would be free.

CHAPTER THREE

The Giant's Fist, Later Jadaren Hold

1461 DR—The Year of Three Goddesses Blessing

During the birthing of the land that mortal and fey would eventually call Faerûn, the earth twisted and buckled, and the rocks that composed Toril melted and re-formed, only to melt again. Volcanoes erupted from the plains, and rivers of lava flowed like water would millennia later. The very elements of the planet were in constant, shifting flux. The crust cracked open, revealing the scarlet and orange chasms of plasma bleeding beneath, and healed itself, only to be torn asunder again and again.

At the end of this cataclysmic time, the rock and fire at the heart of the planet folded in on themselves and were pushed to the surface, breaking through the crust. Mountain ranges hatched like a clutch of dragons out of one monstrous egg. Active volcanoes sprang up wherever the skin of Toril was thin, studding the ribs of the mountains like enormous, fiery gemstones.

One range pushed to the surface, high and jagged. It then became worn down over time by the elements and the restlessness of the earth, and rose again, newly forged in the liquid heat of the mantle. The second time, a volcano rose with it. Made of black rock, it spewed a constant river of bright lava to flood the slopes of the valley below.

A thousand years passed, and another, and the flow of liquid rock from the black mountain slowed, diminished, and finally stopped, leaving miles of rippled stone like a river frozen in time. Now and then a plume of smoke would belch forth, along with a rain of pumice and ash, but with less and less frequency until the volcano became a cinder cone, extinct, an enormous knob of basalt squatting on the weathered side of the mountain range, and the folklore passed on by the tribes that began to settle the area was the only testament to its original primal savagery.

At the base of the cone, years of weather and erosion had hollowed out caves, some shallow, some so deep as to extend halfway under the mountain. There were tunnels where lava had flowed, some with ceilings so low that a halfling child would have to duck its head to go inside. Some were enormous, tall enough to hold houses, roomy enough for any goliath that might choose to dwell there. Particle by particle, rainfall wore away the softer minerals throughout the monolith, leaving it honeycombed with more passages, some smooth as glass, some lined throughout with crystals. Erosion had also carved the softer material of the mountain away from the cone, so it was a discrete structure in itself.

At some forgotten place in history, a race of beings—dwarves, perhaps, or one of their relations—had come and constructed a stair, carved out of the living rock, that circled behind the cone, between the basalt knob and the mountain, and emerged at the top of the monolith. From the flat summit, an adventurous soul could see a dizzying view of the valley and rolling green meadows below, with tributary streams branching and tumbling through them to a distant river, and only traces in the landscape of the solid black lava beneath it all.

The ancient, mysterious delvers had refined the voids and tunnels of the cone, making wide passageways and series of rooms, stairways from base to summit, and hallways big enough to house an entire village.

Some said they disturbed a primordial evil that slept in the passageways and were devoured, while others said they tunneled too deep and broke through to the Underdark, and were killed or enslaved by gray dwarves.

Who they were, no one knew, or would admit to knowing. They left only their stonework, the marks of their tools on the surface of the basalt, a few ancient runes on some of the walls, and legends of their passing.

The folk of the surrounding settlements avoided the place and said that it was cursed, or haunted, or that strange eldritch creatures dwelled in the bottommost depths of its mazes. No treasure was hidden there that anyone knew of, and there was little of value to be mined on or around that basalt protuberance, save for a few pretty quartz crystals. It sat on the border of Erlkazar but was too far from any city of size for any of the baronies to take an interest in it for settlement or even for use as a way station. Twice or thrice throughout the centuries this or that local lordling had claimed it, only to find it too remote and barren to be either a dwelling or an outpost.

Folk called it the Giant's Fist, or the Blackstone, or the Eye of Leviathan, depending on the custom of their village and the fancy of their bards, but unless they were asked about it, or had to retrieve some livestock that had wandered that way, they mentioned it hardly at all.

Gareth Jadaren knew the Giant's Fist was no palace. The wind howled over it in an unpleasant way, like a harpy chuckling over a trove of carrion. It was desolate, gloomy, and unaesthetic. But it was defensible.

"And the work of tunneling is done for us!" he called cheerfully to Ivor Beguine and Jandi M'baren.

Ivor and Jandi looked dubiously at the monolith that loomed against the mountainside. The valley they had come through was ribboned now with streams and well grown with small trees and fields of mountain flowers, but the occasional crunch of the donkey's hooves against pumice and a black tumble of rocks peeking through the grasses told of the lava plains beneath.

They had ventured well south of Turmish when they began to hear travelers' tales of the Giant's Fist, its legends, and isolation. The stories fascinated Gareth, and he persuaded the others to skim the northern border of Erlkazar and seek out the strange monolith.

He patted the donkey's neck with satisfaction while the animal snorted and tore a mouthful of sweetgrass from the ground.

"Does Berendel claim the land all around the base?" asked Ivor, coming to stand beside Gareth.

"He does," said Gareth. "As much as he can. Men set themselves up as barons here, laying claim to a splotch on a map and a handful of villages so others will bob their heads and call them lord. This land's been part of a half-dozen baronies over the last hundred years, as far as I can tell. Not that it matters, for no one cares to come near it or make it their home."

"It's a lonely place," said Jandi, pulling up more sweetgrass for the donkey and regarding the Fist narrowly. "A sad place."

"We'll make it a happy place," said Gareth. "A prosperous place. All for ten platinum and a promise to call Berendel 'm'Lord' twice or thrice a year."

"Strange he would sell it so cheap," said Ivor.

Gareth tugged the donkey away from its lunch. "All the folk hereabouts have lived with it all their lives, and it's just a remote, haunted spot to them. The trading interests want dominance over the established routes, and few think of the wilderness save as a source of occasional good and a breeding ground for pirates. Here"—he spread his arm wide, earning a bleat of protest from the donkey as he accidentally tugged at its tether—"a well-fortified headquarters could command trade from the Eastern Reaches to Turmish and beyond."

Ivor prudently took the lead rope from him. He patted the donkey, and the animal snorted indignantly. "And we fortify it how?"

Gareth tapped the pouch at his belt where the bracelet lay. "Jandi said she could ward a fortress with this."

"That's not a fortress," said the cat-eyed girl. "That's a rock you've bought yourself."

"More of a long-term contract," said Gareth.

"Nevertheless, a rock. A very big rock."

"A rock we'll make a fortress," said Gareth, his eyes gleaming.

Jandi turned to Ivor with a laugh on her lips, and caught him looking at her with a peculiar intensity—a look he didn't intend her to see. When she returned it, he looked quickly at the ground and his tanned cheeks reddened.

"The sun's going down behind the range," said Gareth, oblivious to the silent exchange as he watched the sky turn pink. "I suggest we camp tonight and explore tomorrow."

If he hadn't been so distracted by his plans, Gareth would've noticed his friends' replies were more subdued than was their wont.

Jandi sat at the base of an oak, watching Ivor pile black pockmarked lava stones into a ring for their fire pit. Gareth had ventured into the woods a short way to find firewood.

Ivor positioned a stone and stood up, stretching his back. In doing so, he caught her gaze, as she had done his down on the plains, and like him she felt herself blushing. He smiled at her, and the breath caught in her throat. A strange tingle that had nothing to do with her Art spread over her body.

When he turned to look at the ponderous monolith, she could breathe normally again, and the evening breeze felt cool against her flushed cheeks. She tilted her head back to look at the oak above her. The enormous spread of its branches showed its age, and it looked out of place in a wood thick with elm and birch. Perhaps it was an ancient remnant from the oak vastness of the Chondalwood, surrounded here by upstart trees spreading from the forests at the base of the Cloven Mountains. It was as strange among these younger trees as the black stone of the Giant's Fist was in the softer flank of the mountain range.

She was still studying its interlacing branches when she felt someone approach and stand in front of her. She waited and counted her heartbeats—one, two, three—before lowering her head.

Ivor kneeled in front of her, bringing their eyes to a level.

"You said you could open the inside of a man like a lock," he said.

"I can."

"How?"

Jandi considered him a moment. "By making my will into a key and reaching inside," she said.

He smiled, a teasing smile just short of mockery. "Do it to me."

"What? No!" she exclaimed.

"Why not?"

"Because I don't wish to kill you."

He rocked back on his heels. "I don't think you can do it."

"Then more fool you," she said tartly.

"You can't." His smile was maddening.

"Is that a challenge?"

He bent close. "Yes."

She looked a long moment into his dark brown eyes, studying his face. Then she reached out and placed the palm of her hand beneath the open ties of his shirt, against the bare skin over his heart. Her hand was cool and his flesh was warm; she could feel the strong, steady beat of his heart.

He didn't move, still staring into her eyes. It seemed to that her his breath became quick and shallow, and she felt the blood rush to her cheeks again. She dropped her gaze, concentrating on her hand on his heart.

He didn't move as the sigil on her cheek pulsed once with a green light. Tiny green sparks, bright now in the gathering dusk, danced across her body and down her arm. He felt something insubstantial push through the wall of his chest, between his ribs and through the muscle. His pulse quickened at it.

She raised her eyes to his, and it was as if she held his heart cupped in her hands. He knew she could unlock him, but she wouldn't—not this way.

Jandi closed her eyes, and he felt that gentle, dangerous touch withdraw. When she removed her hand from his chest, the skin it had covered was suddenly cold.

Her lips were warm when he bent forward and covered her mouth with his.

"Where are you laze-abouts? Come help me with the load!"

Gareth's voice tore through the moment and Jandi and Ivor pulled apart, the breeze chilling their lips. Jandi glanced over Ivor's shoulder and saw Gareth, his arms piled high with prickly deadwood, standing by the half-completed fire pit. A log rolled off the top of his burden. He cursed and turned toward them, laughing. The grin froze on his face when he saw them together, and he turned away suddenly. The wood falling on the ground made a sound like the clatter of sticks on a stretched hide being beaten to make soft leather.

Gareth and Jandi stood on top of the Fist while Ivor and the phlegmatic donkey kept watch at the base. Jandi drew her cloak closer around her body and shivered. The autumn wind moaning across the Fist's flat surface was chilly.

"I didn't leave Bane's city to sojourn in Bane's gravel pit," she grumbled, kicking a pebble over the side. It bounced several times against the side of the monolith, making a clacking sound every time it hit. Far beneath them, she saw Ivor's head turn to follow the sound.

"It'll be a paradise by the time we're finished with it," Gareth proclaimed, hopping down from a knot of stone and examining the half-illegible characters carved at its base. "Is there any magic left here, from who—or what—went before? We don't want any residual Power to clash with your Art."

As she had done several times on the hike up the stairs that curved between the cone and its parent mountain, she closed her eyes and held out her arms, elbows at her sides and palms up. She inhaled deeply, and Gareth heard a gentle humming, although she didn't seem to be producing the sound herself.

Jandi opened her eyes. "I don't think so," she said. "Possibly an echo in the depths. It's hard to avoid any trace of magic. Creatures magical by nature pass by, and always leave some kind of trail, no matter how faint. I would be more suspicious of a place completely clean of magic—it takes an effort to burn an area clear. There's nothing here that would interfere with my overlay."

"Well, then, what's stopping you?"

The young mage glared at the grinning ex-pirate and reached into the bag slung across her shoulder. "Nothing," she said. "But you'll need to give me the Key."

Gareth pulled the torque from his upper arm, where it had nested the night before. Jandi had found a spot clear of rocks and sat cross-legged.

Jandi placed the Key cautiously on her lap and took a clean glass vial from her pack. She held it in her right hand and drew her small blade with her left.

"Give me your hand. I'll need some of your blood. Oh, please!" She laughed as he flinched back. "I know you've had worse fighting. You've shed more blood while shaving!"

"That was due to ill-intentioned folk, or an accident," he said. "I'm not accustomed to having those who are supposed to be working for my benefit stabbing me with their little knives."

Imperiously she gestured with bottle and knife, and he sighed.

"Which hand?" he said.

"The one you would hold a key with, if you were unlocking a door."

He kneeled and extended his right hand. She held the bottle close alongside while she sliced deeply across the pad of his forefinger. Thick blood welled, and she filled the small bottle quickly.

"Sorry," she said, giving him a sympathetic smile.

He stood and wrapped the small wound in the tail of his shirt. "It is what it must be," he said.

She sheathed the knife and took the Key in one hand, the glass vial filled with scarlet in the other. Her eyes closed, and the sigil on her cheek glowed briefly with the strange green light associated with her Art.

He retreated to sit on a nearby rock and reached in his own pack for a skin of ale. He watched as Jandi's breathing slowed, the time between her inhaling and exhaling uncomfortably long. Minutes stretched to an hour and he finished the skin, wishing he'd brought another and wondering if anything was going to happen.

Then he saw the tiny green sparks hovering around her body like fireflies. Thicker and brighter they grew, coalescing into a ring around her. The circle of green light moved down her form, spreading as it met the rock. It was followed by another, and another. They moved across the surface of the Fist like slow-moving ripples.

On and on it went. As dusk came on, the glow became brighter. He watched, fascinated, and wondered what it looked like to the watchers below.

Down at the base, Ivor watched the Giant's Fist turn from black to chartreuse, waves of green light drenching it like a strange tide. Although the outside temperature wasn't particularly cold, he leaned against the donkey's neck and shivered.

The walls of the oubliette flared suddenly, red-hot, and the walls of Fandour's prison constricted. Fandour screamed, startled out of a deep state of meditation, and rolled away from the hot metallic surface, trying to be as small as possible. It didn't work; the walls seared Fandour's flesh. The glowing walls sprouted thick iron thorns, and they pierced Fandour's tough hide, sharp pinpricks of pain in the midst of the dull agony as the sullen orange wall pressed, relentless.

Let me die, *thought Fandour, struggling to send a clear tendril of thought through the pain.* If I can't be free, if I must be tormented, let me die and seek release no more.

And in answer to the acute mental cry, he heard a whisper, from a long way off. It was hard to understand, like a message read in an uncouth voice by someone who didn't know the language and was guessing at the sound of the letters; like the language of the gith, muttered by an Aboleth, or an orc with a mouthful of pebbles.

Give, give, *the voice cried, greedy as a baby bird.* Give a morsel of yourself, a piece of your Power, a handful of light and stone torn by strong hands from the core of your essence. Give!

Fandour flung a thought back through the planes: Stop this, or kill me now. *He flinched farther into himself as the hot walls constricted once more.*

Kill you? Never. You will live forever, pressed on all sides by red metal and thorns. Give what I ask for!

Was the voice that of the Rhythanko? Could his bound avatar turn against him so? Or was his tormentor the alien mind that possessed the long-sundered key to his prison?

Fandour could bear no more. Take, *he shouted, opening up and exposing a soft underbelly, going against every instinct to do so.* Take, and stop this torment.

Ah, *the voice gloated as* something, *not another entity but a thought and will made material and animate scooped out a part of Fandour, twisted, and escaped like a small savage fish nipping a chunk of flesh from bigger prey and darting away.*

The thorns retracted, the searing heat was gone. Exhausted and quivering with remembered pain, Fandour sprawled on the floor of the oubliette and strove to understand what had happened.

Someone had used the Rhythanko to tear away a little of Fandour's Power, to mold it and forge it into something of use.

Eagerly, ignoring the waves of pain that still rippled through his essence, Fandour sent tiny thought tendrils along the fragile and ephemeral ley lines that still connected the Rhythanko and the oubliette. Someone was out there, sitting on a great mass of stone, stone from the flaming heart of a mountain, cool and hard now and honeycombed with tunnels. Two people: one had the knowledge of the nature of all manner of locks and keys, magic, mundane and mechanical, in her head and held the Rhythanko in her hand; the other was harder to see, having little magic in him. He reached out, and the other, the mistress of things locked and unlocked, put the Rhythanko in his hand. A jolt of Power struck Fandour's thought tendril, sending it back into him like a blow.

Fandour curled up inside the oubliette, clinging to the memory. The man reaching with tentative fingers for the Rythanko was bound to it by blood. The Rhythanko, in turn, was bound to him by the Power the woman had ripped from Fandour. That small essence Fandour had lost forever, but in that brief contact, Fandour had sniffed out the dark one's blood, a nexus between him, Fandour, and the Rhythanko.

Time was long and until Fandour healed, there was little else to be done. He coiled about the memory of the blood, the nature, the taste, the smell, the tiny components of it.

Fandour would not forget anything to do with that blood.

A troubled expression on her face, Jandi sat silent as the green light of her Art faded. She turned the bracelet round and round between her fingers.

"You'd impress them back in Mulmaster," said Gareth. "Why the glum look?"

She looked up at him, ignoring the hand he'd stretched out to help her up.

"I wish I knew more about how the Key was made, and the exact nature of the Power it taps into," she said.

"Why? It did what you wanted." He wiggled his fingers at her.

She seemed to see his hand at last and took it. He winced as she grasped his wounded finger tightly while pulling herself to her feet. She staggered, and he extended an arm to steady her.

"Are you unwell?"

She breathed deeply and raised her eyes to his.

"It's just . . . I have a feeling I caused pain to something, to some entity or Power the Key is connected to.

I felt a cry of pain, and more—despair. Something with no hope, and nothing to do but watch and plan for . . . for something. A chance to escape, to be free of the Key."

"But you didn't intend to hurt anybody."

"No, of course not. But sometimes you can cause great harm, accidentally. When you were a sailor, and you had to fight a pirate, do you think you ever had to hurt . . . or kill . . . someone who was innocent? Because of the circumstances, or the tools of your trade, just in the course of business?"

Gareth turned away to look at the horizon, black starred silk against black velvet, and pulled on his gloves, for the mountain air was chilly. Neither he nor Ivor had told Jandi they'd served on Ping's ship before they'd met her in Mulmaster.

Gareth found himself wondering if Ivor would tell her, now that she'd thrown her lot in with pirates.

"Yes, I suppose," he said at last. "You can't avoid stepping on every ant. And maybe you did injure something in using the Key, but it's over now, and they'll likely forget."

"Yes, very likely." Jandi's voice told him she wasn't so sure. She swayed again.

"Careful of the edge," said Gareth, guiding her to a stone knob. She didn't sit but leaned on it, still twisting the torque in her hand.

"Are you all right?" He glanced at the rock beneath their feet and wondered if he was imagining the ambient green glow that seemed to cling to the contours of the rough stone. "Did . . . did it work?" He tried not to sound too eager.

She nodded wearily. "It worked, possibly in more ways than we'll ever know. But your palace is warded to you, and I wish you the joy of it."

He looked at the dull metal she wound between her fingers like a snake. Tentatively he reached out for it.

"Shouldn't I—shouldn't I hold that?"

Startled, she looked at him, then down at the torque.

"Yes, of course," she said. "But . . . do you mind if I hold it a while longer?"

Reluctantly he pulled back his hand.

"It's drained me," she said. "But now it's over, I feel some of my strength return. And I'd like—I'd like to find out if it can give me any more information before you take it back."

She looked down at it, brooding.

"I'd like to find out whom I've hurt. May I? Just for a while. I'll give it back tonight."

Suddenly Gareth longed for the brisk walk down and a slap of cool water on his face at the base of the Fist.

"Come on, then," he said, taking her elbow. "Dinner and your sweetheart below, and then you can tinker with that Key as long as you like."

Jandi made it down the rough-hewn stairway unaided, but Ivor persuaded her to mount the donkey for the short trek back to their campsite at the old oak. The donkey grumbled, but Jandi was light and there wasn't far to go. She kept turning the bracelet over in her hands, and every once in a while the mark on her cheek shone green.

"We'll need a name for it," said Gareth to the company in general.

"A name for what?" replied Ivor as Jandi and the donkey were silent.

Gareth gestured with his thumb over his shoulder at the monolith.

"That," he said. "The Giant's Fist is an unwieldy name for a trading headquarters."

"I have a name for you," said Ivor with a suspicious glance backward. "Jadaren's Folly."

CHAPTER FOUR

Near the Giant's Fist, Later Jadaren Hold

1461 DR—The Year of Three Goddesses Blessing

Between the lacework of the oak's branches, Jandi, staring at the sky darkening from lavender to purple, stretched her neck before looking back down at the torque in her lap. The *presence* she'd felt while warding the Fist—or the Hold, as Gareth decided to call it on the hike back to the campsite—was gone, but the memory lingered of a great intelligence imprisoned, all too aware of its confinement. It gave her the unpleasant feeling of seeing a forgotten pet in a cage, staring at her with dumb, tortured eyes, mired with filth and too big for its shackles.

Ivor had ventured under the forest's canopy to restock their wood, taking the donkey with him ("I should've thought of that yesternight," Gareth had remarked), and Gareth was down by the stream, trying to trap a dove or some quail as a change from dried meat. Birds twittered in the elms, and if Jandi listened carefully, she could hear the distant chatter of the stream.

She didn't hear the shadowed figure behind her, nor did she know the danger she was in until the thick leather cord snapped around her neck and was pulled tight. Jandi's eyes opened wide and her hands flew instinctively to her throat, but her assailant's fingers were strong. Jandi tried to wrest the garrote from her neck, but the leather bit deep into her flesh. She reached behind her head to try to grasp her attacker's wrists and pull them away. But exhausted from the day's work, she only batted weakly at the wiry forearms that twisted the cord ever tighter.

Desperately, Jandi tried to suck in air—to fill her lungs and call for help, speak a spell of protection, to live—but her windpipe was wrenched shut. She moved her lips, but no sound came out. The fire before her turned red as the blood beat behind her eyes, and black splotches floated before her. Her throat was on fire, and she felt as if her chest was going to explode. She could hear only the roar of her own heartbeat, desperate and fast, in her ears.

Finding her last reserve of strength, she bucked against the hard ground, thrusting against the figure behind her. The cruel grip loosened for a second, and she frantically drew in what air she could. She tried to focus, to make her will into a Key and unlock her assailant's body.

She couldn't do it. Her assailant recovered and pulled the cord tighter, cutting off her breath for good. Jandi struggled limply a few more seconds, but her vision was blacked out now, with only a few spots of light floating in front of her, and the pressure on her throat hurt like a raw wound. The fire in her breast was fading, and she didn't even want to fight anymore. The roar in her ears slowed and faded until she could hear each individual *thump-bump,* slower and slower, weaker and weaker. Her heartbeat faded, faltered, and stopped.

Jandi was lying on the wet grass, her eyes glazed open, although she saw nothing, a black beyond the darkest night before her eyes. Something seemed to stir inside that blackness, something huge and malevolent. She was paralyzed, as in the terror of a waking dream when nightmare forces advance and the dreamer is powerless to move.

The presence, whatever it was, was made of darkness itself and was therefore invisible, but still she knew it shifted its thick, coiled body, raised its immense bulk, and considered her. Despair filled her as she sensed it gloating.

It was Bane or one of his servants. It did no good to flee Mulmaster and the dreadful bargains with the Dark Lord brewing there. He had hunted her down, and in her death he would take her.

Then, in the center of the blackness, came a spot of light—not the bright painful sparks she saw in her death struggle, but a gentle glow like a hearth fire. It strengthened and lengthened, a long thin oval, and she felt the invisible malevolence retreat, sullen and reluctant. The light grew brighter, until it was almost painful to look at. Then it blazed so brightly that she was as blinded by the light as she had been before by the darkness.

Jandi tried to blink, but her eyes remained open. She was faintly aware of her body, stiff and cooling, in the long grass, the campfire falling apart and dying before her.

She was supposed to keep the fire burning, wasn't she? She tried to remember who had told her that.

The light faded until it no longer pained her eyes, and the shape in the middle shifted and resolved itself into the tall and long-legged figure of a woman. Jandi watched with a detached curiosity as the woman approached and kneeled beside her.

The woman tilted her head and considered her. She wore a garment of some river-green fabric that flowed about her as if a breeze were blowing, and her scarlet hair was cropped close beneath her ears. Her eyes, a slightly darker green than her dress, were almond shaped.

The woman smiled suddenly, and her smile was like sunshine on Jandi's cold flesh. Reaching out, she stroked Jandi's hair, and her gentle touch broke the icy grip that kept her limbs frozen.

She blinked rapidly. The woman's elfin features came into focus, and the blaze of light faded until she could see the grass she lay in, the trees beyond, and the dying, stone-banked fire before her. Everything was imbued with a golden, illuminated quality, as if the light had flowed into the landscape instead of dying away.

Jandi flexed her stiff limbs and found she could sit up effortlessly, although the movement made her dizzy. The woman rose and stood over her, still smiling.

"Who are you?" Jandi whispered, expecting her throat to hurt and surprised that it did not.

The woman reached out a long-fingered hand, and Jandi took it.

"You can call me Mandira for now," she said in a voice that had the tremble of silver bells in it, pulling Jandi to her feet, and seeming to expend no effort doing it. Indeed, Jandi felt as if she were floating.

"I don't remember . . ." she began, then, looking down, saw the crumpled body at her feet. The pale face with the blue lips looked familiar, the eyes slightly protruding and staring at nothing. She had the impression of an insubstantial figure bending over the body.

"I don't understand," she concluded.

Mandira still had her hand, a touch so light she could barely feel it.

"You will in time," she said. "But now you have a choice. You can stay here, tied to the flesh and its memories. Or you can come with me, and dwell a while in Brightwater's gentle realm."

The red-headed woman tugged her hand, the slightest of tugs, and Jandi let herself be pulled away one step, then two.

"Wait," she said. "I'm waiting for someone. I'm waiting for . . ."

Ivor. The name was a whisper in her mind. The woman smiled sadly at her, and Jandi knew she'd somehow heard it.

"It's a cruel thing," she said. "To be struck down when love is fragile and new, uncurling like a butterfly from its cocoon. Flesh is mortal and love is not."

She tugged her hand again. "The lady grants this mercy, because love had found a home in your heart. You may find a home, for a while, with her. You may refuse. You may stay with this body, and see your lover grieve. You may haunt this place, searching ceaselessly for what you can no longer have while your body rots beneath the ground. It is your choice."

Jandi glanced once more at the body. It seemed a thing utterly alien, nothing to do with her, and now it was fading like a face in the twilight. She saw a small circlet of dull metal beside the body, with a haze of sickly green about it.

She felt she should remember something about it, but the memory slipped away like a scarf in the wind.

The oak tree beyond the body was glowing now, its bark burnished gold. The forest beyond faded from view as well, save for individual trees scattered here and there that glowed with the same golden light as the oak. She could see their roots branching beneath the ground, and their leaves were amber and jade.

Jandi made her decision and looked deep into the woman's eyes, drowning in emerald. The light from the trees grew more intense, until there was nothing but brightness and the distant sound of water.

A tall woman kneeled over the body of the young mage, not loosening the braided cord around her neck until she was sure she was dead. Finally, the woman released her grip and looped the garrote neatly, tucking it into her belt. The moon emerged from behind the clouds, illuminating a lean face with a thick red scar twisting the corner of the left eye and marring the cheek to the jawbone. She pressed two fingers beneath the still girl's jawline, trying to detect any trace of a pulse.

Satisfied on that point, she plucked a bracelet from the grass. It had tumbled from the girl's lap in her final struggle. She examined it. It wasn't silver or gold, and the three red stones embedded in it weren't rubies or even garnets. She tossed it away like a piece of trash, then rose to her feet.

She didn't see the bracelet twitch a couple times, elongating and flattening until it became a long chain of links, which crept, snakelike, through the grass and coiled around the dead mage's limp arm.

Helgre stood, silent, listening intently to the sounds of the dusk. She knew one of her quarry was still down at the stream, and she could hear the other foraging along the verge of the forest, heralded by the heavy tramp of the donkey.

She smiled wolfishly. She had spent months nursing her wounds and hatred in the Mulmaster slums. Many tendays she had spent sniffing out rumors of the deserters in the dockside dives and taverns. She had spent almost a year tracking them and the wench they'd picked up in Mulmaster, north through the unfriendly towns of Turmish, and then following them across borders and back again. By chance she had met one of would-be Baron Berendel's men in a roadside inn and heard the tale of a mad ex-sailor who wanted possession of a cursed piece of barren rock.

Hard on their trail, she lurked in the cover of the sprawling forest. When she ventured close enough to see their faces, a fierce joy burned in her veins. It was them, after all—Gareth Jadaren and Ivor Beguine, traitors and cowards who had not only abandoned the ship she loved but set those dreadful avengers on her wake.

That had been more than a year ago now. The second she had found Din and Barneb sprawling on the deck in the early morning, still groggy, she knew something was wrong. She knew Gareth and Ivor were on third watch, and their absence was suspicious. A few quick slaps across

Din's face and a knife beneath his jaw elicited the information that the Turmish man and his friend had come last night with wine. She considered knifing the hapless easterner and dropping him over the side.

Instead, she dropped him in disgust and went to tell Ping of the deserters. She'd just reached his chambers when she heard the chaos on deck.

It was too much of a coincidence. Gareth and Ivor had jumped ship and betrayed them in Mulmaster. I never trusted that Gareth, she thought, as she drew her knife. I should've cut his throat when he signed on.

She expected to see a fighting ship and a pack of Mulmaster bullies, recruited by what passed for the law in that scabby dock town. Instead, she saw a confused mass of crew, some of them sprawled on the deck, unmoving. Standing on the forecastle deck was a tall figure, armed with a heavy bow. He looked rooted in place, his boots wide-side on the boards. The graceful motion of his upper body as he drew his long black-feathered arrows from the quiver strapped to his back, nocked them to the string, pulled back effortlessly, and loosed into the shambles, finding his mark every time, spoke of long practice and a mastery of the art.

On the deck below, the shifting bodies gave her a glimpse of Krevlak, a burly half-orc they'd picked up near Thay, swinging a mace at another combatant. Krevlak's opponent ducked, and the mace swung wide, sending the half-orc off balance. As the figure straightened, Helgre saw it was a woman, dusky skinned with a pale mask across her eyes, and hair braided away from her face.

She held a greatsword two-handedly, and, as Krevlak stumbled, she brought it up in a killing stroke across his torso. The half-orc fell in a red spatter, and the woman leaped across his body with insolent ease, engaging another pirate.

The rest of that nightmare day was a blur. She remembered seeing Ping's head jerk back as an arrow slammed into his throat, and the pain as another ripped into her shoulder as she tried to duck away. She remembered a red-orange ball of fire, like a miniature sun, streaking toward the archer on the deck and the easy movement he made with his hand, as if he were turning away a blow, dispelling it so it sputtered against the rigging. She remembered the sickening impact of the water against her rib cage as she dropped over the side. A man—it was Barneb—had gone the same route and clung to a board floating in the water. With her remaining strength she shoved him away and pushed him under, kicking at him until he sank. She prayed the predatory fish that followed the *Orcsblood* would feast on him and ignore her. She didn't know how she finally reached the shore. She knew only that it was night when she did, and the rocks were slippery and cold under the docks.

But she had lived, and now she waited, patiently, until their guard dropped and they separated for the first time. She took the girl first as opportunity offered.

That's the penalty, my girl, for consorting with traitors.

Now she would track Ivor down as he scavenged for wood. Then she would wait, concealed in the trees, for Gareth to return.

She licked her lips. She must kill Ivor slowly and let him know that his ladylove died first.

A fist knotted into her hair, jerking her head back. She gasped at the suddenness of it, too surprised to scream.

"I intended to take that morsel for myself, until you came and robbed me of my game," a husky voice whispered in her ear. "But perhaps you'll prove better sport."

She tried to twist away from the grip on her hair, but her captor was unnaturally strong and had the advantage of surprise. She managed to get her knife halfway out of its sheath before a powerful hand found hers and wrested the weapon away with almost insolent ease, flicking it away from them both. She heard the metal clang against a stone.

Helgre fumbled for the garrote in her belt, feeling it slip through her fingers. In a desperate effort, she flailed at her assailant, trying to find any weak spot.

But suddenly a warm lassitude flowed through her limbs, as did an odd feeling of well-being. Her attacker still held her firmly but now didn't seem so threatening.

A hand traced the raised line of her scar, caressingly, from the corner of her eye, down her cheek, and over her jawline.

"How does a lady come by such a thing? You must tell me someday."

Helgre closed her eyes, enjoying the feeling. The hand brushed the ends of her hair back, tucking it behind her ear and leaving her neck exposed. She felt gentle fingers against her skin, tracing the line of her jugular down to the base of her neck, where her pulse jumped. There the light touch of the fingers paused.

She closed her eyes, enjoying the sensation.

No. Her eyes snapped open. Something was wrong. She shouldn't feel like this.

Confused, she tried to shake off the feeling of contentment. Her life was in danger. She must fight for it.

Sharp teeth sank into her neck.

Gareth was within sight of the fire pit, a brace of quail on his belt, when he heard Ivor cry out. He ran. The limp birds, still warm, bounced against his hip.

In the gathering twilight his friend kneeled in front of the old oak, clutching something in his arms. The donkey stood a little way off, a load of firewood bound on its back. It stamped its front hoof and whickered.

Gareth stared at Ivor's burden in confusion. Ivor was holding Jandi to his breast, and the mage was looking straight back at Gareth, her eyes wide and unblinking.

What was the matter with her? Gareth took a step forward, then another. He saw that Jandi's eyes were bulging slightly and that her lips were blue.

"No," he said, and took another step. "She's not . . ."

Ivor looked up at him with red, streaming eyes. The horror of the moment flooded him. In an instant he was on his knees beside them.

"She's gone," said Ivor, looking into the mage's dead face. "I came back and thought she was sleeping. I was going to rouse her, tease her about taking a nap all alone, but . . ."

He turned on Gareth with a snarl. "It was too much for her, all that mucking about with that key or bracelet or whatever that cursed thing is you brought from the

Orcsblood. It wore her out, broke her mind. If you hadn't made her do it . . ."

"I didn't *make* her do anything," retorted Gareth, stunned. "This is horrible, but don't look to me for the blame."

He studied the body, trying to avoid eye contact. It was terrible to look into Jandi's eyes when there was nothing, no soul or spirit, behind them. There was no blood, no sign of a wound. The he saw a bruise on her throat, under the curve of her jaw.

"See—look at her neck."

Gently Ivor tilted her head back so she gazed at the sky. To Gareth's great relief, he passed his hand over her eyes, closing them. With her throat exposed, they could clearly see the mark encircling it, where some sort of cord had bit deep.

Gareth touched her chill skin, hoping against hope to find a pulse. There was nothing. She was as dead as the quail he'd trapped.

"Resurrection," gasped Ivor. "If we can reach Berendel's people . . . If they have a priestess . . ."

Gareth shook his head. "It's too late. She's already cold. Even if they had someone powerful enough, or willing, by the time we got there . . ."

"I know," said Ivor.

Gareth sat back on his heels. "Who could have done this, Ivor?" He glanced around them at the silent trees. "Could they still be here?"

"Look no farther than there." Ivor pointed at Jandi's arm.

Confused, Gareth looked past Ivor's shaking finger. The sleeve of the mage's robe had fallen away, revealing the pale skin of the inner arm, branched with blue veins.

Coiled around her arm was a length of dull metal links. A red stone peered out from between the arm and the grass like a tiny bloodshot eye.

"That *thing*," sputtered Ivor. "That cursed, unnatural *thing*. It wrought that creature's doom on the *Starbound*, and now it's taken Jandi. Strangled her."

"No," said Gareth, shaking his head. "It's not possible."

"It crawled around her neck, like it did to you on the *Starbound*. You were lucky then, or maybe it realized it could use you. You've served its ends ever since."

Ivor gestured at the Fist.

"Safe haven," he said, mockingly. "That's all you've talked about for the past year, all you've sought. I was along for the adventure and the hope of profit someday, and Jandi—" His voice broke. "She wanted out of Mulmaster. She wanted to test her skills. I didn't know you'd be willing to destroy her for the sake of your precious security. That dead pile of rock—is it what you wanted? Or what *it* wanted?"

Gareth was peering intently at the marks on Jandi's neck. Something about them looked familiar—something that should have been obvious, that he simply didn't remember.

"Look here, Ivor," he said. "I'm sorry, I know it's hard, but look. Whatever it was left a pattern, embedded in the skin. I've seen that before, but I can't think . . ."

"Idiot," said Ivor. "It's the links from the chain." He laid Jandi's body carefully on the grass and tore the necklace with its three stones from her arm.

"Ivor, it's not," said Gareth, still studying the pattern. "It's not the same shape."

"You cold bastard." Ivor rose and flung the necklace at Gareth's face. Gareth caught it with one hand. It didn't move, but it did feel oddly warm. "She's dead, and you sit there quibbling about the strangle mark. You're as cold inside as Helgre."

A piece of the puzzle dropped into place, and Gareth sprang to his feet. "Helgre . . . she had a garrote, Ivor. Used it sometimes on the prisoners. Very thin and strong, and the cord was braided. It left a mark like that. She's followed us here."

"Are you trying to tell me she tracked us all this way, killed Jandi, who never did any harm to her, and decided to have mercy on us? I don't believe it. I don't believe she survived the *Orcsblood*."

He snorted. "Your associates have more than their share of bad luck, don't they? Especially when it suits your purposes. I should have known, that day on the dock. I should've parted ways with you then."

"That's not fair, Ivor."

Something moved in his hand, and he looked down to see the necklace move and contract, making itself back into the torque-shaped bracelet. It was disconcerting to see the dull metal moving like a centipede on his palm, and he had a sudden urge to drop it on the ground. Instead, he slipped it back into place on his wrist, where it moved no more.

"Fair?" said Ivor. "Talk to Jandi about justice, Gareth, if you can manage it."

"I swear I've seen Helgre leave the same mark. She's here; I know it. She tracked us down, and she killed Jandi out of spite."

Ivor flung out his arms and tossed his head back.

"Helgre!" he bellowed. "Come on out, Helgre! Scared of taking both of us on, you murderous bitch?"

"Are you insane?" Gareth put his hand on his sword and scanned the edge of the forest, half expecting the scarred woman to appear from between the trees, bent upon revenge.

"She's not here. You have no one to blame but yourself. No—that's a lie. I killed her, too. I killed her by trusting you."

Ivor grabbed Gareth's pack from beside the fire pit and flung it at him. "Get away from me—from us. Go and gloat over your fortress, and may you have the joy of it. It's infected by that *thing*."

He looked down at Jandi's body. "I hope you live a long time, rotting in your sanctuary, all alone."

Gareth had caught the pack and held it against his chest, uncertain of what to do. He slung it across his back and became aware of the quail still hanging at his belt. He untied them and held the cool bodies, soft in their feathers, one in each hand.

"Ivor—come back to the Fist tonight. Blame me if you must. But it's not safe out here."

"I take my chance with whatever's out here, even if it is Helgre," spat Ivor. "I prefer the company of beasts to yours."

"What will you do?"

"I'll bury my dead. Under the oak. She loved it. And then—I have my platinum; you have yours. You can't say you didn't do well in the bargain."

Gareth laid the pair of quail on the grass, near the fire pit. "I'll help you," he said.

"Get away from us." Ivor's voice was dangerously soft.

The donkey whickered softly. Automatically Gareth reached out to pat its side. Ivor quickly strode over and struck his arm up.

"I'm keeping the donkey. I don't trust you with any living creature."

Gareth backed away, his hands spread wide. "In the morning."

Ivor turned his back on Gareth and his shoulders slumped. "In the morning I'll be gone. Go to your folly. Jadaren's Folly."

Ivor laughed, a short, humorless bark. "I was righter than I knew."

Ivor didn't move until Gareth's footsteps faded in the distance. When all was silent, he kneeled by Jandi's body. The trunk of the old oak was in reach. He stretched out a hand and placed a palm on the rough surface.

In a single smooth motion, he pulled his arm back and struck the trunk with a balled fist, splitting the skin across his fingers on the bark.

Feeling nothing, he leaned on the tree as the hot tears came.

CHAPTER FIVE

Sanctuary of Shadrun-of-the-Snows

1584 DR—The Year of the Skirling Pipes

A tall figure stood on the flat-topped Watcher's Rock. Below, the crook of the road led to the hollow where the Sanctuary of Shadrun-of-the-Snows provided shelter. The figure, her form obviously that of a woman, set her feet shoulder-width apart and crossed her arms, her stance relaxed but watchful. A sword was strapped diagonally across her back, the hilt just behind her left ear where she could draw it either one- or two-handed at need. Thrust crosswise through her belt was a dagger in its sheath, larger than average with a simple but well-wrought hilt. The pommel of the hilt had a single, smooth, rounded ruby. The dark leather of the sheath was decorated with an elaborate pattern of intertwined snakes. Smaller stones, wine-dark like the pommel, made their eyes.

From a distance it looked as if she wore a mask: a wide strip of pale fabric across her eyes. Closer, it was clear the stripe was part of her natural coloring. Her hair was braided in rows away from her face, and the braids that touched her mask were the same pale color.

She stood still, surveying the view of the road that switched back and forth down the mountain and met the main road in the valley below. Occasionally a plume of road dust betrayed where travelers passed, some with trade goods strapped onto animals or in wagons, and some on foot, looking for adventure or simply a place to stay. Sometimes a lone figure was silhouetted in the distance, and only then did the woman stiffen slightly and narrow her eyes, watching them closely, relaxing when she determined they weren't those for whom she waited.

Although she faced the road, she was acutely aware of the thick woods behind her and heard every rustle that the small animals of the forest made in going about their daily business. She was aware, as well, of the two pilgrims descending the path from the sanctuary, their visit at an end. By sound alone she marked each turn they took, hearing their sandals kicking up small stones, and knew exactly when they would emerge from behind the trees and pass the Watcher's Rock. She heard them emerge from behind the trees and hesitate when they saw her, then continue again, their voices hushed. They were the two women from Turmish, she thought, from the sound of their footfalls and the few words she caught.

As they passed in front of the rock where she stood, she saw she was right. Almost shyly the pilgrims raised their hands in greeting, and she nodded in return. One looked as if she would like to stop and talk, but the other pulled her away, and they hurried down the path to the base of the mountain.

Lakini spotted them as they emerged on the road. She hoped they had the sense to ask to accompany a caravan, or at least to join with other pilgrims. Unless they had more command of defensive spellcraft or protective rituals than she suspected, they would be vulnerable once they were out of sight of one of the devas that protected Shadrun-of-the-Snows.

Her gaze ranged the road before them and froze as she saw the lone figure that passed the pilgrims, turning onto the road that led past her sentry post. The women gave him a wide berth as they went by, although he didn't acknowledge them.

Lakini frowned. Lusk was still too far away for her to see the expression on his face, but she knew what it looked like. The mouth grimly set, the eyes that showed no trace of pity but stared through people as if they were made of glass.

She didn't go to greet him but waited until he came to her. He strode quickly, making little sound nevertheless on the roadway. When he saw her standing on the Watcher's Rock, he paused, then came to its base, staring up at her with the same near-unblinking stillness she possessed.

He had left the sanctuary four tendays since, and only this morning had the rising sun told her that this day he would return.

His hand lay on his own dagger, which, like Lakini's, was secured crosswise in his belt. The gesture wasn't either threatening or combative, but was that of a fighter who would touch his weapons to make sure they were in place and to seek reassurance. The sheath where his dagger rested was plain, but what was visible of the hilt was inscribed with flowing scrollwork and inset with sapphire cabochons. Instead of a greatsword, he had a longbow almost as tall as himself secured across his back, and a quiver full of arrows fletched with feathers so black, they gave no answering gleam to the sun that shone bright above them, reflecting on the snow that clung to the upper slopes of Shadrun's mountain. His mouth was indeed grim, and the stripes across his face made him look the fiercer.

"*Cserhelm,*" said Lakini, placing her hand on her breast and inclining her head.

Lusk stood, regarding her a long minute before his lips curved upward in a small smile, and he did likewise.

"*Cserhelm,*" he replied.

Lakini jumped from the flat-topped rock to stand beside Lusk. She didn't have to ask him to know that his journey had not given him the peace he sought.

And she wouldn't ask. She and Lusk had been companions for much of her present lifetime, which now spanned almost two centuries. She knew they had traveled together in other lifetimes, before their current incarnations. Devas remembered very little of their previous existences, born innocent of what they were before—although in extremity devas could call upon their previous manifestations to guide or protect them. Still, Lakini sometimes had dreamlike glimpses of previous lifetimes, and visions of an entity she identified as Lusk. She knew he had like memories. Many decades ago they had met, recognized each other, and exchanged daggers—she giving him the sapphire-studded weapon and he giving her the dagger with the snake-inscribed sheath.

Since then they had ventured together, parting sometimes for days or months or years as their respective destinies took them. Their paths had always met again. Lakini knew what a rare gift this was, and that most creatures of her kind never had the privilege of meeting another deva, fated as they were to live only with the mortal folk of Faerûn.

But, bonded by forces beyond their understanding, each deva held a solitude deep in his or her heart, a secret place no one else, not even a dagger-mate, could touch. Sometimes that solitude would cry out to one or the other of them, and cause them to step aside from the path they walked together, to quest alone, although they would eventually return to the same path.

There were places in a deva's heart deep and sacred as the sea. Lakini would not ask after Lusk's discontentment.

"The crofters say there's a nest of gnolls denning near Rophile's Crevasse," she said at last. "Shall we go rout them out?"

Lusk grinned. "Nothing would delight me more."

Rophile's Crevasse was a deep slice in the side of the mountain where the ground had cracked open once, exposing the dark gray rock of the mountain's substance. Jagged teeth of layered basalt and granite jutted over a chasm few had ventured far into, and precarious, little-traveled paths wound down, clinging to the sides of the cleft. Sun struck down the slopes only a few hours at midday, and moss and small ferns grew deep. Venturesome folk said one could hear water trickling below.

Rophile was not the name of the discoverer of the crevasse or of an adventurer who braved its depths, but of a sheep that had wandered in one day, never to be seen again. The crofter quickly gave up the errant Rophile as lost, but stories were told of a feral, incredibly tough breed of sheep that roamed the interior.

Lakini had heard, and dismissed, theories that the crevasse had no bottom; that it was a passage to the Underdark and its horrors. She didn't fear attacks by the drow and their allies, not here. But it was an attractive hiding place for the dangerous creatures, sentient or not, that preyed on the merchants, travelers, and pilgrims who braved the road and the wilderness to come to Shadrun. Local rangers, hunters, farmers and crofters, let the sanctuary's guardians know when something more than fairy tales and mythical monster sheep took refuge in the slash in the mountainside. Lakini had picked up a rumor three days ago that a passerby had barely escaped the fang-spike club of a gnoll.

As it turned out, rumor was wrong in this case. There were no gnolls in Rophile's Crevasse.

Lakini kneeled on a boulder that overlooked the drop-off. She breathed deeply, filling her lungs with the air and scents of the wilderness. There was the clean, balsamic smell of the pines, as well as a musky smell from the moss that grew on the cliffside's damp walls and from the leaves rotting on the forest floor. A dank scent rose from the maw of the rift, and she spared a thought for the mass of the bones of clumsy men and animals, ancient and new, that were probably tumbled together at the bottom together with fallen branches and vines. There was nothing unusual here, there being none of the carrion stench of a gnoll pack. She opened her eyes and felt for the lines and letters carved over the top of the boulder—it wasn't uncommon for the area youth to come here to impress their friends, bleat in an attempt to call the flock of legendary feral sheep, and carve their signs or initials in the rock to prove they'd done it.

She sniffed again, catching just a trace of something strange. It was not like an animal, or the charnel smell of gnolls, but something almost like the reagents a mage would use, a whiff of an alchemical process. There was just a hint of it in the air, and then it was gone.

She tilted her head at a rustle in the leaves up the slope. Lusk was casting about, looking for spoor, tracks, or other signs of the gnolls. She leaped gracefully off the boulder and called out between the trees.

"See anything?"

"Not much." His voice echoed, disembodied in the crisp fall air. "No gnoll sign, I think. I found the skull of a deer, but that could be from a big cat, even a wolf. Or it could have just died in the winter—it's full-grown. Wait—no, a predator got it. There's flesh still on it—fresh."

A whisper of a boot on dead dried leaves told where Lusk cast about in the woods above. Lakini loosed her sword in its sheath across her back—ordinary predators were nothing like gnolls, but it was best to be cautious—and leaned against the grainy surface of the boulder, enjoying the heat that the stone had gathered through the day on her back.

"Lakini?" Lusk's voice had a quality that made her stand straight and reach for her dagger.

"What, *Cserhelm?*" she called.

"Keep watch, Lakini. I found the rest of the deer. All of them."

A long, liquid snarl sounded behind Lakini, behind the boulder that overlooked the crevasse. She turned, crouching and reaching for her greatsword, in time to see an enormous wolf round the stone at speed, leaping for her with an intent that had nothing to do with a workaday predator. Caught off-guard, she had the vague impression of cruel, knifelike claws outstretched for her and a mouthful of wicked teeth before it bore her to the ground. Cursing herself for an inattentive fool, she rolled as soon as she hit, avoiding a swipe of claws aimed at her gut, and unsheathed her dagger. The length of her sword on her back pressed into her muscles. Still tumbling, she lashed out with her dagger and saw the creature flinch back. She came out of the roll into a one-legged kneeling position, knife extended, and faced the wolf that slavered a few feet before her, feeling her lips rise into a snarl in return. Dark blood dripped down the wolf's leg where she'd slashed at it, but it wasn't any kind of serious wound.

"Lakini!" called Lusk, somewhere behind her.

"I found the wolf," she called back, not moving from her position, and not shifting her gaze from the creature in front of her. The thing's mouth seemed to open wider in a grin, and saliva pooled in the corners of its lips.

Very slowly Lakini shifted her dagger to her left hand. The outsize wolf's eyes—one brown, one an angry-looking red—followed her every movement. The smell of chemicals—sulfur and something like burned iron—filled the air.

With a smooth motion Lakini grasped the knife hilt in her left hand and reached for her sword with the other. The wolf leaped for her again. She rose to her feet and seized the sword hilt, drawing it and bringing it down in one fluid, powerful arc. The blade missed the creature's skull by a hair, but it bit through the edge of its upright, pointed ear, taking off a third of it. At the same time, Lakini sliced the knife up in an undercut, protecting her left side and cutting deeply through the wolf's forelimb.

The animal howled and jumped back, well out of the range of her sword, farther away than it should have been able to jump. The burned metal smell intensified. She watched as the bones of the wolf's face seemed to melt beneath the surface of the skin and the thing stood upright, hind legs lengthening and forelimbs turning into long, burly arms, still tipped with black claws. Rearing to its full height, it topped her by two heads.

The thing snarled. Its eyes, one still scarlet, were sunk deep on either side of the broad nose. Its face and what parts of the body weren't covered with thick leather armor were as hairy as the wolf. Its right arm was cut to the bone, dark blood coating fur and armor, and part of its left ear was lopped off, the side of its head wet and matted.

Sweet Selûne served with parsnips, thought Lakini. It's a barghest.

Quickly she sheathed the dagger and took the worn, familiar grip of her sword in both hands. "Lusk!" she called, not taking her eyes off the lycanthrope for a second. "Barghest! There might be more!"

"At least one," he replied grimly, and she heard the furious scream of a wounded animal.

The barghest glared at her, and a coldness rose through her body like a tide. Her joints ached and she felt a dull despair, heavy as iron on her shoulders.

You'll die here, a small voice whispered in her head. *This thing will kill you, and you'll never see the sun again.*

She hesitated, confused. The hobgoblin moved a step closer. The smell of sulfur was almost overwhelming now.

It was an invisible attack, as deadly as that mouthful of teeth slashing at her—some barghests had the skill to project despair into the minds of their opponents, dulling their senses and making them easier prey.

Without letting the tip of her sword droop, Lakini concentrated. Part of her still focused on the threat before her, while another sought the river of Astral grace that ran inside her always, sustaining and illuminating. All devas, save perhaps those few who had become corrupted by their experiences in this plane, contained within their spirit the gift of Astral light, born as they were in the hallowed seas.

She visualized two hands scooping the luminous material into a sphere and hurling it at the barghest, straight through the miasma of doom it was inflicting on her. Her unseen counter was effective, and the beast staggered back as if struck.

She pressed her advantage, striking at its midriff, then swung again at its wounded right arm. It jumped back toward the boulder, and she pursued it, unwilling to let it take refuge in some cave in the chasm and heal. It would be madness to let such a dangerous creature survive so close to the sanctuary.

There was a narrow ledge where a person could stand between the boulder and the drop-off. The wounded barghest was crouched against it, grinning at her. She raised her sword to strike it down.

The enormous curved edge of a battle-axe chopped down between her and the wounded barghest. Only by scrabbling backward uriously did she escape the blow that would have sunk deep into her knee. The blade bounced off a stone in front of her, drawing sparks.

Idiot, Lakini thought. He was luring you into a trap.

The second barghest, a female slightly smaller than the first, was covered entirely with black fur, save for two white blazes that started high on the wide, flat scalp and extended down both sides of the body. It growled and lifted the battle-axe again, and Lakini deflected the downward blow with an upstroke of her greatsword. The weapons met with a clash that made the metal ring and sent a great jolt of pain through her shoulder.

Stupid. She had fallen so easily into the assumption that there would be two, that the beast Lusk battled upslope would be the only other danger. Partnering with Lusk and patrolling the limited demesne of the sanctuary had made her soft. She had forgotten about the sheer variety of evil that made Toril its home.

She had thrust the white-striped barghest back with her sword, and while it regained footing, the first darted under her guard and slashed at her with its claws. She cried out as pain knifed into her side. It had penetrated her side armor, leather, skin, and muscle, and opened a gash along her ribs. The blow had flung all her weight onto her right leg, and Lakini used that, delivering a solid kick to the creature's knee with her booted foot. It yipped and sprawled on the ground.

Nausea took her, and the wound in her side throbbed. She was going to die here, and Lusk as well. Shadrun would be cracked open like an egg and the bones of those that sheltered there left to weather under the sky. Lakini looked up to see the female barghest glaring at her, gripping the axe at the ready.

Lakini tried to find the river of light inside her to counter the barghest's psychic attack, but this time it eluded her.

It swung the axe and she leaned back, letting it whistle through the space where her torso had been a second before. When it backswung, she countered it, fighting to remain strong through the pain of her lacerated side and the despair that bore down on her. The thing snarled in her face and its head flattened. Its ears rose on either side, and the snout lengthened. Teeth bristled in the open mouth, and the stench of sulfur was overwhelming. It was changing into a wolf, with its white stripe still blazing down its lupine body.

It raised the battle-axe again, and she struggled to counter, to get in a blow of her own. Something whistled over her right shoulder, and the black fletch of Lusk's arrow brushed her cheek. The bolt buried itself in the beast's furry neck. The barghest froze, a look that might have been astonishment in the beast's eyes. It staggered backward, swayed at the edge of the chasm, and vanished over the side.

The first barghest had recovered its footing and stood at the lip of the cliff, staring down at where its companion had vanished. Slowly it turned its massive, maimed head and pierced her with a look of purest hatred, its red eye glowing like a bloody ruby. With a scream, it leaped for her, a tremendous jump that spanned three of its own body lengths. Ready for it, she braced herself for the attack. Her greatsword pierced the abdomen, and she thrust as hard as she could, feeling the blade part sinew and muscle and then grate against the creature's backbone. It froze for a second, the hairy, bloody head almost lying on her shoulder. Then, without a sound, it collapsed to the ground, sliding off her blade.

A freshening wind came from the mountaintop, blowing away the smell of sulfur and leaving the iron tang of blood behind.

Lakini limped to the edge of the chasm to make sure the other barghest was dead. Half-wolf and half-goblin, the white-blazed body sprawled broken over a root that jutted out of the cliffside. She shivered at the sight of the monstrous hybrid, neither one species nor the other.

Lusk called her away, examined her wound, and wrapped it tightly. "It's not as bad as it might have been," he remarked. "Make sure it's cleaned out well and it'll heal quickly."

She nodded, forbearing to point out to him that after centuries in this incarnation, she was well aware of the necessary care of battlefield wounds.

Together they hiked through the trees to recover Lusk's dagger, stuck firmly between the ribs of the third barghest, a smaller goblinoid sprawled next to a pile of deer bones picked clean.

"Where did they come from?" she said. "How did we not know they were here?"

Lusk, meticulously wiping the barghest's black, sticky blood from his dagger, shrugged. "We're in the wilderness, *Cserhelm.* We can't control every handbreadth of the mountain." He sighed. "I suppose I should get my arrow back, but I don't want to crawl down after that thing."

She stared at the beast's body and at the remains of the deer. There must have been fifteen or twenty. "We should have been aware of this kind of predation. And I didn't expect there to be three." She still heard the big male barghest's last scream, before it impaled itself on her sword, full of rage but also a kind of despair. It was the same kind of despair a barghest could inflict upon its prey, but heartfelt within itself. Why? Was the skunk-striped barghest its mate?

"Perhaps the chasm does extend to the Underdark," remarked Lusk, giving the blade a final polish and sheathing it, "where the eldritch spawn of Rophile roam. Listen!" He put his hand to his ear. "Can't you hear them?"

On the breeze came the faint bleating of sheep, probably from a herd grazing in the meadows below. Lakini laughed, ignoring the pain in her side. At least the lycanthropes wouldn't be preying on the crofter's flocks.

Lakini knew the gouge in her side would heal quickly, but she suspected it would be a long time before the baffled roar of the barghest faded from her mind.

"Come home," she said, laying her hand briefly on Lusk's arm. "You've not even paid respects to Shadrun yet, and the Vashtun will want to see you."

The Vashtun had not always been the Vashtun, of course. His birthname had been discarded and forgotten long before. The sanctuary keeper of Shadrun-of-the-Snows was always called the Vashtun; the name of the first keeper had become a title over the length of years.

Years before, in the Year of Azuth's Woe, that first Vashtun, a quiet, unassuming city scribe, had laid aside his transcription of the bloated history of a rich merchant's ancestors, tied his ink pot and quills at his side, and walked away from the busy streets and commerce of his native place, walked into the heart of the country, down a road teeming with market folk, private guards, and weary would-be adventurers in search of coin to be made honestly or not. He passed dwarves bound for town to negotiate trade treaties, halflings in search of a day's labor and mischief afterward, and farmers taking their town goods home. At night he would sleep by the side of the road in the travelers' shelters raised by local lordlings or town councils for the public good, drinking from public wells and sharing food with fellow journeyers if they had it to spare.

He walked roads farther and farther away from human habitation, and when he came upon a crooked mountain path that pleased him, he turned aside from the main road and climbed up, past oaks clustered thick and twisted at the mountain's foot, past thickets of pine and deep, white-barked, rustling birch to where ferns grew in a sunny meadow stretched in the sun beneath the peaks and ravines of the summit. There he found the remains of a forgotten temple, little more than blocks of moss-grown marble tumbled around the warm trickle of a mineral spring. He found the carved onyx head of some ancient, obscure godling, cleaned the dirt from its time-worn features, and propped it up against the ruins of a retaining wall. He washed his road-sore feet in the warm, slightly sulfurous waters of the spring and found himself a comfortable seat in last season's fallen leaves. Vashtun sat contemplating the long and crooked snakelike road that coiled between the cities of the plains.

He had spent so many days putting one foot before the other in such a steady rhythm that the simple action had become hypnotic. Gone was the strange impulse that made him set aside the heavy parchment, filled with line after line of neat writing, push back the chair from the slanted desk, and leave the rich man's library to walk ceaselessly. Now he wanted nothing but to make his mind a blank, like a blown glass bulb containing a perfect vacuum. He wasn't bored, or frightened. Sometimes he felt a little hungry or thirsty, but to stir from his perch to find berries or water would stir the still, cold waters of his mind, so he pushed such sensations away.

As the sun reached its zenith, a crofter a few miles away spotted crows circling, curious, over the ruins and sent his child to see what went forward. The boy returned an hour later to say a man was there, with strange clothing and nothing but a pouch at his hip, and he had found an old god in the dirt and restored it to the spring. The strange man said nothing but watched the horizon with an abstract smile.

The crofter's wife sent the child back with a bottle of mead and a basket of bread and fruit paste, as well as an old patched cloak against the night chill, for it was clear to her a holy man had been sent to guard the old spring at Shadrun. Word spread to the other crofters in the foothills, keepers of the mountain cattle that thrived on the rough brush and stiff grasses of the slopes, the rangers that wandered the woods, and finally to the villages rooted below, the same villages the scribe had passed in his journey. Folk came to see him, to bring him food and what few items he seemed to need. He looked upon everyone with the same dispassionate smile, and he did not resist placing his hand on their heads when they kneeled before him and asked it.

Some of the men built him a simple shelter with the cracked, chipped blocks of the old shrine. Others restored the retaining wall around the spring, and the steps going up to it, so that again it pooled, warm and steaming, before trickling away between moss-blanketed boulders. Passive as a child fed his dinner and tucked into bed, he watched as these things were done, but anyone who kneeled before him and looked into his eyes knew that behind their benign, blue-sky expression, an encompassing intelligence moved.

Sometimes when someone sat beside him, breathing the same way and able, over the course of hours or days, to focus on nothing, they felt a tickle in their mind, a sense of someone outside of them possessing their senses. Some heard a whispering in an incomprehensible language, drifting through their brain like the cold insinuation of the winter wind. Most who sat and meditated with the holy man Vashtun did not attempt it again, leaving the task of communing with the gods to those with the inclination for it. One, the dreamy son of a stolid crofter, began weeping after an hour of sitting at Vashtun's feet and refused to ever go near the spring again (on the positive side, he became far more industrious in the fields and sheep pens then he ever had been before). But there were those few who seemed to thrive on the same strange state the holy man manifested, who stayed with him as the air thickened with cold and the snows came. With the help of the locals, they added to the shrine shelter, making it a warm place to stay throughout the winter, heated with steam from the spring.

When the thaw came, a trickle of pilgrims, some from the cities of the plains, some from far beyond them, began to arrive. The locals were glad to guide such visitors up the crooked mountain paths for a small fee, and also to house and feed them, likewise for a small fee. Over time, the mountain path became a decent-sized and passable road, and small houses and inns sprang up beside it to take care of the travelers' needs. The tiny ruined shrine beside Shadrun spring was expanded and rebuilt to become Shadrun-of-the-Snows, a refuge for the weary traveler as well as the questing pilgrim. The lords of cities and estates, as well as forward-looking merchants, sent tribute and manpower to Shadrun-of-the-Snows, for here was a sanctuary and safe resting place for those journeying between domains and kingdoms, where one could rest and recover, safe from mercenaries, beasts, and bandits, before proceeding on one's way.

Vashtun became *the* Vashtun, served and protected by those who found comfort in always being in his presence. After the length of his days was done and he was buried on the slopes above the sanctuary, another took his place. Having spent long hours meditating with the Vashtun, the thrumming, insistent whisper that pervaded the holy man's mind possessed his as well. Never himself a scribe, he tied the old pouch of scribes' tools at his belt, and all called him the Vashtun. He was protected and served in his turn, as was the case with the one who came after him, and the one who came after her. There were many who thought, hundreds of years later, that the same silent and meditative Vashtun sat in a quiet room at the shrine of Shadrun-of-the-Snows, and in some ways they were correct.

Nonthal, Turmish

1584 DR—The Year of the Skirling Pipes

"Ridiculous!" Sanwar Beguine, overcome by anger, paced the modest confines of his brother's study.

Unperturbed and ensconced behind the sturdy and ancient desk his great-great-grandfather had brought back from a then-extant Mulhorand, Nicol Beguine watched Sanwar measure the length of the thin, finely made carpet, its ancient, intricately knotted patterns supposedly spellcast with good luck.

"Reasonable, rather," he said mildly, as Sanwar frowned at him. "A fit conclusion to a feud that has spanned generations, hurting both our Houses. A feud I consider, to use your own word, ridiculous."

Sanwar ceased his pacing and turned on his brother. "Their treachery, their sabotage, that is nothing to you? I've devoted my time and what talent I possess in magic to protecting our caravans, trade routes, merchandise, employees and partners, from their machinations. If we lower our guard . . . they could very well wipe us off the face of Toril."

Nicol sighed and wove his fingers together before him on the surface of the desk—a gesture familiar to those who did business with him. It meant he was prepared for a long round of negotiations and would not leave the table until a deal was struck.

"We have taken advantage of them in our turn, whenever possible. And just like you, I've had legends of the great feud dished into my ears since I was a babe. The villainy of the Jadarens is endless, I've been told, and we can never be at peace. Well, I'm weary of this so-called vendetta. Over what trifle, so many generations ago, did it start? No one remembers. And no one cares. And yet, the harm resulting from it has been immeasurable."

"The Jadarens were born of a pirate, and they are still pirates at the core," Sanwar spat. "However they may hide beneath a veil of respectability. Wed one of our own to their ill-bred spawn, and you pollute our House."

Nicol let an expression of impatience pass across his features. "Really, Sanwar. We're not the ruling family of Cormyr. Surely we don't need to pretend that our bloodlines have anything of the sacred about them."

"They might," returned his brother. "They might, if you could bother to pay attention to such things."

"What? Are we to breed ourselves like a pack of yuan-ti? Do calm yourself, Brother. Both our businesses will benefit from this bargain."

"And what does Kestrel say to your proposal? What if she doesn't want to become bound to a pirate's spawn? Will you give her a choice in the matter?"

"Sanwar, what kind of a tyrant do you think I am? Of course, ultimately it's her decision—and that of the Jadaren boy, this Arna." Sanwar winced, as if the given name of a Jadaren scion could wound him. Nicol did his best to ignore his brother's melodramatics. "But Kestrel is a sensible girl. I'm sure she'll see the benefit to both our Houses."

"I pray she'll see reason, and that you'll come to your senses, Brother," said Sanwar, sweeping out of the chamber and slamming the door behind him.

Before he did, however, he glanced at the tapestries behind Nicol's chair, which hid a small arras where the private papers of the Beguine family were kept. A ripple in the fabric betrayed where someone hid, and he would bet the entirety of the latest caravan's profits that it was his niece. He hoped she had taken his words to heart and would take the path of sanity, and not sacrifice herself to his brother's insane desire to treat with the Jadarens.

And if she proved as mad as her father, well—there were precautions he was prepared to take. And any bad situation could, in the end, be made into an opportunity.

Sanwar's heavily booted footsteps had faded down the hall outside the chamber door before the tapestries were pulled aside and a small girl with chestnut hair to her waist stepped out. She wore a simple dress, well made but worn at the cuffs and hem, for Kestrel Beguine was a practical girl. As was customary for the women of her House, she worked diligently at the accounting and record keeping necessary for a merchant family to prosper, as well as taking her turn with kitchen and housekeeping work. Knowing she was there, Nicol didn't look around, but she touched her father on the shoulder as she passed his desk, and he glanced up at her and smiled.

"You heard all, I trust?"

Calmly, Kestrel paced the same length of carpet that her uncle had before her.

"Of course. Uncle Sanwar's not shy about his opinion of the Jadarens."

"You should know there are many who share his views and would be equally shocked—although perhaps not as personally offended—at the idea of your wedding Arna Jadaren. And there are those within his House who despise the Beguine family deeply. We have done much injury to each other over the generations. I disagree with your uncle, but I would have you consider all the disadvantages as well as the benefits of this bargain."

Kestrel clasped her hands behind in unconscious imitation of one of her father's habitual poses, and faced Nicol across the desk.

"I have, Father. By my reckoning, we stand to lose two profitable alliances if I marry Arna Jadaren. House

Andula's matriarch has cared little for Bron Jadaren since she thought he cheated her out of a shipment of cedars ten years ago, and the Spicer's Guild helped us in that little matter in the Year of the Wicked Jailor and will not look kindly upon a reversal of our loyalties."

"Well reasoned. The question is whether the advantages of the match make the price worth it. And if so, is it worth it to you, personally, to sacrifice yourself in such a way?"

Kestrel smiled. "I'm sure House Jadaren considers it as much a sacrifice. I'm sure Arna has an uncle Sanwar of his own, shouting his outrage at the idea of polluting their sacred halls with my unworthy presence."

Her expression grew serious. "I am of a mind with you, Father, in this matter. It's time this feud and the hurts it inflicts ended. I will consent to the match, on one condition."

"Only the one? Name it."

Kestrel looked at the woven patterns of the rug and blushed. "On the condition that I like the boy."

In his elegant and simple chambers, Sanwar fumed, furious at Nicol's dismissal of the consequences of a Jadaren alliance and at his seeming incomprehension of the harm it would do. He was furious at his willingness to unite the proud name of Beguine with the despised name of Jadaren, and furious at his eagerness to sell a Beguine daughter as he would a whore.

He was furious most of all at Nicol's ignoring his arguments against the scheme. In his heart of hearts, that was what smarted the most. His objection should be enough to overcome any kind of argument for the mad plan.

Sanwar had dedicated his life to the family business his brother headed, never demanding the trappings of leadership himself. He took a fierce pride in the Beguine legacy, and for the chief of the House to dismiss his concerns was like a slap in the face. And it hurt. This was his blood, his brother. Raised together, they had learned their numbers and the intricacies of the merchant trade together. It hurt to be ignored.

His pacing took him past the door of his chambers. A solid panel of oak, it was unadorned, save by a small and beautifully carved eye in the exact center. Beside the door he paused, frowning, and listened intently.

For years he had studied the arts of sorcery, independent and alone, knowing most of his House frowned upon the study of dark magic and resentful of the fact that his father—and Nicol's—had forbidden him to travel to such a place as Netheril to study them properly. Despite his application and his ever-growing library of arcane books and scrolls, his skills were nowhere near where he'd like them to be.

He was not yet a master of magic, but his senses had been honed by study, and he was aware that someone lingered on the other side of the door, someone who either hesitated to make him- or herself known or who intended to lie in wait for him to emerge.

Sanwar held out his left hand, palm up and fingers spread, and murmured the first few words of a spell. Heat prickled down his fingers and began to gather in the hollow of his palm. But before he could engage the graven eye and before the spyspell worked upon it, before he could see who lurked on the other side, there came a gentle tap at his door.

Still holding his left hand out in readiness, he jerked the door open abruptly. With a muffled gasp, Vorsha Beguine, his sister-in-law, stumbled into the room amid a flurry of embroidered silks.

With a quick flick of his wrist, Sanwar dismissed the defensive spell gathering in his left hand and caught Vorsha by the elbow with the right. He quickly pushed the door shut, muttering a short silencing cantrip as he did so. It would not do for some curious servant to spy out what he and Vorsha got up to in his chambers.

Sanwar and his brother shared more than Nicol knew or suspected.

Vorsha Beguine was a wide-eyed wisp of a woman, with the thick chestnut hair that her daughter had inherited and a timid manner that Kestrel had not. Sanwar had found, however, that despite her shy manner and diffident nature, she was completely different in bed—passionate and sometimes surprisingly inventive.

Vorsha tried to be a good wife, if not a faithful one. She had remained true to Nicol during the first few years of their married life, but he was distracted much of the time conducting the business of one of the most far-reaching merchant enterprises in Faerûn. It was the custom for the Beguine women to learn and to manage the accounts of the House, and such work wasn't to Vorsha's taste. Her talent was for the small domestic arts that most ignored yet, unknowingly, took great comfort from. She couldn't discuss trade routes or profit margins with her husband, but she could make his House a home. Fortunately, her children—her two daughters and a son now absent in the service of House affairs—had favored their father in their business acumen.

If Nicol was disappointed that his wife didn't share his interest in the intricacies of trade, he never showed it. He was kind to her, always, and had been since their wedding night.

But over the years, they had begun to grow apart. And to her great shame, for Vorsha had been raised a virtuous woman, even in the beginning of their marriage Nicol couldn't excite her as his brother could.

For a long time she'd known Sanwar looked at her with desire. She felt the heat of his gaze as she passed him in the halls, or from across the rooms where he lurked apart while company gathered. For a while, to an inexperienced young wife, it was exciting enough to feel his longing touch her like questing fingers.

And then, finally, he touched her. In a dark corridor in the family quarters of the House, she had turned to find him behind her, his eyes hot on her body. He had pushed her into a secluded corner, almost roughly, and she didn't resist. No—she seized him and pulled his hard maleness against her. The step of a servant down the hallway made them spring apart, both breathing heavily, lips parted and eyes shining.

She had sworn it wouldn't happen again, but it did. Then she had sworn that she would never go to his bed.

But she did. Again, and again, until she finally reconciled herself to leading two lives in House Beguine—as virtuous wife to the master and as wanton mistress to the master's brother.

Today she came to find out for herself the extent of the argument between her husband and her lover, and had sworn to herself—as she did before almost every encounter with her brother-in-law—that she would only talk to him, and resist tumbling into his bed. But it was no use—enflamed by his conflict with Nicol, Sanwar pushed her against the wall, pressing his body against hers with an urgency that could not be denied.

"Stop," Vorsha managed, feeling her limbs melt beneath her and clinging to Sanwar's shoulders in response. "We must stop this madness. It can only hurt us, and hurt the House."

In answer, he cupped her breast with one hand and felt her nipple harden against his palm in response. "Do you really want me to stop, Vorsha?" he whispered, his breath hot on the curve between her neck and shoulder. "Tell me to stop again, Vorsha, and I'll do it."

He pulled away from her a fraction, still leaning against the wall. She snaked a hand around his neck and pulled him against her. "No, please don't," she managed. "Don't stop."

He scooped her up by her thighs and, when she wrapped her legs around his waist, he carried her to the bedchamber with no more preliminaries. Let Nicol have the last word in business matters. Let him hold his brother's wishes of no account. Here in the bedroom he was in control, and he could make his brother's wife respond in ways Nicol had never imagined.

CHAPTER SIX

Shadrun-of-the-Snows

1585 DR—The Year of the Bloodied Manacles

It was early spring, with the pale green buds of mountain flowers fighting through a stubborn crust of snow, when the messenger came for Lusk. The runner, a long, lanky human, almost fell from his foam-flecked horse and staggered exhausted into the gathering hall at Shadrun-of-the-Snows. An attendant ran to him and called for refreshment. The messenger refused to rest, and with his remaining breath begged to see the "tiger-striped deva."

He didn't have to wait long. Lusk was listening to the messenger's tidings with his head bent close, so that no one else overheard, and an expression that brooked no interference from anybody.

Taking the time only to pack a few traveling essentials and to check that his weapons were in full working order, Lusk requested and was granted the use of two of the sanctuary horses. Yet again, as she had a year ago, Lakini stood on the flat-topped Watcher's Rock that marked the turn from the road to the sanctuary path to watch him go.

Bithesi watched with her. She was a slight, shy-seeming woman who had charge of Shadrun's animals and directed the merchants how to shelter and pasture their beasts. Lakini liked her for her hidden strength, her unobtrusive toughness, and the way she could both appear inconsequential and calm a panicked ox seemingly with sheer willpower.

"What does he seek?" she asked.

"I don't know," said Lakini. "It's a place in his heart where I don't wander, and the doors are closed to me."

Together they watched as the tall deva, his robes rippling around his roan's flanks, and the messenger, almost falling off his gray in sheer exhaustion, disappeared around a bend in the road.

"*Ashonithi,* my dagger-mate," Lakini murmured to the spring breeze freshening through the delicate redbud branches. "Until we meet again."

Bithesi looked up at her curiously. " '*Ashonithi.*' What does that mean?"

Lakini considered before answering. She'd never had to translate the phrase before.

"Simply put, 'in this life or the next one.'" Lakini hopped off the flat rock and automatically surveyed the road and the fringe of trees bordering it before she turned back to the sanctuary. Bithesi trotted along at her heels, studying in her turn every bird that hopped beside the path or in the redbud, and noting that the squirrels were thinner than usual coming out of the cold season. It had been a harsh winter on Shadrun's mountain.

"It didn't sound like a simple word," Bithesi remarked, pausing to examine some tracks by the side of the road, where a patch of snow remained. If foxes were about and hungry from the cold season, she would need to double-check the poultry's pens for weakness. If it was something bigger, she'd need to ask an adept for a warding.

Lakini chuckled. "It isn't. You have sharp ears. I can't convey the meaning entirely in Common—best I can do is 'as we have met in other lands and times and lifetimes, and as we have crossed snow and sand to exchange daggers, so we will certainly be together again before or after this world tears our bodies apart.' "

Bithesi laughed. "That's not very poetic, is it? I liked plain cryptic *Ashonithi* better."

"That's what you get for asking for a translation. Next time let the mystery stand."

Bithesi went to find an adept to charm the cages, leaving Lakini to search for the grooming brush in the stable. The deva found the simple labor of tending the horse, whether worn beast of burden or magnificent war charger, soothing, and a good workout for her arms. Having secured the poultry to her satisfaction, Bithesi returned to the stables and watched her tall, mask-marked friend brush the glossy hide of a delicate-footed lady's mount, polishing it to a shine.

"Lakini, forgive me my prying," she said eventually, as the deva lifted a forehoof to examine it. The horse mumbled at Lakini's braids where the pale hair that branched off her mask blended with the dark. "But what you were telling me—the unpoetical part. About meeting in other lifetimes, and the world tearing you apart. I've heard that kind of sentiment before, from bards and books. But there's something about you—and something about Lusk—that makes me suspect it's not some pretty phrasemaker's conceit. And it makes me wonder . . ."

"What do you wonder?"

"What are you?"

There was a long pause, punctuated by the delighted chuckle of a chicken finding a beetle, and the squabble of the other fowl claiming the prize.

What do I tell her? thought Lakini. That such as Lusk and I fall from incarnation to incarnation, like water from a celestial sea poured from one stone jar into another? That we exist, transparent, like crystals in a glass of oil?

Lakini smiled and put the hoof down, gently pushing the beast on the shoulder so she stood square. "Why, Bithesi," she said, "I am nothing of this world."

She looked as if about to say something more, then shook her head and returned to brushing the horse. The animal nickered in contentment, eyes half-closed.

The little woman shook her head. "Cryptic and poetical is overrated," she remarked, hurrying back to her chickens.

The Vashtun sat cross-legged in his chamber, meditating. The flat cushion he sat on was the only furnishing. Across the chamber a shallow trench had been cut, then lined with green glass pebbles. Water flowed in it, a diversion from the main geothermal spring. By the time the water flow reached the Vashtun's chamber, it had cooled, and it made a pleasant sound in the near-empty room.

No portrait, landscape, or tapestry hung on the walls, but their smooth plaster was decorated on all four sides with abstract patterns that integrated fractured circles and angled lines. These designs were the work of previous Vashtuns, beginning with the second, and had been centuries in the making. Much of the pattern was laid in by the second Vashtun and the two that followed him, but each of their successors left his mark. Here a bisected arc; there a triangle of odd proportions was added, and made part of the whole. It was as if a master pattern existed, invisible, beneath the surface of the innocuous white plaster, and those who painted the strange geometries were discovering it rather than creating their own.

It was the custom of the holy man to meditate upon these designs, and often his apprentice-successor would meditate with him. The chamber was private more by custom than law, and any who sincerely desired to contemplate the inner mysteries of the sanctuary were welcome to enter. It was not unusual for a servant of the sanctuary or a visiting pilgrim to stare at a certain coil, or series of fractured lines, and find that many minutes or hours had passed without his being aware of it, and to take away the memory of a conversation that could not have occurred. If one sat in the middle of the chamber, facing any wall, and was very quiet, an insistent whispering would seem to rise like an invisible tide.

Not everyone could stand it. Many of the inhabitants and visitors to Shadrun-of-the-Snows avoided the Vashtun's chamber, never approaching or entering it without great reluctance.

"It's like a voice in your head that won't go away," one would-be pilgrim had told another after paying his respects to the holy man. "Like someone saying things you can't quite hear, so you listen closely. But when the words start to distinguish themselves—you don't *want* to hear them. Even though you don't understand what they mean."

The Vashtun stared at one particular pattern on the wall, and his forehead furrowed. Without looking, he reached out and grasped one of the sticks that lay near at hand—thin, long, and burned at the tips. Rising from his cross-legged position, he stepped over the rivulet of water and approached the pattern—a circle bisected from left to right by a slanting line. He stood before it a long moment, and then with sure strokes sketched three short parallel lines in the lower left half of the circle. That done, he let his hand gripping the charred stick drop to his side.

"That's better," he muttered, studying his handiwork. "That's much better."

Fandour concentrated. The Nexus was engaging the Vector, and he must use the opportunity to strengthen his connections to the Rogue Plane. With luck, the Nexus would add another element to the Vector, giving Fandour a fraction more access.

Fractions added into integers, and integers multiplied into larger and larger numbers. It was a process that had taken centuries, as this plane reckoned time, and it was not yet finished. But each alteration of the Vector increased his

Power. Each mind to which he connected acted as both lens and prism, concentrating his Power within this plane, and at the same time scattering the light of his awareness across more mind prisms.

And now he sensed that other entities, not just the Nexus, were adding to the Vector in different places and that each allowed him to cling ever more persistently to the plane where the Rhythanko, which kept Fandour imprisoned, was kept.

For a long time Fandour simply concentrated on remaining still, meditating within the confines of his prison, until he could control the waves of panic that threatened to send him pounding helplessly at the iron walls the gith had constructed so well.

He wondered sometimes if nothing existed but himself if the oubliette was the universe and he its only inhabitant. But sometimes Fandour could remember, and he clutched at the memory until he could always remember, that there was something that lay beyond the confines of its world—the Rhythanko; the artifact that was the key to his imprisonment. If the fabrication that held it tight lay without, then there was a without, a world apart from Fandour's iron eggshell.

He would never be free until he could control the artifact. He almost had, when the Rhythanko was new and not completely forged. And then that odd race, the gith, had come to possess it, and sealed him in tighter than before. And then, just as he had a hope of gaining control of it again, there was a presence that had mastery of key and lock, and had wrested the Rhythanko from his touch and bound it to an alien blood. Fandour still remembered, vividly, the pain as the red-hot walls of the oubliette seared him.

But the grind of years passing loosened all bonds eventually. In cold darkness and across cold time, mind by mind, Fandour wove himself a presence within the Rogue Plane.

It was autumn, with leaves blazing scarlet and a chill in the air, when Lusk returned. The gray horse was tethered to the roan he had ridden back, and there was no sign of the messenger. Bithesi took the horses back to the stables and found them reasonably fit, but their hooves showed signs of wear, and she would have to send word to the farrier.

When the attendant offered Lusk the travelers' libation, he pushed her hand aside and withdrew into his austere quarters. Lakini was patrolling the slopes above the sanctuary. When she returned, she went straight to Lusk's door, knowing he was there, and stood outside it a long time, not knocking but simply listening to the absolute silence within. Hours she stood there in her still way, leaving only at the bell that summoned all to the common meal. She took a mouthful to sustain her and returned, laying her palm against the rough grain of the wooden door.

In the morning, Lusk found her sitting cross-legged, her back straight against the semismooth stone blocks of the wall, her eyes closed. He squatted beside her, and she opened her eyes, instantly aware.

"Do you want to tell me what happened?" she said.

He shrugged. "*Bondaru,*" he said. "It took place in another life and is sealed from us now." Lakini knew there was no possible answer to that.

They sat in companionable silence. Lakini stared at the wall opposite. Someone had sketched a figure on the plaster, carefully limning in straight lines and precise angles to form an odd asymmetrical figure, something like a star. Lately she had seen variations of basic geometrical shapes appear on the walls of the sanctuary, drawn in various pigments and by various people—both pilgrims and folk of the sanctuary—and always with great care. The Vashtun didn't seem to mind it, and the Diamar, his second, tried to tell her they were a means of meditation much like the great wheels some of the holy people of the eastern lands made out of colored sand.

But she didn't like them. There was something about how their angles were jointed together that seemed unnatural, like the three-legged frogs one found sometimes in spring ponds, swimming ungracefully with their two-legged brethren. There was simply a sense of wrongness, and when she looked at one of them too long, a humming would grow in her head and start to sound like whispers before she jerked her gaze away. She didn't like the way the whispers began to break apart into coherent words, words that made sense at first but that she couldn't remember when she disengaged.

She and Lusk sat against the wall a long time, the adepts of the sanctuary passing them from time to time, intent on their business and occasionally glancing at them in curiosity.

"Will you go again?" she asked, as the shadows shifted around them.

He rubbed his striped forehead before he answered.

"No," he said. There was a long pause before he continued. "They're all dead, you see."

She nodded, glancing at the mathematical figure opposite, feeling the conversational buzz rising in her mind, and looking away again.

"They all die," she said, thinking of Bithesi, her grace with animals, her limited lifespan. She rose and held out a hand to him. He took it and pulled himself to his feet.

"The Diamar has asked to consult with us," she said. "Two of the merchant Houses seek an alliance and ask that Shadrun midwife the negotiations."

Lusk frowned. "Shadrun is a holy place. What has a sanctuary to do with commerce? And we are warriors and guardians, not diplomats."

"The sanctuary is like us, Lusk. We might not be of the world, but we must function within it. Shadrun guards the roads, and while we serve Shadrun, we do likewise. And for better or worse, merchants use the roads."

She smiled at him. "We become responsible for what we protect."

Lusk stared at her so intently, her smile faltered. He didn't appear to see her at all but seemed to be looking through her, as if she were transparent, to some distant scene behind her. If she had the ability to probe his mind's eye, Lakini wondered, would she see his gathered dead ones looking back at him reproachfully?

Then his gaze shifted, and he was aware of her again. He relaxed a fraction and smiled back.

"It used to be simpler," he said. "Back when we were newly born. Which Houses are we to wet-nurse?"

"Jadaren and Beguine, Beguine of Turmish," said Lakini, relieved that his dark mood was lessening. "There is a blood feud between them, going back through their generations, that is rooted in some imagined wrong. Now they seek to marry two children of their Houses and end the dispute."

If Lakini hadn't turned away, she would have seen the tiny shiver that passed over Lusk's frame at the name Jadaren, or the way his eyes narrowed almost imperceptibly, as if trying to puzzle out a riddle.

"I don't know the name Beguine, and Jadaren only in passing," he said, his voice level. "And their bickering means nothing to me."

As Lusk turned to follow Lakini through Shadrun's passages, his gaze fell on the askew star shape. He, too, felt a voice murmur in his head, but when he looked away, the voice stayed, just below the level of consciousness.

Unlike Lakini, he didn't mind the voice. It echoed back his own thoughts, multiplying the words that drifted there until they took on the nature of a chant: *Jadaren,* and *blood feud,* and *revenge,* and over and over again, *the dead, the dead, the dead.*

Nonthal, Turmish

1585 DR—The Year of the Bloodied Manacles

Sanwar Beguine stood in the library, in the circle of light cast by the sun shining through the round window embedded in the center of the roof. The library was not large, but it was a pleasant room, with clean lines, plenty of light, a high ceiling, and shelves lined with a respectable selection of books and scrolls collected over several generations, to which he had added not a few. Here were histories, ancient and modern, of the land of Faerûn in many languages, as well as popular tales and entertainments. Here also were more arcane volumes, spellbooks, as well as atlases of not only strange lands, but of strange planes, to which most people never thought of journeying.

It was these, of all the volumes the Beguine family held, that appealed most to Sanwar's sensibilities. Let his brother deal with the practicalities of trade; he would protect the House with the magic arts.

He knew their enemies did. It tormented him—the knowledge that no matter how he studied the arcane arts, no matter how he tried to advance the interests of House Beguine with magic, the Jadarens possessed something with Powers he could only dream of—something that warded that monstrosity of a Hold they hunkered down in; something that kept them from being destroyed.

He would find a way to best it. He would find a way in.

There was a rustle of silks and the scent of roses threaded the air, but Sanwar didn't turn around until a soft hand touched his shoulder. He glanced down into the wide brown eyes of his sister-in-law.

"Does Kestrel still cleave to my brother's plan?" he asked. "Or by some miracle has she come to her senses?"

Vorsha shook her head. "She's like her father. She looks favorably on the idea of an alliance between the families, whatever her personal feelings in the matter."

“ ‘Like her father,’ ” Sanwar said. “If she’d been mine, Vorsha, her temper would have been different. I wish she were mine. She could have been.”

A hot blush burned across Vorsha’s neck and face, and she turned away. She could feel the heat of his bulk as he bent over her.

Sanwar’s lips were almost touching Vorsha’s ear. She felt his warm breath on her skin and closed her eyes.

“Vorsha, do me this favor,” he said, softly.

“Anything,” she whispered.

“It destroys me to think of that little girl trapped in that den of serpents. I can’t stop her from going—not without a miracle—but I can try to protect her in my small way. I need your help to do it.”

Vorsha did open her eyes then and looked up at Sanwar guilelessly. “I’ll help however I can.”

“I can make her an amulet—something that will give her warning when danger is near, and can turn aside a stealthy blow or curse. It’s not a guarantee she’ll be safe, but if someone wishes her harm, at least she’ll have a fighting chance. But I need something from her to craft it. I don’t want to upset her by asking her myself, but you could get it for me without anyone knowing.”

“What do you need?”

He smiled and put his finger under her chin, tipping up her face to the warm sunlight streaming through the circular window. He brushed his lips lightly against her neck and felt her shiver with anticipation.

“Nothing of any significance. Five hairs from her brush—five long, unbroken hairs. No more and no less.”

She looked into his eyes, and unexpectedly, her eyes narrowed. "For a protective amulet, you say? No more, no less?"

He looked hurt. "Do you think I'd harm her?"

"Not intentionally," she said, considering.

He withdrew, and all warmth and life seemed to go with him, leaving her cold and alone.

"I only want to shield her, Vorsha. It seems I might be the only one who objects to throwing your daughter to the Jadaren wolves. But if you truly distrust me . . ." He turned from her.

"No!" She flung herself into his arms, and, to her inexpressible relief, he scooped her up, embracing her. She felt she could bathe in his warmth. She buried her face in his chest and fought back tears.

"Of course I'll get them for you, of course."

"Good girl," he said, stroking her hair and looking over her head at the rows of books, leather-bound, hide-bound, hinged in steel and locked in silver. The books would tell him what to do.

Kestrel had a big slant-topped writing desk in her chambers. Her mother found her with an accounts book spread wide on top of it. She was sitting at a stool before it, holding a short ivory pointer in her hand and running it down a column of figures. Vorsha had entered when there was no answer to her soft knock, and it didn't surprise her to find her daughter engrossed in numbers. Kestrel had caught her lower lip up between her teeth, and to Vorsha she looked very much like the child she had been seventeen years before, learning her figures and the marvelous written tools of commerce at her father's knee.

At Vorsha's light step, Kestrel looked up from the cream-colored pages, startled, and smiled.

"What are you reading, love?" asked Vorsha, crossing behind the desk and stool to Kestrel's dressing table. There were a few cosmetics scattered across the wooden surface of this other fine piece of imported furniture inlaid with fanciful figures, men riding horses, and small dragons, in brass and silver. She straightened the items, capping a perfume bottle that leaked the smell of summer flowers, and gathered some well-used pens into an alabaster cup. Smiling, she rubbed at an ink blot that marred the tail of a mounted dragon. She knew nothing save sanding that would get it out, and she knew no amount of scolding would stop Kestrel from scribbling at figures anywhere it struck her.

"The accounts from the spice trade two years ago," said Kestrel, lifting the tip of her ivory stick from one column to another. "Ciari told me the price of saffron has jumped extraordinarily, and the Testra clan is claiming the flowers were damaged by hail. But at this time two years ago there were similar storms, and the increase was not nearly so great. They have a new proctor, and we suspect he's taking the opportunity to set a new bar."

Vorsha fingered the carved wooden handle of a brush, examining the bristles for strands of hair, but Kestrel must have cleaned it.

"You can hardly blame the man. You'd do the same thing." She took the brush and went to Kestrel, standing behind her and gathering her thick brown hair behind her shoulders. Kestrel sat straight, as she had as a child when her mother brushed her hair to dry it before the fire.

"I would, but I wouldn't attract attention by tripling the price. A ten or fifteen percent increase would pass by unnoticed or excused. Three hundred percent is simply greedy."

"What do you propose to do?"

"In this case, merely to get my figures in order. Then I'll pass them to Ciari, and she'll have a chat with the Testra proctor."

Vorsha couldn't help laughing. "Poor man."

"She'll scold him up and down the guildhall. Then they'll work out a fair price and drink on it. He's a man of business and a big boy—he can take it."

In answer, Vorsha brushed her hair, with long strong strokes from the hairline all the way to the tips. Kestrel sighed and tilted her head back a little, closing her eyes in pleasure.

Vorsha worked methodically, gathering each section and brushing it until it gleamed. "You have a tangle back here," she said.

"Yes. I'm incorrigible," replied Kestrel, eyes still closed. "What am I going to do without you when I'm married?"

They were both silent, struck suddenly by the casual finality of that statement. Vorsha continued brushing without pause. "Kestrel, are you certain about this? Marrying a Jadaren—yes, I know your father considers this feud outdated. And to tell the truth, I've never heard any evil of Arna. But just as there are Beguines who cannot overcome their hatred for House Jadaren . . ."

“Like Uncle Sanwar.” Kestrel’s voice sounded sleepy.

Vorsha hesitated, holding a thick skein of hair, and her hand trembled. But she forced herself to continue, and her internal shaking stopped. She desired Sanwar, yearned for his desire, and despised herself for it. But when it came to her brother-in-law, it seemed she couldn’t control her body. And Sanwar had promised to protect Kestrel.

“Just like Sanwar, yes,” she said, banishing the quaver from her voice. “Like your uncle, there are Jadarens who hate us, and will hate you, and will have you at their mercy in that great hulking hold they hunker down in. Who knows what could happen to you there?”

“They aren’t monsters, Mama,” Kestrel said, rising and embracing her mother. “And I plan to overcome them with my irresistible charm.”

Vorsha hugged her, suddenly and fiercely. In the brush she held over Kestrel’s shoulder, she could see the brown gleam of hair in the bristles. Kestrel pulled back and smiled.

“I’m tired with talking, and if I don’t stop looking through the account book, I’ll have visions all night of columns of figures swirling around me. I have to go to bed now, or I’ll fall asleep on the floor and you’ll have to carry me to bed, undress me, and tuck me in, as you did when I was five. Oh, Mama,” she said as the bright water sprang to Vorsha’s eyes. “Please don’t cry. It’ll be ages yet before I go. We have to negotiate, and I want to close the leatherwork accounts. And maybe Arna won’t even like my face.”

Vorsha wiped her eyes with the back of her hand and laughed. “I can’t imagine that, my sweet.”

She kissed Kestrel on the cheek and went to the dressing table, placing the brush next to the cup with the pens. With her back to Kestrel, she pulled out the hairs that clung to the bristles and tucked them into her palm.

Outside Kestrel's room she examined her prize. Some of the hairs had broken, but she had at least ten, whole and complete, that shone with tints of walnut wood and amber. Holding them carefully to her breast, she walked quickly along the hall to the room where she would try to wash the smell of Sanwar off her thighs and pretend to sleep before Nicol came to bed. The hot tears came unbidden and streaked along the side of her face, as if driven by the wind.

CHAPTER SEVEN

JADAREN HOLD

1585 DR—THE YEAR OF THE BLOODIED MANACLES

Arna Jadaren held a twisted coil of paper between his thumb and forefinger and frowned at it.

"So far I'm not impressed," he told Vidor Druit, who snorted and snatched the paper back.

"Nor was your uncle," he said. "Which is why we're going to see if House Beguine is more forward-thinking than you stick-in-the muds."

Arna stirred the rest of the bits of paper that were piled in the small soapstone box his friend had brought.

"Careful," Vidor told him. "They're designed to be easy to ignite, and that's all the samples I have at hand."

Arna withdrew his hand. "So show me. What makes these marketable?"

"Watch," said Vidor. He took the twist of paper and, with a quick jerk of the wrist, flicked it on the surface of the table. As it hit, there was a thin *pop,* and the paper blazed up in a tall flame, bright yellow, then blue as the paper crumbled to ash and the flame died. Curious, Arna rubbed the surface of the table with his finger, feeling only a slight warmth and a few grains of grit. There was a faint brown mark where the paper had flared.

"Useful, no?" said Vidor, his freckled face stretched in a grin.

Arna shrugged. "For what? A couple seconds of light? A trick for the children?"

Vidor shook his head. "You're spoiled from easy living in this monstrous rock of yours. Come on the road with me, or a tenday exploring the wild, or even spend a day or so in a crofter's hut. Somewhere where a servant isn't ready at hand to light a fire whenever you want one. You can spend a few minutes striking flints together, and gods help you if they're wet. Or maybe you have live coals left from the night before, but most likely not. Or if you're very lucky, you have a spellcaster to hand. Or you might have a box of these, cheap and handy. All you need is a bed of twigs and tinder, and snap! The cantrip's already spelled on it. Your weary goodwife needs no spells nor skill, just one of these to flick on the hearth. There's another to sharpen a dull blade, and another to test if your well water is pure. And we're working on more."

"Hmm." Maybe Vidor had a point. Arna took a twist and imitated Vidor's action, flicking his wrist as he'd seen his friend do. The paper bounced against the table and emitted a weak fizzle. There was a singed smell in the air and the paper was blackened, but no flame showed.

"Ah, yes." Vidor looked a little crestfallen. "Unfortunately, the success rate of the lots we've produced isn't as high as we'd like."

"You mean the fail rate's *higher* than you'd like."

"You need a wizard to impregnate the cantrip papers with the spell. Wizards don't come cheap—none of the ones worth using, at least. Your workaday goodwife or man-for-hire doesn't have the coin to pay for a box of these. And those with coin often enough have staff to light a fire, or sharpen the knives, or rid the room of fleas. We need to make them cheap enough to sell to market, so the wizard must work quickly. Out of a lot of twenty, one or two, three maybe, are duds. It won't matter to the goodwife. She'll just swear and reach for another, for she can afford plenty."

He replaced the lid of the soapstone box on the little hoard of cantrip papers with a resigned air.

"Five to fifteen percent," said Arna. "That's a little high for a middleman to want to deal with. And the big Houses have their reputations to think of."

"Hypocrite," returned Vidor. "We all know the fruit seller who, stuck with a crate of spoiled plums, puts one in each basketful he sells, for no one cares about one bad plum, and that way all share the burden and lose nothing. We all do the same to one degree or another. Finding a shipment of cloth not up to standard and with the seller long gone, doesn't your uncle sell them as 'rustic-weave,' and command as high a price as he can?"

Arna laughed. "Fair enough. So your goodwife might have to use flints for her fire, and sharpen her kitchen knives on her own whetstone. But what if the cantrip fails to tell of the bad water, when folk thought it would?"

Vidor flushed. "I had thought of that. I've told my cousin that those spells mustn't fail, even though we must charge more for them. But as for the rest, they're a way for those without riches to have the conveniences you and I take for granted."

"It's a clever idea, I'll grant you that," said Arna, distracted. "Vidor, when is it you go to Turmish?"

"I leave with the mule train tomorrow morning and join the Andula caravan that afternoon," said Vidor, putting the small box with the fire cantrips away in his leather sample pack.

"And you are determined to solicit the Beguines?"

Vidor gave him an odd look. "We need backing and the promise of a substantial market to produce the cantrip papers, especially if we're going to improve the reliability. House Jadaren has the scope to support the venture, but your uncle's not interested. House Beguine's an obvious place to try before I go farther abroad."

He pulled the strap tight. "I know there's bad blood between your Houses, but business is business, and you can't expect—"

Arna laughed. "I wouldn't dream of asking you not to go to House Beguine. In fact, I'd like to come with you."

Vidor shouldered his pack. "As far as Sespech, you mean, as before? And have your uncle skin me alive for not nursemaiding sufficiently far from that merrow-den?"

"No," said Arna. "I mean to go to Nonthal with you, as your assistant, to trade with the Beguines."

"Funny," said Vidor, flatly.

Arna hurried behind him as he left Arna's rooms, through the maze of passageways that threaded the family quarters of Jadaren Hold.

It was many years since Gareth Jadaren had claimed the Giant's Fist, shed the name of pirate, married the daughter of one of Beredel's thanes, and exploited the nascent trade routes branching between Erlkazar and the Unapproachable East, and had finally died old and fat and prosperous, surrounded by his descendants and assured that the name of House Jadaren would endure. Between then and now, the tunnels that threaded the monolith like worms through cheese, excavated by some race lost to recorded history, had been cleared out and expanded by Jadaren workers. Caverns at the base of the gigantic rock were hollowed out further, creating shelter for caravans and great chambers to serve as meeting halls and places to feast and entertain. Additional hollows functioned as storerooms for trading goods as well as for supplies to meet the ongoing needs of the household, the servants, guards, and visitors. Tunnels that branched from both the base of the rock as well and the summit were enlarged until they resembled the hallways of some great palace, with steps carved out of the living rock leading from level to level, allowing easy passage from kitchens to banquet hall, bathing chambers to guest quarters, storerooms to the family's chambers. Here and there large voids in the body of the monolith were broken into, and proved to be mirror-smooth bubbles of obsidian, or chambers full of white and amethyst crystal.

Sometimes in walking through the passageways that generations of Jadaren chatelaines had striven to make both comfortable and magnificent, laying carpets to cushion the feet and tapestries to delight the eye, it was easy to forget that one was in the center of a block of volcanic rock. Only the lack of outside light and the constant light of spellcast torches, flickering in the currents of air that the ventilation holes drilled perpendicularly through the monolith, spoiled the illusion that Jadaren Hold was like any other merchant's house.

"I'm serious," Arna told Vidor as they both squeezed against the wall to allow a servant girl bearing an oversize tray of soiled crockery to go by. "I don't intend any prank or game. I've a good reason to see the Beguines for myself. Or at least one Beguine in particular."

"Why is that?" asked Vidor. The hallway was clear, and he slowed to allow Arna to catch up with him.

"Because I'm supposed to marry her."

Vidor stopped so abruptly that Arna had to stumble backward to avoid bumping into him, earning them both a glare from a second servant who was trying to balance a load of clean linens on her head. They both muttered an apology and let her pass before they proceeded, Vidor grasping Arna's sleeve.

"Marry a Beguine! Are you mad? Your entire family would expire of shock!"

Arna shrugged. "It's Uncle Bron's idea. Or possibly Nicol Beguine's. I don't know who had it first. Not many, not even our trading allies, know about it, but we and House Beguine have been in negotiations for at least a year to bring an end to the feud."

"But the feud has lasted for centuries!"

They were near one of the many alcoves scattered throughout the Jadaren Hold tunnel system, crafted for the convenience of any who desired to step away from the human traffic that sometimes streamed through the passageways, busy as any traveler's path on a sunny day. Arna pulled his friend aside as yet another linen-laden servant—it must have been one of the twice-tenday cleaning days his aunt mandated—went by, glancing at them curiously.

"Yes, it has," said Arna. "But can any tell why?"

"Well . . ." Vidor furrowed his brow in thought. "There was the matter of House Andula's entire season of cider shipments being undercut, with House Beguine having a stake in it. And the disagreement with the Jeweler's Guild. And that ship at Mulmaster, with Clan Testra's half stake in it, burning after the crew fought one of House Beguine's."

"Yes," Arna interrupted. "And we both could point to a double handful of fights, and raids, and downright sabotage throughout the years without even thinking hard. Some of them are even legendary, and the subject of songs and ballads—very dirty ballads, I might add. But is there a reason for them?"

"Pursuit of profit," answered Vidor, with the confidence of a merchant's child.

"Ah, profit, the blessing of Waukeen," said Arna. "But does this bickering profit anyone in the end? We do dirty by the Beguines because they do dirty to us, and each expects it in return. The only reason for the feud is the feud itself. But the lives lost, people injured, and the good—gods!—the goods that might be sold or traded, wasted for the mere satisfaction of hurting an enemy. What's the good of it?"

"There must have been a reason for the feud once," said Vidor.

"Oh, likely. A very good reason, I would guess, considering the strength of the hatred, and how long it's lasted. Even through wars and Spellplague and the fall and rise of cities. But does anyone remember it now? It's buried beneath the fall of the years, forgotten, and it's time we forgot the feud it spawned."

"So you agree with your uncle, and with Nicol."

"Of course. Why should a baker in Sespech have her flour spoiled by beetles because a Jadaren is trying to ruin a deal? Or a sailor's wife be widowed because a Beguine mage cursed his ship and her load of Jadaren lumber? Why, in fact, should my beauteous self be endangered by a forgotten wrong?"

"Or my beauteous self for that matter, for the sin of being your friend?" said Vidor.

Arna grinned. "Correct entirely. Oh, Uncle Bron is wise as a serpent in this matter. But there is a complication. He and Nicol want a public testament to the end of the war. They want the advent of a new harmonious era to be crystal clear to everyone, family and ally as well as stranger. And what better way to do it than to marry the children of both Houses together?"

Vidor leaned against the polished stone wall and folded his arms, regarding his friend with sympathy.

"And what do you think of being the sacrificial ox?"

"I am of two minds. One agrees with Uncle Bron. An alliance with House Beguine will mean a new era of prosperity, and linking our two Houses together through marriage is a small sacrifice to pay—and no sacrifice at all, really, since the Beguine daughter would come to Jadaren Hold to train as its chatelaine."

Vidor nodded. "That makes sense, since House Beguine has two daughters and a son to manage their affairs. And your other mind?"

"My other mind is selfish, and concerned with my own comfort, and would like to see my proposed bride before I commit myself for life. Sad, and I blush to admit it, but true."

Vidor laughed and gave Arna a light shove.

"So you would like to come with me and spy out whether the Beguine girl is pretty enough for your exalted tastes, is that it?"

"Alas, but I am flawed. And think of this: it's not fair for her to have to marry a man who doesn't find her to his liking, is it?"

"Ever the gentleman," said Vidor. "Very well, pack your gear and meet me in the caverns. We have to leave soon, and I won't wait for you. And I expect you to do your share to sell my cantrips, by the way. None of these snide comments about quality and shoddy goods."

The sun was just shy of being overhead by the time Vidor Druit and Arna Jadaren, accompanied by three seasoned guards, who had served the Druit household for a decade, and a pair of laden mules passed Jandi's Oak. Over the years the way to Jadaren Hold had grown from a barely perceptible path to a wide road, capable of letting a small army pass. The long tongue of trees that once reached out from the branching of the Chondalwood and Thornwood had been pushed back, cleared for its wood and to allow the road to expand.

The great oak, so alien amid the other trees, was spared, and now grew flourishing and massive-trunked by itself, standing like a gigantic rooted guardian overlooking the road and the distant anthill of Jadaren Hold. Beneath the stretch of its branches was a small shrine, waist-high to a human, made of stacked lava stones. Before the shrine was a circle of similar stones, making a small fire pit that was now filled with cold black char.

"Wait," called Arna, sliding off his horse. The horse, a short fat draft form, which Arna had tumbled off on a regular basis since the age of nine, snorted and rooted for grass at the stones at the side of the road.

"We're late enough," called Vidor.

Arna waved back in reply, but didn't pause on his way up the slight slope to the shade of the oak above.

Under Jandi's Oak it was very quiet, as it always was. Even when the road was busy, all sounds seemed to be muted to those who sat under its branches, and today, with the Druit party the only travelers nearby, the sole sound was the faint twitter of finches, invisible between the dark green leaves.

The black lava-rock shrine was little more than a simple pile of rocks, fitted together without mortar, and topped with a big geode that was broken open at one side, leaving a hollow area lined with a haze of tiny gray crystals. It was likely formed at the same time as the Giant's Fist, in the same frenzy of volcanic activity that had made the black river of lava at the bottom of the valley.

Inside the crystal-lined hollow was a tiny figure, like a small doll, exquisitely braided out of dried grass stems or fine wooden fibers. Knotted around its neck was a length of green thread with three knots at the end. Arna ignored it and pulled out a small round of copper from an inner pocket of his jerkin. The tiny coin was pierced through, and a length of red string threaded it. Arna quickly tied a square knot in the middle of the string and laid it inside the geode, next to the straw figure.

From the road, Vidor gestured impatiently. Arna waved again, but he placed his hand on the rough bark that girdled the immense trunk of the tree, over a scar that looked as though it might have been a carved letter before age and growth had obscured it.

Briefly he bowed his head. "Guard my days, Jandi," he breathed. The words felt strange. He hadn't uttered them since he was a child, and he was a little embarrassed at saying them now. Jandi's Oak had always been here, and it was a tradition for travelers to ask the protection of the nymph, or dryad, or whatever fey creature Jandi had been—if she had ever really existed.

It was also a tradition for the local folk to leave a tribute in the shape of small coins when they were about to embark on great journeys or changes of life. Girls from the local farms would leave their coppers, marked by a uniquely knotted or colored thread, to ask if they would marry their lovers, or leave their homes to find their fortunes, and were answered by the appearance of tiny works of intricate craftsmanship, designated with the same thread they had left with the coin, which were supposed to be signs from the spirits of the nearby forest.

Arna has his own theory about the coins and the figures. He imagined they were made not by spirits but by some reclusive forest dwellers, a race with clever hands and some small magic of concealment. Sometime long ago this method of barter—payment of small coins for their craft—had arisen, a way for folk who didn't want to be found, yet who desired to sell their goods, to do trade. Somehow the idea that the small figures were a means of fortune-telling was born, and bandied about, and became for all intents and purposes the truth.

Yet he desired to make the gesture of leaving the coin, of asking Jandi's protection. Coming events would be momentous, both for him and his House. He wouldn't scruple to seek aid anywhere.

Returning to the road, he mounted his horse. The animal huffed indignantly at being pulled away from the sweet grass at the verge.

"When you're quite ready, Master Arna," said Vidor, wheeling his mount westward with an annoyed glance at his friend.

"I had to ask Jandi's blessings on our enterprise," replied Arna. "And with the quality of the goods in your packs, we'll need all the help we can get."

"You risk a beating for your insubordination," said Vidor, raising a fist in mock rage. "And you'll kindly remember that you're here by my goodwill alone."

"Forgive me, Master Druit," said Arna, kneeing his horse until he caught up with Vidor. "I'll make every effort to watch my tongue."

Beneath Jandi's Oak all was still, save for a whisper of wind along the grass that whirled and spiraled as no honest wind ought to do. And from the line of trees that over time and by human traffic had been hacked, burned, and driven farther and farther back, something patient and hungry watched the party as it disappeared into the dust of the road.

Nonthal, Turmish

1585 DR—Year of the Bloodied Manacles

Sanwar Beguine twisted a strand of long chestnut brown hair around his finger, letting it bite deep. He watched, fascinated, as his pinched skin grew red, then purple before he released the hair.

Four more hairs lay on an unmarked piece of paper on his desk. He put the one he had been playing with down and contemplated them. Each was at least the length of his forearm, from his elbow to the tip of his middle finger: thick hairs, almost coarse, that varied from the color of the very wood of his desk to pale amber. They were strong hairs, unbroken. He picked up his jeweler's glass and examined them minutely. Under magnification, the substance of each hair looked like thick glass, with a clear core in the center. The ends of all five hairs had the tiny bulb that had rooted the hair in Kestrel's scalp.

Vorsha had wept when she gave them to him the night before.

From a slot in his desk Sanwar pulled another length of clean, thick paper. He took three of Kestrel's hairs, looped them neatly, and folded them securely inside the paper, making a tiny packet. He tucked this in a pocket inside his coat and returned to his contemplation of the other two.

It *was* his intention to make Kestrel an amulet. He'd told Vorsha the truth about that. But that required three of her hairs. He had different plans for the other two. They would help him answer a question that had lingered in his mind ever since he'd seen his niece toddle down the hallway outside the children's wing, clutching her nurse's hand. Now, when he saw the girl in unguarded moments, laughing with her sister or reviewing a vendor's tally sheet, he wondered.

He yanked at a tuft of his own hair, wincing. Examining the resultant hairs between his fingers, he selected the two that were longest and placed them next to Kestrel's, flicking the rest off his fingers and onto the floor. His hairs were coarser and curlier than the girl's and of a more uniform brown. He looked at them through the glass. The tints were similar, but then, his hair was the same color as his brother's.

The simple-seeming construction of his desk hid many small drawers and compartments. Sanwar tapped an inset, smooth-headed wooden screw on the right side with his middle finger, giving three discreet, forceful taps. In response, a small, spring-loaded door opened on the side, revealing a small space just big enough to hold a rounded ceramic bowl, the size of a man's cupped hand.

He placed the bowl on the flat surface of the desk, beside the paper that held Kestrel's hairs and his own. The glaze on it was uncrazed, the green of corroded copper. The bowl was otherwise undecorated. Sanwar pulled a clean, soft cloth from his pocket and wiped the already-clean interior until not a speck of dust could possibly remain.

Quickly he coiled all four strands of hair into the bowl. Another compartment in the desk held small glass vials filled with various powders. He removed two—one filled with a yellowish white powder. The other contained a powder so dark it looked black, but when grains of it were exposed to the light, it proved to be a deep red.

Sanwar sprinkled a goodly amount of the light powder into the bowl, and a scant smatter of the red. He paused and took a deep breath.

Arna knew that Nonthal was nowhere near the glory it had once boasted, years ago when Turmish was the center of trade of a significant portion of Faerûn, and that its central market was like as not a mere shadow of what had existed there before. How glorious must that age have been, therefore, when the remnant was so brisk, and bustling, and filled with all manner of shops and stalls hawking everything from spices to silks, amulets to baskets of many varieties of apples. Here was a farm-woman selling poultry: chickens in willow-wand cages and quail and ducks as well, all cheeping and quacking in their precariously stacked quarters. He paused to glance at a countertop piled high with used armor, some of it scored with ominous-seeming burn marks. The merchant, a dwarf with elaborate braids in her autumn red hair and arm muscles that easily surpassed Arna's own in girth, glanced up at him from her task of hammering out the dents in a breastplate, ran her eye over him, and turned back to her work, obviously dismissing him as a likely purchaser of fighting gear.

"Stop gawking like a country cousin on his first trip to a town temple," muttered Vidor, hitting him lightly on the shoulder. "It's not your first venture outside that rock you call home. And you've seen more goods in the caravans bound for Imaskar."

"Sespech isn't like this," returned Arna. "And trade goods are packed tight when they come to Jadaren Hold."

"Nonsense," said Vidor distractedly, pulling a roll of paper the length and thickness of his finger from an inner pocket of his stained traveling jacket. "When the caravans come in, the undercaves of Jadaren Hold are like a pasha's treasure trove. You and I hid there between the bales as youngsters often enough, spying out the bargaining."

He unrolled the paper partway and frowned at it.

"Nicole Beguine's manner is as pretty and noncommittal as his handwriting," he said. "He salutes my clan and pedigree. He pats me on the head for my clever cantrips, as if I were a deserving student. He apologizes that he cannot make the time to discuss the matter with me in a timely fashion, and begs the pressures of business. He refers me to his daughter Ciari, who is empowered to act for the family in all ways."

Arna snorted. "He's good."

"The Beguines are all very good at what they do. It's a brilliant reply, really. Very kind, nothing you could claim was insulting, and yet it's perfectly designed to put me at a disadvantage—to make me a petitioner begging for a favor."

He nudged Arna, who was still looking about him at the panoply of merchant's stalls and sniffing hungrily after the aroma of meat cooking over an open brazier.

"It doesn't help that you refuse to let me meet the Beguine daughters at their quarters, and instead hunt them down in the market like some opportunist carpet seller. They'll never take me seriously."

Arna shrugged. "My apologies, but I can't take the risk some member of the household won't recognize me. It's not the safest place for a Jadaren. There are those hell-bent on keeping the feud alive. And if Kestrel finds that I came spying after her . . ."

"If so, it's only the truth," said Vidor, tartly.

"And should you keep an appointment with Ciara at House Beguine, there's no guarantee that Kestrel will accompany her, while all are agreed that every third and seventh day they go marketing together for the needs of the House."

"Our innkeeper is agreed," muttered Vidor. "That's hardly all."

"Look, Vidor, if this falls through, I'll take up the issue with my uncle. Fair enough?"

"I'll hold you to that." Vidor peered through the increasing mass of people, while Arna looked around for the source of the delicious smell. "Say, Arna, are you sure of your source? I see no pair of sisters bargaining at stalls, and I can't imagine a Beguine not arguing for the best price."

"It's early in the day yet," replied his friend. "And neither of us knows them by sight."

He moved three paces to the armory stall, where the dwarf still hammered diligently at a breastplate, wielding her hammer with a delicacy at odds with one so muscular. Arna made a polite bow and addressed her.

"Your pardon, goodmistress dwarf," he said. "We have business with the sisters of House Beguine, who are to go to market this day. Would you know the ladies?"

The dwarf paused in her work and contemplated him from under bristling eyebrows, unsmiling. Something in his boyish, open face must have struck her as harmless, because she pointed over his shoulder with the head of her hammer.

"It happens that the Beguine girls are over there, at the Widow Bejuer-Vaud's pie stall," she said, her voice deep and surprisingly musical.

Arna turned to look, with a certain sense of foreboding. His promised bride was closer than he had thought, and he hadn't a notion of what to expect.

Vidor had turned to look as well. "There," he said.

Arna tilted his head to look between the milling mass of folk who had come to do business this day: respectable-looking housewives, sleek upper servants restocking their masters' pantries, knots of travel-stained adventurers looking to renew their supplies, pickpockets looking for distracted targets.

There was the stall, with neatly wrapped stacked of pies high on the counter, and a portable stove glowing behind it—the source of the tantalizing smell. Several folk—man-size as well as a brace of halflings who mounted a wooden step set out for such as them to view the wares—clustered around the pie shop.

Without turning around, Arna leaned closer to the dwarf. "I don't know them. Can you tell me which is Kestrel Beguine?"

The lump in his throat, which had been bothering him since the morning, seemed to double in size at that moment. He was about to see the woman he would cleave to for the rest of his life—or would if his uncle and a phalanx of interested parties from both Houses had their way. He felt hot and cold at once, and his forehead felt clammy, as if he were a small boy before his uncle's desk, being tested in his numbering.

Everything depended on the color of the flame. A yellow flame would simply mean that a close relative of Sanwar's had sired Kestrel. It would prove Nicol's paternity, since Sanwar was not aware of any other brothers he might have lying about. A blue flame—well, that would be an extremely interesting situation. It would mean Vorsha was far more duplicitous than he could imagine, and had betrayed both brothers by admitting yet a third man to her bed.

But a green flame would prove the matter of his suspicions true, and Kestrel would be revealed as his daughter, and as her supposed father's niece.

He lifted his hand and spoke a word, soft and sibilant. Heat flared at the tip of his index finger, and he held it over the green ceramic bowl in time to direct the flame that spurted out into the hairs and Powers within. There was a faint sizzle as the strands, short and long, crisped black and coiled in on themselves like maggots cast into a fire, and then there was a smell like burned meat.

A flame, small yet steady, pulsed over them—a flame green as the cracked heart of an emerald.

"Ouch!"

Kestrel's hand flew to her head. At the cry of pain, Ciari Beguine left off looking at the stack of savory pies and turned to her sister.

"What's the matter? Did someone pull your hair?" Ciari cast an angry eye at Widow Bejuer-Vaud's customers clustering around the stall, as if to force a confession from the culpable party. A halfling standing near her on a convenient stepstool drew back in alarm, but no one looked guilty.

"No, I don't think so." Kestrel rubbed at a spot just over her right temple. "It was more of a little jab—as if something bit me."

She glanced at her fingers and saw a tiny speck of blood.

"Look, Ciari," she began. "Something did. . . . Oh!"

She clasped her head again, wincing, and the ledger book she always bore on market days thumped to the ground at her feet.

Concerned, Ciari took her sister by the shoulders and pulled her away from the crush of folk at the counter.

"What's the matter, my love?" she said, her voice gentling. Ciari was at least a head taller than Kestrel, and built on broader lines. It was a running joke among the Beguine caravan guards that Ciari could take any of them on, male or female, in a fair fight.

"It burned!" Kestrel rubbed at her temple. "It's much better now. It hardly itches."

Ciari shifted the market basket on her arm. "An insect?"

Kestrel shook her head. "It felt like someone held a lit straw to my head, but now it's gone. Sorry, Ciari. I don't know what the matter is with me. Pay it no mind."

She bent to retrieve her ledger book, thumbing through it to check for loosened pages, while Ciari efficiently glared away a street urchin who was contemplating an attempt on the sweetmeats she carried in her basket and turned back to her assessment of Widow Bejuer-Vaud's pies.

The dwarf, engrossed in her work, didn't look up this time. Without taking her eyes off the silver-chased steel over her knee, she pointed again.

"Mistress Kestrel is the one at the counter over there," she said.

Arna swallowed hard, braced himself, and looked, holding his breath. Then, impressed, he let his air out with a *swoosh.* The marriage alliance between House Beguine and House Jadaren, brokered by seasoned merchants with little care for romance and its inefficiencies, wouldn't saddle him with an unattractive wife—quite the opposite, in fact.

Kestrel Beguine was tall, straight of back and well built, with reddish brown hair braided into an elaborate bun at the nape of her elegant neck. She wore a simple dress, deep blue with a tiny repeating pattern worked in gold thread, a modified version of those the more modish women of Turmish wore. His merchant's eye told him it was well cut and of fine fabric. A wide leather and brass belt clasped about her waist was hung with all manner of keys and small useful tools—and also served to accentuate her figure. She bore a market basket—his aunt had one similar, although Jadaren Hold had no market—hung over one arm. She was currently speaking intently to the small wizened woman, so shrunk and wrinkled that he would make no wager that she was fully human. Kestrel gestured at a neat stack of pies before her, and the wrinkled little woman shook her head.

Vidor's hand on his arm made him stifle a shriek.

"Easy, fairlady," said his friend. "The lovely Beguine sisters are at hand, and it is time to do some business. Many thanks, my friend," he added to the dwarf behind them, who grunted without looking up from the dent she was coaxing into true.

Together they wound their way between the folk streaming between the market stalls. Arna could hear Kestrel as she addressed the pie shop owner. Her voice was penetrating—not unpleasant, but he suspected it could become shrewish with time and usage.

"Why should I pay so much? Our kitchens are sufficient. I buy for convenience, nothing more, that our cook can turn her attention to more important matters. But she can make our pies at need."

The little widow's reply sounded amused, and not at all offended, as if they had had this conversation many times.

"The day your kitchens can turn out pies like mine, I will close my shop, young mistress," she said. "You well know your cooks, skilled as they may be, could never do better."

"It's not their practice to use cats-meat as the main ingredient," said Kestrel dismissively.

Arna and Vidor paused at the outskirts of the stall, where the fringe of the striped cloth hung to shelter customers from the sun shivered in the slight breeze. Arna turned to his friend and quirked an eyebrow. Vidor didn't see it. He was staring at Kestrel Beguine as she bargained, his mouth slightly open, like a small creature hypnotized by a snake.

A girl stood just behind Kestrel, slighter than the Beguine girl and wearing a dress a rich brown tint. She was brushing dust off her skirt and carried a leather case or book beneath her arm. She was Kestrel's maid, perhaps, or given the quills strapped on her wide belt beside her purse, her accounts keeper.

She glanced up to see the Vidor staring, looked to Kestrel and back at him, and lifted her eyebrows in turn. Arna saw the resemblance then. The hair, gathered at the nape of her neck and left to tumble down her back, was of a similar tint to Kestrel's chignon but with more chestnut and fewer red highlights. Her eyes were of a similar shape, although a different color. The curve of the cheek was also similar to Kestrel's, as was the way she held her shoulders. Arna narrowed his eyes, recalling the Jadaren records room and the innumerable rolled parchments that recorded the families and genealogies of all the merchant families his own had dealings with. This must be Ciari, Kestrel's elder sister.

She noticed him looking at her then, and he swallowed, thankful she didn't know he'd mistaken her for a servant. One corner of her mouth quirked up into a wry smile, and she winked at him. Perhaps she did know at that. He shrugged in apology.

He wondered if she was herself betrothed. She and Kestrel were the only Beguine daughters, he recalled, their only sibling an elder brother of an adventurous mind who had elected to look after the family interests in Imaskar.

"Twenty delivered to the House the day after tomorrow—fresh that morning, mind. I won't serve the stale leavings of your storehouse to my guests or family, goodwidow, especially not at the price you demand. And you'll give me one to take home now, for goodwill."

She took a length of clean linen from her basket and slapped it on the counter.

"Waukeen forgive you for abusing a poor woman at the end of her life," replied Mistress Bejuer-Vaud, with perfect good cheer, as she took the cloth and wrapped a pie in it, deftly tying the ends into a neat knot before she slipped it into Kestrel's basket. "Soon I'll be dead, and you may burn candles to light my passing to temper your many sins," she added, looking more than ever like an elderly gnome.

Kestrel grinned. "Never change, Mother Bejuer-Vaud," she said, sweeping her basket up and turning to go, her sister beside her. The old woman beamed, having made a profitable sale this day.

Vidor had been looking for his chance. As the Beguine girls left the stall, he stepped before them with a polite bow. Arna hastened to stay beside him.

"Your pardon, goodlady Beguine," Vidor began, bending toward Ciari. He must have deduced that the girl in autumn brown must be Kestrel's sister, Arna noted. Both girls halted, Ciari holding her leather packet to her breast and Kestrel starting to frown.

Perhaps she wasn't frowning, thought Arna. Perhaps she was just preoccupied. No, she was frowning. Arna tried not to think of how it would be to wake up next to that frown every day for the rest of his life.

"Pardon my intrusion, but I've come at the behest of your good father," continued Vidor, offering Ciari the coil of the paper from Nicol Beguine. "My family has been developing portable cantrips, suitable for anyone to use at his convenience. Perhaps you received our gift of a box of samples."

Ciari took it between her long, slim fingers, one of which, Arna noticed, had a blot of ink at the knuckle. He stifled a smile, thinking of how often he'd missed a similar blot until he spotted it out in public. Ciari must do the accounting after all.

Kestrel exhaled impatiently and snatched the paper from her sister's hand. She glanced at it and thrust it back at Vidor, who took it, startled.

"Vidor Druit, is it?" she snapped. Arna saw she had fine eyes, so brown they were almost black.

"Well, is it? Speak up, man," she continued, as Vidor only stared up at her, nonplussed.

"So I am, goodlady," he stammered. "It's my honor—"

"I'll have you know two of your so-called fire starters fizzled out with nary a spark," Kestrel interrupted. "You can hardly expect us to put our good name to shoddy goods, can you?"

"I wouldn't ask you to," returned Vidor with some of his accustomed spirit. "Yet two failing meant eighteen worked, correct? For I'm sure you tried them all."

She only frowned in answer. It was a pretty enough frown, Arna conceded. Still, he hoped she didn't make it a habit, although he feared she did.

"How often must one strike a flint until the fire catches?" Vidor pressed on. "Many times, and if the flint is wet or worn, one might never get warm."

"Ten percent is not acceptable," she said with such finality that Arna felt he must defend his friend's venture.

"But it is, for something that can be sold so cheaply and is not convenient in the main," he interjected, then blinked as Kestrel turned the full force of her gaze on him. His argument, so clear before he spoke, became muddled in his head, and he grasped at what Vidor had told him at Jadaren Hold.

"We've all had a basket of bad plums that must be disposed of," he continued, struggling for coherency, "and no one complains if each customer has no more than one."

"Bad plums?" said Kestrel. Arna glanced at Ciari, who was shaking her head with a slight smile. Kestrel drew a deep breath, as if she were about to plunge deep into a cold pool, and proceeded to tell him and Vidor exactly what she thought of bad plums. It took a long time, and was very skillfully done, and both men felt fairly bruised when it was over.

When Kestrel ended her diatribe, or perhaps was just drawing breath for another go, Vidor jumped in.

"We'll get the failure rate below one in twenty, goodlady. We can do it more quickly with backing from House Beguine, however."

She only stared at him as if he were a particularly unattractive slime mold, tossed her head, and turned away.

"Bad plums, indeed," she muttered.

Ciari was looking at Arna with an expression of amused sympathy, and he made bold to lean in close to her.

"What *do* you do with your bad plums?" he whispered.

"We cook them down into plum butter to sell in wintertime," she whispered back, with a glance at her sister, who was tapping her foot impatiently. "Enough brandy, and a little overripeness is easily forgiven."

She looked a trifle distracted, as if something were bothering her, and her hazel eyes narrowed slightly, as if she were in pain.

"Are you all right?" he asked.

She smiled at him and touched the side of her head briefly. "It's nothing. A slight headache, which is passing."

"Come," called Kestrel. "I want to get home and see to your head."

With a final glare for Vidor and Arna she hastened away.

"I'll send word to your House, then, when the shipments are ready," called Vidor after her, but she only stiffened her shoulders.

So now he knew for sure.

There was nothing but pale ash in the green bowl now, and the smell of burned hair hung like a miasma in the room. But there was no doubt about it; the green flame, though short-lived, was unmistakable. Kestrel, Vorsha's youngest, was Sanwar's daughter.

He drummed his broad-tipped fingers on the side of the desk and contemplated that information, what it meant and, most importantly, what to do with it.

Some use must be made of the fact that the Beguine maiden Nicol so blithely proposed throwing to the enemy was Sanwar's child.

Arna and Vidor watched as the sisters walked away, Kestrel clutching the market basket to her side, Ciari with her ledger book tucked under her arm. Once Ciari glanced back at Arna with a rueful smile on her lips and sympathy in her hazel eyes. Arna felt his heart thump against his ribs. Kestrel put her hand firmly on her sister's shoulder, and the older girl turned away, looking forward obediently. The swirl of their long skirts beat the dry dust of the market street into a small cloud at their feet, and as the clamor of dozens of sellers rose about them, they looked neither right nor left, their backs straight, strong, graceful, and uncompromising as they vanished into the morass of carts, people, and trade goods.

Vidor drew a long, shuddering breath and grasped Arna's elbow.

"Arna Jadaren," he said, his voice tinged by wonder.

Arna snorted. "Yes, I know. Come, let's get out of the thoroughfare."

But Vidor, like a man under a spell, didn't move, still gazing, at the spot where the girls had disappeared between a glassblower and a booth hawking many colors of thread. His fingers tightened over Arna's flesh and bone, and the youth winced.

"Arna Jadaren," he said again, slowly, as if puzzling out the words. "You bastard."

"No need to break my elbow," said Arna, pulling his friend from the path of a pair of inebriated-looking mercenaries and a pack of giggling children. Vidor complied passively, continuing to look past the thread merchant as if he had a hope of bending his vision around the booth and seeing where the Beguine daughters had gone.

That would be a useful spell to package and sell, thought Arna incongruously as he pushed Vidor between the stall where apples were piled red, yellow, and green on the counter and the secondhand armor merchant. The dwarf looked up at them, shook her head, and bent back to her hammering.

"You lucky, lucky bastard," said Vidor.

"You needn't make fun," said Arna. "She can't be as bad as that all the time."

"As bad as . . ." Vidor turned to him, and Arna saw he still held Nicol Beguine's note curled between his fingers like a talisman. "You lucky piece of . . ." He gestured in the air as if tasked with explaining advanced accounting to an idiot. "That *creature,*" he continued. "That magnificent, gorgeous creature. That's the kind of bride a man could search the world over for, and kill for, and die for. And, you lucky bastard, she's yours for a handshake."

"You mean Kestrel Beguine?" said Arna, nonplussed.

"No, I mean the Queen of the Goblins! Who else could I mean? I wish my family had an age-old feud with House Beguine, if such a thing meant marrying Kestrel."

"The woman who just scolded you in a public street for having shoddy goods?"

Vidor smiled as if remembering his first kiss. "Oh, she never meant all that," he said. "She's just setting the scene for bargaining advantage."

"Didn't sound like that to me," said Arna. "Sounded more like she never wanted to see your face again. Or mine, for that matter." It occurred to him, at this belated moment, that Kestrel was likely to remember his face when they were formally introduced—and she didn't seem to have much of a sense of humor. Ciari would certainly recognize him. Not much escaped her observant gaze. He could tell that much. Would she be offended on behalf of her sister?

Suddenly it seemed important that Ciari not despise him, and he wondered why.

"You're dense as a post," said Vidor. "And it's not fair, because you still get to marry her. Don't tell me you regret the bargain, because I won't believe you for a moment."

By Waukeen's purse, Vidor seemed ready to fight him over the matter. Arna lifted a placating hand.

"She's a magnificent woman, of course," he said. "I am very fortunate. Let's get back to our rooms, and contemplate my good fortune and your stock of cantrips. I still don't feel entirely safe in Beguine territory." He tugged at Vidor's sleeve.

With a final longing glance down the market, Vidor complied, following Arna blindly and muttering beneath his breath. Arna was glad he'd taken special note of the street turnings that would take them back to the inn.

"Vidor," he said as he nudged his friend around a corner. "Vidor, are you reciting *poetry?*"

"I wish I could recall more," Vidor said. "What's that verse in Tomas of Meryton's poem about the eladrin princess who married a mortal man? 'Child of night and starlight, her beauty as a crown . . .' and then I can't remember. 'Something something something down . . .' or was it 'town'? I know you've read it."

"What will I do with you?" said Arna, amused. He had a wild idea of switching identities with Vidor, of trying his hand at furthering the Druit cantrip venture and letting his friend wed his promised bride, since he seemed to have fallen violently in love with her. No, it couldn't be love, not so soon. Let it be infatuation, then.

"Did you mark her sister?" he said innocently. "Very pretty, wasn't she? A sweet face and manner."

Vidor shook his head impatiently. "Yes, yes, she looked well enough. But a pale shadow, my friend, to your promised bride. If you had hopes of my aligning myself with the Beguines, that is not the path to it. If Kestrel refuses you, however, at the altar or before . . . that's a path I'll gladly tread. 'Down roads of man, to mortal town . . .' No, that's not it."

He suspected Vidor would agree to a switch of identities, but it would never do. He'd hurt his family and House Beguine in the end. It would be best to go through with the bargain, for the sake of peace and the business.

There were worse fates, after all, than marrying a beautiful woman, however hard her tongue.

There were two more coppers in the lava-rock shrine beneath Jandi's Oak, one knotted with green thread; another with blue. The small doll figure was gone, and in its place, topped with his scarlet string with the square knot, was a box, intricately woven of tiny strips of bark. It fit easily in the hollow of his hand.

Carefully he opened it. The close-fitted lid lifted away to reveal another box inside. He laughed to himself when the second box proved to contain another, no bigger than his thumbnail.

He managed to pry off the tiny lid without destroying it. Inside was not, as he half expected, another box but a rough white crystal, such as one might find in the streambed below. He shook it into his palm and rubbed his thumb over it. It was just a small fragment of quartz, smaller than a pebble, with no special quality about it.

Smiling, he restored the stone to the smallest box and nestled them all inside one another as he had found them. He was at a loss to decide how to interpret the Jandi's gift—or the craft of the forest folk—as an augury of his future. Could it mean he was to look past his bride's brash exterior? That was an uncomfortable thought; it could mean she had a heart of stone. Or the bit of quartz could indicate a hidden jewel when it came from the people of the woods.

He slipped the box into his pocket. It was well made, even if it told him nothing, and he didn't intend to drive himself mad trying to guess the future.

CHAPTER EIGHT

NEAR SHADRUN-OF-THE-SNOWS

1585 DR—THE YEAR OF THE BLOODIED MANACLES

At the lip of the ridge two figures crouched. One was so close to the edge, she seemed almost suspended at the crux of falling, but she was rooted at the crest, still as the statue of an archer on the turrets of Belcaine Castle. Not a strand of her silver-marked hair, bound back in braids, stirred, and her face, which was marked with a wide pale band across her eyes like a mask, was impassive. Her hands were empty, and a greatsword was slung across her back.

At her shoulder a taller figure was poised, a golden image on one knee. His hair, steely in the late-afternoon sun that slanted through the pines clustered on the crest, hung free about his shoulders, and his face was also marked, with four thin stripes slanted and branched like a tiger's over each cheek. He held a longbow gripped loosely in one hand.

Below them, in the fern-choked gully that bordered the road, there was a stir of hunched, muscular figures, and a clatter of weapons. Then all again was still.

Lakini felt Lusk tap her shoulder: once, twice, thrice, seven times. Seven brigands were hidden below. She nodded once. It matched her count. He withdrew his hand, and she heard a faint twang as he nocked an arrow to the string.

Down the road came the clatter of horses' hooves and the sound of people calling to one another—a merchant caravan, about to venture into a trap. Lakini wondered at the rogues that lay in wait, about to ambush the caravan so close to the Sanctuary of Shadrun-of-the-Snows, but risky as it was, it might be a clever plan. In more hostile territory the guard would be on the alert, but here they were so close, they were probably relaxing and eager for a rest, a meal, and a soak in the mineral springs. And the thieves might not know two devas patrolled the slopes around the sanctuary.

The company came into view around a distant bend. Her sharp eyes saw that the four riders in front were clustered together, instead of spaced out so they could watch for attack from the side as well as in front. She wondered if the rear guard was slackly organized.

Internally, Lakini shook her head at their folly. If they had any experience at all, they should know to be vigilant always, even when they thought they'd reached the heart of safety. If they didn't have experience, their employers were foolish to put their lives and goods in their hands.

Some would say they deserved their fate. Lakini wouldn't. She reached back for her greatsword and drew it, slowly so the metal wouldn't ring out against the scabbard. At the same time, Lusk nocked a second arrow to his string.

The jingle of reins could be heard clearly in the cool air, and there was the faint but unmistakable sound of a woman's laughter. Five horsemen in blue-gray livery led the group, still ranged in their sloppy formation. A wagon drawn by a matched pair, heavy-boned draft horses by the look of them, brought up the rear, flanked by two more guards. Several riders, men and women both, clustered between the wagon and the foreguard, and one, a slight figure in a long, dull red dress, had dismounted and led her bay by the reins. Lakini watched while she bent and plucked some stalks of lupine by the side of the road.

Yes, she would make it a point to have a word with those guards—if they survived the experience. It was foolishness to allow a traveler under one's protection to stray by the side of the road in unknown territory.

She flexed her hands around the worn leather of the grip, waiting. The birdsong stilled and each second stretched impossibly long. Each step the horses took seemed interminable, and she entered that state of perfect awareness of everything around her: the rough bark of the twig that pressed into the leather of her legging against her knee; the smell of the leaves the heavy feet of the brigands below had crushed; the body heat of her companion behind her. If she concentrated, she could hear the raspy breathing of one of the rogues. Either he was very nervous or had a head cold.

The feeling, the result of waiting, ready for battle, many times over many lifetimes, was familiar.

The guards in front were almost beneath them before they sprung the ambush. With fierce shouts, three of the brigands leaped into the road. The horse of one of the blue-clad guards squealed and reared, more from its rider's panicked reaction than anything else. The centermost man, a burly, bearded fellow who looked older than the rest and might have been in charge, drew his sword and advanced on the attackers.

Three more rogues charged from the ditch, leaving one behind to cover them. Lakini leaped from her perch, lifting her sword overhead in a two-handed grip. She felt the wind of Lusk's two arrows as they flew by her left shoulder, and an instant later she heard the hiss of their passage. They hit the back and shoulder of one of the attackers, who screamed and crumpled into the road. Lakini landed on both feet behind the centermost rogue. Just as she did, he lifted his arm, took aim, and a crossbow bolt pierced the chest of the burly guard.

Using the force of her landing, Lakini brought her blade down slantwise between the neck and shoulder of the man before her. The thick metal chopped into the soft flesh, almost severing the spine. Over his head her eyes met those of the mounted guard. The short, wicked shaft of the bolt quivered in the center of his chest; it had pierced the leather and mail he wore like a pin through paper. His face held nothing but astonishment. He stared at her, uncomprehending, and groped blindly for the shaft with one gloved hand.

He looked as if he was about to tell her something, and a scarlet trickle bubbled from the corner of his mouth. With no alteration of expression he slid off his jittery horse, lying unmoving in the dust of the road.

She tore her eyes away from his body as another brigand leaped at her, slicing at her with a curved, eastern-style blade. She couldn't pull her greatsword from the body quickly enough; she maintained her grip with her left hand and drew her long-bladed dagger with the right, deflecting the light blade as it bore down on her. Letting her blade slide down his sword to the hilt, she flicked the tip of the dagger in a circular motion, slicing the man's wrist. He jumped back with an oath, grasping the wound with his free hand. Blood spurted between his fingers. She hoped she'd cut through a sinew.

Putting her foot on the first man's back, she pulled the sword free, using her left hand to slash at her opponent with the same movement. He stumbled backward.

"Meddling bitch," he snarled. "I'll have that mask off you, and teach you to use parlor tricks in a fair fight." He had the protruding lower canines of a half-orc.

Lakini grinned and flipped her dagger, grasping it by the blade.

"Mind your manners," she replied, and tossed the dagger with a strong arm and a sure aim. It pieced the half-orc's throat with a satisfying *thunk.* He staggered backward, his crimson-streaked hands clutching at his neck.

Lakini glanced behind her and saw another of the brigands lying limp at the lip of the ditch, Lusk's arrows bristling from his body. Lusk kneeled by his side, making sure he was dead.

Three of the brigands remained. Lakini saw that two of the mounted guards had recovered control of their horses and were attempting to box in one of the attackers, a female tall and bulky enough to be another half-orc.

The fourth blue-clad guard, who had slid off his horse to check the body of the burly man, was now engaged in a desperate clashing of swords with another rogue. It was clear that the guard was formally trained and had the advantage of youth, and that the brigand was older and had the inferior weapon. But Lakini's keen eye told her the brigand had years of fighting experience under his belt—street fighting and raids, fights where the goal was to overpower, to draw blood and kill, not to score points under an instructor's eye in an exercise yard. If Lakini had the inclination to gamble, she'd bet the guard had never fought for his life before.

Lakini retrieved her dagger from her opponent's throat with a deft twist, the big ruby on the hilt smooth to her palm. Wiping the blade clean on the brigand's shoulder, she considered interfering but decided to let the boy fight it out. If he lived, he'd learn several valuable lessons. Never let one's attention slide on the trail. Make sure all enemies are accounted for before succoring the wounded or attending the dead. Never give up the advantage of horseback before necessary.

That left one rogue unaccounted for. Quickly she sheathed her dagger and gripped the sword in both hands, scanning the scene before her. The caravan was in chaos. Horses and riders milled about, calling out in confusion, and the wagon was stopped aslant the road. One of the mounted rear guard had forced his horse through the shambles and joined his companions in trying to corner the half-orc, while the other stayed behind, frantically looking around in case of an attack to the rear.

Lakini spotted the seventh brigand. The girl in the garnet dress had lost her mare's reins and, knee-deep in purple lupine and yellow flowers, stood by the side of the road, looking unsure whether to flee on foot or to pursue her mount. The rogue was charging straight for her, holding a long knife at his side. She stared at him wide-eyed, her mouth an "O," frozen in shock.

One of the mounted travelers, a tallish woman perched sidesaddle on her gelding, saw what Lakini had seen.

"Kestrel!" she shouted, and, wheeling her horse away from the confusion in the center of the road, she urged her horse toward the girl and her attacker.

Behind her, Lakini heard Lusk mutter an oath. The mounted woman came between the deva and the rogue, and he was unable to release his arrow.

The girl in the red dress, Kestrel, backed away from the man with the knife. In her right hand she held a bunch of lupines, their purple blooms incongruously cheerful, and she raised them as if she were going to strike him down with her bouquet. He reached for her arm and raised his knife at the same time. Lakini raised her sword to her shoulder and ran at them. She couldn't be sure of her aim with the dagger, not at this range and not with the mounted woman between them.

The man seized the girl by the wrist and jerked her forward. The mounted woman wheeled her horse about so violently, Lakini was surprised she didn't fall off. The mounted woman uttered an oath and slashed at the man with her riding whip.

Startled, the man also swore in his turn and, without releasing Kestrel, turned and lashed at the woman with the long knife. He might have meant to slice at her leg, but he cut into the gelding's side. The horse whinnied shrilly and shied away from him, while the woman fought to stay mounted.

He turned back to the terrified girl and raised his knife, streaked with the horse's blood, once more. Two strides and Lakini would have him.

In that instant, the black-feathered shaft of an arrow sprouted from the man's back. His head flung back and his spine arched, but he still held Kestrel by the wrist. The knife slipped from his fingers, and he flopped to the ground right at her feet. Kestrel wrenched her arm out of his grip as he fell. She looked ahead and flinched back, her eyes wide. Lakini turned to see Lusk before them, another arrow ready, pointed straight at the girl. He lowered his bow to cover the man sprawled before her, but seeing no movement, loosened the gut string.

A glance told Lakini the girl was unhurt. The other woman had subdued her horse and dismounted, her blue dress streaked with the gelding's blood.

Lakini turned to survey the situation at the center of the road. The rear guard, armed with a pike, managed to knock the half-orc's sword away, but she had drawn a wicked-looking dagger and was slashing at their horses' heads. Lakini clucked her tongue in annoyance. It should not be such a task for three horsemen to take down someone on foot, even if it was a half-orc.

She cupped her left hand at her mouth. "You, with the crossbow! Yes, that thing slung on your back. It has a use." The guard—like the others, little more than a boy—threw her a bewildered look.

"Don't look so confused!" seconded the pikeman, who seemed to know what he was doing. "Shoot her in the leg, and get this over with."

The young guard nodded, urged his horse back a few paces, and retrieved the crossbow, inserted a bolt, cocked it, and promptly sent it into the ground a man's-length from the half-orc's foot. Lakini stifled a groan and looked for the guard engaged one-on-one with the rogue.

He had managed to survive thus far. Blood streamed down his cheek, collar, and blue tunic from a cut beneath his eye, and he had a desperate look. The brigand was pressing him hard and Lakini was about to step in, when the guard's stance shifted slightly and the panic vanished from his face, replaced by an expression of intense concentration.

Lakini paused, interested. Training and more, a fighter's instinct, had taken over for the frightened boy, struggling for his life. Anyone who might make the warrior's art his life's work experienced this moment, being at once fully engaged with the opponent and detached from the battle, able to see it from all angles. The boy might make a fighter yet.

Behind them, she saw Lusk nock an arrow and look at her inquiringly. She gave him a slight shake of her head, and he nodded.

The guard let the brigand swing high and came, swift and deadly, under his opponent's guard, slashing his sword across his midriff. With a piercing scream the man staggered back, clutching his belly. Without giving quarter, the guard swung at his foe's shoulder, laying him down in the road.

Panting, with his sword raised, the guard stared down at the still body of the rogue. His face was once more that of a bewildered boy. As Lakini approached, he lifted his face to look at her, and he let the tip of his weapon fall.

In that moment the brigand, still gripping his sword, drew a last dying breath and with a convulsive movement lunged at the young guard's leg. The blade was a hand-breadth from his knee when Lakini kicked the rogue's arm, deflecting the blow, which went wide. At the same time she plunged her greatsword into the base of the outlaw's neck, delivering the coup de grâce. Facedown in the dirt, the man convulsed, sighed, and was still.

There was a strangled cry from the cluster of horses as a crossbow bolt hamstrung the half-orc. She fell to the ground heavily, and the guard with the pike kicked the knife from her hand. Crouched on her hands and knees, she snarled ferociously, until the pikeman brought the butt of his weapon down hard on the small of her back, pinning her in the dust of the road while the other two bound her arms to her sides.

Lakini pulled her sword free and crouched, carefully wiping the blood from the blade with the dead man's tattered sleeve and sheathing it only when it was clean. When she stood, she was a headspan taller than the young guard, who still held his sword as if expecting an attack.

"What's your name?" asked Lakini as gently as she could.

The boy swallowed. "An . . . Ansel." He looked up at her and frowned, trying to puzzle her out. "Ansel Chuit, ma'am." He started to shake.

She made her voice stern. "Clean your blade, Ansel Chuit. Now. Never sheathe it soiled."

He blinked at her, and his trembling ceased. Mechanically he pulled the edge of his shirt free from under his tunic and wiped the sword.

"Your first fight?"

He sheathed his weapon and straightened. "I was trained at the Three Fists Academy in Nonthal. First in my class at free combat."

She cut him off. "Playing at swords. Your first kill, then."

He slumped. "Yes."

"You did well. You lived. Perhaps next time you'll learn to guard what you're hired to protect. But not bad, for the first. You'll have a lovely scar to remember it by."

Ansel felt his face as if he hadn't noticed the wound. In the heat of battle he probably hadn't.

"Don't worry about it. It's clotting up. They'll take care of that at Shadrun."

"Shadrun-of-the-Snows," he whispered. "We're almost there, aren't we? Captain Nimor . . ." He glanced at the big man who lay with the bristles of the crossbow bolt protruding from his chest. "He said it was close, and we could relax."

Lakini frowned. "He was wrong."

Having retrieved her mare, Kestrel stood at the gelding's head, stroking it to keep it calm while the woman in blue who had come to her aid examined its side. The gelding shifted restlessly but was otherwise still.

The guards slung the captured half-orc, trussed like a goat for the roasting pit, over their dead captain's horse. The rear guard who'd come to the aid of his fellows was taking command, barking orders at the others to flank the sides of the road and look out for more attackers.

Lusk, still holding his lowered bow at the ready, came to her, looking intently at the trees on either side of the road and sniffing the air.

"There may be more," he told her, barely sparing a glance for Ansel, who looked from his striped face to Lakini's in puzzlement. He had probably just realized the band across her eyes was not a mask.

She nodded. The faster they got the caravan to the sanctuary, the better. The rear guard with the pike, having marshaled everyone into some sort of order and remounted, urged his horse next to them and nodded.

"From Shadrun?" he asked. His face was lined and he had his own set of scars. His eyes, alert, flickered from them to the fallen brigands to the forest around them. He knows what he's doing, thought Lakini. Why wasn't he in charge?

"Lakini and Lusk, in the service of the sanctuary," replied Lusk. "It's one hour's ride up the mountain path. We'll stay with you and come back with horses for the bodies. We should hurry. We haven't seen any others, but there might be another attack regardless."

"Kaarl vor Beguine," said the guard, and Lakini swiftly searched her memory for various naming customs and determined that Kaarl was a descendant of an illegitimate but acknowledged child of a Beguine scion.

"You've come from Turmish as part of the wedding negotiations?" she asked, and he nodded.

"I'm acting captain now, I suppose," he continued, with a glance at his dead predecessor. He pursed his lips. "By the helm, what folly. I thought him too old a campaigner to let his guard down like that; to let the men play at ladies' afternoon stroll, without a thought of the danger. I spoke to him of it, and he told me to get behind and not play nursemaid. Almost got the young mistress killed, if not for your skill with the bow, sir."

He shook his head and spotted Ansel, still staring at the odd pair. "Wake up, Chuit. Catch your mount and fall in." Kaarl vor Beguine gave the field of slaughter an appraising glance. "Pretty efficient, for holy folk," he remarked.

Ansel obeyed, and Kaarl vor Beguine trotted over to the two women—the girl in the red dress must be Kestrel Beguine, betrothed to Arna Jadaren. The woman in blue, with the injured horse, looked too young to be her mother or governess and too self-assured to be a servant, and she wasn't dressed as a bodyguard. Perhaps she was her sister. She turned from examining the horse to speak to Kaarl, making emphatic motions with her hands.

"Yes, Mistress Ciari," Lakini heard the guard say.

Lakini stood beside Lusk. "Notice anything?" she said.

Lusk nodded. "Of course. It's not customary for a raiding party to be in uniform," he said, nudging the man at his feet with his foot. Lakini winced internally. It was against her nature to disrespect the dead, no matter the path they took in life. It used to be against Lusk's nature, as well. But increasingly she noticed that her deva companion seemed to cherish the divine spark that existed in all living creatures less and less, and to regard his fellow creatures with a cynical air.

She would not think less of him. Lusk was her daggermate, as the knife at her belt and his proved, and had been for a matter of lifetimes. But it did distress her.

"Sage tunics, with a chevron on the sleeve," she said. "The livery of House Jadaren."

"Attacking the scion on House Beguine, on her way to negotiate her marriage to Arna Jadaren," said Lusk. "Interesting, to say the least."

"And I've heard nothing of the Jadaren party's arrival," said Lakini. "Curious that they're not here yet."

Again, she sensed rather than saw Lusk's reaction to the name "Jadaren," so small that it might have been merely his blinking at a gnat near his face.

"Very curious," was all he said, securing his bow in its place across his back, and Lakini wondered if she had imagined it.

Under Kaarl vor Beguine's urging, the caravan gathered into some sort of order and turned from the road to the winding path that led to Shadrun-of-the-Snows, following Lusk as he led them on foot. Before she fell in behind them, Lakini waited for the girl in the red dress to pass by, leading her bay mare. This must be Kestrel Beguine, soon to wed an enemy of her House and make him a friend. Lakini had the impression of intelligent green-brown eyes in a smooth, olive face. Kestrel still held her bouquet of lupines, and gave Lakini a hesitant smile. She slowed her horse.

"Thank you," she said in a low voice. "You, and your . . . partner . . ." She indicated Lusk's back. "I'm sure that man would've killed me. His face . . ." She shuddered. "I was foolish to dismount. I thought it was safe. I know better now."

"You'll be safe at the sanctuary," said Lakini.

The girl glanced at the place where the late captain lay. One of his men had thrown a sage green cloak over the body. Her green-brown eyes filled with tears.

"Poor Captain Nimor," she said. "He used to lead me on his horse when I was a child, and he a guardsman. My uncle will be especially saddened. They were close friends."

"He didn't suffer," said Lakini. "I saw it, and I promise you that. Quick and clean."

He had also died very *surprised,* even after the fight began, a fact that made Lakini suspicious. But this wasn't the time to make mention of that.

The woman in blue was close behind, gentling her gelding. The animal was rolling its eyes nervously at the vociferous objections of the half-orc prisoner to being tied on the back of a horse. Lakini doubted the horse thought much of the idea, either.

"Can any at the Shadrun see to Goldstone's wound?" The woman addressed Lakini, but she was clearly concerned about the animal, so the deva took no offense.

"We have a stable-mistress skilled in tending animals," she said, studying the woman's face. She was taller and more solidly made than Kestrel, with determined eyebrows and a redder tinge to her hair, but her features were similar enough that Lakini thought she must, indeed, be the girl's sister. "She'll treat your Goldstone well."

The woman nodded.

"We are much beholden to you," she said in her straightforward way, gathering her skirts and tugging the gelding forward. "Thanks to the incompetence of our guards, my sister was almost killed this day."

As she let the caravan precede her up the slope and fell in after the wagon passed, Lakini wondered. If the rogue intended to kill the Beguine girl, a long knife was a poor choice. It was more likely he would put it at her throat and take her hostage. He had tried to grasp her wrist, after all.

Was it coincidence that it was Kestrel he had targeted? Standing by the side of the road, was she the easiest mark? Or did it have something to do with her betrothed state? Many would profit from this proposed alliance, but many, too, would profit from the chaos that would result if it fell through.

What of the sage green livery? Were they ex-Jadarens, gone rogue? Had they plotted to meet the Beguine emissaries as friends but changed their plans midway?

And then there was that Captain Nimor, that expression on his face of surprise and more—betrayal.

It bothered her to think of Kestrel Beguine as a target. She liked the girl's face.

Bithesi met the party and took charge of Goldstone personally, examining his wound while the children who helped her in the stables saw to the rest of the horses. As the simple stone buildings of Shadrun-of-the-Snows came into view, a messenger came to first Lusk, then Lakini, telling them that Sanwar Beguine, brother of Nicol—and Kestrel's uncle—had arrived in the morning, while the devas were on patrol in the woods at the base of the mountain, and eagerly awaited the arrival of his nieces.

Sanwar Beguine regarded the bodies laid in a row outside the courtyard before the sanctuary.

"The livery of House Jadaren," he said, his voice shaking in rage. "They dare set an ambush for my niece, on her way to make an alliance with them! Kestrel!" He turned to the girl next to him, who surveyed the bloodstained corpses with a pale but resolute face. "You see the madness in this plan now, I hope, even if your father does not."

Lakini studied the man's face—handsome, and indolent in a way she suspected was just for show. She wondered again why he hadn't made part of the caravan.

He had said that once the traveling party had left, he feared treachery and had a premonition of an assassination attempt, and so had ridden to the sanctuary on his own, risking the dangers of a solitary journey out of love for his niece.

Commendable enough, Lakini thought. But it was strange he had missed the caravan along the way and had chosen instead a back route to reach Shadrun-of-the-Snows before Kestrel and her escort.

Instead of replying to Sanwar directly, Kestrel left her sister's side and crouched beside the body of the man Ansel Chuit had killed. She took a bit of sage green cloth gingerly between her fingertips. Ansel, having taken Lakini's lecture to heart, stood close by her side, his hands on the hilt of his newly bloodied weapon. His gaze flicked across the gathered folk, which included those who dwelt at the sanctuary, as well as curious pilgrims. Among them was Diamar, the Vashtun's right hand. Long ago he had given up family name, status, and inheritance to serve at Shadrun-of-the-Snows and would eventually take on the duties of his master.

Better Ansel take his duties too seriously than neglect them, thought Lakini, as the young guard glanced at the forest stretched below them, at the white-marbled entrance to the Great Hall of the sanctuary, and at the human and half-orc bodies as if their deaths were an elaborate ruse and they were likely to jump up and fight again. If he lived long enough, he would learn balance.

"This cloth is terribly worn," Kestrel said. "Look. The seam is torn halfway up and has been repaired with crude twine."

She rubbed the tunic between her forefinger and thumb. "And it has a strange feel to it, as though it's been churned in the washing like work clothes."

She straightened and rubbed her hand on her skirt, frowning in concentration.

"What of it?" said Sanwar. "It's unsurprising that a crew of brigands would take poor care of their clothing."

"Unsurprising for brigands," broke in Lakini. "But what of the guards you hire in your household? How do you clothe them? I'll wager their uniforms are kept in good condition. And likewise I wager House Jadaren is no different."

"Our worn livery is stripped of its insignia and sold down-market," said Kestrel. "I know, because I keep the records. I wonder if those chevrons are real."

"They're not."

Kestrel started as a slender young man, perhaps in his mid-twenties, with a thin face and mouse brown hair, spoke behind her. He grinned at her startled expression and made a low bow.

"Arna Jadaren, at your service, my lady," he said.

Ansel started and drew his sword a few inches from its scabbard. Lakini managed to catch his eye, and at her fierce look he reddened and let it slide back, taking his too-ready hand from the hilt as he did so.

Lakini didn't miss how Sanwar Beguine, flushed with anger and sputtering at the appearance of the Jadaren heir, looked eagerly at the young guard when he seized his weapon, and frowned when at Lakini's look he stood down. An attack on Arna Jadaren by those sworn to House Beguine would be disastrous at this point. Lakini was reasonably sure Sanwar knew that.

Kestrel rose, looking at Arna with a puzzled expression.

"But . . . I've seen you before," she said, her voice uncertain.

Ciari strode over to the young man and peered closely at his face. "As have I," she said flatly. "On market day in Nonthal, with the Druit boy with the cantrips."

Arna turned beet red as she put her hands on her hips and lowered her brows at him. "Just what did you mean by that, sneaking under false pretenses into my town? You're lucky you weren't found out."

"In my defense, fairlady," said Arna, with all the dignity he could muster, "I never said I wasn't who I am."

He glanced at Kestrel's bewildered face with an abashed smile. Then he made a deep, formal bow to Ciari.

"Forgive my curiosity, Mistress Kestrel," he said, "but when the opportunity to see the maiden that might become my bride arose, I couldn't resist."

Ciari looked from the back of his reddened neck to her sister, and back again. At her silence, Arna looked up from his bow, puzzled. She had turned as red as he and made a sputtering noise not unlike the hiss of a kettle.

Arna turned to Lakini, bewildered.

"She's not going to hit me, is she?" he said.

"She might," the deva replied.

Ciari didn't hit him, bursting into laughter instead. Her sister went to her and placed a solicitous arm around her shoulders, a rueful smile playing on her lips.

Arna blinked. "Perhaps someone might tell me the joke?" he asked mildly.

Ansel Chuit had taken his hand from the hilt of his weapon.

"It might have something to do with the fact that you were addressing Mistress Ciari, not Kestrel," he said, somewhat tartly.

Arna opened his mouth, considered what to say, then shut it with a snap.

"I'm sorry for your disappointment," said Kestrel, as her sister quieted, "but it's no more than you deserve for trying to spy us out in the first place."

She sounded amused, but there was an edge of hurt to her voice.

"I'm not disappointed . . ." sputtered Arna. He stopped and turned to Ciari. "That is, I wouldn't . . . You're both very . . ."

He gasped and looked a little like a fish, unable to stop an expression of delight from passing over his face.

"Get over yourself, Jadaren," said Ciari, pushing Kestrel toward him. "You well know you're not man enough for me."

Arna recovered himself and inclined his head to her. "I have no doubt you are correct, Mistress Ciari," he said.

He turned to the rest of the party.

"My apologies for my early and unceremonious arrival," he said, acutely aware of Kestrel standing beside him. With an abashed expression he addressed Sanwar. "And to you, sir, for not knowing who you were when you arrived and making your acquaintance."

Sanwar found his tongue. He was as red as Arna, but with anger instead of embarrassment.

"Am I to understand that you came to Nonthal to spy upon my niece, to see if she was fair enough for you?" he said. "And that you came by stealth to a place of negotiation, seeking to find the advantage of the ground?"

He spat on the ground at Arna's feet, drawing a low protest from Kestrel. "It shouldn't surprise me, considering that you sent your men to ambush my niece."

Lakini tensed, feeling Lusk do the same. But before they could interfere, a voice came from the crowd.

"Arna Jadaren is a guest in this place." Diamar, clad in a simple white robe and barefoot, stepped forward. In response to his voice, which was at once mild and full of authority, everyone stepped back a pace.

"I gave my name freely when I arrived," returned Arna, angry in his turn. "I came without guards, only a representative empowered to negotiate for my family. It's not my fault you didn't inquire after the guests of the sanctuary when you arrived—as quietly as I did, I notice."

"Calm yourself, Uncle," said Kestrel, moving between the two men. "He has no reason to harm me. And he was merely curious."

Sanwar was still fuming. "So, Jadaren, this ambush was no plan of yours?"

Ciari broke in before her uncle could speak again, and her voice was forceful but not accusing. "I assure you, sir, and my lady, neither I nor my House would contemplate such a thing," said Arna, keeping his temper in check. "As Mistress—as *Kestrel* suspected, these uniforms are castoffs, and these chevrons are nothing like those our guard wear. Ours are crafted as a piece, while these"—with his toe he indicated the scraps of fabric on the half-orc's sleeve—"are bits of ribbon sewn directly onto the cloth. They're also the wrong color."

He gathered his courage and looked directly at Kestrel. "I assist in the record keeping as well."

A corner of her mouth quirked up. "Do you also decide what to do with the bad plums?" she said.

"I've given orders that they be made into plum butter," he replied.

Kestrel placed a tentative hand on his sleeve. "Shall I give you my source for brandy?"

"I would be grateful."

At a gesture from Diamar, two of the Beguine guards manhandled the surviving rogue, her arms bound tightly at her back. She was cocooned in yards of rope. Kaarl vor Beguine stood nearby with his pike.

"Sanwar Beguine has a quick temper at the best of times," he confided to Lusk and Lakini. "And Nimor, Captain of the Guard, was his picked man." He nodded at the shrouded body that lay apart from the brigands. "He has no love for anything Jadaren at this moment."

Sanwar pushed past Diamar to confront the half-orc, who still wore the tattered tunic that mimicked the Jadaren livery.

"Out with it," he growled. "Who sent you? Which of the Jadarens? Bron?" He indicated Arna with a jerk of his head. "Or was it this upstart?"

"Look," breathed Lusk into Lakini's ear.

"I saw," she mouthed back.

During his tirade, Sanwar had made a gesture with his left hand—a closed fist with the thumb outside along the knuckles, and then a shift to a fist with the thumb enclosed. It was at an angle where only the half-orc—and the two of them—could see it.

Lakini didn't know what it meant, exactly, but she knew what it was. She and Lusk were very familiar with the various kinds of hand signals used to communicate in secret. She'd never seen this one, but she could guess—*Keep it inside. Don't reveal the truth.*

The brigand grinned at Sanwar, her lower tusks protruding over her upper lip. "Who and what you are don't mean a thing to us, worm," she said in the guttural accent of her kind. "We were just looking for the easy pickings."

"Liar," thundered Sanwar.

Lakini and Lusk saw his left hand move again. This time the fingers curved half-open, with the thumb tapping the palm.

More coin for you, Lakini guessed.

"Sir," said Diamar, touching Sanwar gently on the shoulder. "Her kind's not susceptible to angry words and threats. Let me try."

Sanwar's mouth twisted, but he stepped aside, not without a quick, meaningful look at the brigand. Lakini thought she saw the brute nod briefly in response. No matter. Diamar would have the truth out of her.

The Vashtun's Second pulled his homespun cowl back from his head and stood before the half-orc, his face completely blank. The brigand threw him a look of utter contempt and tried to pull away from her guards. They both hung on, and Kaarl prodded her meaningfully over the kidneys.

Diamar closed his eyes a long moment and suddenly opened them. They had the particularly blank look that Lakini had noticed in the Vashtun.

The half-orc stopped struggling and, ignoring the pike at her back, seemed to relax, returning the Second's blank look. When Diamar spoke, his voice seemed to come from a long way away.

"What did you mean to do?" Diamar asked, almost offhandedly.

The half-orc opened her mouth, then shut it with a snap, pulling her left-hand guard almost off his feet. Diamar raised his hand, palm out, and closed his eyes again, his forehead creased in concentration. The half-orc relaxed again.

The Second repeated the question.

"We meant to kill the guards and take the girls," she replied, with a voice as detached and unemotional as Diamar's had been. "Kill the others if it was convenient, and if we cared to. We could take the goods. But the girls . . . not them. They were worth more alive than dead. Let the older one go if she struggled and take the little one.

Especially make sure the older guard in blue, the fat man, make sure he was dead."

"Were you working for the Jadarens?" Diamar asked.

The half-orc furrowed her brow, as if puzzled. "I shouldn't tell you," she said, a little indignantly. "You know it's a secret."

"I told you it was the Jadarens," snarled Sanwar, glaring at Arna, who looked at Kestrel beside him and shrugged, shaking his head in denial.

"Let the man do his work, Uncle," said Kestrel, with some asperity.

Diamar's tone was that of a kindly teacher to a promising but recalcitrant student. "It's better if you tell me, you know that." His eyes narrowed, as if he were shuffling through the brigand's mind as he would through loose papers on an untidy desk. "*Garush.* That's your name. It's easier if you tell me. Whom are you working for, Garush, yourself, or the Jadarens?"

While both the Vashtun and his Second's ability to shake the truth from someone was always a matter of fascination for Lakini, she always had the unpleasant sensation that her mind was being probed as well when she was in their presence, as if some remote, utterly alien entity were examining the inside of her skull like a curiosity. The Vashtun had almost entirely disappeared from any public appearance, and she must admit it was a relief, for she fancied she could see some other consciousness, infinitely aware yet infinitely distant, looking out of his eyes. She preferred dealing with Diamar, but lately she had the same feeling when he spoke to her or to Lusk.

"The girl was wearing a red dress," remarked the now-docile Garush. She glanced at Kestrel and she flinched back. "He was right about that. Don't hurt her much, he said."

"Who, Garush?"

The half-orc's eyes bulged, and her entire body convulsed so violently that she pulled free of her startled guard, sprawling to the ground.

"Can't . . . breathe—" she managed, and struggled to her knees.

Diamar's palm was still raised, and his expression was bemused. With a single smooth movement, Kaarl cut the ropes binding Garush's arms down the middle with the point of his pike. Her hands free, the half-orc grasped at her throat. Her face was purple now, and a trickle of blackish blood trailed from her nostril.

The movement was small, but Lakini saw it. The fingers of Sanwar's left hand were flickering rapidly. A leather cord, studded with intricate knots, was looped around his wrist. As Garush's mouth stretched open in a silent scream, Sanwar slipped his hand underneath his tunic, but the movement of his fingers continued.

Lakini tensed, ready to stop Sanwar, but paused when she felt Lusk's strong hand circle her upper arm.

"It's not our quarrel, *Cserhelm,*" he whispered. "Let the merchants find their own way."

"He's killing the witness," Lakini hissed back. "Are you seriously suggesting we let that happen?"

"Perhaps he is. Perhaps he's trying to signal to her again. Perhaps it's your imagination. It doesn't concern us."

With a final shudder, Garush fell over. Her hands remained locked about her throat, and a bluish tongue protruded from between the swollen, purple lips. Kestrel turned away, and Lakini noticed that Arna had his hand on her shoulder.

Diamar looked down at the half-orc's body, sprawled between the nonplussed guards, who looked back at Kaarl as if asking him what they should do now. Kaarl laid his pike on the ground and kneeled by the body, gently loosing the huge, battle-scarred hand from the half-orc's throat and forcing the jaw open. He took his short, practical knife and pressed the back of the protruding tongue down, peering as best he could down Garush's maw.

"There's nothing down her throat that I can see, sir," Kaarl told the Vashtun's Second, closing the mouth and wiping his knife on his leggings. "Nothing that's not supposed to be there already. If she was killed by magic, it was an invisible sort."

"Interesting," remarked Diamar, in his dispassionate way. If he was angry that some sorcerer had killed on the very steps of the Shadrun sanctuary, he didn't show it. "It does appear very clear that House Jadaren, in its official capacity, had nothing to do with this unfortunate attack."

"I will swear under any penalty we did not," declared Arna.

"A pity we couldn't find out more," said Diamar, pulling the cowl back over his shaved head and turning to the Shadrun's entrance. "But to many who plague our guests, crime is its own reward, just as our gift of sanctuary is ours."

Lakini was tempted to call out to him, to accuse Sanwar of killing the witness, but she forbore. It was a relief to have the oppressive feeling of something watching and waiting gone from her mind. And Lusk was right. It was none of their concern.

Kill the big guard, the one in charge, Garush had said, referring to Sanwar's picked man. This was the one who had told the younger guards to relax, that they were within the realm of safety now, that there was no need to be alert. This was the one who had placed his more experienced guards at the rear, knowing an attack would come from the front.

This was the one who must have realized, the moment before the crossbow bolt had killed him, that he'd been betrayed—betrayed by an old friend.

She let her gaze trail over Sanwar Beguine, now in intent conversation with Diamar and Ciari, probably making his demands about the conditions of the negotiations Shadrun-of-the-Snows had condescended to host. The knotted leather cord had vanished, but a light sheen of sweat remained on his brow. As if he knew someone had noticed, he mopped his forehead with his sleeve.

Lusk was right. It would complicate matters to make an accusation, and their sworn duty was the protection of the sanctuary and its visitors from the dangers that were all too common in Faerûn.

Diamar had turned to lead the others into the sanctuary. As he looked back, casually looking at the folk ranged behind him, his gaze brushed across hers. She felt something, gentle but insistent, touch her mind.

Get out of my head, she growled internally, with an annoyance she had not allowed herself to feel before. Like a sea anemone touched roughly, the invisible tendril withdrew.

"Your friend—the Clan Druit boy with the cantrips—did he come with you?"

Startled, Arna glanced up at Ciari. "No. He's on family business."

"A shame. I liked him. Tell him to see me about investing in the venture once the knife-sharpening cantrip's improved."

"I think he's planning to," said Arna, masking his surprise. On impulse he went on. "He hasn't seen me in some tendays. I think he's been jealous. And he's been writing poetry of late. I think he'll be very glad to hear of this . . . unexpected development."

Ciari grinned and patted his cheek. "That's my boy," she said.

In the quarters assigned him by the sanctuary's steward, Sanwar Beguine raged internally. The plan, which had seemed so foolproof before, was a disaster. When he had shared his dismay at his brother's insane determination to ally the House to their longtime enemy, Harilpina Andula had been sympathetic and referred him to a company of mercenaries that had proved useful to her in several situations requiring both force and secrecy. He had met with Garush and her crew, supplied the cast-off uniforms, and instructed them to kill whomever they wished as long as they spared Kestrel and Ciari and eliminated Nimor.

He regretted the necessity of removing the captain of the guard, who had always been loyal to the House and, since he had a sister who was ruined because of a debt the accountants of House Jadaren had held over her head, understood together with Sanwar who House Beguine's enemies were. But he had assured Nimor the mercenaries' mission was to scare, not to kill, and, once blood was shed, he could not be sure the man wouldn't betray him.

The beauty of the plan was that whatever the outcome, his goal should be accomplished. If men in the livery of House Jadaren savaged a Beguine caravan and kidnapped the daughter of its head, or if the same men were killed but had evidence of being from the enemy House, the result was the same: a rending of the tentative truce between the Houses and an end to this mad plot of marrying Kestrel to the Jadaren whelp.

He had not factored in the interference of those two fighters, those tall, preternaturally still, bizarrely marked creatures who'd attached themselves to the sanctuary. He'd not factored in Garush's allowing herself to be captured.

And he'd not factored in Arna Jadaren's already being here, ready to defend his House, to confirm Kestrel's suspicions about the uniforms. Damn the boy, making moon eyes at Kestrel! It was bound to affect her judgment.

He must assume the worst would happen and make his contingency plan. He drew a deep breath, sat on the simple pallet, and mastered his temper.

There were strange figures painted on the white plaster wall before him. Despite his agitation, he studied them with interest. They were lines drawn in a flat black pigment, and shadowed with another color that looked either blue or purple, but it was hard to determine. It was a color rather difficult to look at. The lines looked as if they had been drawn randomly within a square roughly the length and breadth of Sanwar's forearm, but, when he looked at them for a minute, they seemed to shift and form a mathematical figure, unknown to him but certainly drawn with some sort of intent.

As he looked at it, the last of his anger dissipated. He didn't know how long he'd sat there before he realized the lines were vibrating, quivering in time to a hum that had built up, almost unnoticeably, in his head.

The figure couldn't be moving or making a sound. It must be some kind of trick of the light. When he rose and went closer to examine the sharp angles and interwoven circles, the illusion of movement vanished and the sound died away.

He reached out to touch it. When his forefinger was just shy of the pigment, he heard a voice in his head, an articulate voice that spoke carefully as if it were translating from one language to another.

Why your anger? the voice queried.

He should be alarmed at the notion of an alien voice in his mind, he knew. But it didn't seem real. It seemed simply a fancy, a way of one part of his consciousness communicating with another.

He concentrated, playing the exercise of ordering his tumultuous emotions for the examination of an outsider, trying to find a way to victory through defeat.

The members of House Jadaren were little better than pirates, and had found ways to cheat House Beguine over and over again. More than one competitor and jealous noble had tried to infiltrate them from the inside, to find a way to strike at them from within. But the House's headquarters, the heart and brain of their organization, was within a tunnel-riddled volcanic lump, thoroughly protected and warded with powerful spells set in place by the Jadarens' buccaneer ancestor. How he was able to do it no one knew; the Jadarens were not well-known for their spellcraft.

Send an agent. The thought surfaced in his mind, and he laughed. He well knew many had tried. He himself had tried.

Send an agent who doesn't know she is an agent. An agent of your blood. Send . . . What is the word? Your daughter.

Sanwar sat and stared at the odd glyphs, feeling as if he'd been given the last half of an equation that had stymied him for years; a formula breathtaking in its simplicity.

He reached into his shirt for a soft leather pouch and with the tips of his fingers pulled out a slip of parchment, folded lengthwise. Inside were five long hairs, brown with glints of amber. He held them carefully between forefinger and thumb, considering.

He remembered when Vorsha, weeping, had brought them to him, trusting he'd do what he promised. At the time, he had every intention of doing just that: creating a charm of protection that would ward Kestrel in the midst of her enemies. A good idea, he realized now, but not ambitious enough. He could do more.

You can do much more. Especially since you sired her.

It would take planning and careful timing, and would test and tax his skills. But he could do it. With Nicol's simplicity, Kestrel's trust, and a few men still loyal to him and his cause, he could do it.

Folding the strands of Kestrel's hair back into the parchment, he steeled himself to leave the room and meet the others, to feign that he had bowed to fate and intended to support the alliance. At the door, he paused and looked back at the figure on the wall. Some strange decoration, that was all; nothing but the random artistic musing of some pilgrim.

As he turned his back, the blue-purple lines glowed, intensely and briefly, and faded away.

Fandour cautiously probed the hard surface of his prison and contemplated this new information. Since beings from all across the Rogue Plane had journeyed to the place, the sanctuary, they called it, that housed the Vector and the Nexus, Fandour had been able to collect an astonishing amount of information. His imprisoned mind, strengthened by roots inextricably bound into the brains of the first Vashtun and all his successors, probed and questioned and sometimes was able to plant a seed into the folk who visited and revisited Shadrun, bringing news, gifts, sensations, and their own personal histories. Over several hundred years, the fragmented pieces of Faerûn's varied folk were beginning to fit together, like a puzzle picture that would begin to become distinguishable once partially completed.

Fandour had gleaned information and influenced these little minds to bring him more. The Nexus—the Vashtun, and to a lesser extent his Second, remained Fandour's primary links to the Rogue Plane, but increasingly he was able to influence other inhabitants of Shadrun. This latest entity—the human who began to engage the small Vector drawn in his room—Fandour could plant a seed in this one. He didn't understand its emotions. But he could use them.

Over the years, Fandour had become aware of a shadowy place, a fortress warded by enchantments. He couldn't see into it, but he was connected to it by mortal blood, by pain, by a stripping of its Power. Someone inside that dark place, he knew, was the Rhythanko.

This new entity desired to breach that fortress, and Fandour would help it.

Late that night, Kestrel Beguine sat cross-legged by the light of a single candle, her traveling desk in her lap. Ciari snored gently on the pallet in the corner of the simple room.

The parchment on the sloped surface of the traveling desk bore but one line of writing:

My Dear Father:

Kestrel sat a long time, her quill still in her hand, and contemplated what else to write. Her legs were beginning to cramp, and the flickering light of the candle danced across all surfaces, making her work difficult to see.

Finally she smiled and wrote quickly.

I like the boy. And the boy likes me.

She let the ink dry and put away her quill, rolling up the letter to give to one of the sanctuary messengers tomorrow at first light. Before she blew out the candle and crawled next to Ciari's warmth, she paused, frowning at the dark line someone had drawn on the clean white plaster wall.

That was a shame. In thanks to the sanctuary, she would try to clean it off in the morning.

CHAPTER NINE

Nonthal, Turmish

1585 DR—The Year of the Bloodied Manacles

"Is this a time to be doing the accounting?" Vorsha's voice broke into Kestrel's concentration. She checked her last column of figures, drew a line under the sum, and blew on the ink to dry it before she looked up at her mother in the doorway of her chamber.

"All done now. I didn't want to leave it incomplete for Ciari."

"Not the saffron prices still?"

"Even so. But I think I've given her enough information to go by. And I need to stay in practice. Niema Vral Jadaren sent me a letter, welcoming me in advance to the family, and at the same time making it clear that I'm expected to help with the records."

Vorsha ventured into the room. "Good thing you like that kind of work."

"I'm also supposed to keep custody of something. I forgot the name of it. Some artifact that keeps the spells surrounding that big rock of theirs intact."

Kestrel looked up at her mother with a rueful expression.

"Don't look at me like that! It's something to do, at any rate."

"I don't blame you. I spent the night before my wedding picking apart the needlework vest that was my gift to your father, and stitching it, and picking it apart again."

A clouded look passed across her face, but she forced a smile and changed the subject.

"Have you seen your sister? I checked her rooms, and she hasn't packed a thing! I know she's not taking her earthly goods and dowry to Jadaren Hold, but she must take something for the road and the ceremony. Why the smile?"

"Ciari was closeted with Vidor Druit all afternoon," said Kestrel, stifling a giggle. "They're negotiating each House's percentage in investment and expected profit for the cantrip venture. I'm sure she'll be ready by the time we must leave."

She didn't mention that she suspected that Ciari and Vidor were negotiating more than a trading agreement. That day Ciari had greeted the emissary of Clan Druit at the door, scolded him up and down for trying to cheat her House, cataloged a number of ambitious trade ventures that had been the ruination of local business, and scoffed at his ability to keep accounts straight. She'd then marched the bewildered but delighted Vidor Druit off to a private chamber and locked the door. Kestrel, restless with the prospect of tomorrow's journey, paced past the barred room more than once and heard noises of a curious nature, together with snatches of what she suspected to be poetry.

"I see," said her mother. She seemed about to say something else, then smiled.

"Shall I brush your hair one last time, before you are a married woman?"

Kestrel laid down her quill. "Please do. It will help me sleep tonight."

Vorsha took up the hairbrush and lifted Kestrel's tresses back over her shoulders, gathering them together and smoothing them down until the girl's shoulders started to relax.

"You're tangled again."

"You should come and live with us, so you can take care of that."

"I wish I could."

For a few minutes there was no other sound but the soft whisper of the brush through Kestrel's hair and the crackle of the embers in the fireplace.

"Kestrel," said Vorsha, pausing in her work so that the bristles of the hairbrush were entangled in the mass of her daughter's thick hair. "Kestrel, I want you to promise me something."

Kestrel opened her eyes, alert. "What is it, Mother?" she asked.

She couldn't help but notice that Vorsha had seemed distracted all day. Although she had busied herself in helping Kestrel pack for the journey, and making final repairs to the dresses Kestrel had decided she couldn't leave behind, Kestrel thought her eyes were darkened by some inner shadow, her smiles veiled with a secret fear. Perhaps it was merely her concern at sending her daughter so far away to live in what had been enemy territory.

Vorsha laid down the brush and drew something from a pouch that dangled on her belt. "You know how concerned your uncle is about your safety. How distrustful he still is of House Jadaren and their motives in this alliance."

Kestrel sighed. "Yes, I know. He's made it perfectly clear."

Vorsha put her hand on Kestrel's shoulder and held out her hand. On the upraised palm was what looked like a glass bead, looped on a delicate gold chain.

Curious, Kestrel took it between her fingers. The bead was smoother to the touch than it seemed glass could be, as if there were no friction between its surface and her fingertips. The middle was thicker than either end, and inside were swirled tiny ribbons of color—green and blue, and an intense purple so dark it looked black.

She held it up before the embers of the fire. Embedded in the glass between the colored ribbons were what looked like strands of metal wire: gold, bronze, and copper, all thin as hairs.

"It's a protective charm—an amulet," said Vorsha. "Your uncle Sanwar has spent a long time making it. It's to shield you from magical attack."

Vorsha's hand tightened. "I want you to promise me—and your uncle—that you will wear it at all times. On the journey to Jadaren Hold, and while you live there."

Kestrel's thumb rubbed the curve of the bead reflexively. "Oh, for heaven's sake, Mother. You don't seriously think Arna's family—or Arna—wish me harm."

"Honestly? I don't suspect that boy of anything but loyalty to his family. And it's clear he's fond of you. I think you have as good a chance for happiness as anybody. But this feud has lived longer than any of us, and there might be those in that fortress they call home who still believe in it."

Like your uncle, she thought, and she knew Kestrel thought it as well.

"Please, Kestrel. Sanwar's very fond of you. He was most insistent that you should wear it."

Kestrel sighed and put the charm carefully on the desk beside her ledger book.

"Very well. At the least, it's very pretty."

She closed her eyes and let her head dip back. "Brush my hair some more, Mother. It's the last time you'll be able to do it for a while, and I don't want to shock my future in-laws with my hellion appearance. They might back out of the deal."

"I doubt that," said Vorsha, picking up the hairbrush, while thinking it might not be a bad thing, after all, if they did.

Early the next morning, the traveling party assembled in the courtyard outside the stables. The new brick paving protected their shoes and the hems of their cloaks from the dust that, no matter how often the area was swept, wisped across the packed dirt where the wagons passed. Ansel Chuit stood near Kestrel, his blue uniform newly pressed and every button shining. His eyes were in constant motion, surveying every corner of the yard as if brigands were likely to be lurking there, and his hand was near the hilt of his sword, as if he would fight every one of them.

"I think I'm safe enough here," whispered Kestrel, amused.

"We thought that on the road to Shadrun," replied the young guard, without looking at her. "And I don't intend to make that mistake again."

Ciari was directing the servants in their loading of bundles and trunks onto the wagon with her accustomed vigor, but Kestrel couldn't help but notice she had a satisfied, satiated expression on her face, not unlike a cat's. Vidor Druit was not in evidence, but she wouldn't be surprised if Ciari announced her own intention to marry within the next season or so.

Nicole Beguine spoke to Sanwar, with Vorsha standing a little apart. Kestrel's parents, along with Ciari, were to accompany her to Jadaren Hold for the wedding, while Sanwar would stay in Nonthal to supervise the thousands of minutiae intrinsic to a merchant's business. It was a relief to Kestrel and, she supposed, to her uncle that he would not attend the wedding, openly hostile and distrustful as he was toward the Jadarens.

Kestrel watched her father and her uncle speak, and it suddenly struck her how worn and gray Nicol looked next to Sanwar. The brothers were only two years apart, but Nicol looked twenty years older at least, his complexion muddy and his face gaunt, whereas Sanwar had kept the ruddy olive Beguine coloring, and his shoulders beneath his cloak were wide and muscular. Kestrel felt stricken that she hadn't noticed her father's ill health before. He'd seemed well enough when she left to journey to Shadrun-of-the-Snows. When she returned, he was under the weather, claiming to have only a slight cold. She thought he'd recovered, but perhaps he never quite got over it, losing a little more strength every day.

She saw her mother glance from Nicol to Sanwar, and a frown creased her forehead. She must have noticed the difference as well. Perhaps a journey in the open air, away from the cares of business, would be good for him.

The brothers clasped hands, and Sanwar came to Kestrel.

"I wish you the best, Niece," he said as kindly as he had when she was a little girl and he brought her and Ciari little trinkets from his travels abroad. He hadn't spoken to her like that for a long time, she thought as she embraced him. He held her by the shoulders, and Kestrel realized what he was looking for beneath the ties of her new traveling robe.

With a laugh she loosed the ties and showed him where the charm lay on her breast, the gold and copper wires inside glinting in the sun that was breaking through the morning clouds.

"Not to worry, Uncle, I have it," she told him. "And I've promised Mother I'll wear it always."

He breathed a sigh of relief and touched the glass bead with the tip of his finger, pressing it slightly so it indented her skin. She felt a vague prickling sensation, just short of a sting, at the close contact. Perhaps it was the magic.

"This eases my mind, Kestrel," he said. "Even if your husband's motives are pure, there are still those who might seek advantage in harming you. My little charm won't turn a blade aside, and it won't neutralize poison—you must still watch against those—but it will ward off a curse or a malicious spell. Thank you for listening to an old man's request."

Kestrel smiled in return. Over his shoulder she saw her mother, now beside Nicol, staring at Sanwar's back. Of late Kestrel had wondered if her mother and Sanwar had argued. The odd tension that always seemed between them had intensified. Still, Vorsha had brought her the charm at Sanwar's behest. She hoped that whatever disagreement they had had, they could resolve it. Family ought to get along.

Sanwar felt the magic from the amulet tingle through his finger and his hand and up his arm, painful yet pleasurable at the same time. It had taken a day of concentrated work to craft the object—weaving three of Kestrel's hairs and one of his own into the correct configuration, adding the proper elements, making his will and desire a tangible thing, and melting it along with the glass. All the time that strange geometrical figure that he'd copied from the wall of the sanctuary cell glowed dark purple on parchment, pulsing before him like a steady flicker.

He had begun constructing the charm with knowledge gleaned from his books, but as he progressed, words formed in his head, droning with a steady rhythm like that on the parchment and stringing themselves like beads on a thread until they made coherent instructions of how to bend a strand of melted glass so; how to pull a grain of pigment through the charm's substance; how to make such a small object brim with unrealized Power.

He hadn't lied. The charm would protect his daughter from magical attack until the time was right, and all his pieces were in place. . . .

Patience, whispered the voice from the sanctuary. Sanwar had patience and briefly cupped Kestrel's cheek in his hand.

"Come, Kestrel," called Vorsha. "Ciari says the horses are ready."

"Your mother calls," said Sanwar, winking, and Kestrel winked back.

Shadrun-of-the-Snows

1587 DR—The Year of the Long Silence

The seasons passed, as they always had, at the sanctuary in the mountains. The Jadaren-Beguine marriage was accomplished with no more disruptions other than the fluctuations in the market values of certain goods, adjusted to account for the new friendships, enmities, contracts, and opportunities taking place in the mysterious alchemy of the merchant trade. Even Sanwar Beguine, it seemed, had bowed his head to the inevitable and not opposed his niece's wedding. Rich gifts and plentiful supplies were sent to Shadrun-of-the-Snows from House Jadaren and House Beguine in token of gratitude for the sanctuary's help.

The Vashtun died, and his Second, Diamar, took his place, by custom losing his name in the process. He designated a new Second, who took in his turn the name Diamar, strengthening the rumors that the Vashtun of Shadrun and his Second were immortal and eternal.

It seemed to Lakini that the new Vashtun, through his Second, took more of an interest in the doings and machinations of the outside world than the guardians of the sanctuary had done before. Emissaries from the ruling families and councils of the surrounding lands often visited now, following the example of the Beguines and the Jadarens, and were closeted with Diamar in a chamber, the walls of which were almost completely covered in strange and elaborate mathematical figures. Merchant families other than Houses Jadaren and Beguine came to the safe and neutral space Shadrun provided. Travelers arrived from all over Faerûn, as they had in the past, but now they seemed to come more to gawk at the sanctuary's increasing treasures and to listen to the stories itinerant bards told in the Great Hall than to meditate in the presence of the holy.

Time after time, Lakini almost brought herself to ask Lusk to take to the road with her again, to tread the dust of Faerûn, to seek evil where it laired, to come to the aid of those who prayed for help, to become the earthly embodiment of the will of the gods. But Lusk seemed to relish the increased prominence of Shadrun-of-the-Snow, and he spoke whenever he could with the councilors to faraway kings, queens, protectors, regents, thrones, and dominions. Lakini considered pressing the point, or taking to the road herself, but whenever she steeled herself to it, some voice in her innermost mind would object, telling her to stay, telling her that her duty lay in remaining the sanctuary's protector, and that this was the will of the gods that she sought.

That changed the day she and Lusk were patrolling the wooded slopes below Rophile's Crevasse, and her sensitive deva's nose caught an ominous, coppery smell in the air. Lusk caught it as well, and after they cast about and sniffed at the small breezes that danced about the mountain, Lakini pointed out a clearing a half mile away that pilgrims sometimes used as a camp spot.

The dull, heavy smell of blood grew stronger as they approached the clearing, and Lakini twitched her nose and shifted her shoulder into the position she took in battle stance, so she could more quickly grasp the hilt of the greatsword slung over her back. Lusk walked behind her and slightly to one side, glancing left and right into the darkness between the trees with a distracted frown.

Almost to the clearing, an unpleasant tang undercut the oppressive copper smell of blood. Lakini laid her right hand on the hilt of the sword, its familiar, worn, warm feel a comfort. Without thinking about it, Lusk shifted to the left behind her, out of the reach of the backswing the blade would make if she drew it. It was a move that grew naturally from years of experience fighting together, where knowing each move one's partner was likely to make was as important to survival as predicting one's enemy's tactics.

At the lip of the clearing Lakini stopped.

"Ah, Sweet Mother," she swore, taking in the scene before her.

Only one of the halflings had had time to draw his weapon. The short dagger lay loose in his fist. Rigor had worn off several hours before. In death he must have clutched it tightly. He sprawled near the edge of the clearing, his eyes still wide and surprised. Lakini kneeled beside him and shuddered to see ants crawling across the dull-filmed surface of his eyeball. Carefully she shifted his head, and it lolled back loosely, half-severed from the neck by a deep slice. The killer—or killers—must have taken out the lookout first. He was lucky. He had died quickly, unlike his companions.

In the center of the clearing, beside the ashy remains of a dead campfire, another diminutive figure lay crumpled. Lakini's gaze was drawn, however, to the dreadful sight splayed across the trunk of a large tree that stood, bare of branches ten feet up, at the opposite end of the campsite.

Cautiously she rose, forcing herself closer to the blood-soaked nightmare, listening always for the rustling of leaves that might betray the return of the creatures that did this deed, aware of Lusk on the alert behind her.

The halfling's arms had been bound at an unnatural angle tight around the tree, so tight the rough bark had torn the sleeves of his homespun shirt. His feet were tied together with many loops of rope and also anchored around the trunk. His head dangled limply between his wrenched shoulder blades.

A sheet of hundreds of blackflies clustered like a moving sheet of black armor on his torso, buzzing loudly, and there was an unbearable reek of blood and feces this close to the body. Lakini waved away the flies, which lifted a bare few seconds before returning to their ghastly feast. It was enough to see what lay beneath: the halfling had been gutted from neck to crotch, and his intestines pulled out in untidy loops to dangle at his knees.

Lakini reached out to cup his chin and lifted his head. A dirty rag had been stuffed into his mouth, and his eyes were glazed open in the extremity of pain and fear. A few black drops of dried blood spattered the pale face. Unable to look closer, Lakini let the head loll back on the chest and stood back, trying to keep her gorge from rising.

"This one was hamstrung," said Lusk from behind her, and she turned to see her companion crouched next to the figure lying beside the ashes. Keeping an eye on the perimeter of the clearing, Lakini backed away from the disemboweled horror tied to the tree.

Lusk examined the third victim dispassionately.

"His hands are bound behind him, and he's gagged as well. And look at this."

Beside him, Lakini glanced down, taking in the deep vermilion slashes at the back of the halfling's knees that sliced through cloth and flesh and sinew, and the deep gash in the throat that cut right through to the bone. She noted something else about the way he'd been bound. The halfling had long braided hair, and it had been knotted cunningly into a rope that went from the hair to the hands secured in the small of the back.

"He was forced to watch. Couldn't get away, and the killer—or killers—secured his head so he'd have to watch . . . that"—she indicated the gutted halfling on the tree, unwilling to look directly at it as this pathetic corpse had been compelled to do—"and then, I'll wager, killed afterward." She stole another look at the body at her feet, her mind temporarily unable to process what had happened to these people, incongruously noting the decorative beads woven into the wheat-colored hair. An image came to her, sudden and vivid, of the three little people, gathered around a cheery fire, caution forgotten in the comfort of fellowship, singing a song from their native land. Oblivious to the evil that stalked them, waiting for its chance to strike. Her eyes prickled, and she blinked the tears away.

Lusk nodded. "Only one or probably two, or else the clearing would be more torn up than it is. They must have acted quickly. Killed the lookout, immobilizing one so they could have their fun with the other."

He rose, wiping his hand on his trousers.

Lakini swallowed the sharp-edged lump in her throat. "Who would do such a thing? We haven't heard of bandits in this vicinity, and besides, they haven't been robbed. It's something a demon would do, or an acolyte of Orcus."

"A quarrel between thieves, I'd say," said Lusk. "Perhaps these stole from their clan, or cheated their partners or employer. Perhaps someone wanted to make an example of them."

"No," said Lakini. "Look. He's not been robbed." She pointed, and Lusk nudged the bulging pouch at the halfling's belt with the tip of his boot. "Any thief worth his salt might kill, but quickly, without all this fuss," she said. "And certainly a thief would not have left coin behind."

"Not fellow thieves, then," Lusk conceded. He gestured at the shambles in the clearing. Sunlight slanted golden through the tops of the trees, and birds twittered and warbled in the growth above. It would have been a peaceful scene if not for the butchered bodies and the incessant buzz of the flies.

"Rangers would be stealthy enough. Or"—he pointed at the fire—"they cut wood. Druids, perhaps?"

"We have to alert the Vashtun and warn the travelers to be alert. Tell them to make sure they have double lookouts and not let them get distracted." Lakini set her jaw. In her many lifetimes she had seen many tragedies, and brutality beyond imagination. This was not the worst thing one person had done to another, and it wouldn't be the last in the great weave of time. "And we have to tend to the bodies. The sooner they have a decent burial, the better."

She drew her dagger and bent to cut the rope that bound hair and hands together. To her relief, Lusk went to free the gutted halfling from his crucifixion. She didn't think she could bear to touch that rope, thick with clotted blood.

They laid out the bodies as best they could and started back to the sanctuary. In the morning, acolytes from Shadrun-of-the-Snows would return, bury the bodies, and perform the proper rites, assuming the scavengers of night left anything to bury.

Halfway home, something occurred to Lakini, something Lusk had said before, that at the time had only just registered.

"Thieves," she said. "You mentioned fellow thieves. How do you know they were thieves, and not simply pilgrims, or friends in search of adventure?"

The deva shrugged. "It's a logical assumption. Halflings incline toward thievery, whether as a profession or a hobby. Or so I've always found."

Lakini didn't reply. Halflings made clever thieves, certainly, but it seemed to her a sweeping statement to make about an entire people.

When had Lusk become capable of thinking such things about an entire race? There was a time when he would have wept at the sight of such injustice.

Lusk was similarly silent until they reached the stones and pounded the earth of the established road.

"Nasty little creatures," he said, glancing up over his shoulder at the green impassivity of the forest behind him.

Startled by the venom in his words, Lakini stifled a reply. The sight of the butchery in the clearing above them, in woods that were supposed to be sacred, must have upset him more than she thought.

Lusk glanced at her, concern as well as amusement roiling over his striped features.

"I shock you," he said, baldly.

"A little," she replied.

"Lakini," he said, "do you regret destroying the barghest?"

She concentrated on the path and didn't reply.

"And the werewolves of Wolfhelm, so many years ago," he continued. "Should we have allowed them to live?"

"Of course not," she snapped.

"Those lying dead beyond," he said, pointing at the path behind him, "were thieves. Few halflings aren't. Why else would they camp so close to the sanctuary without making themselves known? They intended to prey on the pilgrims. They chose their path, and met the consequences of their actions. Like the werewolves. Like the pirates on the *Orcsblood*."

Lakini had a sudden, vivid memory of the baffled look of the barghest she'd killed a year ago, staring down at its dead, half-lupine mate, with Lusk's arrow in her throat. She still felt a primal revulsion at the nature of the goblinoid's lycanthropy and their need not only to rend their prey but to destroy all hope and joy within them. But now she felt a disconcerting, almost illogical pity.

Pity. The only hope of mortals in a world where divine forces held sway was the pity of the supremely powerful for those who could not oppose them. Pity made the gods protect the mortals who bound themselves to them, and compassion had caused them to create the deva race, souls of angels in fleshly form, sent to protect the innocent and pursue justice.

"Where is the justice in killing them, even if they are thieves?" she whispered.

Lusk's sharp ears caught her question, and he laughed bitterly. "Tell the good folk of Wolfhelm about justice," he said. "Those that died before we got there, those whose fathers and sisters and children were eaten. Should we have had mercy on their killers?"

She stopped, and he turned to face her, a mocking look on his face. Shocked at herself, she had to stifle an impulse to slap it off.

This wasn't what she was supposed to be, or what *they* were supposed to be.

"That's not the same thing," she managed.

"No?" he said. "Explain that to Jonhan Smith. Explain it to his donkey."

Suddenly she couldn't look at him. She walked on, faster and faster until she was running, her breathing heavy in her ears as she left Lusk behind her on the path.

That night while she meditated in her rooms, she remembered Wolfhelm, a village in one of the remote Erlkazar baronies, nestled in the foothills between the Thornwood and the Cloven Mountains. Built on the ruins of some ancient town more prominent in its time, it was a pleasant place, trading the lavender from the sun-warmed fields around it to the bigger baronies.

But Wolfhelm, as its name suggested, was founded where lycanthropes once claimed their territory and bayed beneath the moon. And one season, while the lavender ripened and children were sent into the fields to harvest it, the werewolves came back.

Jonhan Smith and his donkey.

She and Lusk had mustered out the inhabitants of the village, arming them with any weapon that could be found and sharpened with Jonhan Smith's skill. They knew the community's only hope lay in driving the lycanthropes back, mercilessly, until they had killed them all.

Lakini and Lusk, needing little sleep, were on patrol. For the last two nights the weres had howled unrelentingly, from sunset to dawn, at the very gates of Wolfhelm, and the villagers had huddled awake, unable to rest and without anything tangible to attack. The devas knew the lycanthropes were softening up their victims for the kill.

Lusk held his bow at the ready, an arrow to the string. The village had three gates: north, south, and west, and a tall wall that was unreliably warded by old spells that the local priest of Chauntea did his best to maintain. As they approached the west gate, they spotted a figure, still and pale in the moonlight. Lusk had raised his bow and Lakini had her knife in her hand before they heard the chanting and realized it was the priest, trying to weave the wards back together.

He turned when he saw them and lowered his hands, looking abashed.

"It's dangerous out here," said Lusk, gesturing past the gate to the hills visible beyond. "If you're alone, a were could take you and we would never know."

"The wards used to be so strong," said the priest. "But now I haven't the strength—"

His words were drowned by another howl and the sharp tearing sound of an animal screaming.

The cold silver moonlight bathed the village, making everything light and shadow. Here and there lights flickered on behind shuttered windows. The screaming was coming from the north gate, and Lakini tore the sword from its sheath as she ran, sensing Lusk close at her heels.

Jonhan the blacksmith was there in his nightshirt and bare feet. He clutched the neck of a donkey, trying with all his might to pull it from the grasp of an enormous wolf that had its claws buried deep in the animal's sides.

The donkey was the one screaming.

The wolf was unnatural, its forelegs like muscular human arms; its head huge. It tugged once, twice, and the donkey brayed desperately as it was pulled half out of the gate. Blood, black in the moonlight, ran in glistening rivulets down its heaving sides. Jonhan lost his grip and fell on his knees in the dirt. The lycanthrope opened its maw and lunged at the animal's back, about to tear the flesh from its spine.

Lakini moved in fast, taking her sword in an instinctive two-handed grip and swinging it underhand and up. It skimmed the top of the unfortunate donkey's back, passing under the werewolf's gaping jaw and through the sinewy neck. The creature's head arced through the air and landed with a wet *thunk* between the gateposts—not far, Lakini thought, from the place where its many-times great-granddam's skull had been staked for all to see. The body remained for a second, poised over the animal's haunches, claws still flexing in and out of its hide. A gout of blood pulsed from the severed neck, mingling with the donkey's blood that trickled down its sides. Then the beheaded were slowly slid to the ground. The donkey kicked it as it went down, and it flew like a giant rag doll to lie next to its own head.

Lakini turned to Jonhan, still on his knees before the donkey. He was staring over her shoulder, and his eyes widened in alarm.

The feathers of the shaft of Lusk's arrow almost brushed her face as it sang past her, over Jonhan's head and into the chest of the were that had loomed out of the darkness behind the blacksmith. The creature arched backward with a cry somewhere between a growl and a human scream. Jonhan rose and stared at the werewolf as it twitched on the ground behind him.

Blindly, he grasped a halter around the donkey's neck and pulled it away from the gates and the dismembered werewolf.

"Rosebud gets out sometimes," he muttered, half to himself and half to Lakini, examining the wounds on the donkey's sides. Lakini had seen the animal tethered behind the smithy, snatching at some flower boxes. "I woke up and thought she might have wandered, and then I heard that . . . howling. And she screamed."

"Were you bitten?" Lakini asked the smith, as he patted Rosebud's trembling neck.

"No," he said.

"Think very carefully," she said. "Are you sure?"

"That one only touched Rosebud," he said, nodding at the body between the gates. "And then your friend killed the other before it could touch me."

"Good," she said, and meant it. She didn't like the idea of killing the smith, but she and Lusk would have little choice if he'd been infected with lycanthropy.

"But what about Rosebud?" he said, looking at her in concern. "It clawed her. I don't know if it bit her. Can donkeys become werewolves? Or . . . or weredonkeys?"

Rosebud whickered at him, and he scratched her ears reassuringly.

"No," said the priest, his voice shaking as he looked at the dead werewolves. "Only the human-shaped can catch the curse."

Lusk was circling the area, bow at the ready, making sure no more werewolves lurked in the darkness. Once he looked at Lakini, then shot an inquiring look at Jonhan, lifting a ready arrow. She shook her head at him.

Jonhan ascertained that Rosebud's wounds were more scratches than gouges, and led her home. Lakini stood guard at the gate all night after the moon had set, beneath the cold starlight.

In the morning they burned the bodies of the werewolves, and the thick, greasy smoke of the burning rose straight in the air like a beacon and a warning. The priest who tended the small chapel of Chauntea, after hastily consulting books and scrolls he hadn't touched in years, began to reconstruct the north gate wards.

In her room at Shadrun, Lakini blew out her meditation candle impatiently and leaned against the rough wall, the plaster surface pulling at the thick, slick fabric of her robe. She didn't like to remember Wolfhelm. What had possessed Lusk to remind her of it, so many years later?

Should she have shown mercy to Jonhan Smith, later, when the time came?

Or was her crime in even considering it?

She tried to sleep, although devas rarely slept. It was a way of forgetting the despairing cry of the barghest, the glazed eyes of the murdered halfling, the mournful bleat of a donkey.

Lakini had no sleep that night. She wondered if Lusk had even bothered to try.

And when she closed her eyes, she saw geometric forms glowing purple on the walls, although none were scrawled within her chamber.

The next morning, Lakini packed her gear in a worn leather pack and sought out Lusk.

"I'm going away for a time, *Cserhelm,*" she told him when he opened the door. "Will you come with me?"

He opened his mouth, and for a second she thought he would assent, take a few minutes to grab the bare necessities, and measure his stride against hers on the road into the wide world. But he paused, and the gray eyes looking down at her had a clouded look.

He closed his lips and shook his head.

"No, my dagger-mate," he said. "One of us must stay to protect this place. One day you will see the truth of that and return."

She knew him too well to argue. She left Shadrun without a word, although as she passed the stables, she almost turned aside to bid farewell to Bithesi. But as she paused, she felt that tickle in her mind of that voice telling she should stay, must stay, must not leave Lusk alone. Any longer here and she wouldn't be able to ignore it, so she struck out on the road, passing a cluster of grimy, white-clad pilgrims and a saffron-robed, prosperous-looking woman on a donkey. As she turned the corner at the sentry rock, the voice faded and she walked faster and faster, Faerûn spread like a map before her.

CHAPTER TEN

Nonthal, Turmish
1600 DR—The Year of Unseen Enemies

The small study in the headquarters of House Beguine had changed little over the years, its fine carpet and tapestries still intact, although a little faded with time. The man behind the elaborately carved Mulhorand desk, looked up from an age-yellowed, closely written sheet of paper, and frowned.

"Let me get straight to the point. My niece is in danger, and I need your help to protect her."

Sanwar Beguine steepled his fingers together and contemplated the man who had served the House as captain of the guard for the past fifteen years, ever since the mysterious raid on the party that brought Kestrel Beguine to meet her future husband at Shadrun-of-the-Snows. There was more white in Kaarl vor Beguine's beard now, and gray streaked Sanwar's hair as well.

Kaarl stood on the other side of the desk, in the relaxed stance of an old soldier, and frowned. "I don't understand. Is Mistress Ciari . . . ?"

After Ciari had wed Vidor Druit, half a year after her younger sister's alliance with House Jadaren, the family home in Nonthal had been enlarged with the purchase of the shops of a grocer and a wine merchant to make room for an additional wing for Ciari, Vidor, and their growing brood of children. The Beguine-Druit clan was under the protection of the Beguine House guard, and Kaarl should have known about any threat against her.

"No, no," said Sanwar, leaning back. "That girl is perfectly capable of taking care of herself. I mean Kestrel."

"Kestrel!" The astonishment on the old soldier's face was plain. "But surely . . . Jadaren Hold is impregnable, everybody knows that. What possible danger—"

"The danger doesn't come from outside the Hold, but from within," said Sanwar. He held his right hand spread over the yellowed paper, hovering just above it as if it were a source of heat.

"I had hoped it wouldn't come to this," he continued. "It's no secret I opposed the alliance. But I hoped I was wrong about the Jadarens, and all this time it seemed I was."

Taking the edge of the paper carefully between the tip of his forefinger and thumb, he lifted it slightly from the surface of the table.

"Now I fear for my niece, more than I ever did. I wish I could have obtained proof like this before my poor brother's passing."

In the months after the alliance was negotiated, Nicol Beguine had sickened, although on the voyage to Jadaren Hold for Kestrel's wedding, his appearance and strength had improved. Some months afterward, however, he fell into a decline, and the physicians suspected one of the mysterious wasting diseases that sometimes struck down seemingly healthy people with no outside indication of what could be ailing them. He grew weaker and weaker, and Sanwar took branches of the business under his management so his brother could rest. Finally, the winter after Ciari's wedding, Nicol died in his bed, with Vorsha holding his hand.

Business continued with barely a ripple—Sanwar already controlled so much of House Beguine's dealings that transitioning power from his brother to himself was an easy task. After a decent interlude, he married Nicol's widow, a decision that engendered some enjoyable gossip amid the more prominent families of Nonthal but was in the main considered good business sense.

The Beguine girls kept any opinion they held of their uncle's marriage to their mother, good or bad, to themselves.

Sanwar still held the edge of the paper gingerly. "What do you know about the history of House Jadaren?"

Kaarl's forehead wrinkled in thought. "I know something of the routes they've forged over the years. And the feud, of course. But the history of the merchant families isn't chronicled the way that of the noble families is, of course—although it's my opinion they influence the course of history just as much, if not more."

Sanwar smiled faintly. "That a man of war is wiser than a chronicler doesn't surprise me."

He frowned down at the paper. It was of a curiously thick texture, and the writing on it was strange to Kaarl—all slanted, angular lines, rather like dwarf runes.

"The feud," he continued. "This vendetta we pretend is finished. It's old news to the merchants we deal with, both those that aligned themselves one way or another and those that managed to stay neutral. But does anyone know why it started?"

Kaarl shrugged. "Ivor Beguine partnered with a man named Jadaren, long before the Spellplague. I'd heard they had a shipping business, and one cheated the other."

Sanwar nodded. "My father told me Gareth Jadaren cheated Ivor Beguine out of a contract to deliver cedar to Waterdeep. My grandfather claimed a Jadaren poisoned a Beguine when they were rivals in love. I never cared why. I had plenty of reason to hate Bron Jadaren and his sniveling nephew on my own, the smug, self-satisfied—"

He bit his lip and stopped, looking up at Kaarl with glittering eyes.

"Here." He lifted the paper fractionally. "A scribe in Old Nonthal took this down from Ivor Beguine's son, as the son lay on his deathbed. It tells why his father hated Gareth Jadaren and why he warned his generations against his. There's a dark secret at the heart of House Jadaren, within that riddled rock they call their home. It explains the protective magic of the Hold. It explains why the alliance will prove disastrous to my niece."

He let the paper settle back on the table. "They are patient. They're willing to wait years for their plans to bear fruit, to see a crop from the seeds they've planted deep within the bosom of our family. I know of at least one spy that we all trusted with our lives."

Sanwar smiled as his quick eye caught Kaarl's shoulder muscles tense and his right hand flex automatically. "Yes,

I know you've always suspected that Boro Nimor had something to do with the raid on the party to Shadrun, so many years ago. You can speak honestly to me."

Kaarl took a moment to marshal his thoughts. "He was so insistent I keep to the back," he said. "And he let the others slop around, out of formation, that distance from the sanctuary. It wasn't like him. It wasn't like a man of his experience. It's always bothered me. It's not my place to say so. But it did."

"You're a Beguine as much as I am," Sanwar told him. "Wrong side of the blanket or no. You have every right to state your opinion, to me or anyone else, Cousin."

The captain of the guard bent his head. "Thank you."

Sanwar studied Kaarl dispassionately, aware it wouldn't be as easy to trick him as he had tricked Nimor.

"They will attack you as you approach the sanctuary," he had told him. "Keep the experienced men in the back, with the girls and the wagon. You'll know them by the green uniforms—Jadaren uniforms."

Nimor had frowned at that. "I don't understand."

Sanwar had sighed internally and put an expression of patient concern on his face. "I know the Jadarens intend something sinister in this so-called alliance. How they've convinced my brother baffles me. If he didn't live so transparent a life, I'd suspect blackmail. I do believe they've wrought an undue magical influence upon him, and I have tried to nose it out, to no avail."

"My lady Kestrel . . . she has no such concerns?"

Sanwar had bit back an impulse to tell the captain of the guard to concern himself with martial matters and leave the thinking to him. "She obeys her father's wishes. And the spell might extend to her as well. I would do so, if I had cast such a thing.

"I need to put doubt in my brother's mind, just to crack the surface of whatever it is they're doing to him. Just so I can talk some sense into him, and have a chance of his listening." Sanwar studied Nimor's face, seeing obstinacy in his lowered brows. Carefully, he composed the tonalities of his voice, pitching his words in such a way as to make everything he said seem eminently reasonable.

"Do you think the Jadarens would be any kinder to my niece than they were to your sister?"

Noting the involuntary widening of the eyes and the clenched muscle at the side of the jaw that betrayed a sudden flare of rage, he adjusted his voice accordingly, making it more insinuating. "Forgive me, my friend. I don't wish to prod such a painful wound. But you can't deny that they entangled that poor woman into debt, encouraging bad decision after bad decision, until everything had been stripped from her and she was destroyed."

In fact, Boro Nimor's sister had been an extraordinarily unlucky and poor businesswoman, in debt to many before ill health and despair had cut her life short. At the end, the agents of House Jadaren she had cheated had been dunning her, as were half a dozen other merchants.

But Nimor loved his sister and couldn't bear to believe her lack of business acumen was her own failing. He needed a scapegoat to blame, and Sanwar had long since convinced him that Angharah Nimor was the innocent victim of Jadaren manipulation.

Sanwar chose his words carefully, cajoling the captain into believing that his plan was the only sensible solution.

"If Nicol thinks there's a chance Jadaren guards would attack Kestrel, he'll delay the wedding. The more time I have, the better chance I have of convincing him to call the whole thing off."

Nimor shifted his weight, considering. "I would not like any of my guard to be hurt in this charade. Many of them are young and untried."

"My men have orders to retreat when you fight back. Make it last a little, though. Enough that your guards see the uniforms."

"Are you sure of them?"

"I would not risk the safety of my niece. Or that of your guards, either. They're actors, playing at bandits, no more. I doubt they could hurt any of you if they tried. I would ask that on your end you avoid killing any of them."

The burly guard had grinned. "I can't guarantee they'll escape unscathed."

Sanwar spread his hands. "What can one do? They're well paid and take on the risks of their profession. I would appreciate it if you could manage to avoid killing any of them, though. Good actors are hard to find."

Not a tenday later Boro Nimor's body lay under a ragged piece of cloth, just outside the sanctuary, apart from the corpses of the ill-fated raiding party. The fabric was tented slightly where the base of the crossbow bolt that had killed the Beguine captain still protruded.

The mountain air had an edge of frost to it, but Sanwar felt his face burn. He was drained from the working that had killed the she-orc, preventing her from betraying him to that damned insidious monk. And more, he was furious that his plan had failed. Not only had those two guardians, unearthly in their strange facial markings and preternatural stillness, interfered with the raid, but Kestrel, ironically enough, had spotted the false uniforms for what they were.

The bandits, under his orders, were to rough up the party, kill the one Beguine besides himself who knew of the plot, and kidnap Kestrel. The survivors were to struggle on to the sanctuary, where they would meet him, fortuitously having arrived early and suspecting foul play. He would feign outrage, take a couple of the surviving guards, and hunt down the bandits and their prey at a prearranged spot, claiming to use a locator spell and Kestrel's hair, saved for the amulet, to do it. After an impressive display of battle magic, he would rescue his ersatz niece and bring her safe to Shadrun, where she would repeat the bandit's carefully scripted threats and gloating—all of it implicating House Jadaren. Trust would be shattered, and any proposed alliance between the Houses would be stillborn from the start.

Instead, the wedding seemed more likely than ever to go forward—curse that fresh-faced Jadaren cub's playing up to Kestrel like that! And the girl fell for it—and Sanwar's man, the closest creature he had to a friend, was dead for nothing.

He kneeled, the pebbles of the unpaved path biting into his knee, and lifted the cloth away from Nimor's face. Someone had tried to close his eyes, but the lids weren't completely shut, and a dull gleam peered from beneath them. A scarlet bubble had dried in the corner of the man's mouth.

Something about the half-open lips and the arch of the eyebrows spoke of astonishment. Sanwar wondered whether, in his last few seconds of life, Boro Nimor knew that he'd been double-crossed by a man he'd trusted.

From the inception of the plan, Sanwar had regretted, most profoundly, the necessity of eliminating the captain. It would have made him very happy to find a way to allow him to live. But he couldn't. Nimor would never have betrayed him intentionally, but it would have been too easy for him to let his secret slip when he was in his cups, or talk in his sleep, or have the truth coaxed out of him by a man such as that Diamar. And if that happened, any power Sanwar held within his merchant clan would be gone.

Thank the gods all the bandits were dead, Garush among them, and none could know his secret. Harilpina Andula would suspect, but she had her own interests to protect. He flexed his hand, which was still aching after the working that had blocked the half-orc's throat. He had feared that one of the queerly marked guardians, the male, had seen him cast the spell, and that perhaps the female had as well. But they said nothing, and he dismissed the thought. He had plenty to worry about without being paranoid.

A hand closed lightly on his shoulder and he stifled a yelp. Looking up, he saw Kestrel standing beside him. A tear sparkled on her cheek.

"I'm so sorry, Uncle," she said. "Captain Nimor was always kind to me, and I know he was your friend."

He stood and took her hand, drawing her into an embrace against him. He could try persuading her against the wedding again, but instinct told him the effort would be wasted.

Later the voice within him whispered to him, setting a clear path in his mind. Let my daughter marry him, he thought then, remembering the weight of her head on his shoulder. She will be my agent, unknowing. If I can't prevent her from joining with the Jadarens, I'll use her to destroy them from within.

Fifteen years he had waited, and now it was almost time. He must set his chess pieces carefully.

Carefully, agreed the inner voice that he'd first noticed at Shadrun-of-the-Snows; the voice that sounded within him infrequently but was always insistent when it did come.

"They corrupted Nimor," he told Kaarl. "But that was nothing to what will happen to Kestrel if we don't stop them."

He leaned back and fixed Kaarl with his glittering gaze. "They intend to sacrifice her, and likely her children as well. They're willing to do anything to maintain their precious wards. Oh yes," he said, as Kaarl shook his head in incomprehension. "They've done it before. It's all here.

"In a way, it was about a woman. But it was a woman Ivor loved. And to Gareth, she was just a tool; a means to an end.

"She must have been a mage, and a highly skilled one, Ivor's ladylove. Ivor and Gareth must have been friends at that time, because the mage agreed to set the wards that would make a desolate chunk of rock a Hold. And she did it. She wrought magic that stands to this day.

"And to thank her? Gareth Jadaren killed her."

"What? Why?"

"To bind the wards more closely to him, and to ensure she couldn't undo what she had done, or do it for anyone else. He cut out her heart under an oak—a tree that still stands outside Jadaren Hold. They still call it Jandi's Oak. I'm sure Gareth and all that followed him—Bron and Arna among them—find it amusing to call it by the name of the woman who died by Gareth's hand."

"And Kestrel?"

"With time, the wardings fade. To renew them, they must shed the blood of a woman bound to them by marriage and more. They have Kestrel. They have her eldest child, Brioni, who mingles the blood of both families within her."

"I don't believe Arna Jadaren would hurt Kestrel, much less his daughter."

Sanwar waved a dismissive hand. "Perhaps not. Perhaps I malign the boy. But his uncle has a shrewd eye and a heart of stone when it comes to business. And maintaining the wards, to him, is simply good business sense."

Kaarl frowned and was about to object. And then a tiny voice that must have come from somewhere within him whispered, small in his ear, *He's right.*

"What should we do?" Kaarl stifled an urge to shake his head, as if dislodging an insect from his ear. Nothing was there. It was simply his common sense.

Look at the evidence. He's right.

"I simply want a contingent of you and some of your picked men to have a presence in the woods beside the Hold. I don't want you to attack it without provocation. But be ready, in case Kestrel has need of you."

"We can do that," said the captain. "We can. But it would be easier if we knew the lay of the land better."

"I think we can ally ourselves with some natives of the place," said Sanwar. "Those who can find an opportunity in the downfall of House Jadaren."

Fifteen years the alliance and his inability to stop it had gnawed at him from the inside like a gall worm—fifteen years that would soon be over.

Fifteen years, *thought Fandour.* What is that? Less than an instant in my prison. How impatient the creatures of this world are, but then, how short their lives. It seems incredible that beings with the span and experience of gnats can help, hurt, or hinder me at all. It's because of the Rhythanko, of course—that part of my soul within their world. But it's been so long, it's forgotten me. It thinks it's a thing apart. I must bring it to the Vector so it can remember me, and recall its purpose, and free me.

As if fifteen years meant anything at all.

At the North Border of the Plains of Purple Dust

1600 DR—The Year of Unseen Enemies

The messenger found Lakini before she could vanish into the desert west of High Imaskar. The deva was alone at a greasy table in a tavern of dubious repute in a scrubby little oasis at the lip of the sands. Others clustered in the inn, and fearsome and scarred folk among them, but they avoided the tall, strangely marked woman in the corner.

The messenger was a young woman with pale red hair tied neatly back and a forest green cloak. Around her sleeve was a tan band, inscribed with a simple sigil not unlike some of the figures scrawled about the sanctuary. Unperturbed by the insalubrious locale or company, she stood by Lakini's table until she raised her mark-marred face to acknowledge her.

"The Vashtun asks that you return, my lady Lakini," she said, without preamble.

Lakini pushed the chair opposite her out from the table with her foot.

"Sit," she told the messenger.

The messenger paused.

Lakini sighed. "Even should I decide to oblige the Vashtun, I am sure he can hardly expect me to venture forth by night in this area. And you have come nonstop. I see the red clay of the east-fork hills still on your boots. And you are covered with the dust of travel. Sit and keep me company."

Somewhat reluctantly, the messenger girl perched herself on the battered chair. Lakini nodded at the geometrical figure about her arm.

"So Shadrun has a crest now?" she asked. "I remember when the sanctuary was not of this world, but apart from it."

The red-headed girl looked puzzled. "Many come to Shadrun to seek the advice of the holy man," she said, as if such a thing were natural. "The Vashtun helps keep peace in a troubled region, and the roads safe for all travelers."

Lakini waved her hand. "Yes, yes. Well I know it. And the safety of those who came to Shadrun was ever our duty."

One of the men leaning on the bar with his fellows, a great ruffian in leathers with what looked like an impractical number of knives sheathed about his belt and diagonally across his body looked over his shoulder at the deva's table and grinned ingratiatingly. Lakini narrowed her eyes at him and he turned back to his companions. He said something under his breath, and crude laughter rang out.

"Will you come?" said the messenger. She had a faraway look, and although her jaw was firm and she held herself alert and poised, as if at a summons from the Vashtun she would dart halfway across Faerûn, her face was white and drawn with exhaustion.

"You must be tired," said Lakini. "Here."

A big brass key was looped around her wrist on a worn length of leather. She handed the key to the messenger, jerking her head toward the hallway that led into the darkness of the inn behind her.

"Third door to the left is my room. Take my bed and sleep. You're in no condition to go back to Shadrun, whatever my answer."

The girl held the key in fingers that shook slightly from weariness, and made no move to obey her.

Lakini sighed. "You serve the Vashtun best by resting. No need to kill yourself on this quest. I will not need sleep this night, and I will consider my course of action. In the morning, I will either leave with you or send you back with my answer."

The girl nodded and made her way to Lakini's room. The brute with the excessive knives rose and stepped toward the hallway as if to follow her. Lakini caught his eye and shoved the table aside, exposing her hand on the hilt of her dagger.

The brute paused, as if considering his options. His hand wandered across the weapons strapped to his buckler. Lakini leaned forward and rose just a little, balancing on the balls of her feet. The brute's companions, becoming aware of the tension in the room, quieted their chatter and turned to see what entertainment would result.

The man shrugged and, laughing as if it were all a good joke, returned to the bar. Lakini relaxed and sat back down, glad to avoid a fight this night. She placed her back square against the rough wood wall, slitted her eyes, drew up her legs in a meditative pose, and did not stir until morning.

Sanctuary of Shadrun-of-the-Snows

1600 DR—The Year of Unseen Enemies

"The Vashtun is concerned about the stability of the Beguine-Jadaren alliance," said Diamar, or the person who had taken the name of Diamar, different from the last one she'd seen. This Diamar was a woman, with the elongated ears and smooth features of a half-elf, and something about her eyes made Lakini deduce her human parent was an easterner. Lakini shifted uneasily next to Lusk, and eyed the familiar pillars of the Great Hall. Once smooth columns of unmarred stone, they were now incised with rows of figures that, from a distance, looked like lettering, and, close up, were revealed to be geometric sigils of the same kind as the messenger's armband had sported.

The Second continued. "Shadrun did its best to assist the joining of these two great families, because the conflicts between their Houses fostered unlawfulness in many of the lands they do business in. A scion of one of the Houses has expressed concern that despite the current harmony, there is a danger to Kestrel Beguine within Jadaren Hold."

A figure behind Diamar moved out of the shadows, and Lakini felt a thrill of recognition. It was Sanwar Beguine, whom she and Lusk had suspected of engineering the attack on his own niece to disrupt the wedding negotiations.

The man was wearing a rich red traveling cloak, and, in the few years since she had last seen him, his dark hair had started to streak gray.

She glanced at Lusk, wondering if he found Sanwar's presence as disconcerting as she did. But she could not read his face. He had stayed at Shadrun while she had wandered. Perhaps he was aware of the politics of the situation.

Why had she returned, after all? Perhaps because she missed Lusk, and the years of their companionship. Perhaps because of the red-haired girl's mute appeal after she had delivered the Vashtun's request. Perhaps because of a feeling of loyalty to Shadrun and the safe haven it sought to become. Perhaps because at the sight of the messenger, and the sign on her arm, the persistent voice had begun in her mind again, faintly, as if it didn't want to be invasive. *We need you, Lakini,* it had said. *We need you home.*

At first she had pushed the thought away. Devas didn't have homes, not in a physical sense. They had causes, loyalties, companions. It was ridiculous to call a place in the world "home" when one wasn't of the world.

And yet . . . How was it she longed for home?

Maybe the voice was a god, recalling her to duty.

Sanwar's voice interrupted her pondering. "My niece and her father were determined upon the alliance," he said. "I've cause not to trust the Jadarens, but for the good of the House I consented."

Only after a handful of rogues and your own sworn man were dead, thought Lakini. And one killed by sorcery by your own hand.

Sanwar's eyes shifted to her and he frowned, as if he'd heard her thoughts. She felt Lusk shift closer to her.

"I did take some precautions," continued Sanwar. "For one, I crafted a charm to protect her from a treacherous attack. It's not as infallible as I'd like, but it's a modicum of protection. Second, I have a source inside Jadaren Hold who informs me that a rogue element of the House seeks to harm not only Kestrel, but her family—her husband and children."

"For what purpose? Why harm a scion of their own House, after all this time?" Lakini asked.

"To empower themselves in the absence of the heir, and to take advantage of the chaos that would ensue," he returned. "Great Families are like nations in a way, and their conflicts are like wars, and there is always a profit to be made in wartime."

As you would well know, thought Lakini. You could school them well on that. And I thought the wards of Jadaren Hold were impregnable to spies.

"It's the Vashtun's wish that the two of you go to Jadaren Hold and offer your services on Shadrun's behalf to protect the family," said Diamar. "You are not bound to obey him, of course. No one here is. But the sanctuary would count it a great favor if you assist it in this manner, and enter House Jadaren's service for a time."

"Enter their service?" Lakini glanced up at Lusk, who shrugged almost imperceptibly.

In her mind, the tiny god's voice sounded. *Please.*

"It's part of the ancient warding," said Sanwar, looking displeased. "Who enters the Hold must pledge service."

Lusk looked down at Lakini and mouthed an echo of the god's voice. *Please.*

Fifteen years she'd wandered Faerûn—a long time in the life of a human but not very long in the life of a deva. Still, while she had been Lakini and Lusk had been her *Cserhelm,* they'd never been separated so long.

She was tired, she realized. It was not a weariness of the body, but of the mind. She was tired of being alone. In the greatness of the world and its populations, it was almost impossible to be alone, but there was none other like her. In her travels, she'd never met another deva.

Casting her mind along the fragmentary memories of her reincarnations, she had only known Lusk.

Lakini nodded.

⁂

They went to the stables to get their mounts. Lusk took the roan similar to the one he'd ridden years before, on his mysterious mission. Bithesi, her round face creased by a few more wrinkles than Lakini remembered, brought her a sturdy bay mare, already saddled. She passed the deva the reins in silence.

"Bithesi," said Lakini, "not a word of greeting?"

The little woman paused at the stable entrance, her back to Lakini, and seemed to gather herself before turning.

"You left without saying good-bye," she said, her face expressionless. "Why should you mind now?"

Lakini considered explaining, considered telling her that had she stopped to take her leave she would never have been able to leave Shadrun, to wander until the despairing cry of the barghest had faded. But no words came to her to say it, and she folded the thick leather straps of the reins over and over between her fingers until the mare whickered in her ear.

Bithesi went into the stable, Lakini mounted the mare, and the devas rode at an easy trot down the mountain.

"She can't understand," said Lusk, after they'd cleared the sentry rock. Lakini had a vivid memory of the travel-stained pilgrims she'd passed the last time she was here. "No one can understand how it is with us—except us."

She nodded. They were silent for a time, but it was a companionable silence, their horses' cadences matching and each deva keeping all senses alert for danger without having to speak of it. It reminded her why she and Lusk seemed to come together, year after year, lifetime after lifetime.

CHAPTER ELEVEN

Jadaren Hold

1600 DR—The Year of Unseen Enemies

They saw the shape of the giant black rock from many leagues away. It loomed on the horizon before they were even close enough to pick out its features. There was little traffic on the road that afternoon, and their horses' hooves crunched in the road's crushed obsidian, making a sound like tiny beads of glass breaking.

Lakini saw that the imposing facade of the monolith, a forbidding and uniform black from a distance, was threaded all over its surface with greenery. Pockets carved by man or nature held, like great black bowls, clusters of ferns; bright green moss studded the dark rock like peridots in a matrix. Threads of spring water crawled silver down the monolith, and here and there the stone had been carved to divert the moisture away from the openings that served as doors and windows and into basins on the ground where it pooled, fresh and ready for use.

At the base of the side facing the great volcanic plain, the entrances of great caverns yawned. Animals—beasts of burden as well as cows and goats—were tethered outside, and Lakini realized the caves served as stables as well as storage chambers. She studied the structure with a practiced eye, as she would a fortress, and saw that as long as there was a way to block entry from the underlying caverns, the place would be all but impregnable. A wide path curved around the lava cone, presumably merging into a stone staircase that led to the summit—but a few defenders on top could hold off many attackers.

As she and Lusk approached, she lifted her eyes to that summit. It was flat, but at the rim rough rocks were silhouetted against the blue sky like jagged black teeth. Although the day was pleasantly warm and the light against the mountains was golden, a shiver went down her spine at the sight. She blinked and thought she saw a flicker of green, bilious and alien, unlike the natural green of the plants that clung to the side of the Hold. She watched carefully and saw it dance, like the ghost lightning that played in ships' masts, over the jagged stones.

Lakini glanced at her companion to see if he noticed anything. If he did, he didn't mention it, although his gaze flickered over the surface of the rock as fast as the strange green lightning. She wondered if Lusk, too, felt that the closer they got to the maw of the caverns, the more they were being *examined* by something curious and unearthly, something that resisted their approach, and made the warm air congeal slightly and resist their passage.

Several figures waited for them at the base of the Hold. Lakini recognized Kestrel Beguine and her husband. Standing beside Kestrel was a well-grown girl of about fourteen, with enough of Kestrel's eyes and cheekbones and Arna's mouth to prove she must be their daughter. Kestrel also had a baby cradled in her left arm, most of its weight supported by a sling she wore across her shoulders.

Someone with the bearing of a fighter stood beside Kestrel. Lakini smiled, and she recognized Ansel Chuit from the way he held his shoulders, ready to turn in any direction, and from how close he held his hand to the hilt of the sword on his belt. She hadn't forgotten his lesson.

As Lakini and Lusk dismounted, stable hands—or should they be called cave hands? she wondered—ran to them and took their mounts by the bridles, guiding them into the chambers at the base of the rock. Lakini wondered how far underneath they went, and if there were subterranean chambers below this one.

The hands seemed to know what they were doing, taking the time to gentle the horses as they led them. Of course, with the kind of traffic from across Faerûn that Jadaren Hold saw, they would have to care for many strange beasts of a variety of temperaments.

Their careful handling of her horse reminded her of Bithesi, and she felt a sudden pang.

Kestrel and Arna stepped forward to greet them. Lakini felt the resistance that she associated with the green light increase as the Jadaren scion held out his hand, and then suddenly ebb away as she touched it. Did the light, and the odd feeling in the air, have something to do with the wards that were said to bind the monolith?

"Welcome, devas," said Kestrel. "Welcome to Jadaren Hold."

To Lakini's surprise, she found she liked the familial chaos of Jadaren Hold, and the bustle of a place that was a trade center as well as a home. Children ran in and out of the archives where records of goods, their origins, destinations, and prices were kept. The private chambers and hall of records were securely warded, but there were public areas where those on business for their Houses and employers gathered to bargain and negotiate and often enough that there was a festival air to the place.

Kestrel and Arna's home proved to be a happy one, not the least because the Jadaren heir had the sense to allow his wife to keep the records and manage accounts how she pleased. Kestrel seemed happy in her new home and family, which included twin boys as well as the daughter, Brioni, and the baby, who was named Bron after his uncle. Lakini sensed none of the hidden dangers that Sanwar insisted were menacing his niece.

"It's a puzzle to me as well," said Kestrel, later that night, as she showed Lakini to her accommodations in the family quarters.

She had aged since Lakini last saw her, but the lines around her eyes were laugh lines, for the most part.

"I know my uncle Sanwar keeps the welfare of the family foremost in his mind, and sometimes I wonder . . . Well, I'll say it: I wonder sometimes if his obsessive nature has addled his good sense, together with his animosity toward my husband's family." She touched a charm at her throat. It was glass bead, with dark colors swirled together, and threads of metal or a similar material embedded within. "Still, he did insist this charm would keep me safe, and maybe it has, all this time." She laughed. "He is so proud of his skill with sorcery. I wouldn't like to take credit away from him."

"He said the danger to you was deeply buried, and the Vashtun and the Second of Shadrun thought his concerns legitimate," said Lakini. "Perhaps its source is not a rogue element within the Jadaren clan, but a visitor or rival."

Kestrel shrugged. "Perhaps. I don't intend to live in fear, especially under the protection of Shadrun-of-the-Snows."

After Kestrel departed to see to the evening meal, Lakini examined her assigned room with interest. She didn't usually pay much attention to her living space. So long as it was clean and quiet, any room would do. Devas didn't sleep overmuch and had few possessions to clutter up a bedroom.

This room was simple in its lines and luxurious in its appointments, with a soft bed piled with cushions and rich tapestries over two of the walls. One portrayed a hunting scene, with weaponless horsemen pursuing a unicorn that looked back at them over its shoulder, as if enticing them on, and one a mountain lake with many pairs of colorful birds embroidered about it. It occurred to the deva that in a place with few windows, such decorations provided a view of the world that was otherwise lacking.

Two walls had been left bare. One, with the door to the labyrinthine tunnels outside in the center, was dull and rough to the touch, although any sharp ridges had been ground down. The other wall, smooth, flat, and polished to a mirror-bright finish, was a floor-to-ceiling surface of shining black glass.

Lakini's reflection stared back at her, looking like her own dark twin frozen in ice. As she stared, the markings across her eyes shifted and changed, splitting apart and becoming Lusk's stripes. Lusk stood before her, rimmed in green fire.

Startled, she reached out to him, her fingers touching only the cold surface of the wall. His hand lifted to meet hers. The green flame surrounding his form swelled and consumed him, and as he burned, she saw his face twist, and melt, and re-form.

Lusk stood before her with a tiger's face.

She jerked her hand away from his. She blinked, and Lusk was gone. It was only her own reflection in the wall, her eyes burning in the pale mask across her face.

She'd laid her sword on the bed, thinking she didn't need it inside the safety of the Hold. Now she slung it on its accustomed place on her back, and strode out to walk the unfamiliar halls of Jadaren Hold, wondering what bothered her most about her vision—that Lusk was burning, or that he didn't seem to care.

The Docks, Llorbauth, Erlkazar

1600—The Year of Unseen Enemies

The warehouse roof arched high overhead, supported by thick timbers of hundreds of years' growth. Small spaces between the timbers exposed only the black night sky overhead.

Sanwar wondered if Saestra's intention in using and maintaining it was to suggest a royal audience chamber. If so, the shifting of the floor beneath his feet as it floated on its supports and the whiff of the livestock that had been tethered here, waiting to be shipped out of port, gave the lie to any claims of grandeur. His nose wrinkled. Pigs—there had definitely been a herd of pigs here recently.

He tried to decide if he preferred the perfume of the pigsty to the constant sulfur stench of the Lake of Steam they'd had to cross to get here. Three days of rotten-egg smell and moist heat had sickened some of the crew. He concluded that the aroma of pigs was more intense, but that the range was limited, and that pigs had the virtue of being absent at this particular time.

He wondered if Saestra was keeping him waiting on purpose, then laughed at himself for having doubt about it. Of course she's making me wait. She has the power here, and she wants to make sure I know it. I would do the same thing.

He shifted his stance slightly and wondered if he should have brought some guards with him, after all. Those he'd left behind on the cutter didn't like him going alone. He'd told them the head of the syndicate, who was offering House Beguine the barley monopoly from three of the Erlkazar baronies, wanted to deal in secret, since if word of the deal was nosed abroad it would imperil several other contracts. They subsided, grumbling, and the woman Kaarl vor Beguine had handpicked to captain the contingent of guards Sanwar had taken on this journey promised that if Master Sanwar hadn't returned within two turns of the hourglass, she would order the guards out of the docked ship and search every warehouse until he was found.

He didn't argue with that. If he wasn't back in the prescribed time, it meant he was dead and beyond all earthly cares, and the guards must look after themselves.

There was a glimmer in the shadows in the back of the warehouse. Sanwar narrowed his eyes and tried to make out the details, wishing his night vision were better. The hairs on the back of his neck and his forearms prickled, and he took a deep breath, willing himself into calm.

Guards would be no good here, not in Saestra's domain on Saestra's terms. Her almost infinite resource here would overpower any resistance his fighters could offer. It was far more impressive to come alone, unarmed, giving himself casually over to her power while he offered her his bargain.

At least that was what he was gambling on. He tried to swallow, his mouth suddenly dry, as the glimmer shifted and became discernible forms, advancing toward him.

Saestra was tall, with the dark good looks and bold features of her Karanok ancestors. She wore a simple gown of burgundy damask, fitted to her slim form, with an elaborate pattern of crystal beads the same color across her breast. The tiny gems, invisible when she stood still, glittered in the faint light when she made any movement. Sanwar bowed deeply, stifling the instinct to price them. It was not lost to him that her feet made no sound as they glided across the rough boards.

Sanwar saw that between her long, elegant fingers she held the missive he had sent her. She gripped it casually, as if it were of no importance. Only a deadly paleness beneath her rather dusky skin and the glint of an elongated tooth when she spoke betrayed her undead nature. She stood, surveying him a long minute before inclining her head gracefully in return.

Just behind Saestra's right shoulder stood three women, also with the deathly pallor of vampires, each dressed in silks of opulent colors that boasted a vivid, splendid barbarism. Their hair was respectively black, chestnut, and a rich, garish red, and it was piled high on top of their heads in a more exaggerated version of their mistress's hairstyle.

At Saestra's left stood two more figures, not nearly as exotic. One was a huge, muscle-bound, mace-armed fighter, a human big as an orc, who glowered at Sanwar. The other, who barely came to Saestra's waist, was a diminutive female figure. The halfling wore a tunic and trousers of the same material Saestra wore, without the glitter of crystal. She stood with her feet apart in a ready-to-fight position, arms folded across her chest, and her thick hair was tightly braided in a complex pattern away from her face. Sanwar would wager that she had knives close to either hand under that burgundy tunic, and that of the two fighters she would prove the more dangerous.

"I am honored to be granted the grace of a visit from you," the vampire said, in a rich, deep voice with a sardonic edge. She turned the missive around in her fingers. "Even in this backwater I have heard of House Beguine.

Your caravans thread the countryside, and your agents are in every city. But surely if you wish to do more business in Erlkazar, it would be more expedient to speak to the barons directly?"

The barons governed by day. But Saestra was Queen of the Night Barony of Erlkazar, the shadowy organization composed of both the undead and the living. Saestra ruled the Night Barony, and the Night Barony from its lairs beneath the Daylight Baronies ruled Erlkazar and terrorized its neighbors.

It was Sanwar's understanding that she interfered very little with the common people of Erlkazar, and bade her people leave them be—although she could hardly be blamed if foolish folk risked being away from the safe haven during the darkness. She could not manage every bandit, vampire, or lycanthrope.

"With respect to all the noble sirs," replied Sanwar evenly, "you are the only power worth consulting in Erlkazar."

Saestra smiled at him coldly. "You are too kind. And well-informed."

"I bring a small gift, not worthy of you, but perhaps of interest." From inside his robe he brought out a cylindrical case, made of ancient leather and capped with brass. Red lettering, flaked with age, circled it. He didn't miss that the halfling woman watched closely when he reached under his clothing and that the human didn't.

"I'm a collector of old texts and chronologies," Sanwar said. "I came across this—a genealogical scroll of the Karanok family. To anyone but a scholar, it's not that valuable, I admit—more an antiquarian curiosity. But such as it is, it's yours."

"Ponta," said Saestra, and the halfling at her side stirred and came to him, reaching out her hand to take the container. She examined it, gave the leather a sniff, and presented it to her mistress.

Saestra in turned handed the leather cylinder to one of her ladies, who took it with long-clawed fingernails.

"Many thanks for the thoughtful gift, Sanwar Beguine," she said, an amused smile quirking the sides of her mouth. "But you didn't come all the way and into the lair of a vampire simply to give me a present, and you have the air of a man who intends to say more."

Sanwar swallowed, steeling himself. "If you know the name of House Beguine, you know the name of House Jadaren," he said, and saw a gleam of recognition in her eyes. "And you know of the enmity between them."

Saestra tilted her head. "But surely that's a thing of the past? Did I mishear, or was there not an alliance made? A wedding celebrated?"

"It wasn't celebrated by me," Sanwar said through set teeth. "And I acknowledge no alliance."

He said it more forcefully than he intended, and the vampire trio to Saestra's right stirred slightly, out of their unearthly stillness, like leaves touched by a breeze. He heard a faint giggle.

The human guard tightened his grip on the mace and furrowed his brows.

The vampire stared at him a long moment, her eyes so smoky dark they looked like pools of darkness one could fall into forever.

"I see," she said at last. "You cling to your ancient hatreds. And yet an alliance means more trade, and more goods moving across the land, and more for my people to share with the virtuous folk of Turmish and Camlishan." Her voice hardened. "What do you journey so far to ask of me, merchantman?"

Cold sweat prickled across his body, and for a moment he regretted the absence of his guards. They would have stood no chance here, however.

Stand firm, urged the voice inside him. *There's no profit for her in your death.*

"My niece's family live in Jadaren Hold now," he said. "You know how well it is warded."

She made a slight, palm-up gesture with her hand, her meaning clear. *So?*

"I have sources who tell me she's in danger," he continued. "I am prepared to overcome the spells that protect the Hold to ensure her safety. But the Jadarens are well manned and have had years to plan their defenses. We are only a merchant house, with guards we employ to protect our goods and ourselves—and their numbers are limited. I have no army at my command."

"And I do," said the vampire.

"And you do."

There was another long, deceptively lazy pause.

"What interest have I in your petty squabbles, merchantman? Let Jadaren Hold stand for all eternity, if the gods will let it. I have little interest in what lies within."

"Perhaps. But I have a sweeter bargain to offer you."

What he thought of as the voice within him welled up, silently, and became a presence, reaching out to the mind of the vampire before him.

Listen. Listen to what he says. He saw her blink, then frown, and he knew she had heard.

"How long has it been since the Sanctuary of Shadrun-of-the-Snows made it its duty to protect travelers? How long has it interfered with your affairs, right on your borders?"

Her face tightened, and his heart leaped at the confirmation that he was right. The gamble paid off. The existence of the sanctuary was a sore spot for her.

"That hovel in the mountains, with its chanting monks and caravans of stinking donkeys? I have no interest in it whatsoever."

"With all due respect, my lady Saestra," said Sanwar, "you are lying."

Her entire body stilled, and he could feel the cold emanating from her very bones. The vampire trio behind her froze as well. Ponta did nothing whatsoever.

"That's enough lip from you," snarled the human fighter to Saestra's left. He shifted the mace and lashed out at Sanwar, a blow meant to drop him.

Time seemed to slow to a torturous crawl. Sanwar watched with dispassionate interest as the weapon approached his face. He had no time to duck, and he knew he should be afraid, horrified—but he could summon no emotion.

Like an afterimage, something flashed behind his eyes—a geometrical figure drawn in deep purple. In an instant it was gone, and he felt invisible hands seizing his shoulders and pulling him aside so that the mace missed him. The fighter, overbalanced, sprawled on the floor.

Time snapped back into place, and Sanwar staggered, dizzy.

The brute swore and attempted to get up, but the halfling Ponta slipped past Sanwar as neatly as a cat and kicked him deftly under the chin. He grunted and fell back down. The mace clattered from his hand and didn't move again.

Saestra turned her attention back to Sanwar as if nothing had happened.

"Did I just hear you call me a liar, Master Beguine?" she said lightly.

His back hurt with the effort of facing her. "Yes, my lady," he said, schooling his face to look unafraid. "My regrets, but I did."

She laughed. "You are quite right. I did lie. I care very much about Shadrun-of-the-Snows and its place on my borders and its interference with my people."

He stifled the impulse to lick his lips. "I can give you the key to Shadrun-of-the-Snows, my lady. It lies within Jadaren Hold."

Sanwar couldn't determine when he began to realize that the loci of the warding that must lie within the Hold had something to do with the Power that pulsed beneath the seemingly placid surface of the sanctuary. But his inner instinct told him he must bring one to the other and—

Burst the bond of my prison.

Before the cold eyes of Saestra he almost frowned, distracted. Where had that thought come from? *How* did he know one was related to the other? Whose prison?

Something coiled within his mind touched his jumbled thoughts, and they quieted. His books and studies had told him along the way. One did not always know where one's fragments of knowledge came from.

Saestra tilted her head, considering him. "Interesting," she remarked. "I wonder if you are lying in your turn."

"I might be," he said. "It would be risky."

"It would indeed," said Saestra. "But then, a promising investment is worth some risk, as we both know."

Saestra turned her head toward the shadows behind her. "Come," she commanded.

There was another pale glimmer in the darkness, and a tall figure drifted toward her. It was a woman, with the pale mien of a vampire and clothing that would not look out of place aboard a ship. She wore her hair braided tightly at the back of her neck and a terrible scar twisted her face out of true, a slash that started at the corner of her left eye and ended at her lip. On a human, the scar would have been a vivid pink. On her, it was white as a salamander's underbelly.

She turned her burning eyes on Sanwar, and now he knew true fear. He wanted to run even though every fiber of him knew he had no chance of escaping a predator like this.

But then those disembodied hands touched his shoulders, very lightly, and he managed to face her without flinching back.

"Helgre has little love for the Jadarens," said Saestra. "And she possesses a certain familiarity with the woods around the Hold." Her mouth quirked, as if she had remembered an old joke.

Looking at those eyes, rimed with frozen flame, Sanwar thought perhaps Helgre had little love for the Beguines as well.

The interview over, Saestra waited until her preternatural instincts told her the merchant was halfway back to his ship. The human fighter who had tried to discipline Sanwar still lay on his back, blinking stupidly at the rafters. Followed by her three ladies, who seemed to move without taking a step, Saestra drifted to him and looked down.

"What is your name?" she said gently.

He struggled to answer, and the halfling answered for him. "Holba, my lady."

Saestra nodded. "Well, Holba," she said, "I don't allow my men to attack my guests unless I order it. I would teach you this lesson myself, but I haven't the time, so I'm afraid you will not be able to use this knowledge at a later date. Ladies, if you would oblige?"

She made another elegant gesture and floated away, accompanied by Ponta and Helgre. Shrieks rang out behind her, heralding the short-lived education of Master Holba.

Just short of the relative safety of the ship, Sanwar heard the screams and shuddered.

CHAPTER TWELVE

JADAREN HOLD

1600 DR—THE YEAR OF UNSEEN ENEMIES

Lakini wondered if Lusk would pine after Shadrun-of-the-Snows, but he seemed to be as comfortable at Jadaren Hold as anywhere. She did notice he always seemed to be watching and waiting for something to happen—an impatient edginess she had never before associated with him.

The mountain in which the Hold was rooted was covered in primal forests, and the devas returned to their old habit of patrolling together. Lakini reflected upon the sanctuary's red-haired messenger and her determination to track Lakini down, and discovered that all in all she was content.

Her peace was shattered the day a delegation from a halfling merchant family from Waterdeep arrived to negotiate an exclusive contract for the silk trade to High Imaskar.

Lakini and Lusk were returning from patrol at dusk. They entered through the common passages at the base of the Hold that opened into enormous storage chambers, stables, and public gathering areas. The members of the newly arrived Waterdeep delegation were grouped together loosely, unpacking their animals and checking their goods. Lakini caught a glimpse of folds of deep, smoky blue silk, and greens shot with threads of gold—gifts to encourage the Jadarens' permission to use long-established routes. There was a bustle of stable hands converging on the delegation to unbridle and tend their animals, and a braying of donkeys and shouting of orders. Through careful maneuvering, Lakini and Lusk made it through the crowd without incident.

Toward the rear of the caverns, a halfling richly dressed in crimson silk was speaking to the stable master. As they approached, the halfling made an elaborate bow and hurried back to his delegation. As he passed them, nodding distractedly and politely, the close quarters made the hem of his silk robe lap over Lusk's boot.

Lusk snarled and spun around to face him, half drawing his dagger. Folk sometimes joked about Lusk's facial markings looking like a jungle cat's, just as they said Lakini's looked like a mask, but at that moment he looked truly tigerish.

The folk around them quieted and stared, and Lakini stared herself, too startled to react at first. The halfling looked puzzled, then, as it became clear the deva's wrath was directed at him, alarmed. He muttered an apology and bowed low to the ground. Lusk looked at his defenseless back as if he'd like to smash the hapless halfling's spine into the ground.

Truly alarmed, Lakini reached for Lusk's arm. He jerked under her touch and turned on her, his teeth bared. Still she pulled him away, toward the back passages and away from the harmless creature that had somehow offended him so deeply.

With a snarl of disgust, he sheathed the dagger, shrugged her hand off, and walked away. She trotted after him as a murmur swelled to fill the silence of his wake. The halfling, no doubt thinking he'd had a narrow escape from retribution for some fancied offense, scurried off to rejoin his party.

Halfway up the slope of the corridor, Lusk slowed his pace to let Lakini catch up. Still flushed with anger, he gave her a sheepish look.

"I probably shouldn't have done that, but the filthy thing touched me. I don't like halflings overly much."

He said it as if it were natural to treat the race like toadfolk, defiling all they touched, and as if she'd understand and agree.

She wondered if she would have been able to react in time to stop him if he had tried to kill the halfling. In that first red moment, that had certainly been his intent. If he'd been alone, she suspected, he probably would have done it.

If he'd been alone . . .

Pieces fell together like a puzzle: the halflings murdered in the woods near Shadrun, and Lusk's indifference; the gutted body of a halfling thief outside an inn in Cormyr; a dozen, a hundred tiny things Lusk had said over the years, mildly disconcerting in themselves but taken together and considered impartially, deeply disturbing.

"It was you." Lakini's voice caught in her throat like a physical thing. She halted in the dark corridor, and Lusk turned back to her. "The halflings in the forest outside

Shadrun. The little thief butchered in the alley. It was you the whole time."

She wanted him to frown at her, to deny it, to call her ridiculous, deluded, even traitorous to make such an accusation. But instead he shifted, leaned against the wall, and folded his arms, smiling at her.

She was horrified. "You're a deva. We abjure evil and fight for the good. How could you do such things?" Her voice felt ragged, torn by the sharp lump in her throat.

"What good do we fight for?" Lusk retorted. He pointed down the corridor, where the sound of commerce mumbled through the stone walls. "Down there they buy and sell the same goods and lands, back and forth, back and forth. All a hopeless, unrelenting cycle. It doesn't *mean* anything. Such as you and I are born, over and again, into this world of petty bickering and squabbling after gold, land, and power. Nothing changes and nothing will. Where's the good in that?"

His raw anger seemed as deadly as his half-drawn dagger a few minutes before, ready to plunge into the hapless merchant.

"You're arguing against our nature," she retorted. "And why hate the halfling? Enough to do what you did in the forest at Shadrun, so near a holy place . . ." Suddenly her knees felt like water. She felt as if she was going to be sick.

"Halflings are filthy vermin," said Lusk. "You don't know, Lakini. You don't know what they are. Not a one of them is worth saving. Listen, *Cserhelm*—"

He took her arm and pulled her to him. She was helpless to do anything but listen. The world had changed, with the dreadful knowledge that Lusk had done these things—could even consider doing these things. She wasn't ready to live in this new world yet.

"Infection exists in this world," he whispered roughly, his lips to her ear, his breath hot on her skin. "If a body is not to die, it might fight off its infections. Some you cannot reason away. Some you must cut from your flesh."

He released her arm, and she didn't realize until the blood rushed back into it how tight his grip had been.

"If you don't realize our nature is to carve away evil like a cancer from the body, then learn it now. We destroyed the cancers in Wolfhelm. You should remember that lesson better."

The werewolves, more of them, five or six at least, had struck at the south gate this time. Lakini beheaded two and watched two boys and a very fierce and muscular girl, who usually was stationed behind the baker's counter kneading the dough, deal with the rest. The Wolfshelm youth acquitted themselves well, but Lakini was uneasy. These werewolves were small and weak, little more than cubs, and she suspected the south gate assault might be more a distraction than an attack. Beckoning the sturdy baker girl to follow her, she told the rest to watch the gate and keep alert. Then she trotted around the village wall, weapons at the ready.

She was right. The previous attack was a feint, and fierce, full-grown wolves were leaping the wall that had seemed so secure. She impaled one, and the girl clubbed another's head to a pulp, but many slipped between them and into the streets of the town. Lakini ran down the main thoroughfare, beating on doors and bellowing a warning, the baker girl on her heels, and presently she heard the bell of Chauntea's temple peal a warning, echoed by the shouts of the villagers in their houses steeling themselves to fight. All down the streets of Wolfshelm, firelight, torchlight, and witchlight glowed between the slats of the windows and through the chinks in the doors. The werewolves that prowled through the lanes and alleys, expecting easy prey, were met with a fierce and desperate resistance.

Lakini heard the scream of a donkey and ran through the maze of streets to the smithy. An amber witchlight shone at the apex of the building, and by its glow she saw Rosebud flailing with a wicked determination at two werewolves that were circling her. She spun about, lashing at one, then at the other, as they tried to sneak in under her guard. One almost managed to grab her leg, but she evaded it and landed a hoof square in its gut. Yipping in pain, the lycanthrope was bowled head over heels. But, recovering quickly, it sprang to its feet and returned to the attack, growling fiercely.

It saw Lakini too late, and a quick slash of her blade liberated its head from its shoulders.

She looked back to the donkey and saw what she hadn't before: a figure lying on the ground, limp as a bundle of rags. The remaining werewolf made a lunge for it, and Rosebud let out a fearsome bray and circled the body, kicking madly. She was tiring rapidly, however, her reactions slower and slower. Lakini knew it was only a matter of time before the beast would overcome Rosebud and rend her limb from limb.

Lakini stooped and grabbed a handful of dirt, the thick, gravelly clay that defined Wolfshelm's streets. Waiting until the donkey was clear, she hurled the dirt at the werewolf. The big clot landed hard on the side of its face.

The thing snarled and turned on her, its great yellow eyes full of hate. Standing upright, it might have come as high as her chin, but it crouched, its long, muscular arms outstretched and tipped with wicked claws. A charnel smell rolled off it, befouling the air.

It rubbed at its face and then looked at its hand, rubbing grains of dirt between its foreclaws. It charged her, arms reaching for her like the mandibles of a spider. Rosebud aimed a final kick at the thing, but she was tired and the blow was weak, missing its mark.

Lakini let the creature charge. At the last moment, when she could smell its carrion-befouled breath, she lifted her sword, still streaked with the other werewolf's blood, braced herself, and let it impale itself on her weapon.

A mouthful of teeth snarled at her, and its spittle flicked her face. It lashed at her, and one of the claws hooked into her tunic, tearing the fabric. She forced the blade in deeper. The beast shuddered and jerked away from her with a force that almost tore the sword from her fingers, but it was the werewolf's dying spasm, and it slid to the ground.

The supine figure stirred, moaning, and Lakini kneeled next to it. It was the smith, who still clutched the hammer he'd seized to defend himself. With a dreadful feeling of foreboding, Lakini squeezed her hand shut and opened it again, causing a small ball of light to appear on her palm. By its pallid light the man looked as pale as the undead.

“You’ve been hurt,” she said. It wasn’t a question but a statement. “Show me.”

Shaking, the smith held out his forearm. It was already swollen, and a dreadful purple color. The tattered flesh around the punctures had turned black.

“I wasn’t so lucky this time,” said Jonhan Smith, and tried to smile.

Lakini stared up into Lusk’s eyes a long moment. Then she pushed him, sudden and hard, both hands on his shoulders. Startled, he stumbled back into the wall.

“Stay away from me,” she said, shaking with anger. “You are an abomination.”

Without turning to see what he did, she ran down the corridor, through the crowded common rooms, past the startled guards, and up the wild paths of the mountains where the clean air could scour and cleanse her.

In the woods outside Jadaren Hold, a human captain of the guard stood beside a vampire with a disfiguring scar. The captain wondered how his employer had ever, ever thought this might be a good idea.

Still, the creature made no threatening gesture toward him and his men, and she kept the disorganized-appearing mob she’d brought with her in order.

She stirred against his shoulder, and he tensed. She pointed at the monolith that loomed in the darkening sky before them, orange flickers of campfires springing into life at its base. A little more than halfway up its side, a tongue of green flame shot forth and faded.

"Soon," whispered Helgre in her beautiful voice that had never sung. "Very soon now."

Nonthal, Turmish

1600 DR—The Year of Unseen Enemies

Sanwar sat cross-legged in the middle of his private study. The room was close and hot, and he was stripped to the waist. Sweat trickled down his back and spotted the floor, but he made no move.

He was staring at the wall. One of the luxurious tapestries had been torn down and lay rumpled in a corner. On the bare wall, which was just a skim of plaster over thick and solid brick, a geometrical figure had been sketched in chalk. Purple light flickered across it, in stark contrast to the white chalk.

Sanwar had a single hair, the chestnut, honey-highlighted hair of a woman, wrapped so tightly around his finger that it cut into his flesh, making the pinched skin turn purple.

Someone tapped at the other side of the door.

"Sanwar?" Vorsha's voice was puzzled, afraid. "Sanwar, dear, is everything all right?"

Sanwar didn't stir at the sound of his wife's voice. There was a scraping sound as she tried to open the door and failed.

Go. He didn't turn to the door but projected that voice that now lived always within him at it. *Go away, and leave me be.*

The tapping stopped, and, after a pause, he heard Vorsha's feet padding down the corridor.

He flexed his finger, tightening the wind of the hair around his finger. Fine as a wire, it started to bite into him, and a small wound split apart on his skin. It gaped up at him like a tiny, eager mouth.

Sanwar smiled at the sensation. A small drop of blood welled from the cut and ran down his finger.

Now, he thought. *This is the time. Now.*

Miles away, deep in the bowels of the labyrinthine monolith, Kestrel lay sleeping beside her husband in their private chamber. She lay on her back, her hair tumbled about her, and Arna slept on his side facing her, one arm draped across her body. The bead around her neck suddenly flared with a deep purple light. Brighter and brighter it grew, then faded until it glowed like a strangely colored ember against her breast.

Kestrel's eyes snapped open and stared at the ceiling. Her eyes were completely black, with no white or iris, as if her pupils had swallowed everything up.

A faint green haze was gathering in the room, like mist on a cool evening. The green particles, each so faint that singly they couldn't be seen by the human eye, swirled around one another and coalesced until they became a transparent ribbon. The ribbon reached for Kestrel where she lay, eyes still open.

It hovered over her face, and an end of it paused over the glowing charm. The ribbon reached for the charm as if to touch it, then reared back, like a startled snake.

The green ribbon floated a moment, sinuous as a flag in the wind, as if deciding what to do. It thinned out until it was simply a mass of green specks again. The particles retreated to the walls and soaked through as if the stone were porous.

Kestrel rose and pushed back the covers, not bothering to put on her slippers, but going straight to the little table where she kept her cosmetics and little trinkets. Here were her comb and the brush she used to untangle her daughter's hair, as her mother had before, and a little woven box containing a chunk of dirty-white quartz that her husband had given her on her wedding night.

There was a box there, a beautifully inlaid piece made of a curious wood. It was a present from her uncle, sent on her birthday this past year. The note said it was a puzzle box, with a prize inside, and challenged her to open it without breaking it apart.

She had fiddled with it almost nightly, but the solution eluded her. Sometimes she was tempted to take the lazy man's way, and pry the end off.

She pressed the lid of the box, and it popped open with no effort at all. Inside was a knife with a long, thin blade and a grip that fit all the curves of her hand as if it were cast for it. Kestrel looked at her own hand and opened and shut it reflexively.

In the bed, Arna muttered to himself and rolled onto his back, snoring faintly with his hand dangling over the side.

She took the knife and walked around the bed to Arna's side. Her bare feet made no sound on the cold stone floor. With her left hand she stroked his hair, all that black, silky hair he had. She ran her fingers through it, and cupped the back of his head. He opened his eyes and smiled sleepily up at her.

She took a handful of his hair, pulled his head back, and slit his throat. The knife was so sharp, it cut right to the bone. He died still looking at her.

It was only a few steps to the nursery, where little Bron was sleeping. The nurse had a bed beside the crib. She woke when she saw the shadow at the door and rose to see what her mistress wanted. She was a short woman, and the top of her head barely reached Kestrel's shoulder. All Kestrel had to do was swing the knife up, under her jaw, through the top of her mouth, and into her brain.

The weight of the woman falling pulled the knife from her hand. She walked to the side of little Bron's crib. The boy was sleeping on his back, his arms spread-eagled in that utter sleep they are capable of at that age. She took the blanket from the foot of the crib, wadded it up, and covered his face.

When the baby was still, she left him covered. She pulled the knife out of the nurse's jaw and shoved her inside the nursery door, so the alarm would not be raised right away. Then she went to Brioni's room, next to the nursery.

Brioni was so proud when she was old enough, just that past year, to have her own room. But her covers were cast aside, her bed empty. Kestrel waited awhile, but Brioni didn't return to her room. So she went on to the boys' room—to Geb and Shev. Geb was fast asleep, and a quick blow finished him, just like his father. But though she could swear she made no sound, Shev was awake when she went to his bed. He stirred, and she saw his eyes glitter up at her, puzzled. She grasped his jaw before he could make a sound and put the point under his ear. Like his father, he was still looking up at her when he died.

Miles away, poised at the rocky edge of the cliff with the wind roaring through her hair, Lakini felt something twist in her stomach.

Something is wrong at the Hold.

She had sworn to serve and protect them, and then she had run away, and now the Hold and everyone in it was in danger.

She turned from the wind and the view and ran, surefooted over the rocks and the places where the path disappeared.

Lusk needs you, sounded the familiar voice from the sanctuary. *He needs you, and you've left him behind.*

Jadaren Hold was stone and should never have burned; yet from the basalt mass beneath her, a haze of smoke emanated. She ran faster, almost flying over the ground as she let pure instinct take over where she put her feet.

There was fighting, and knots of people were at the top of the Hold. Before her eyes, a couple ventured close to the edge and a body, attacker or defender, fell twisting to the ground below.

The wards, she thought. The wards have been broken.

An image of Lusk burning with green fire flared in her mind, and she forced herself to run faster.

"Lusk, Lusk, I am coming for you," she whispered to herself as she ran, as if he could hear her. *And yes, I am waiting for you,* she heard, as if he bent again to speak roughly in her ear.

Almost there. Something rushed her from the side, and she ducked and drew back, letting her assailant's weight unbalance him.

There was an angry snarl, and a set of razor-sharp claws slashed in the air over her head. Lakini drew her sword overhead in a single smooth motion and lunged at whatever it was.

A werewolf, here at the Hold—how was that possible?

There was no time to wonder. A single thrust and her sword pierced the slavering creature's throat.

Reaching the Hold, she paused before a body sprawled across the threshold of one of the doorways carved out of the black rock. The face was turned up to the sky, the eyes open and expressionless. One hand was flung upon, palm up, as if in his last extremity the owner had appealed for mercy to some passing god.

The face was Ansel Chuit's.

She stepped over him, into a mass of fighters, some in the sage green of House Jadaren, some in the blue of House Beguine. What was happening? Had some outlaw element of House Jadaren turned against Kestrel, and House Beguine come to rescue her?

She must find Kestrel and the children.

She pushed and fought her way past clusters of fighters, horrified to see that werewolves fought there as well. Servants and family members, confused and terrified, ran back and forth, and everywhere there was a choking haze of smoke.

Where was Lusk?

Finally she shouldered her way into Kestrel and Arna's private quarters, with the chamber where their children slept adjoining. Their door was slightly ajar. Had they hid inside?

She shoved open the door. Kestrel was not there. There was a bed, with a pale cover streaked thickly with red. Under the cover, his calm eyes staring sightlessly at the ceiling, was Arna Jadaren, his throat slit open like a second mouth.

"Lakini."

She whirled, bloodstained sword upraised, to see Kestrel, standing in her nightclothes. She was barefoot and her skirt was stained with blood. She held a small knife, clotted to the hilt, in her right hand. In her left, she held a dull silver bracelet with three red stones.

Lakini appraised her quickly. She was pale and her eyes were cloudy, but she didn't appear injured.

"Come," said the deva. "We'll get the children, find Lusk, and get you to safety." First things first—she could tell her of Arna's death later.

"The children are taken care of. They're safe now," said Kestrel, in a voice strange and unlike her own. "You needn't worry about the children. Except Brioni. Have you seen her?" She reached to touch the charm at her throat with the hand that held the bracelet.

"Kestrel," said Lakini firmly. The girl must be in shock. "We must go."

Kestrel's unfocused gaze sharpened. She suddenly seemed to recognize the deva. Urgently, she held out the strange bracelet.

"Lakini," she said. "Take this, and get it far away from here. It's what they're after, and they mustn't have it."

"Later." Lakini shifted her sword to the right hand and reached for Kestrel's arm with the left. Shouts and screams were echoing down the corridor. "You can tell me about it after we get clear of this."

"No!" Kestrel grabbed her hand and shoved the bracelet into it. At the touch of the cold metal, an alien whisper passed over Lakini's mind. "You swore to serve my family."

"I swore to protect your family," said Lakini gently.

It was as if the woman didn't hear her. "I order you to take it away. Don't let them get it."

Lakini hesitated, nonplussed. Kestrel's eyes went back out of focus, and she walked past the deva into the bedroom, still holding her bloody knife.

The metal in Lakini's hand felt strange, like the hint of lightning in the air, and it seemed to be vibrating. She tucked the bracelet inside her tunic.

"Give it to me." Lakini looked up, and her hand tightened again on the sword. Lusk stood there, a stained short sword in his hand, his bow gone. He was staring at Kestrel.

Lusk. She should be relieved to see him.

But his voice, hate-filled and gloating, was the voice he used when talking about the halflings he'd killed.

"No," said Kestrel. I've hidden it where you'll never find it."

He snarled and advanced on her. Lakini stepped between them.

Lusk's eyes narrowed. He tilted his head, very like a big cat. Then he smiled. "Why do we argue, *Cserhelm?*" he said in his normal voice. "She has a bracelet. Just a little thing, but it doesn't belong to her. There's a lot of Power in that bracelet, Lakini. Get it from her, and we'll go. We'll take the children and go."

She said nothing, and once more his face changed, and he lunged at her.

She was ready and beat his blade up. She should have struck him then, under his guard where his side was exposed, but she hesitated too long. He smiled at her mockingly and slashed back, and then it was feint, parry, and thrust, down the halls of sundered Jadaren Hold.

It was like a training exercise gone terribly wrong, with death, instead of merely a sharp rap from one's opponent, being the consequence of inattention. First Lusk, then Lakini, were shoved up against rough walls, smooth walls, and once Lakini nearly stumbled into a room lined completely with razor-sharp crystal. Sometimes she could glimpse the fighting that didn't concern her directly, and saw more lycanthropes, and some shambling horror that looked like a ghoul.

An infection in the body of the world.

A fresh breeze stirred her braids. A passage leading to the top of the monolith loomed near. Lakini turned sharply to go inside and ran for the roof, hoping Lusk was not so far gone as to stab her in the back.

On the top of the Hold they faced each other. She lunged. He hopped back, avoiding the sweep of her blade with a sinuous twist of his torso. Recovering quickly, he slashed his weapon down, but she'd seen that trick a thousand times and slipped backward, out of reach of his long arms.

They both knew with a dull certainty that one of them must die. The paraffin lantern, hanging on an abandoned watchman's pole, flickered and spurted a gout of strong-smelling smoke. Up the passage echoed the voices of people shouting in desperation, anger, and grief, and there was the sharp staccato sound of a woman sobbing.

Lusk swung again, and she lifted her blade sideways, catching his weapon on her hilt. She pushed as hard as she could. He had the advantage of weight and height, but she was more stable, closer to the ground. The force of her thrust flung him up, and he staggered against the rock wall. Taking advantage, she charged, her sword aimed at his 'midsection. He regained his footing and jumped sideways, bringing the hilt of his sword down hard on her back. She cried out in pain and slashed at his ribs, slicing through his tunic. They circled each other, breathing heavily. A slow flow of blood stained the edges of his damaged clothing.

Dull pain pulsed where he'd hit her. Something was injured inside, muscle torn and bleeding internally. She didn't have time to worry about that now. Without lowering her guard, she inhaled, forcing the pain into a place down and away. That she would deal with later, if she lived.

Again he struck and again she parried, and she struck in her turn, until both their arms trembled with the strain. Then he snarled and struck fast, blows like the strike of an axe, faster than she could return them. Her grip weakened and with a final blow her sword clattered to the ground. She leaped back while he paused, too exhausted by the effort to push his advantage.

"Lakini!"

The deva spared a quick glance behind her. The slight figure of Brioni Jadaren was framed in front of the flickering light of the torches that still ranged around the perimeter of the roof. Her skirt was kirtled almost to her waist, and she clutched a pole inexpertly in her hands, as if she'd been using it as a staff.

There wasn't time to apologize for not teaching her sword play, as Lakini had promised.

Brioni turned and shouted, and figures assembled behind her, dressed in sage green. She'd managed to rally some of the guards.

Brioni pointed at her. Lusk shouted something, and two of the guards started toward them, bloodied weapons raised.

Lakini turned to look at Lusk. There was her opportunity—he was distracted by the guards and his shoulder was open. Lakini feinted left, then right, then lunged at him, dagger in hand.

But at the last instant, her knife turned in her hand. She struck him in the shoulder with the fist that was wrapped around the hilt. She felt him stagger.

They grappled at the edge and wrestled their way back. Breathless, she drew back and saw that he didn't realize how close to the edge he was. Finding a second wind, she shoved against him again, and Lusk began to topple.

He wrapped his arms around her as he went backward, pulling her against his chest in a deadly embrace. She felt a sting in the back of her shoulder. There was a despairing shout behind her, from Brioni or one of the guards.

As they went over the edge together, it occurred to Lakini that never, never in this incarnation had she ever been so close to him, flesh to blood-slicked flesh, the hard muscles in his arms locked around her, the curves of her body fitting so intimately against his. They would both die, clasped breast to breast.

Then Lusk uttered something in a language she hadn't heard for years, but recognized—Astral, the tongue they had known with every rebirth.

Something that burned with a cold flame surrounded them as they fell—wings, enormous wings of ice-cold flame, feathers that burned faint yellow. Their velocity slowed.

They had no soft landing. Both were stunned with the impact. Lakini was on top, but Lusk beneath her took the brunt of the landing. Still, the air was driven from her lungs and she gasped, trying to suck it back in. She was aware of two of her ribs cracking like dry sticks; pain blossomed white-hot in her side.

She drew back, gasping, stumbling away from him while she still could. He lay prone on the ground. Again she could have killed him. Again she did not.

Staggering like a ghoul, she limped away from him, clutching her dagger in her blood-wet hand, fire in her side and shoulder. She headed over the road to the woods, where she had a chance of hiding from him. It took a thousand years to walk that mile. She was doubled over when she passed the wide-spreading branches of Jandi's Oak and the fringe of the shadowy forest.

CHAPTER THIRTEEN

NEAR JADAREN HOLD

1600 DR—THE YEAR OF UNSEEN ENEMIES

Lakini leaned against the trunk of a tree and tore a strip of fabric from her tunic. Folding it into a pad, she pushed it against the wound in her shoulder. The dull, pulsing pain grew sharper and deeper. She steeled herself and pushed it harder against her flesh, fighting the urge to cry out. The pain was ferocious, but she couldn't risk the wound's bleeding any more and leaving a trail to follow. The tracks she's left behind her were obvious enough. No matter how she tried to focus, her injuries distracted her and she stepped clumsily, breaking twigs and disturbing leaf-fall to show where she had passed.

She wondered why Lusk hadn't tracked her down yet. Perhaps he was hurt as badly as she was.

She felt the prickle of fallen pine needles beneath her, and she smelled the balsam as her weight crushed them. She should tear apart more fabric to tie the improvised bandage to her shoulder, but she didn't have the strength to do anything but hold it in place.

Her head fell back against the bark, and she looked up through the branches at the night sky. Pockets of black, spangled with distant stars, peeked between the dark gray of the close-twined tree limbs. Her vision blurred, and the dim specks of light shifted. She blinked in a futile attempt to focus.

She felt something stir within her tunic against the skin of her unwounded shoulder, something sinuous and cold. A snake, she thought, with a dull flare of alarm that soon faded into indifference. A snake has crawled beneath my clothes, seeking warmth. Poor worm. Soon I'll be as cold as it is.

As if thinking about the cold had summoned it, an icy chill gripped her legs and passed up through her body, through her leg bones, her gut, her torso. The broken places inside her sparked with pain as the cold passed through them. The skin of her shoulders and neck prickled as if in response to the winter wind on Shadrun's mountain. She breathed as deeply as she could, half expecting to smell the sharp scent of new-fallen snow, but instead she smelled the mingled scents of decaying leaf mold, crushed pine, and the dull copper of her own blood.

There were the stars, then nothing, then the stars, then an ever-greater nothing as her eyes closed and didn't open.

She woke to a deeper night and a dull pain that penetrated every inch of her flesh. Her arm was locked into place across her body, still clutching the wad of fabric to her shoulder. As she became able to distinguish one sensation from another, she realized her improvised bandage was completely drenched, and that a small, steady trickle pulsed from beneath it with the rhythm of her heart.

Lakini let her right hand fall away, and the sodden fabric fell. There was something around her wrist, something metallic that glinted in the faint light of the stars that still shone down from between the tangle of branches.

Her arm seemed to weigh a ton. With great effort she shifted it, blinking at the object that coiled there. It was a bracelet, wound round her wrist several times, made of small flat links.

She didn't have the strength to be curious about it.

She needed to find more cloth, find a way to stop the bleeding, find help and healing. She needed to regain her strength, get back to Jadaren Hold, and stop Lusk from his mad descent.

He would destroy two families, if she couldn't prevent it. And he would destroy his own soul, if any remained to wreck.

There was no one here to help her. She couldn't even help herself. She tried to meditate, to find the inner core of peace and strength from which she could summon and enforce her own healing, and push back the black tide that was rising to engulf her. But the ability eluded her.

She felt very light now. Although her shoulder still throbbed and her side ached where her ribs had snapped, the pain seemed almost a distant thing, something belonging to a body of flesh and feeling that was increasingly not part of her.

I am dying now, she thought. She wondered why it had taken her so long to realize that. Surely, after so many centuries, after taking so many bodily forms and shedding them like a tattered cloak at the end of the day, she should recognize death when it came for her.

This husk is finally fading now, she thought without terror. I will go on and forget my life as Lakini.

The throbbing pain radiating from her shoulder slowed and stilled, replaced by a gentle warmth that gradually suffused her entire body. The ache of her cracked ribs faded as well. She felt weak as a newborn kitten. Any number of dangerous beasts or beings, Lusk included, might be on her trail, but she felt no need to move. She knew it didn't matter now.

Now she was ending, and soon enough she would begin again, and all this would be nothing but a faint memory.

She looked across the copse at the mazelike tangle of tree limbs opposite. It seemed that as her body faded, her sight grew ever sharper, even in the darkness, until she could see every vein in every budding leaf, each tiny insect that crawled across the twigs, the very sap as it pulsed beneath the bark. She could see faces in the mosaic the brambles made, female and male both. Faces that watched her, witnessing what was happening. Faced with markings across them, none exactly like hers or like Lusk's, but unmistakably similar—each a sigil the Astral Sea crafted upon its own children.

Faces that were hers in previous lives, each shed like a snake's skin when it grew dull, revealing the new patterns of a new life beneath it.

Devas rarely remembered, except in extremity, the lives they shed. Lakini could remember the drifts and the currents of the Astral Sea that had birthed her, millennia ago, better than the life and body she inhabited before this one. But now, on the cusp of death, staring at her own past faces witnessing her passing, she remembered. Images flickered through her consciousness, as if someone showed her the illuminated pages of a book depicting animate scenes from history—her own history.

She watched, impassive, as fire and melted rock poured down a mountainside, and man-size, serpentine creatures frolicked joyously in the lava. One turned to her and stretched out its arms covered in scales, imploring and mocking her at the same time.

She remembered the taste of wine made from grapes that grew and froze on an ice-bound rock that floated over isolated reaches of ocean, and the onyx-carved cup she drank it from, and the cruel, beautiful smile of the creature that had poured it out for her.

She ran with another, an incarnation of the deva who in this time had become Lusk, ran full pelt at the edge of the cliff rimmed in pale green grass and tiny white flowers, the dirt and rocks beneath their feet crumbling and falling into the sea far below. They were at the point of falling themselves but ran too fast for gravity to catch them, and the sunlight winked diamond-bright on the waves for miles before them.

She stood on a beach, on golden sand lapped by silver water, and bowed her head as she kneeled to an immense winged beast. She bore no weapon, and her body was very new. The beast's warm breath stirred the hair at the base of her neck. She raised her head and saw the beast's clawed hand holding out a sheathed sword. The sheath was white leather with a repeating leaf pattern stitched in gold, and the hilt and pommel were silver and gold worked together to form waves like the liquid fire in the heart of a mountain. The beast spoke, and in her memory she couldn't hear the word it uttered, but she knew what it meant.

Dawnbringer.

It was both a naming and a benediction.

It was her first incarnation as a creature of the mortal plane, never remembered until now. Dawnbringer—her purpose to bring hope and justice, like the new sun spilling light at the edge of a darkened world.

Lakini could name her faces. Lakini. The one who had no name but was known as the Lady of the Sparrows. One of her rare male incarnations. Pashia the Golden.

Dawnbringer.

A thick mist clouded the edge of her vision, bright and shot through with silver. She blinked, but the mist didn't go away, spreading instead and obscuring the faces so that one by one they faded away.

There was a great weight on her chest—not on, not exactly, but inside it, pressing against her heart. Beat by beat the flow of blood through her veins slowed. The pressure would have been painful if not for the warmth and lassitude that served as a drug, numbing all sensation.

She closed her eyes and drew a deep breath, knowing that as she exhaled, the mortal components of her body would dissolve, each tiny particle returning to the bosom of the land she'd wandered for so long. Like all things living and unliving beneath the sun and moon of Faerûn, she was composed of star-stuff, and as a dying star she would scatter for a time before being remade as something, someone else.

Everything changes. Everything dies. She had been an instrument of that cycle of killing and dying often enough to know. Dying, she remembered Wolfhelm and the smith.

There was a smell like gangrene in the smith's small neat hut behind the smithy. His eyes were yellow, and thick black hair had sprouted all over the arm that had been bitten.

She sat by him a long time as he tossed and cried out in his sleep. At one point his lips drew back, and she saw long yellow canines were sprouting from his gums, over his normal, human teeth.

He lunged at her and snapped. She drew back just in time.

Jonhan opened his eyes and looked up at her, startled. Lurid yellow eyes looked back into her gray ones.

Her voice was gentle. "How do you feel?"

"Terrible," he said. "But I was dreaming, and that felt good."

"What did you dream?"

He grinned wolfishly. "Killing. Eating." He looked startled at his own words.

"Killing what?"

"Rosebud. You. Everybody. All meat. All rabbits to be eaten." He drew a great, shuddering breath, then looked at her, stricken by what he said. "You're going to have to kill me."

"Yes," she said, and then, "Are you ready?"

He swallowed. "Yes. Can you make it quick?"

"Yes," she said.

"You've done this before."

"Yes," she said, drawing her dagger.

Outside, the donkey's braying sounded like weeping.

Lakini was floating in the warm waters, each ripple moving her body as if she were composed of water herself. This is death, she thought. It's not familiar to me, although I've done it before.

Something tugged at her right wrist. She ignored it, and it tugged again, insistent.

Blinking her eyes open, she looked down at it and frowned.

There was no sea, no feeling of peace and contentment. Pain lanced through her again. She sprawled against a tree in the middle of the dark woods, cold and alone. The bracelet around her wrist tightened again and, as she watched, one end of it uncoiled from the rest, reared snakelike, and jabbed the skin of her palm.

It wasn't painful, but her body jerked against it. She no longer felt as if she were dissolving. She was all too corporeal.

A voice, clear and implacable, came from the center of her being.

Your work is not done here.

Let me go, she thought, despairing.

Your purpose is unfulfilled. You must remain.

Reborn, she would be whole again, an unblemished weapon ready to do the will of the gods. She would remember nothing of the sanctuary, of the Houses of Beguine and Jadaren, of Kestrel or the Rhythanko. She might remember Lusk, even if he took a new form. She knew that the beings that were Lusk and Lakini had found each other again and again over the centuries, bound together in a time mortals would consider ancient.

Lusk . . . He had tried to kill her, at the behest of something outside them both. She knew, with a wisdom older than her Lakini body, that Lusk had begun to walk apart from the path of his deva nature long ago.

Should Lusk die, he would not return as a deva, but as a rakshasa, a tiger-demon, his outer form betraying what his inner nature had become.

If she denied her rebirth, would she take the first fatal step off that path, condemning herself as well?

Outside her, the Astral Sea called on her to let all go, to dissolve. The voice inside her called on her to remain. Lakini herself was trapped between them.

I must decide.

Another vision came to her, this one not of her past lives or the dwelling places of the gods. This was a mortal face; Kestrel's face, with nothing divine about it. It was a human face, touched with the hands of time.

The thing on her wrist moved again. If she had had the strength to pry it away and cast it aside, she would have.

No. It was too much. She took everything that remained to her and flung it at the cosmos. *No!*

The cosmos struck back with a flash of white light. It erased all her senses. She was blind, deaf, paralyzed. Nothing existed but the light.

Then, slowly, she was aware of her body again. There was no pain. She lay half-curled on her side. She had a sense of a circular chamber, of huge, hand-wrought stones, and of powerful presences standing around her.

She should get up; she knew it. But she couldn't, whatever the consequences.

One of the presences reached out and touched her mind. It felt cold, slightly alien, but it spoke to her gently.

What are you doing, child? By now you must have learned to accept death.

I have unfinished business here. Even to her, Lakini's thought sounded childishly stubborn. Well, let it be so.

This body is finished, and so, too, all business it may have.

I . . . do not agree.

It cannot be that you refuse your reincarnation.

But I do.

She heard another thought-voice, imperious and impatient.

You dare contend that a few mortal creatures and their concerns are more important than the will of the gods? More important than the purpose for which you were created? A deva is more than herself. In you is contained the entire nature of life, death, and rebirth. In shedding your body and its wants, desires, and histories, you symbolize that everything can become pure again. Denying this is blasphemy.

Let her refuse, and so cease.

This voice came from something that seemed to coil through the air like thick, greasy smoke, overpowering the senses. It was amused, taking satisfaction in her distress.

She will dissolve into the aether, and it will be as if she never was, all her lambent memories fading. There was an underlying hunger to the voice. *If that's what she wishes, let it be.*

She felt it pressing into her, as if it would crush her in its coils. Then something broke it apart, as a fresh breeze clears a smoky room. Lakini felt the new entity kneel beside her and touch her hair gently. She had a sudden vivid impression: green eyes in a pale face, with hair the color of sunset.

Lady, she thought at the entity. *The human woman has lost everything she loved. Does that count for nothing?*

Mortals lose everything, eventually. The goddess's thoughts sounded resigned. *Love, even that of a mortal for a mortal, is a spark in the world's darkness, and a precious thing. Most love, but all die.*

She claims unfinished business.

A sharp, silver thought; a bright light penetrated Lakini's blindness, and she both cringed away from it and craved more. This light was hard and white, like the surface of the full moon on a clear night.

It continued. *I may have unfinished business with her.*

Lakini was deeply weary. She couldn't fight them all. *Shall I die then, Moonmistress?*

She felt a cool touch on her face.

As the smith died at your hands? The thought was like the tinkle of silver chimes in a jeweler's window.

What could I do? He had become a beast.

You didn't give him his chance.

What chance?

All creatures of the night are mine, to some degree. You didn't give him his chance to give himself over to my power, to control the beast inside.

Many are not able, and become dangerous.

But some can. There is hope for any infected with the curse of lycanthropy, so long as they seek help before they are sunk too deep in their bestial nature. I might have saved Jonhan Smith. You were too arrogant to let him try.

I thought it was for the best.

Even as your apostate companion, Lusk, thinks what he does is for the best.

It was Jonhan Smith, shaking with sweat and fever, his mangled arm scarring over unnaturally, his face changing to a beast's.

It was Jonhan Smith, looking up in mute appeal as he drew her dagger, kneeled, stroked his hair, and slid it into his brain.

It was Jonhan Smith, who could have been saved.

So I have committed murder, thought Lakini.

She was as guilty as Lusk, slaughtering the innocent.

No, returned the silver voice. *You did what you thought best. Now you know better.*

Lakini felt them all withdraw from her, the silver presence and the red-haired goddess, and the coiling horror, the imperious one. The first presence, still patient, remained.

If you refuse this, you deny your entire nature. Are you prepared for the consequences?

No, I am not prepared. But I will face them.

A pause, then came the following words:

Because you understand this, it will be permitted. It will be harder than you know, Lakini, for so you will remain. Your path will be difficult.

She felt a touch between her eyes, and everything exploded into white light.

.:^:.

She kneeled, alone in the clearing. Her shoulder and her ribs throbbed, but when she tentatively touched the wound, she found it had stopped bleeding, and the edges were already beginning to scar. The night was graying as dawn approached. From the shoulder to the hip, her tunic was stiff with dried blood.

The bracelet was still wound tight around her wrist, and she took a moment to contemplate it. The links were narrow, long, and flat, and embedded along the bracelet's length were three dull red stones—rubies, perhaps, or more likely garnets.

Now she remembered. It was the bracelet Kestrel had given her in the Hold. *Take it away,* she had said. *Don't let them get it.*

And then Lusk had come, demanding the bracelet.

She remembered tucking it inside her clothing, more to keep Kestrel quiet than for any other reason. How had it come to be around her arm? She had a vague memory of movement against her skin, of it questing like a snake, sometime before she had refused her reincarnation and faced the gods' judgment. She must have been hallucinating.

But, as she watched, the bracelet flexed again and undid itself, wind by wind. It was very like a snake as it crawled up her arm, the small links tickling her skin.

She felt a wave of inquiry from it, not enough to distinguish words or even feelings, but certainly a sense that it possessed some sort of intelligence and wondered where it was. It was almost the feeling she had at Shadrun-of-the-Snows, that of some invisible presence quietly manipulating everyone it could.

When it got to her shoulder and started to wind around her neck, she tensed. She considered pulling it off and flinging it away, but it had had all night to strangle her, so she let it be. And, indeed, it simply looped around her neck, invisible beneath the neck of her shirt, and lay still.

She could find out more about the artifacts of Jadaren Hold later. Now she needed to concentrate on healing herself. The chill air was growing warmer, and the dull gray light was brightening as the sun rose.

Dawn was coming, and she was Dawnbringer.

As such rapid healings were, it was painful. Lakini used all her powers of meditation to find her still center of grace, and drew the lambent, pulsing Power she found there throughout her body. Now and then she felt a gentle touch to her Powers, a gift, she decided, from the sister goddesses, and the strength and duration of the healing increased.

Split flesh rejoined. Shattered ribs came back together. Broken vessels were whole.

She would live on as Lakini. But her face, although she didn't know it yet, would never be the same.

Jadaren Hold

1600 DR—The Year of Unseen Enemies

Lusk paced, uncharacteristically impatient. The pain across his ribs where Lakini had slashed at him stung, and the bruised place on his shoulder ached where she had struck him with her fist closed around the hilt of her dagger.

He glanced at the Hold. The late-afternoon light was casting purple shadows against the surface.

Why had she done that? She could have stabbed him rather than punching him. Instead, she turned the point of the knife away at the last instant, giving him the advantage, letting him strike back in return.

He wasn't grateful. She should have struck swift and true, the deva way.

More and more he suspected that his path, twisted though it seemed, was the right one, and that Lakini, companion of his many lives and dagger-mate, was straying away from the gods' plan for them. He had tried to convince her to listen to the Voice, the Voice of the sanctuary that had set him and so many others on the course to meet their destiny. Instead, she had rejected its guidance and left the sanctuary—left *him*—to wander among the useless people of the world. She was convinced to return and join him in his quest to bring an artifact, a coil of metal stolen many years ago, back to the sanctuary where it belonged. But when he had revealed himself to her, his true nature, the things he had done to make the world safer, *purer,* she had rejected him.

She had called him an abomination.

She had forced him to fight her.

She would pay for that, if she was still alive.

Kaarl vor Beguine stood a little way apart, watching the pacing deva with a wary eye. The Beguine guards were stationed at intervals around the Hold, their bows at the ready for any of the besieged that might try to escape. The great doors that led into the caverns at the base of the monolith had been barricaded, and they had already learned that any attempt to break them down would be met by a volley of arrows.

Kaarl had vowed to rescue Kestrel and her family, and it broke his heart that they had failed to get them safely out. He knew Arna was dead, killed by some Jadaren treachery, and had heard terrible rumors about the children.

It went against his every instinct to fight beside the terrible creatures he'd seen preying on mortal men last night. But his guards were too few. As he'd told Sanwar, they were no army. Without the help of the bandits and ghouls, they'd stand no chance against the Jadaren forces. Someone within the tunneled monolith had taken charge last night, organized the defenders, and managed to push them out and keep them out until dawn, until the bulk of the bandits, unable to tolerate the sun, had slunk away.

He'd told Lusk, and the deva had snarled at him that he must wait until dusk, until the creatures of darkness could use darkness to their advantage. And so Kaarl waited, reflecting on the irony of having to fight beside a vampire.

Lusk suddenly felt Lakini's presence behind him, warm as if she touched his back. He whirled, his hand on the hilt of his dagger.

No one was there. But across the way, on the other side of the road beaten wide by the passage of trading caravans, beneath the spreading limbs of an immense, lone oak that stood apart from the edge of the woods, a shadowed figure stood.

Lusk shaded his eyes and peered at it. It was standing still in a way few creatures that walked on two legs could imitate—the way a deva stood.

"Wait here," Lusk called to Kaarl vor Beguine, earning a startled look, and hastened across the road to meet the figure waiting there.

CHAPTER FOURTEEN

Jadaren Hold

1600 DR—The Year of Unseen Enemies

Walking the mile or so down the crushed-lava road to the oak, Lusk remembered the halfling thief in Cormyr, and a smile curved his mouth. How naïve Lakini was about it.

He had felt the slight tug of the thief's sly fingers on his coin pouch.

The deva turned on the unsuspecting thief, quick as thought. The halfling found himself gripped around the throat, his air cut off before he could react, then lifted into the air and shoved hard against the rough, slick stones of the alley wall. His eyes widened as he stared into the eyes of his erstwhile mark, the golden eyes and the slanted streaks across the face. What was this creature? He had taken it for an oversize half-elf.

The little thief grinned ingratiatingly. The deva was stern but would turn him over to the tender mercies of the city watch. Day watch would be problematic, but dusk watch was well bribed by the guild and would let him go for a reasonable fee and a few light cuffs for show. The deva might be angry, but he wouldn't harm him. The creatures were ridiculously law-abiding.

Nothing could express the little thief's astonishment when the deva's knife pierced his entrails, deep, ripping up, up, up. Lusk leaned close to the halfling's ear, his lips almost touching it.

"In your last few moments of life, maggot," whispered the deva, "it will be my duty and pleasure to teach you a very valuable lesson."

It was only a minute before the halfling was beyond all education.

The sun had long passed its apex, and the figure under the tree stood in a pool of shade. Lusk's fingers itched for his bow, but the figure didn't move, and he forced himself to relax.

He climbed the slight rise to the base of the oak, passing without a glance the small shrine of lava rock that had stood through all time and weather.

Lakini stepped forward to meet him. Despite himself, Lusk stopped, shocked at the sight of her face.

The pale band was still across her eyes. But now she was further marked. It was as if her face were a porcelain mask that had been dropped and shattered, and then repaired, leaving a pattern of cracks.

"By the Sea, Lakini," he whispered, forgetting for a moment his anger at his once-companion. "What happened to you?"

Her expression remained placid, but she lifted a hand to her face, tentatively touching it as if she could feel the cracks. He saw her sleeve was brown and stiff with dried blood.

Her hand fell back to her belt, to the hilt of the knife he had given her, now her only weapon. It was an automatic gesture, not meant to be offensive, so he didn't react to it.

"I began to die, Lusk," she said. "After I got away, I went to the woods."

"We tracked you to the edge," he said. "There was a lot of blood."

"Why didn't you go farther?" There was a genuine curiosity in her voice.

He paused, frowning, unable to answer. The truth was that he thought he had killed her. And although they had become enemies, he couldn't bear the thought of desecrating a deva's death, which was simply the beginning of the process of reincarnation, by hunting her down like a wounded deer.

After a long pause to allow him to answer, she went on. "I started to die, Lusk. I felt myself dissolving. And then, when it came to it, I refused my reincarnation."

"You—" Lusk swallowed and looked past her shoulder, at the rough patterns in the bark of the oak, at the ancient letters carved there. "How?" he asked.

"It's hard to remember everything," said Lakini. "But I was . . . scattering, I suppose you'd call it."

Her voice grew bitter. "You can't remember, because they take that memory away from you, don't they? All the memories of living and dying. How it must have maddened them that we remembered enough to come together within each lifetime. How it must have gladdened them that we turned against each other."

Frowning, Lusk looked into her shattered face, searching it. "Who?" he queried.

"The gods, Lusk, that make us play this game of life and death. When it was time, I told them no. I refused to reincarnate. And since they made me to be reborn, they couldn't let me die."

A corner of Lusk's mouth turned up. "Were they angry?"

She toughed her face again, as if self-conscious. "Yes. They were very angry."

"Why, Lakini?" His voice was stern. "Why did you defy them?"

"Because I realized you were right."

Unconsciously his hand brushed the hilt of his own knife. "Are you speaking the truth?" There was a thread of hope in his voice.

"I've been well marked for speaking the truth," she said. "These human families do nothing but sell the same goods back and forth until everyone forgets what they have and buys more. I know now why you were sent here."

She nodded at the dark stone eminence over his shoulder. "That bracelet. Shadrun needs it, and I know where Kestrel hid it. I saw her. Let me go inside and get it."

"Where did she hide it?"

She shrugged. "Nowhere original. A box on her dresser. I can find it for you, *Cserhelm.* For Shadrun."

He tilted his head, dubious. "How? They're well organized now, and fortified. And they still have . . ." He hesitated, then went on. "The bracelet. The Rhythanko, it's called. It's the source of the warding. It holds the spells about the place together, lock and key."

That's why it was so important to Kestrel, thought Lakini. She was its keeper. She was acutely aware of the slight weight of the Rhythanko about her neck, although it wasn't moving now. But then, if the Rhythanko *was* the lock and the key to Jadaren Hold, how was it Lusk and his forces hadn't been able to move right in?

Perhaps some of its Power remained with Kestrel. Whatever the truth of the matter, she had to get inside the Hold, by any means in her power.

Even if it meant lying to another deva.

"They'll let me in," she said. "Last they saw, we were going over the side together. Tell your men to fight me, and I'll break through their line and make for the Hold. They'll let me in."

He considered her a long moment.

"Your sword is somewhere up there." He waved an arm at the top of the Hold. "You have your dagger, but . . . how will you fight convincingly?"

"I am a deva, and they are but men," she said. "But tell them not to press too hard. I don't want to hurt them."

Lusk grinned then, a sharp-toothed smile.

"My mother? You want to see my mother, who killed my father and my brothers and would have killed me if she could?" Brioni Jadaren demanded.

The surviving daughter of Kestrel and Arna paced the stone floor of the chamber. Lakini had been stunned and amused to find that she had organized the defenses of the Hold the night before, taking advantage of the confusion caused by Lusk's and her tumbling off the top of the monolith, for despite the wings Lusk had been able to conjure out of thin air, many thought both devas had been killed. Under her command, the Jadaren guards had been able to push back the forces of both the Beguines and Saestra, and although the wards that Lakini now knew the Rhythanko controlled were compromised, much of the magic lingered.

"I do want to see her," said Lakini calmly. "I didn't make my way past the Beguine guards for a lark."

She had learned that a body healed of horrific wounds wasn't as quick as one newly made, but he had managed to get by five of Kaarl vor Beguine's best men without lasting injury to either side. And they'd put on a good enough show—eager hands had helped Lakini over the doors into the caverns, and archers had discouraged the Beguines from coming closer.

The girl flashed her an odd look, and Lakini knew it was because of the crazed pattern on her face.

Brioni bit her lip. "You can imagine that it's not pleasant to know that the woman who gave birth to you is a traitor to the core."

"I don't think she was."

Brioni's head snapped around at her. "Really? Killing my family and letting the enemy into the heart of our Hold was not the act of a traitor? You have strange ideas, Lakini."

"I suspect, Brioni, that she was under a spell."

"How can a spell make you hurt your children? I saw my baby brother. She smothered him in his cradle. She killed his nurse."

She scrubbed at her eyes with the back of her hand, a gesture that recalled to Lakini how very young she was. "The men won't let me see my father or my brothers. I did see the blood."

"Fifteen years. What spell lets you live with a man fifteen years, and bear children with him, and then slaughter them all one night?"

"A very evil spell," said Lakini.

Brioni blinked rapidly and looked down. "I'll let you see her. I'll take you there myself."

Lakini nodded and turned to go.

"Wait," said Brioni, and went to a corner. She lifted a white-wrapped bundle from the floor.

"It's your sword," she said. "We found it on the summit, afterward."

The girl, older than her years, studied Lakini's shattered face as she nodded her thanks and unwrapped the sword, examining the blade for cracks and the edge for nicks before slinging it into its accustomed place across her back.

"How did you live, Lakini?" Brioni asked finally. "You fell all that way. I saw the two of you, like a ball of fire falling past a window. And the men say you were hurt very badly."

She studied the bloodstain on Lakini's shoulder with frank curiosity.

Lakini waited until the girl's eyes met her own.

"I'm a deva," she said simply. "It's not my nature to die."

She followed Brioni down a series of passages. Now and then they passed an armed guard, each of whom nodded at Brioni and touched his or her forehead. She recognized some of them, and some greeted her by name.

"What's the deva doing with Mistress Brioni?" she heard one guard say to another, both of them thinking they were too far up the tunnel to be overheard.

"Maybe she's here to exact divine justice on that filthy bitch," responded the other guard, with considerable venom.

Lakini's keen eye caught Brioni shivering.

"Why hasn't she been killed, Brioni? Emotions are running high."

Brioni shrugged. "No one understood, at first, that she had let in the attackers and killed my father and my brothers. She was in her bed, lying next to my father. She wouldn't speak, and we thought she was in shock from what she'd seen. But she had the knife in hand, and she didn't deny it."

She had left Lakini at the top of a passage that led down to Kestrel's prison and a guard, gnarled and taciturn, led her the rest of the way.

They'd put Kestrel in a chamber on the lowest inhabited level of the Hold. There were lower tunnels, carved from the rock when the place was still called the Giant's Fist, but no one ventured there, and despite the tales the children whispered to one another at bedtime, no subterranean horrors came crawling out from beneath. The prison chamber was, like the rest of the quarters at

Jadaren Hold, hewn out of the living rock. The walls down here were rough, not smooth and finished, and the room was ten paces wide in either direction.

A woman sat against the wall, her hair hanging over her face, her hands folded on her tattered skirt. From a small subchamber to the side came a smell that showed it served as a privy.

Lakini stood in the middle of the room, waiting for Kestrel to notice her. When the woman made no movement, she finally spoke.

"Kestrel."

Kestrel looked up. Lakini started in shock. Kestrel's gentle brown eyes looked at her from a ruined face that was torn all over with scratches and gouges. In the witchlight that hung from the ceiling, she could see that her arms were similarly marked.

Lakini felt a flare of anger. No prisoner, no matter his or her sins, should be treated like this. It would be better to kill the individual and have it over.

Then she saw Kestrel's nails, broken and stained, and the dark semicircles of dried blood and tissue beneath the nails. She had done it to herself.

"Have you come to kill me?" croaked Kestrel hoarsely.

"No," said Lakini, and crouched down so the woman wouldn't have to strain her neck looking up.

"Why don't you kill me, Lakini? I should have died. *She* should have died."

"Who?"

"The woman who did it. Who opened the wards, who took the Key, who killed"—she swallowed painfully—"who murdered my children. She was in me, so how else could you kill her but by killing me?"

Lakini crossed her legs in the posture of meditation. "Can you tell me what happened?"

There was another long pause, while Kestrel looked down, rocking back and forth slightly. The silence stretched out, and Lakini waited patiently, without moving a muscle.

"It was as if I were imprisoned in a glass chamber, while an alien creature possessed my body," Kestrel began, her red-rimmed eyes staring at the wall past Lakini's shoulder as if she saw the dreadful scene reenacted as a lantern show. "At first I didn't understand. I thought it was one of those dreams, those half-awake dreams, where you lie paralyzed while shadowy figures creep about the room. But I realized I was watching myself, my own body, from a place just outside of it. I couldn't stop it. But I could see everything. I—" Kestrel stopped and shook her head as if to clear it. "It was a gift from my uncle Sanwar, that knife. He was so very angry about my marriage. He's one of those Beguines who hate anything to do with the Jadarens. But for my birthday this year, he sent me a box. It was a puzzle box, he said, and I'd have to figure out the solution—or smash it open. I laughed, and promised him I'd never break it apart."

Kestrel looked at Lakini suddenly, hard, the intensity of her gaze like a blow.

"Where were you? You had sworn to protect me, and you left me helpless. Against *her,* against the thing I was forced to be. Why did you go? You came to me only when it was too late, when it was over."

"I am sorry," said the deva, and meant it. Sorry for that. Sorry for Jonhan Smith. Even sorry for lying to Lusk.

"The knife was in the box," said Kestrel. "Why would Uncle Sanwar send me a box?"

Sanwar.

"The Key," continued Kestrel. "Something told me to find and take the Key, and give it to the other, the deva with the tiger stripes. Lusk. But I didn't, did I?" Her ravaged, bloody face looked suddenly panicked. "Where's the Key? Do you know? I mustn't lose it. Niema told me, before she died, that I must know where it was, always."

"It's safe," Lakini told her. "You gave it to me."

Kestrel shut her eyes.

"I remember you there, and giving you the Key. And then I was very tired and just wanted to lie down with Arna. He was very still, and cold, but I lay with him, anyway."

"Kestrel, you said your uncle Sanwar gave you the knife. Did he give you anything else?"

Kestrel looked puzzled. "No."

"Anything? Ever? A wedding gift."

"I remember now. He gave me a charm. A charm against harmful magic. My mother made me promise to wear it always."

Kestrel looked away. "Uncle Sanwar married my mother, did you know that?"

"Where is the charm?"

Kestrel reached for something at her breast, then screamed.

"It burned," she said, gasping. "Something searing over my heart, liquid fire. It hurt, but a pain like a hunger, distracting."

Her torn, bloodstained gown was fastened up the front with simple bone buttons, and she pulled at the closure, tearing two of them away. Beneath the cambric, the smooth skin of her breast was fearsomely scarred. Either glass or metal so hot as to be liquid had poured on her. Embedded in her skin were blue and green fragments of glass. The charm had melted into her as it fulfilled its true, diabolical purpose.

"Sanwar," said Lakini. "He gave you that and saw that you would wear it always, until it suited his purposes to activate the trigger. He planted you as an innocent weapon in the heart of his enemy's fastness. But there's something behind him. He didn't know it, but he was being used himself, by a being that considers us nothing but puppets. It's using Lusk, too."

Kestrel blinked.

"Yes, I know. It was . . ." She shut her eyes tight like a child trying to remember a lesson. "Fandour."

"How do you know that?"

"I don't know. It's a name that's come to me, an echo from the magic of the Key. I know it sounds strange, but I don't think that even the Key knows who Fandour is."

The chain around Lakini's neck stirred and unwound from her. Lakini grabbed at it, but it dodged through her fingers, stretching still thinner as it went. Completely animate now, it landed on the stone floor and wound its way to Kestrel's feet. By the time it reached her, it had thinned to the diameter of a bowstring, and the links were gone. It was as if a child had taken a figure made of soft clay and rolled it thinner and thinner between his palms, until it had lost all shape and feature. The three red gems along its length winked dully in the grass, spaced unevenly.

The Rhythanko strand, no longer any kind of bracelet or armband, coiled around Kestrel's ankle and ascended whip-quick up her body, beneath her shift, and emerged at the neck. Kestrel smiled at Lakini, her thin face resembling a death mask. The now-threadlike strands of the Rhythanko nosed at the raw skin around the base of her neck.

To the deva's horror, the gem-studded thread reared back and stabbed into one of the wounds Kestrel had carved into her flesh. She reached out and tried to grab it, but Kestrel pushed her away, staggering back against the wall.

"It will kill you, Kestrel!" Lakini lunged toward Kestrel again, with the vague thought of throwing her down underfoot and winding the cursed threads inch by inch out of her body.

"It's not killing me," Kestrel gasped, wrapping her arms around her body. "It's becoming a part of me."

She threw her head back, as if in pleasure, as the last of the Rhythanko and the third gem forced its way into her body. She stretched out her arms. Lakini could see the tiny threads writhing under the skin of her neck, shoulders, and arms, burrowing like worms, and leaving bruised flesh in their wake.

Kestrel relaxed and lifted her arm, watching the Rhythanko move under the dead white, blue-veined skin of her forearm, marred by the scratches she had inflicted and the pool of red and purple-brown where the insistent metal threads were tearing the fascia. She lifted her head and smiled at Lakini with her hollowed eyes. The deva flexed her hands, feeling helpless. She couldn't get the Rhythanko out without tearing off Kestrel's skin.

"They can't take it now," said Kestrel. "Not without ripping me apart." Her gouged face looked lost again. "Do I still have a daughter?"

"Yes," said Lakini.

"Sometimes I think I killed them all. Lakini?"

"Yes?"

"Have you ever killed the innocent?"

Lakini remembered Jonhan's eyes. "Yes."

"How do you forgive yourself?"

Lakini didn't answer for a long time. "I don't," she said finally.

The rock knew fire.

It was made in the swell and ebb of fire from the center of the world, born from molten stone that pushed a fiery tide at the surface until it burst forth. The rock pulsed liquid within the volcano that formed there, a mountain's heart beating slower and slower while it solidified. The mountain slept, and the rock within it, until time and the elements stripped the skin and the sinew and the flesh of the mountain away, leaving the rock naked in black basalt solitude.

Now and then, in the ages that followed, small fires were lit on top of the rock, and the tiny creatures that lit them huddled against the cold. They always moved on, for the rock was a barren place overlooking a desolate plain, far away from anybody's hearth and home.

Then more creatures came, skilled in sculpting stone to their ends. The rock burned again, worms of fire tunneling deep inside it, deeper and deeper until the delvers burrowed to the root of the mountain. There, beneath the spine of the world, they broke into chambers sealed before the current age was imagined. There they found the raw treasures of the earth—gemstones and rare metals—but also they woke horrors that had coiled there, sleeping. Those few who were not devoured fled for their lives to distant lands, never to return.

More recently a green fire had passed through the rock, not hot but cool as water as it flickered through the long-abandoned passages. The fire came from something small, but, like the sharp tip of a dagger, it had great Power behind it. A human wielded it, locking the substance of the rock and its tunnels to the blood of another, down to the caverns at the foot of the rock, down to the tunnels bored out of the substratum beneath.

But not as far as the voids and passages deeper, which over time had been colonized and abandoned and found again by dark-dwelling creatures rarely thought of by those that lived in the realm of the sun. The green fire sealed off those corridors below, but they remained, like scar tissue deep beneath a healed wound.

The small fires that made a dwelling place for men and their kin—hearthfire, coals for cooking, and torches to light the night at the heart of the rock sparked in it now. And deep underneath, where those who came before and delved too deep had died, beneath the giant anthill of rooms and tunnels, beneath the caves where caravans could shelter, beneath doorways sealed and spelled in a language men had forgotten long since, more fires burned, cold and smokeless.

The ways and desires of men, dwarves, halflings, or elves meant nothing to the rock—nor did the things they made or bought or sold, or their songs and stories, their good deeds and evil, their lives and deaths. Let them hew out tunnels, cast spells, dwell within, or be cast out by fate or a stronger clan. It didn't care. It knew only the forces that made it: the liquid center of the world, the thrust of continental plates, the force of a volcano, the slow but inevitable grind of wind and water on its surface. It knew fire.

Now a small cold fire burned in the hand of the deva that walked with Kestrel along one of the deep tunnels, an ancient escape route burrowed in time unimaginable.

"You must leave here," Lakini had told her. "So long as Lusk knows the Rhythanko, the Key, is here, he won't rest until he has it. Do you know a way out?"

Past the privy chamber was a tunnel, and the tunnel led deep into the woods. "The children told me about it," said Kestrel. "Brioni and her friends."

Her voice choked a little on her daughter's name. "They play in every part of the Hold. There's nothing they don't know. You can learn a lot if you listen to children."

It seemed like hours they walked the tunnel before a haze of green light showed where a mass of overgrown vines hid the entrance. Lakini closed her hand, stifling her light, and they shoved past the blockage until they were free.

This was a different part of the woods than the place in which she'd almost died the night before. There were fewer close-growing pines and more birches, so the remaining sunlight dappled the white trunks of the trees.

Lakini breathed in the fresh woodland air.

"You lied to me, Lakini," said a voice. She whirled, reaching overhead for her sword without a moment's thought.

Lusk stood a little ways away on a hillock, an arrow to the string of his bow, but he was not aiming it, not yet.

"It appears we're not in agreement, after all," he said. "You think I'm an abomination, and I think you're a fool."

CHAPTER FIFTEEN

Jadaren Hold

1600 DR—The Year of Unseen Enemies

"Get behind me, Kestrel," said Lakini. She pulled her dagger from her belt. At this distance she had a chance of bringing Lusk down with a knife throw before he raised his bow.

He lifted an eyebrow at her. "I'm going to give you one more chance to understand."

"Try," she responded.

"Listen, Lakini." He lowered his bow and removed the arrow from the string.

"Before I met you, during the time when you were Lakini and I was Lusk, I found a family, a family of my own. They took me in, thinking I was merely a beggar. Not a warrior, not a celestial. A dirty, smelly beggar from the road, looking, as they thought, for a meal. It did not occur to them they would benefit from taking me in. They weren't filled with stories of disguised princes rewarding those who succored them. It was because they were that improbable thing—good people. Farmers, very simple folk. I left them with a blessing, and then when

I passed that way again, I had an urge to see them. And they welcomed me in, as before. I never stayed long, and never frequently. But I knew they would always be there. If I had stayed with them longer, I could've kept them safe. But no—it's my nature to wander. You know."

Lakini, despite her horror, winced at the self-hatred in her fellow deva's voice. She felt Kestrel shifting in the leaves behind her.

Don't let him see you, she thought at the woman, although she knew she couldn't hear. *He'll see the wires beneath your skin and know.*

"You can't know what it was like, Lakini," continued Lusk, "to know that whatever the time of year, no matter the hour, if it was midwinter or washing day or harvest season, there was always a place for you, a seat at the table. A cup kept especially for you on the shelf. A child, seeing you across the fields, who ran to greet you. In those years, I knew what it was to have a family. My own folk.

"But one spring—it had been a hard winter on the country folk, that one, with frozen crops and flooded fields—I came to them again. I had gifts for the children in my pack, gifts I'd brought from toymakers in the East. Magic things, exotic, unheard of there."

He was looking past her, not at Kestrel but at the pattern of vines at the mouth of the tunnel, his voice almost dreamy, as if he saw what he narrated.

"I didn't understand what I saw, at first. The house, half-gone, the rest like a broken eggshell, made of burned timbers. They were still smoking. There was another smell, too—burned meat. I found them all inside the house, what remained of them. The woman was clutching one of the children to her. I couldn't tell which one. I found the others, the man, the rest of the children. All save one. I found, later, from the neighbors that a band of halfling thieves had been plaguing the district. So far they'd just robbed houses and crofts in the owners' absence—a quick raid to steal cattle, or supplies, or the coin under the bed. Nothing like this."

His face hardened, and his voice seemed to come from a long way away. "Those bandits gave me a great gift. They taught me that the gods care nothing for us. In return, I give halflings, when I can find them, another gift—the gift of oblivion. And each time, I rid the rotten world of another maggot that burrows in its flesh."

He looked back at her.

"That time, when the messenger came, and I was gone two seasons."

"Yes." Her throat was dry as sand. "I remember."

"He brought word of Darla. She was the littlest, a girl no more than eight, the one I couldn't find. When I found their spoor, I thought, perhaps, they'd taken one away, a child they could sell. I followed them, but the trail went cold. But I left word with folk I knew—folk who owed me their lives—that I wanted any word of her.

"The messenger brought me word that it was four years since a halfling gang took a few children to be sold at market not a hundred leagues from the slaughter. It sounded too alike to be a coincidence. It took a long time, and many false trails, but I found a man who had bought a little girl, just like Darla, as a maid for his wife.

The child died a year later from the bloody flux. I also found the name of the slaver who bought Darla from the thieves and sold her to the merchant."

He spat out the word: "Jadaren."

"No," Kestrel whispered behind her. "None of us has ever dealt in slavery."

Lusk ignored her. His faraway eyes focused on Lakini, and his voice became steely.

"So you tell me, Lakini. Where is your good in any of this?"

They looked deep into each other's eyes for a long moment before he nocked the arrow back to the bow, lifted it, and loosed it straight at her heart.

She was expecting it and had already begun to fling herself to one side, pulling Kestrel with her. The arrow missed, whispering into the leaves at the mouth of the tunnel.

She had to decide, lightning-quick, whether to throw the dagger or charge with the sword before he got another arrow to the bow. Clasping dagger and sword together, two-handedly, she ran up the hillock. He dropped the bow and drew his own sword, parrying her aside as she struck.

She was still healing. But so was he. She ignored the pain in her shoulder as she bore down, two-handedly, again and again against his one-handed defense. Once he managed to push her off balance and struck with the dagger in his left hand. She dodged aside and, ducking, hit him with the hilt of her sword in the back of the leg.

Lusk staggered and went down on one knee. She forbore to press her attack, and he took advantage of that, striking at her sword from beneath and knocking it out of her hand.

She drew her dagger and crouched. There was no time to retrieve the sword. Lusk launched himself at her, chopping at her left side. She met the blow with the dagger, letting it slide down the length of his sword. With a familiar twirl of her weapon, she circled the hilt and slashed the tip into his wrist, opening the artery.

He dropped the sword and gasped, gripping his damaged wrist. His mad eyes glittered at her. "I can't believe I fell for that trick," he said.

He drew his own knife with his left hand and leaped on her, letting his useless right hand dangle. She sliced her weapon up and felt it meet resistance, and then as she thrust with all her strength, it penetrated. At the same time he bore down on her, and the pain in her injured shoulder returned with a vengeance. She could do nothing but push the weapon deeper and deeper into him. Her left side felt numb.

For a moment they were locked together, breast to breast, hip to hip, as they had been when they fell in the cold flame from the Hold. As the last of their strength faded, they relaxed and staggered apart. He stared at her, and the glitter went out of his eyes. She saw the hilt of her blade protruding from beneath his sternum. The tip had pierced his heart.

He blinked, as if puzzled, as if he didn't understand what had just happened. He opened his mouth as if to speak, and a great black bubble welled between his lips and burst, sending a red trickle down his chin.

Unbending, like a tree, he fell. He did not move again.

Lakini crouched by his side. His eyes stared, unseeing at the forest canopy above.

"*Ashonithi, Cserhelm,*" she whispered as she closed them.

"That's one of you gone, anyway," spoke a beautiful voice from behind her. Startled, Lakini turned.

A woman with the waxy face of a vampire and a scar twisting her mouth out of true stood at the mouth of the tunnel. Her hand tangled in the girl's hair, she held Brioni tightly against her, pulling her head to one side so her neck was exposed.

Kestrel stood before them, her arms extended in mute appeal.

The vampire ignored her and spoke over her head to Lakini.

"Ironic that one of you killed the other, isn't it? Very piratical. Ping would have approved. Oh, that's jogged your memory, has it? Probably wasn't much to you, just a ship at sea with a dead crew."

Lakini did remember, and she heard again the sound of Lusk's arrows finding their targets.

"Don't hurt her," said Kestrel. "You can have anything you want. Just don't hurt her."

The vampire ran a pale finger over Brioni's neck, just over the jugular, speaking to the Kestrel now. "But this, my dear, is what I do want. You don't know this, but your ancestor did me a very bad turn some two hundred years ago. And I don't forget easily."

She grinned, showing her fangs. "The delicious irony is this—his friend, his very dear friend, his bosom friend—he also did me a very bad turn at just about the same time. And while your great-grandsire was a Beguine, this one's great-great—so many greats—grandsire was his good friend. A Jadaren.

"Yes," she said, grinning at Kestrel's wide eyes. "They were friends, until I gave them a reason to hate each other. And they were both, you will be delighted to know, pirates. And"—she sighed—"not very good pirates."

"So this is what I am going to do. I'm going to kill this little chit in front of you, and then I'm going to drain you. But first, I think I'll take your shatter-faced friend's sword."

Still keeping her grip on Brioni, the vampire maneuvered over to where Lakini's sword lay. As she passed Kestrel, two long, thin cords leaped from the back of the woman's wrists. They looped themselves around the vampire's legs and pulled hard. With a shriek, she stumbled and fell, releasing Brioni as she did.

In a single movement, Lakini scooped up her sword and cut off the vampire's head.

Kestrel clasped Brioni tightly to her, and the girl's arms were locked around her mother's waist. As Lakini watched, Kestrel stroked her daughter's hair and took her by the shoulders.

"You followed us," she said gently.

Brioni nodded and hiccupped. "I knew about the tunnel. When I came back and found your empty cell, I didn't want to call the guards. I thought they'd kill you."

"They'll always want to, said Kestrel, her voice dark and bitter. "And I don't blame them."

Nonthal, Turmish

1600 DR—The Year of Unseen Enemies

At the entrance to House Beguine, Lakini asked for an audience with Vorsha Beguine. The doorkeeper was very polite, very ingratiating, and said the mistress was busy with the kitchen, or with her husband, or in her private chambers. Could the fairlady come back another time?

Lakini bent close to the doorkeeper's ear and informed him that if he didn't tell Sanwar Beguine, immediately, that a deva late of Shadrun was here to tell him of the Key, she would not be responsible for the state of his guts. The man paled and hurried away.

Sanwar received Lakini in the library of House Beguine, with the sun shining through the domed glass overhead. Since she'd seen him at Shadrun a few months ago, he'd gained a little weight and had more white in his hair, but he was still a good-looking man.

He frowned, obviously not expecting her.

She knew she had to act quickly, before his caution overcame his greed.

"You're not whom I expected," said Sanwar.

"The other sent me," she said smoothly, still walking toward him. She was almost to him before his eyes widened and he raised his hand and a smell like lightning on a hot day filled the room. Before he could manifest the spell, she smashed him to the floor.

He groaned and tried to roll away, still gesturing with his fingers. She already had a thin rope in hand. Kicking his hands apart, she seized him by the wrists and bound them together. She reached for his feet and he kicked at her.

"Do that again and I break them," she growled, and he subsided.

There was a gasp, and Lakini looked up to see a servant in the doorway, mouth open as she looked as her master trussed like poultry on the floor.

"Bring Vorsha Beguine here, now," Lakini told her.

The woman hesitated, obviously unsure whether to obey or raise the alarm.

"Now!" Lakini growled.

The woman scuttled away.

Something plucked at her throat. She turned to see Sanwar muttering a spell. She kneeled next to him and clamped her hand across his mouth.

"Unless you want to be gagged," she said, "you won't try that again."

"Sanwar—? What are you doing?" said a voice. Vorsha Beguine stood there, looking bewildered. Lakini could see some of Kestrel's features in her mother's pretty, now-worried face.

"I've come to see you. Your husband can wait there for now," Lakini said, nudging him with her toe.

Open-mouthed, the woman looked from Sanwar to the deva. "But . . . you can't just—"

"But I can, and I did."

"I'll fetch the guards." Vorsha turned to the door.

It opened and Kestrel stood there.

"Kestrel! I thought—! I had heard—"

Vorsha flung herself at her daughter. Hesitantly Kestrel's arms went around her mother. Lakini saw thin wires vibrating beneath her skin.

"So it's not true?" said Vorsha.

"I'm sorry, Mother. It is."

Vorsha drew back and cradled her daughter's ravaged face with the palm of her hand. "Then Arna?"

"Is dead. And Geb. And Shev. And little Bron."

With each name Vorsha flinched as if she'd been struck.

"And the worst thing, Mother, is that I killed them."

Vorsha looked at Kestrel as if she were mad. At her feet, Lakini felt Sanwar stir, and she put a cautionary foot to his throat.

"How is that possible?"

"Like this."

Kestrel held out her hand. On her palm was a lump of melted glass. With trembling fingers Vorsha took it.

"Look inside," said Lakini.

The woman blinked at five strands of brown hair that twisted inside the ruined charm. Lakini saw she didn't have to explain. Three of the hairs fused inside, Vorsha had plucked herself from her daughter's hairbrush. The other belonged to Sanwar.

Vorsha's lips pressed together, tight and white, and her eyes were enormous. She turned her unblinking gaze on Sanwar.

"What did you do?" she said, her voice cold.

"He made Kestrel a weapon, against her will and inclination, to strike against the Jadarens from inside," said Lakini.

Vorsha clutched the ruined charm so tightly that part of the glass cracked apart and sliced her palm. She ignored it.

She kneeled by Sanwar. "It's not true. Tell me it's not true."

"It isn't true," said her husband.

But Vorsha saw the truth in his face.

She seized his hair, yanking it back fiercely. A terrible expression distorted her placid face.

"I'm a wicked woman, Sanwar, but I love my children. I never loved Nicol, and I was unfaithful, but I thought if I married you, if I was a better wife to you and a faithful mistress of the House, I might do honor to a good man's legacy. And now I find that I desired a monster, and opened my legs to the worst kind of traitor."

She spat in his face. "I would've done better to sell myself at the yuan-ti market. Whore's business is more honest than this."

She rose and moved away from him. There was a bloody handprint on her silk shirt.

"Kestrel," she said. "Will you stay? You'll be safe here."

Her daughter shook her head. "I killed your grandchildren. I can't face you, my sister, our friends, our servants. I know you would be kind, Mother. But I can't."

"I can take her somewhere," said Lakini. "Somewhere she can heal."

Vorsha nodded, tears streaking down her face.

"I came to give him over to the goddess for punishment," said Lakini. "But perhaps you will say he doesn't deserve that kind of mercy."

The small woman prodded Sanwar with the toe of her elaborately embroidered slipper. Casually, she turned and strode over to the row of weapons displayed on the wall. She ignored the greatswords and the thick-hafted spears that would be an effort for a half-orc to wield, passing her hand over the long knives and the daggers. She let her fingers finally touch a blade small enough to slip in one's sleeve, an assassin's weapon with a wickedly sharp, thin blade the length of her palm.

She pried it from its mount and turned back to Lakini. Sanwar saw the weapon and grunted at her feet.

Her face was wet with tears, but her back was as straight as a birch tree. She was Vorsha Beguine, mistress of the House now.

"I think you can leave any matter of mercy to me, deva," she said. It was a dismissal. Lakini only inclined her head in response. It seemed that Ciari Beguine was in some ways very much her mother's daughter.

Vorsha watched as Lakini and Kestrel left the room.

"Do you want to see your sister?" asked Lakini.

Kestrel shook her head. "No. She would try to be kind, if she knew, but she would still hate me."

When they reached the dusty street outside the compound, Lakini thought she heard a cry from inside the dwelling. She saw Kestrel's back stiffen, but neither of them mentioned it.

"Is there really somewhere you can take me?" asked Kestrel.

"More like to someone," said Lakini.

CHAPTER SIXTEEN

SANCTUARY OF SHADRUN-OF-THE-SNOWS
1600 DR—THE YEAR OF UNSEEN ENEMIES

Bithesi examined the cut in the dog's side. The big mongrel cur lay on its side, panting heavily and whimpering slightly when Bithesi's careful fingers probed the edges of the wound. It kept as still as it could, however, and never snapped at her, even when she dipped a rough rag in a bucket of warm water and washed away the clotted blood.

She muttered an apology, and the dog's tail thumped lightly in the straw that mounded the floor of the stable. Then its gaze went over her shoulder, and its eyes narrowed. Its body tensed, and it lifted its head. Its lips drew back, exposing impressive white canines, and a liquid growl rumbled up its throat.

Bithesi laid her hand, damp with water, on the animal's neck.

"Hush, Torq," she said. "They're friends."

The dog quieted and laid its head back down, but it kept a distrustful gaze on the two figures in the doorway.

Bithesi didn't turn around, keeping her attention on the wound in Torq's flank.

"Come in, Lakini," she said. "And your companion as well. It's chilly outside."

It was. The warmth of the autumn day had fled with the setting sun, and the mountain air now hinted of the bone-cold winter to come. The barn, occupied by a dozen-odd horses as well as their keeper, the dog Torq, and the usual contingent of cats, was warm, with the pleasant earthy smell of a well-kept farmyard.

"Bithesi," said Lakini.

"You never said good-bye," said Bithesi, breaking in on her.

"I don't—" Lakini began.

"Good-bye," Bithesi said. "It's a thing friends say to each other when they part. A grace note, in the midst of our small business, our comings and goings, our mortal squalor. A simple thing to say. You're not mortal, but you might try to remember."

Lakini had no answer.

Bithesi glanced up at Kestrel, and her gaze lingered. The wounds on her face were healing, and the scars were forming pink on her hands, but her cheekbones stood out and her eyes glittered as if fevered.

"Would you like to help?" Bithesi spoke to Kestrel as she would to a small child.

Kestrel reached out a trembling hand to the dog. She paused, looking searchingly at Bithesi, her hand suspended in the air.

She touched the dog's side. Torq jerked in response, then quieted as she gently stroked his short, coarse fur.

Bithesi waited until the dog's breathing grew regular before raising the threaded needle with her right hand and pinching together the sides of the cut with her left. She muttered something that sounded like a short prayer or invocation before she bent to her work, stitching the animal's skin back together with tiny knots, delicate as the embroidery on a lady's court dress.

Torq's eyes jerked open and he whimpered, but Kestrel placed a firm hand on his neck and kept stroking his side, and he didn't stir.

"Good-bye, Bithesi, my friend," said Lakini.

She would not say *Ashonithi.* She knew she would never see Bithesi again.

Lakini waited a long time at the barn entrance, feeling the cold air on her back and the barn warmth on her face. From one of the corners where the wall met the ceiling, a nesting dove cooed. Bithesi focused on the dog's wound as if nothing else existed. Kestrel glanced up at the deva once, a serious look that recalled the grave manner of her daughter.

"Good-bye, Lakini," said Bithesi, not looking at her.

Kestrel turned toward her, still keeping her hands on the dog's side. She gave a small, tight smile.

Lakini smiled back and slipped away.

Standing in the mud outside the barn, Lakini became aware that she held within herself the small hope of staying at Shadrun, of finding for herself the idea that the mortal races called "home." But with the realization came the knowledge that hope lay stillborn inside her. However many years she had spent at the sanctuary, even if she stayed here a century more, she would always be apart. The place would be familiar, even comfortable to her. But she would never cherish it in her heart, or long for it when she was away, as a crofter did his hovel or Bithesi her stables.

Home . . . Lusk had tried to find it with his adopted human family, until the chance violence that always threatened to engulf the mortal destroyed them and made him the twisted creature he had become—and was doomed to be forever. Kestrel had found it, and it had been torn from her. Bithesi wove her home around the animals she tended, finding a warm place inside the meditative task of caring for them.

The moments she had spent in Bithesi's company were her home, Lakini realized, and the many years she had spent with Lusk. But Lusk's madness had taken one home away from her, and Bithesi's mortality the other.

Something stung her eye, and she halted, blinking. The sting became a mild burn, and the burn gathered into liquid within her eye, and as she shut it briefly, a drop of moisture fell to the dust at her feet. The burning was gone.

Lakini touched her cheek in wonder, feeling one more drop there. A tear. She had wept. Was that one of the consequences of denying her reincarnation? Would she become more mortal?

Was it a punishment or a reward?

Fandour was puzzled. Two of his vectors had winked out, one soon after the other, just at the point of seizing the Rhythanko.

But now the Rhythanko was close—closer than it had been in millennia, although it was . . . changed, somehow. It had taken refuge in a different form.

Fandour went over his connection in the Rogue Plane like knots in a fishing line, finding none broken until he tried to touch those vectors, then . . . nothing.

He was patient. He still had his foothold. And the Rhythanko was near.

Foothills of the Curna Mountains, Beastlands

1600 DR—The Year of Unseen Enemies

The heat of the day still lingered, cloying and oppressive in the still air. In the tall, dry grass, a few insects chirped wearily. Now and then a birdsong sounded from the low trees that clustered in deep, stream-cut ravines that threaded the foothills.

A figure trotted through the dry grasses, casting a long, thin shadow diagonally over the ground. It was a human boy. He had the scrawny frame of a child, but his face, gaunt and anxious, hinted that he was older. He was clothed in worn leggings and a thin shirt, and his feet were bare and calloused.

The Boy—he had had a name once, but his masters had called him nothing but "Boy" for so long, he'd forgotten it—cast a worried glace at the sun, reddening low over the foothills of the Curna Mountains. If he didn't find the runaway swarm and capture the queen by nightfall, one of Lord Mahijith's hives would be lost.

The Boy didn't think that Skreetchu, the raven-headed kenku overseer that supervised the lord's outlying estates, would show mercy to a slave who lost a valuable swarm.

For one thing, busy with the extra task of changing out soiled straw in the stables, he'd been late going out to the hives. Despite the heat and his weary shoulders, he enjoyed the walk to the outer fields. A rare, refreshing breeze tumbled past him, cooling his sweat-soaked shirt, and the wheat was ripening in great golden knots on top of swaying stems. The Boy strode down the worn path between one furrowed field and the next, spreading his fingers at his sides to touch the stiff stalks on either side. Past the thick rows of grain the world fell away in gentle curves, humping and mounding in the distance until the foothills reared up and became the Curna Mountains, with their sharp, white-capped precipices and knifelike, purple-shadowed sides. He paused and breathed deeply, fancying he could feel the mountain's icy breath in the hot air.

Sometimes he pretended he came from a cool climate and would someday return to a place where a handful of chilled snow could cool a hot face after the labor of the day. Perhaps he did. He had been sold into Lord Mahijith's household as a child, and he remembered little before that. He didn't know if his dim impressions of a protective father and a gentle mother were real or simply products of his imagination.

The haystack-shaped hives were arranged in two even rows. His first task was to check the perimeter to see if the wards that protected the combs and their sweet treasure still held. Only Skreetchu knew the cantrips that would keep bears and other hungry animals from scenting and tearing apart the hives, but the charmed crystal in his pocket would tell him if they needed renewal.

The Boy frowned. In the distance, a black cloud hovered over one of the farthermost hives, a cloud that flexed and compacted into a black ball and then spread out until he could see its component parts. Bees—thousands of bees, hovering over their hive, when they should be returning from their labor and settling in for the night.

Giving the quieter haystacks a wide berth, he trotted toward the cloud, keeping his breathing in check. That was one of the first things he'd learned after Skreetchu assigned him to care for the hives—it never was wise to panic around bees.

The contented buzzing of sated bees, always an undertone in this section of the fields, changed as he approached the golden speckled mass. The sound was higher, not threatening, but excited, and the hive in question was not, as he feared, smashed by some marauding animal whose craving for honey had overcome its fear of being stung. The woven straw dome on its stand was whole, and bees still crawled in and out. Some perched in rows near the entrance, cooling it with their furiously vibrating wings.

The cloud of bees over his head swooped left and right, looking for all the world like a single entity rather than a disparate swarm.

Realization struck him like a sharp blow to the belly. The hive was swarming, half its inhabitants splitting off from its mother and old queen, and this was the new queen's mating flight.

The Boy had not expected such a thing—bees swarmed in spring and early summer. If the queen led her followers and mates into the hills now, just at the point when summer was turning into autumn, they'd be lost to Mahijith's estates. They might even die. Bees that swarmed out of season often died.

In the spring, Skreetchu would have been prepared with new hives and tools—smoke and instruments—to capture the queen, to create a new hive and increase production, and there would be more honey for the master's stores. Now, however, not only would they lose the nascent colony, but the honey production from the mother hive would be halved for the season.

The pitch of the swarm rose, shrilling in the autumn air, and the cloud started to move. Individuals broke apart and rejoined, but the center of the mass remained compact. The new queen was somewhere in the middle.

He kept the crystal inside a crude box he had hacked out of a chunk of wood that fell from the pile by the fireplace in the cold of winter, knowing the punishment would be dire if he lost the magical trinket. If he could track the swarm and capture the queen, he could use it to return her to one of the empty hives.

Should he follow them now, or let Skreetchu know what had happened? He risked a beating either way.

The Boy made up his mind. He drew a deep breath and ran, leaving Mahijith's estate behind him, following the black cloud of bees into the reddening sky.

Hewn blocks carved with worn runes lay scattered, half-buried in the sandy soil. A lizard ran across the rough surface, pausing with its tail lying half in the depression made by an ancient sigil. It lowered its blue-sheen belly to the hot surface of the stone and up again.

Before it, between the rocks that were tumbled carelessly across the sand, the air began to shiver. As if someone had cast a stone into the still surface of a pond, ripples formed and spread from a turbulent center located a man's height from the grassy sand. Like glass heated and pulled this way and that in a glassblower's kiln, the air took transparent shape.

The only witness was the lizard, which pushed up and down a few more times, flicked a pale pink tongue, and vanished in a quick scuttle between the slabs of stone.

In the still heat, the column of air warped and flexed. There was a smoky smell like green sticks burning. Slowly the ripples took on a humanoid shape, as if a figure made of glass moved underwater, all but invisible in its transparency.

Something small and yellow-brown buzzed heavy-bodied through the air, making a lazy circle around the coalescing transparent figure. Then came another, and another, until a dozen bees were making their drowsy sound between the ruins.

The Boy stopped, catching his breath, bent with his hands on his thighs. He reached down to pull a burr from the hem of his leggings and paused. On the ground by his boot a disoriented bee crawled, falling from one thick blade of grass and crawling up another. Bigger, more elongated than a worker, it was a drone, dying after a mating flight.

They couldn't be far. He plucked the burr away and started off again in an efficient jog-trot, instinct telling him to follow the faint breath of a breeze that freshened the unseasonable evening warmth. His foot almost turned against a half-buried stone block, too regular to be natural. There must have been buildings here once, long before Lord Mahijith and his ilk had laid claim to the Durpar lowlands. He scanned the landscape constantly for the blur of the swarm, aware he had ventured farther from Skreetchu's domain than he ever remembered having done before. The tall grass thinned here, and the soil looked to be mixed with sand. What had stood here, and what happened to the builders? Had a town grown here once, and died over time like an out-of-season swarm? Or had a conquering race like Mahijith's destroyed them?

There! Was that the flicker of the black cloud, vanishing behind the crest of the next hill? He hurried ahead and saw that the bosom of the hill hid a hollow, as if some giant had scooped an enormous handful of the sandy earth out of its side, leaving a gentle depression large enough to hold a manor and its grounds. The Boy could hear the consistent hum, louder and louder as he approached the lip of the hollow.

If they had settled to rest, or to spend the night, in some foliage in the hollow, he had a chance. He probed his pocket, feeling the rough surface of the box inside. *If* he could find the queen in the center of the swarm, and *if* he could manipulate her into the box without hurting her, and without the defensive worker bees turning hostile . . . He muttered a quick prayer and pulled out the box. He reached the edge of the hollow, looked down, and gasped.

His first impression was that some elemental horror, a story told to frighten children around the fire in the dead of winter, had risen from the ruins of a cursed habitation. A primal bolt of fear, ice-cold, shot through his bowels. A tall humanoid stood just below him, featureless save for a vague indentation where its eyes should have been. Although the figure was still as stone, its black and tawny flesh was moving, like a goat's carcass alive with maggots, and he felt a prickle over his own skin in response.

It stood as a supplicant, facing the setting sun with arms upraised as if in appeal. The lumps at the ends of the outstretched limbs looked like hands from which the fingers had corroded and fallen away. As he watched, a golden brown mass of the thing's skin fell to the ground in a clump and fell apart. It disintegrated into many small bodies, some crawling over the grass that grew between the squared-off stones and some flying back to rejoin the hideously quivering mockery.

Then he heard the hum and drew in a great gulp of the warm, summer air. It was only the bees lighting on a statue. The scattered stones were the ruins of a temple where once a deity had stood, depicted in stone, arms spread to receive its worshipers. Or perhaps a great house stood here, with the image of an ancestor preserved in granite, now covered with the questing swarm.

Feeling foolish, he scrambled over the lip of the hollow and picked his way over the tumbled stones that had once made a wall. The bees' buzzing grew louder, and he gently waved aside a few that flew around his face. He knew he was safe. It was rare for a swarm to sting an intruder, so long as one moved slowly and unthreateningly. It wasn't until they'd found a home to defend that they'd be dangerous. In front of the bee-encrusted statue he paused, smelling the honey-scented tang of the insect mass, searching the quivering, moving surface for the long-bodied queen. The statue was a head taller than he. The Boy looked up into where its featureless face should have been.

There was a quiver as two handfuls of bees fell away. From the blunt-featured face, two eyes blinked open and looked at the horizon. They blinked again and looked down at the Boy. Round eyes with golden yellow irises and a black, black center looked down at him, reflecting two tiny images of the reddened sun. No other part of the statue moved.

The Boy opened his mouth to scream, but only a harsh whistling sound came out. He felt as if a blow of Skreetchu's baton had struck his ribs, knocking away his air. He wanted to scramble away, but he felt as if his limbs had frozen in place.

The Boy had nightmares like this—nightmares of goblins and worse chasing him, close enough so he could see their leering faces and yellowed teeth, and him unable to move, or moving unnaturally slowly, knowing in a few seconds he'd be seized and devoured. Drenched in sweat, he'd wake, sitting bolt upright on the thin pallet he was allotted in the stables.

But this was no dream, and he wouldn't wake. A bee-covered arm reached up before he could move, and a strong hand grasped him about the throat. He grabbed at the arm, feeling a few bees crushed beneath his fingers and the dull shock as his hand was stung. This time he managed to scream, a shrilling cry that rang in his ears. He tried to yell again, but no sound came.

As if reacting to his scream, the bees sprang away from the figure, swirling up and away like a thick mist. The Boy's neck was still clasped in a firm grip as the statue's head turned to watch the bees as they spread out so one could see them as individuals instead of a solid mass. They merged into a solid black column, then dissipated again, vanishing over the edge of the hollow.

I'll never catch the queen now, thought the Boy, despite his terror. The figure turned back to look at him, and the Boy would have screamed again had the pressure on his throat not increased, choking off his cry. He felt a warm trickle against the inside of his leg as he lost control of his bladder.

Yellow eyes in a fierce face stared into his own. The figure's head was furred, with deep black stripes across the burned orange and stark white of its cheek, chin, and muzzle. Stiff, wirelike whiskers jutted beneath the flattened, flaring nose of a predator, and the feline-split upper lip quivered in a snarl, exposing thick ivory fangs. Tufts of tawny fur framed its ears, the backs of which had jagged black stripes while the inside of each was snow-white. The ears swiveled slightly to catch every sound: the distant buzzing of the bees, the occasional chatter of a bird, his own subvocal whimpering.

It was a tiger's head, square on a thick neck and muscular body that was a man's, save that it, too, was covered in short tawny, black-striped fur. The tiger-man pulled the Boy up by the neck until his toes barely touched the ground. The creature growled in his face. The Boy's breath was cut off, and black dots danced before his eyes. He could feel the tips of sharp claws biting into his skin.

He thought he'd been afraid of Skreetchu, with his species's cruelty and his baton always at the ready for an errant slave. But he'd willingly go to the kenku now and confess to losing the swarm and to a passel of other sins if only he could get free of this monstrous creature.

Just as the pressure on his neck grew intolerable, the tiger-headed creature snarled and tossed him aside. The Boy fell heavily against an inscribed slab of rock that tilted, broken, half-buried in sand. He struggled to regain his breath and wrapped his arms around his battered ribs, knowing that if the creature decided to kill him there was no defense.

He squinted up at the creature, which stood rooted in place, ignoring the Boy. The tiger-headed thing was staring at its own hands, turning them back and forth. They were strange hands, unnatural—somewhere between a human hand and a paw, elongated with claw-tipped fingers mobile enough to hold small objects, but powerful enough to wrap around the hilt of a weapon.

The hand-paw was covered with fur, striped tawny and black on the back and white on the palm. As the creature turned its hand over, however, it became apparent that something was wrong: the palm faced back, and the large, clawed thumb was reversed. It was as if some clever trickster had severed the tiger-man's hands, flipped them over, and skillfully stitched nerve, bone, sinew, and skin back into place, backward.

The Boy closed his eyes, and a small groan escaped him. He'd lived too near the Beastlands for far too long not to know what stood there; a rakshasa—a demon with the body of a humanoid and the head of a jungle cat, and most telling, those awful backward paws.

Lusk looked at his hands in baffled rage and horror.

He looked at the small human who had witnessed his rebirth, whom he had seized upon in his anger and tossed aside. A boy, he saw, grown too tall for his shabby clothing and a face too thin for his eyes. He was thirteen, perhaps; no older than sixteen, surely. The child struggled to his feet, breathing unsteadily and cradling his side as if it pained him.

Lusk's nose twitched. His sense of smell was acute, like the predatory cat whose shape his incarnation had taken. He smelled sun-baked grass and rock, and a strangely strong, sweet musky smell.

Honey . . .

He remembered the bees. They were gone now, but he remembered—the blackness of the void, all his senses muffled, the only sound his own voice inside his conciousness, shrilling in terror. Then, a stab of light came through the void, tearing away his blindness, painful and unrelenting. He floated, helpless, inside that merciless light, until he felt ground under his feet and warm sun on the body that was emerging, molded like clay from the very air where nothing was before. Then came countless tiny vibrating bodies, humming insistently and covering his new, raw skin from head to foot, hurting him with their thousands of tiny clawed feet but sheltering him from that excruciating light, that too-warm sun. They cooled him with their wings until he could stand in the world without experiencing the agony of the new, raw flesh the gods had given him.

The bees had flown away and the child stood there. Lusk smelled sweat and the stables and urine, and also a trace of the dried-sugar musk of the bees. The skin of the boy's throat was bruising where Lusk had seized him before, and there were small drops of blood where his claws had pierced. Lusk wondered if he should kill him.

He took two strides and stood in front of the boy. It would be very easy to break his neck. Or . . .

Lusk's belly growled with the hunger of his new body. He could find a use for the child, skinny as he was.

The boy's eyes widened, huge in his thin face, as the rakshasa approached him. Lusk knew the child was aware there was no use running. The boy straightened his back and faced him, looking up into Lusk's tiger face, and steeled himself to die.

Lusk remembered a time long ago in his previous life as deva-Lusk, early in that incarnation. He remembered a farmhouse, and a family who welcomed him, however far he wandered. He remembered finding the burned-out farmhouse, and the bodies, and his soul torn away from his body.

He remembered the children of that family. He found all the bodies save one. The eldest, a girl, was about the age of this boy, and something of his height.

Lusk spoke, carefully shaping the words in the unfamiliar contours of his new mouth, lips, and tongue. Although catlike, his new mouth was sufficiently humanoid so he could speak.

"What is your name?" he said gruffly.

The human boy blinked rapidly. "I don't—" he began, then faltered. He looked at the ground, at Lusk's great clawed feet. "They always call me Boy."

"Look at me," growled Lusk.

The Boy drew in a breath, held it, and looked up into Lusk's inhuman, golden eyes. Lusk looked back. The child's eyes were muddy brown at the edge of the iris, lightening to hazel surrounding the pupil. It reminded him of something, a lake, with round, polished brown-green agates in handfuls on the shore.

"Tamack," he said after a long pause. "I'll call you Tamack."

The child was mute, staring at the rakshasa with a terrified wonder.

"I won't eat you, Tamack," Lusk continued, "if you can find me something to eat. Soon."

The Boy—Tamack—found his voice.

"Can you eat honey?" he said in a very small voice.

Lusk grinned, and Tamack flinched back from the rows of sharp, ivory teeth.

"For now," he said. "I shall require something more substantial, but for now, honey will do."

Someone had sheltered this boy, although not well. He was a laborer, and very likely a slave. Where there were slaves there were masters, and where there were masters there were estates of a sort, whether great or mean.

Insignificant as he was, the child Tamack was now his. The property of his former master would be his as well.

For good or for evil, the gods did nothing without a reason. That was something devas knew. It was part of their nature, part of the faith that kept them in service to the deities through the continually rotating wheel of their life and death.

For a long time, he had been warring with his deva nature, even as he tried to embrace it. With his understanding of the fickle nature of the gods, they had punished him by denying the peace of true death, and rebirthing him as this monstrosity.

Very well, he thought, following Tamack as he led him through the twilight over the foothills to the habitation that would soon be his. *The gods do nothing without reason.* He heard Lakini's voice in his head, Lakini who had chosen promises made to mortals over his friendship, who maintained a foolish faith that her existence was anything but a cruel joke. She had betrayed him and would pay the price. In the meantime, he would acknowledge a kernel of truth in what she said, ignorant that it would destroy her.

If the gods had a purpose in condemning him to a lifetime as a rakshasa, doomed to be born a demon again and again, he would twist the curse into a gift. He would find his place and cultivate his Powers. He would serve no master but himself.

The gods would regret this poisoned gift.

Near the Sanctuary of Shadrun-of-the-Snows

1600 DR—The Year of Unseen Enemies

When Lakini left the stables, she took the descending path that led away from Shadrun, not giving the buildings of the sanctuary a glance. She walked down the mountain and out into the world, paying no mind to where she went. Sometimes she walked alone. Sometimes she fell in with other travelers.

One evening, she came upon a group of horse traders stopped for the night and preparing their dinner. They called on her to join them, and so she turned aside, happy for the companionship this time.

She watched while one started the fire for the stew.

"Watch this," he said.

He drew a box from inside his pocket and took out a twist of paper. He flung it onto the kindling, producing only a sad puff of smoke.

The others laughed.

"I'll fetch my flints," said another.

"Wait," said the man with the box, taking another twist and flinging it in its turn. This time the paper blazed, and a good fire flared up at once.

"Always a couple duds in the bunch," he said with satisfaction. "But they're worth it."

She stood watch all night, not needing to sleep. Before the sun rose, the cook woke up to start the breakfast and Lakini wandered away, through the meadows starred with yellow and purple blooms, past where flat slabs of sandstone thrust at an angle from the soil. Past these she found the soft purple of foothills at sunrise and stood, unmoving, taking it all in.

Dawnbringer, she thought.

The edge of the horizon looked like a transparent bowl filling with liquid gold. The sight warmed her before the actual rays of the sun could heat the night-chilled air. The great mechanism that made the world and all within and all without it cycled round and round, like all she had been and was going to be, born again and again like each day that dawned over village and ruin, city and sea, army and gravestone, rock and jewel.

ACKNOWLEDGMENTS

Many thanks to Susan Morris for her inspiration and Mark Sehestedt for his patience, to Martin and the girls for their love and understanding, to the readers for reading, and to Pastor Nelson for not making me write the sermons.

ABOUT THE AUTHOR

Samantha Henderson is the author of the Scribe Award-nominated Ravenloft novel *Heaven's Bones,* and her short stories have been published in *Realms of Fantasy, Strange Horizons, Fantasy,* and the anthologies *Running with the Pack, Steampunk II: Steampunk Reloaded,* and *The Year's Best Science Fiction & Fantasy.* She is the co-winner of the 2010 Rhysling Award for speculative poetry. For more information, visit her website at www.samanthahenderson.com.

MANY ROADS LEAD TO NEVERWINTER™

RETURN WITH
GAUNTLGRYM

Neverwinter Saga, Book I
R.A. Salvatore

NEVERWINTER

Neverwinter Saga, Book II
R.A. Salvatore
October 2011

CONTINUE THE ADVENTURE WITH
BRIMSTONE ANGELS

Legends of Neverwinter
Erin M. Evans
November 2011

LOOK FOR THESE OTHER EXCITING NEW NEVERWINTER RELEASES IN 2011

RPG for PC
Cooperative Board Game
D&D® Roleplaying Game

HOW WILL YOU RETURN?

Find these great products at your favorite bookseller or game shop.

DungeonsandDragons.com

NEVERWINTER, DUNGEONS & DRAGONS, D&D, WIZARDS OF THE COAST, and their respective logos are trademarks of Wizards of the Coast LLC in the U.S.A. and other countries. ©2011 Wizards.

Enjoy these fantasy adventures inspired by
***The New York Times* best-selling**
Practical Guide series!

MONSTER SLAYERS

A Companion Novel to ***A Practical Guide to Monsters***
Lukas Ritter
978-0-7869-5484-1
Battle one menacing monster after another!

NOCTURNE

A Companion Novel to ***A Practical Guide to Vampires***
L.D. Harkrader
978-0-7869-5502-2
Join a vampire hunter on a heart-stopping quest!

Aldwyns Academy

A Companion Novel to ***A Practical Guide to Wizardry***
Nathan Meyer
978-0-7869-5504-6
Enter a school for magic where even the first day can be (un)deadly!

The Faerie Locket

A Companion Novel to ***A Practical Guide to Faeries***
Susan Morris
978-0-7869-5562-6
The locket will whisk you into the world of faeries—and the adventure of a lifetime.

DUNGEONS & DRAGONS, D&D, WIZARDS OF THE COAST, and their respective logos are trademarks of Wizards of the Coast LLC in the U.S.A. and other countries. Other trademarks are property of their respective owners. ©2011 Wizards.

BOOKS FOR YOUNG READERS

Get More Out of Your D&D® Experience.

D&D INSIDER™
Become a member today. DungeonsandDragons.com

Add more to your characters and campaigns with a constantly growing source of new and exclusive tools and online applications like:

D&D Character Builder
D&D Compendium
D&D Adventure Tools

Plus articles, art, maps, galleries, and other exclusive content.

Level up your game at
DungeonsandDragons.com

Dungeons & Dragons, D&D, Wizards of the Coast, D&D Insider and their respective logos are trademarks of Wizards of the Coast LLC in the U.S.A. and other countries. ©2011 Wizards.

EPIC STORIES

UNFORGETTABLE CHARACTERS

UNBEATABLE VALUE

OMNIBUS EDITIONS — THREE BOOKS IN ONE

FORGOTTEN REALMS

Empyrean Odyssey
Thomas M. Reid
February 2011

The Last Mythal
Richard Baker
August 2011

Ed Greenwood Presents Waterdeep I
July 2011

Ed Greenwood Presents Waterdeep II
December 2011

DRAGONLANCE

Dragonlance Legends
Margaret Weis & Tracy Hickman
September 2011

EBERRON

Draconic Prophecies
James Wyatt
October 2011

Find these great books at your favorite bookseller.

DungeonsandDragons.com

DUNGEONS & DRAGONS, D&D, FORGOTTEN REALMS, DRAGONLANCE, EBERRON, WIZARDS OF THE COAST, and their respective logos are trademarks of Wizards of the Coast LLC in the U.S.A. and other countries. ©2011 Wizards.

LEWIS, the master of all video games
PAUL, the sports star
SARA, the straight-A class president
JAKE, the juvenile delinquent

They'd played at being heroes—casting magic missiles, fighting back dragons and goblins, conquering terrible villains. And then one afternoon, this unlikely group stumbles on a secret door and slips into the world they'd only imagined. Ready or not, the Nentir Vale desperately needs them.

It's Time for Them to Learn It's More Than a Game

DUNGEONS & DRAGONS®

Nentir Warriors

The Lost Portal
A.M. Jenkins
September 2011

The Hidden Shrine
Ree Soesbee
November 2011

Find these great novels at your local bookseller.
Also available as ebooks.

DungeonsandDragons.com

DUNGEONS & DRAGONS, D&D, WIZARDS OF THE COAST, and their respective logos are trademarks of Wizards of the Coast LLC in the U.S.A. and other countries. ©2011 Wizards.

BOOKS FOR YOUNG READERS

THE ABYSSAL PLAGUE

From the molten core of a dead universe

Hunger

Spills a seed of evil

Fury

So pure, so concentrated, so infectious

Hate

Its corruption will span worlds

The Temple of Yellow Skulls
Don Bassingthwaite
March 2011

Sword of the Gods
Bruce Cordell
April 2011

Under the Crimson Sun
Keith R.A. DeCandido
June 2011

Oath of Vigilance
James Wyatt
August 2011

Shadowbane
Erik Scott de Bie
September 2011

Find these novels at your favorite bookseller.
Also available as ebooks.

DungeonsandDragons.com

DUNGEONS & DRAGONS, D&D, WIZARDS OF THE COAST, and their respective logos are trademarks of Wizards of the Coast LLC in the U.S.A. and other countries. ©2011 Wizards.